RED MOUNTAIN RISING

BOO WALKER

ALSO BY BOO WALKER

A Marriage Well Done

Red Mountain

Red Mountain Burning

An Unfinished Story

Writing as Benjamin Blackmore:

Lowcountry Punch

Once a Soldier

Off You Go: A Mystery Novella

For Leila Meacham,
my pen pal, mentor, and sage

1

A WOMAN'S BEST FRIEND

Late June, Washington State

"Oh, God, Adriana, you know how sometimes you're watching TV with the remote in your hand, and you get up to do something and accidentally take it with you? Then it's lost until an hour later when you find it in the fridge or a cabinet? I've lost something, but it's not the remote, and it's... Ahh, I'm going to rip my hair out looking—"

"What is it, Ms. Pierce?" her new housekeeper asked, their backs to each other as she polished the faucet of the porcelain farm sink.

"It's *Margot*," she insisted, rifling through her dried beans and specialty pastas in one of the wicker baskets that organized her open shelving next to the refrigerator. "Adriana, call me Margot. Please don't remind me how I'm withering away to sags and wrinkles."

"Okay, Margot. What did you lose?"

"Oh, never mind. Just please keep doing what you're doing. I'll find it." Margot blew out a blast of air and crossed her arms. She'd torn her kitchen apart and searched every basket on the espresso-stained wooden shelves, every inch of the fridge, every drawer under the counters. Not that the item she was missing had any business in the kitchen, but where else could it be?

Because of the open floor plan, she could see most of the downstairs from the island in the kitchen, so she looked over all the places she'd already scrutinized: the entrance with the matching ficus plants in rustic clay pots, the far corner with the delicate French furniture around the television, the main living area with the linen drapes that fell all the way to the floor, the brick fireplace with a stack of new wood waiting for winter, and the long dining-room table with the linen runner and elaborate candelabras.

Margot noticed her young terrier mutt Philippe panting and staring up at her from the kitchen floor like she was crazy.

"Do you know what I'm looking for?" Margot asked. "Have you seen it?"

Philippe perked up his ears.

"It's not a bone. I'll tell you that."

In only a few hours, guests would be traipsing all over the house and if Margot hadn't returned the missing item to its hiding place, someone was sure to discover it and ruin Margot's night—the night of the solstice party she'd dreamed of having for so many years. Not to mention she had other things to be doing. If she spent the entire day turning over every pillow, who would ensure the crystal glasses and silverware were polished? Who would ensure the caterers understood the timeline? Who would create the perfect solstice playlist? Who would ensure every flat surface hosted a bouquet of flowers or fresh herbs? Who would ensure the candles were lit, the patio swept, the mirrors sparkling? Who would? Who would? Who would...?

With Philippe at her heels, Margot entered the powder room down the hall for the third time. She looked at the white space around the tiny vase holding a dahlia on the back of the toilet. She scanned the surface of the yellow table painted with chalk paint. Nothing there but her curated selection of soaps and sprays.

She caught a glimpse of herself in the turn-of-the-century gold mirror above the sink and gasped at the unsightly Chia Pet staring back. *Ugh, look at me.* Her nervous habit of tugging at her long blond hair was worse than usual today. Trying to ignore the wrinkles around her eyes, she looked down and was reminded that she'd forgotten to change out of her yoga pants and tank top. She locked eyes with the Margot in the mirror. "This is me. This is what you get." She wet her hands in the sink, smoothed down her hair, and returned to the kitchen.

Adriana stopped spraying cleaning solution on the counter and turned to Margot. "I'd love to help you, Ms.—I mean, Margot, but I don't know what *it* is."

Margot paused and analyzed the woman, debating internally the level of trust she was ready to bestow upon her new employee. Was the embarrassment worth the extra pair of eyes?

Adriana wore a lavender housekeeping dress with a white apron wrapped around her tiny waist. Both women shared noticeable curves, but Adriana had this hourglass figure that surely turned heads. Her dark chocolate hair was pulled back, a few strays floating free up front. Her forehead was painted with a fine sheen of sweat. Margot still couldn't get used to the pink scars that marked the left side of her face. It was hard not to be overwhelmed with sadness every time she saw them. The poor woman looked like she'd been through so much to only be in her mid-thirties. Margot still had no idea where the scars came from and wouldn't dare ask—even she had boundaries.

Margot quickly thought of how, when they first met, Adriana had been working for a local maid service, cleaning for several of the wineries on Red Mountain. She'd run into her while attending a tasting room managers' meeting and then approached her out in the parking lot to ask if she wanted a job "off the books." Adriana had jumped at the opportunity, and their arrangement had been perfect so far. She was fast, efficient, trustworthy, and most importantly, pleasant to be around. Margot wanted to hire her full time but needed to get to know her a little better first.

Ready to share her burden, Margot said with a sigh, "You might as well find out sooner than later what a mess I am, not that I've hidden it well so far."

Adriana raised her hands, the right one covered with a yellow rubber glove. "I'm not one to judge. Believe me."

"Well," Margot said, her embarrassment showing on her reddening face, "it's long—like really long—and purple and made of silicone. And it vibrates."

Adriana's eyes widened.

Margot held her hands out in front of her like she was showing the length of a prize cucumber from her garden. Dropping her chin, she said, "Do you know what it is now?"

"I do," Adriana admitted, recommencing the cleaning of the counter.

"It's okay, you can laugh at me. It won't be the first *or* the last time. I've been the butt of jokes since my Virginia kindergarten days."

Adriana shook her head, obviously suppressing a laugh.

"Go ahead; let it out."

They locked eyes for a moment.

A sharp cackle—nearly a shriek—escaped Adriana's mouth.

"Yeah, I'd laugh too. I'm going to walk next door to check the inn. I can't imagine I walked over there with a vibrator in hand, but it's worth a look. These days, I wouldn't put anything past me." Before walking way, she added, "I'm going to leave Philippe here. Just make sure he doesn't sneak out. He's a magnet for trouble."

"No problem," Adriana said.

They were in Margot's home at the western edge of her twenty-acre property. The eight-bedroom inn she had recently opened stood a little farther down the gravel drive. Her farm sanctuary, where a collection of rescued farm animals would spend the rest of their pampered lives, was farther east, on the other side of the property.

Tonight, Margot was hosting her first summer solstice party. It was a night she'd been looking forward to since she'd started building her dream—this inn and farm sanctuary—two years before. For a long time, wine enthusiasts had known Red Mountain for its world-class cabernet, merlot, and syrah, but the infrastructure had never been there to support the tourism. Not until now. Every part of her knew she'd turned up at the perfect moment. Even with all the doubt that had axed away at her self-confidence, she was proud of herself for taking this journey. And it felt right, like she'd embraced the grand design.

In the move to Red Mountain, Margot hadn't expected the uniqueness of the characters with their giant personalities, their big beautiful minds, and their many skeleton-filled closets. She fit in well with these people, and they brought out the wild side that she'd almost lost during her last years in Vermont. She had discovered that on this mountain you could be whomever you wanted to be, and she needed that kind of freedom like a bird needed wings.

When Margot and her teenage son had decided to leave her cheating husband in Vermont and move west, they'd discovered a wonderful opportunity to be a part of a growing community. Rediscovering her entrepreneurial spirit, she'd found the perfect spot to fulfill her dream of opening a little inn, and as a bonus, it would be the first real place for guests to stay on Red Mountain.

Despite a conniving contractor who'd delayed construction, she'd eventually caught up with her previous completion and financial projections and, after two agonizing years of going through all sorts of tribulations, she was ready to open on April 1. Something, however, about launching her dream on April Fool's Day made little sense, so she'd opened the inn for booking starting April 2. Once she flipped the switch, the people had come out in droves to support her, and the inn had been full ever since. Her guest book in the lobby was filled with names of people from Seattle to New York and even a few from England and Scandinavia. Nearly three months after opening, she'd surpassed her own expectations. Her life had finally come together.

For the most part.

This evening was also a going-away party. Several people were leaving the mountain, including her son. Tomorrow, Jasper would be off to college at the Berkeley School of Music. Margot was about to find a new level of loneliness.

Before leaving her house, Margot stopped by the table in the foyer, where she kept a tube of her favorite body lotion. She squeezed a generous portion into her hand and walked out the door. Stopping on the stoop outside, she rubbed the lotion into her hands and breathed in the hot desert air. Was all of eastern Washington one big dry sauna? It was still hard to believe that it was only June and that July and August would be even more intense.

She'd taken a few trips out west during her lifetime but had never understood dry heat until she lived in it. Where the East Coast humidity steamed her like broccoli, eastern Washington heat baked her like kale chips. In addition to the desert sun, the skies only graced this place with a few inches of rain a year. There weren't many drier places in the United States, an absolute blessing for her hair, but a nightmare for her skin.

As part of her arsenal to battle the elements, she kept organic skin lotions in every room in the house, and if you searched her Volvo, you'd find lotions in the center console and in each of the doors. Probably even under the seat. These small sacrifices were worth it for her hair, though; no more of those unruly frizzy flyaways.

Thank goodness it would cool off before people arrived. What she liked most about June on Red Mountain was the slight chill of the evenings, the diurnal shift that could drop a sweltering ninety-five-degree day into the low seventies by the time one sat down for a late dinner. It turned out the grapes liked the diurnal shift as well, and it's part of what made Washington State famous for its grape growing. The cool nights would slow the ripening process, allowing the berries to mature with more complexity without becoming too sugary too soon.

As her friend and mentor Joan had taught her, she must stop every day to appreciate what she had. *Slow down. Look. Listen. Breathe.* Not an easy concept when you're missing a purple vibrator the size of a baseball bat that someone would surely stumble upon at the most inopportune time.

Forcing herself to slow down, she rested a hand on the iron railing.

Breathe. Listen. The here and now.

The distant purr of a weed eater told her that Enrique, her landscaper/handyman/just-about-everything man, was working along the tall grass by the main road.

Margot looked toward her inn. Halfway there, her hens, all named after Broadway characters, pecked the dirt looking for worms. Those birds meant more to her than anyone could ever know. They symbolized the freedom she'd found since leaving her husband, an ordeal that had nearly snapped her soul in half.

The caterer's white van was parked near the giant wooden doors leading into Épiphanie. Margot did most of the cooking, but tonight she wanted to enjoy the company of her visitors and friends, so she'd employed a renowned chef and her team from Seattle to prepare whatever they'd like, as long as they used Margot's vegetables from the garden.

Margot twisted her head left and right, amazed at how many more vines farmers had planted since she'd bought her land. New wineries had popped up too. The vineyard blocks, separated by dirt roads, reached all the way from the highway far off to her left and nearly to the top of the mountain to her right. The contrast of the lush green of the vineyard blocks and the arid desert-brown land-scape could make a person wonder if farmers were meant to be there at all. Up past the highest vineyards stood the proud, treeless ridge-line of Red Mountain, the only part of the mountain not covered in vines.

Well, not yet. Every spot that was easy to plant in the growing region had now been purchased, which left ambitious vignerons to plant in less optimal spots just to get a piece of this prized land, to be a part of the gold rush. Looking at the western side of the ridgeline, Margot could see people planting a new vineyard, a formidable task considering the shallow loess soil, the harsh higher elevation winds, and the giant chunks of granite and basalt.

She dropped her eyes back to the vineyards stretching across the lower elevations. This time of year, the leaf canopies running along the trellises burst with life. Depending on the position of the sun and clouds, most of the vineyard blocks bore some shade of green, but there were the occasional blocks of white that marked a new vineyard. Farmers placed white grow tubes around newly planted vines to protect them in their youth, the collective forming a white sheet floating in a sea of green. Between the green and white vineyard blocks, Red Mountain looked like an Irish chessboard.

This chessboard buzzed with life today. A man inspecting his irrigation lines through Aviator sunglasses bounced through the rows on an ATV. One of Margot's neighbors crept along his roof, repairing shingles damaged by the April winds. Up near Col Solare, a woman dressed in red led a group of tourists through the vineyards. Directly ahead, Sunset Road had turned into a tractor highway. Farmers chugged along in their John Deeres and Kubotas and Mahindras, and the wine tourists sped past them in the other lane. Margot had heard of times when a tasting room might see one or two visitors all day; now, the weekends brought tour buses, limousines, and even horse-drawn wagons.

Trying not to stress over the vibrator, Margot strolled down the gravel drive, which was lined with young black locust trees. She took a moment to chat with her chickens and *still* reached the inn in less than two minutes. The shortest commute to work in the world. She stopped to flip the water switch on the porcelain fountain of a young girl on her tiptoes reaching for a drink. As the stone girl enjoyed her first sip of the day, Margot took a moment to appreciate the rose beds on either side of the stairs. To her delight, she'd found that roses grew like weeds on Red Mountain, so she and Enrique had created rose beds that wrapped around the entire inn.

She looked up. Épiphanie was plastered with an authentic cream stucco applied in the Old-World tradition, sans the modern tools and materials that pushed most stucco done in the United States into dangerous Olive Garden or cookie-cutter Mexican restaurant territory. The pastel yellow hand-built wooden shutters were built to be used, to be effective, to protect from climatic extremes. Within the last fifty years, builders had often forgotten why we do things, and aesthetics trumped effectiveness. Below each ground-level window hung a wooden box overflowing with purple geraniums, scarlet begonias, and accents of trailing sweet potato vines that fell down the sides like locks of hair.

Margot climbed the steps and placed her hand on the iron pull of one of the wooden doors. The candied scent of the short-rooted honeysuckles climbing the walls on either side of the doors touched her heart like a sunrise kiss from a lover. "Good morning, beautiful," he might say. *If* he'd actually existed.

As she pulled open the door, ready to embrace the chaos of her caterers running around the kitchen, the madness of a lost item, her needy guests chasing her tail, and even the joys and sadness of having her son for one last day before he set out on his own, a smile rose from within. This was Margot's dream—all of it: the inn lively with people, the solstice party among the vines, the tables of glorious food and wine, the children playing.

Her lovely French-inspired dream was coming to fruition.

THE HOWLING INSIDE

Otis Till had a fascination with the moon that bordered on obsession. That big bright ball was inside him. It spoke to him like it spoke to the coyotes at night. He'd watched it rise and fall for sixty-four years. When he had been barely double-digits, his family had relocated from London to Bozeman, Montana, where he'd first met a coyote, his spirit animal. He had finally discovered why that cursed moon had been talking to him all those years: he was a wild dog himself. And when he learned to howl with his brethren, he could finally speak back.

The summer solstice, the longest day of the year—a symbol of rebirth for many—was extra special tonight. For only the second time in his life, the day would coincide with a full moon. Otis could feel the energy of the universe bubbling in his veins as he made his way along the gravel road in between two vineyard blocks behind Épiphanie. He could hear the craziness of the party behind him: loud Gypsy jazz music, laughing, hollering. He'd been in the midst of it until a few moments ago, when he'd decided to take a stroll. Something about a few fingers of Scotch always made him want to meander into the dark.

With a tweed cap covering his balding head, he let his hands fall to his sides and gazed above, slightly swaying from too much Lagavulin. Like his father, the original silver fox, used to say in his beautifully intellectual British accent, "Drinking whiskey is always a good idea, but it's never a good decision." Out in the desert, so far from city life, the full moon and stars glowed and twinkled with an immenseness that city dwellers could never know. Tonight, the moon was strong and loud and wicked.

That damned moon had seen Otis grow up and fall in love. It had seen his life fall apart. It had seen his wife and sons die way too young, the previous vintage of wine destroyed by an angry and evil neighbor, and the new love of his life shot by that same neighbor. And all that moon had done was watch like a sadomasochistic spectator absorbing a death match. Otis's life was a canvas of disaster, each beautiful scene he tried to paint trashed by buckets of black falling from the sky.

This time, he already knew where and when the next disaster was going to happen. After a brilliant start to this vintage, he was about to leave his vines for the summer. Right when the sun was shining brightest—his grapes' formative years—smack in the middle of berry set, he was taking off. For the first time since he'd moved to Washington many years ago, he was leaving during the summer, only months before harvest. He wasn't terrified of the potential of something going wrong; he was absolutely sure of an imminent, unpreventable collapse. Fear had owned his thoughts for months leading up to these days, that ever-present black cat in his path winking at him with a sly smirk. *Ready to get knocked on your arse again, Otis?*

Still, he'd committed to leaving, and that's what he was going to do. *It's only for a few weeks,* he kept telling himself. It's not like he was going somewhere terrible. He was off to see the world and spread his recently deceased aunt's ashes. His aunt Morgan, the vibrant force of nature that she was, had left the request in her will. Otis was to embark on a first-class trip around the world, spreading Morgan's ashes in the places she'd missed during her lifetime. In order to earn his inheritance and prove he hadn't cut corners, Otis was required to have his picture taken while holding the local paper at each specified location.

The moon glared at Otis like he'd done something wrong. He surveyed the surrounding ground, looking for that black cat. In his still lingering English accent, Otis looked back up and said, "What are you going to do about it? Why am I even talking to you?" He jabbed his finger up into the night. "You're a son of a bitch, and you've brought me nothing but hell. You and I both know I'll return to this place in six weeks, and the whole bloody mountain will have burned to the ground."

The sounds of the night whispered back.

He shuffled his feet in the gravel and threw up his hands. "What! I'm not going to howl to you tonight. If I could spit on you, I would. I know you're up there waiting. Waiting until I get on that plane. And then you're going to laugh as my vineyard falls apart." He spat on the ground. "Fine, just stare back and don't say a damned word. Take everything and everyone I love and watch me crumble!"

Otis turned down a vineyard row and felt the gravel change to soft dirt on his feet as he disappeared into the vines. The coyotes around the upper ring of the mountain called out, but he didn't feel at one with them tonight. He continued on, stopping, starting, listening. Over and over again. There was a fear inside him that had wedged its way to near permanence, and it was almost like he was out here tonight searching for the truth of it.

After thirty minutes, he wound his way back down to the inn and noticed a group of seven winemakers sitting around a table on the patio caught up in a lively discussion. As Otis paused to listen in, Elijah, the young intern who would care for Till Vineyards in Otis's absence, pushed an open seat out with his foot. "Take a chair, Otis. This conversation's right up your alley."

"That right?" Otis asked as he sat down. He felt grumpy and needed more to drink.

"Yes, sir. We're talking about the future of Red Mountain," Elijah said as he poured Otis a glass of red.

Otis set his cap on the table, took a sip, and sat back to listen to the new guard of Red Mountain argue for a while. He looked at Elijah laughing and partaking in the conversation. The young man wore the same tattered Irrigation Specialists hat every day, and his black jeans and boots were covered with dirt from the day's work. Was his student ready to watch the vines? The young man had problems of his own. Was he strong enough to overcome his home life and put all he had into the new crop?

Christophe Hedges, an outspoken visionary farmer who ran Hedges Family Estate with his sister Sarah, a fermentation artist of the highest caliber, was speaking of context in wine, a topic he never tired of discussing. He was a tall brute, built rock solid from his days of stacking stone and pouring concrete. In his typical animated fashion, Christophe raised his hands in the air to finish his point. "I'd rather drink a bad wine that has contextual significance—something *real* to say—than a perfectly crafted wine that has no story, no backbone. Like those Drink Flamingo wines," he said, referring to a winery out of California that was filling glasses across the pop world, touting themselves as the leaders of the box wine Renaissance —*Renaissance* being their word, one heard repeatedly in their endless television commercials. Their motto, *Drink inside the box. Drink Flamingo.*, was plastered on boxes in every supermarket in America— or every supermarket that could legally sell wine, anyway.

Christophe continued, "Nobody knows the source of the grapes. And look who's behind it. A board of directors studying trends. I don't care if people say their wine is the best in the world, I'm not putting it in my body. That's not art."

Otis agreed with Christophe. Though he was a young hothead, Christophe's thoughts and visions were as pure as the Hedges wines.

Jake Forester, owner of Lacoda and the resident celebrity on Red Mountain, turned to Otis. Despite years of leading a popular band and touring the world, he'd aged well. He kept in good shape by running and working outside, and he'd told Otis one day that he kicked most his bad habits more than twenty years earlier in his thirties. Otis sensed that Jake had found true happiness in this life—this intoxicating sense of peace—and Otis always valued their time spent together. Of course they shared a deep love for Red Mountain and a dedication to the pursuit of truth in wine.

Jake had this unshaven, unkempt look, but he did it with style. The man crossed one leg over the other, raised his tattooed arms, and asked with true curiosity, "What do you think? What do we need?"

Otis took a moment. Where to even begin? It's all he thought about. Finally, he said, "We need to figure out a way to find some common ground. We need places to stay and farm-to-table restaurants. We need more Épiphanies. The eight rooms here are a start, but we have to keep it going."

Otis sat up. "And we need to start using the same type of bottle. Like the one Jake's using—his squat bottle. Just imagine if every winery on Red Mountain, hell even every winery sourcing fruit from Red Mountain, had to use the same bottle shape. By law. We could have the Red Mountain triangle etched into the glass." He wagged his finger. "The squat bottle could be a sort of trademark for Red Mountain. That's marketing. That's big-picture thinking. That's putting the mountain before anything else. We need to figure all this out before someone richer than us comes in and decides the future for us."

Otis often had the last word. The others at the table simply nodded their heads. Otis hid the fear in his belly, that cold sweat shiver that kept beating from inside his bones, telling him not to leave, telling him that he couldn't leave his vines, telling him that these guys needed him now more than ever. It amazed Otis that such a small group of winemakers and owners who shared the same soil could have such diverse wants and needs. Some might like to see their wines on wine lists in Tokyo or Berlin, while others simply wanted their tasting rooms to be drowned in foot traffic. Otis hoped that diversity wouldn't create too many divides as the growing region developed.

Jake Forester's wife, Carmen, came through the open French doors leading out to the patio and approached the table. The former supermodel hadn't lost much in regard to beauty or fashion. She shared the same sway as Otis, though she pulled it off with much more elegance. All the men turned but tried hard not to stare. Her beauty was in every cell of her body, especially the way she moved. The catwalk seemed to always be unfolding in front of her, even when she was slightly intoxicated.

Not out of character but certainly out of nowhere, Carmen sat on Otis's lap. They didn't know each other well enough for the intrusion, but she wasn't one to respect the typical social rules of interaction, and Otis was far too much the gentleman to embarrass her by nudging her away. The others at the table watched with smiles and laughter at her invasion into Otis's space.

The first thing Otis noticed was that the woman barely weighed anything. Had his eyes been closed, he might hardly have noticed her sitting down on his leg. Her head was a few inches above his, and he had to look up to meet her big brown eyes. Thick waves of cinnamon hair reached well beyond her shoulders.

Her full red lips turned up into a smile, and she touched his cheek with her slender fingers, one of them adorned by a diamond nearly as bright as the night's full moon. In a sultry voice, Carmen asked, "Why the sad face, handsome?"

Otis cleared his throat. "Do I look sad?"

"You look on the verge of tears."

He glanced behind him. "Sorry, I meant to leave it out there in the vines."

"What troubles you?"

Otis could smell the liquor on her breath, but he knew Carmen hadn't lost total control. She was honestly concerned. He looked around the table at the others, who were now half paying attention.

"Ever feel like you can't drink enough to make it go away?"

She laughed. "Not really. I find there's always a point where the poison works." She wrapped her skeletal arm around him and twisted her head toward his face. "You're this mountain's mascot, Otis. You can't get down, or we all will. We need you to be bright and cheery." Between the martinis, white wine, and the alleged pills coursing through her system, Carmen was a hot mess ready to explode.

Otis offered his most sincere effort at a smile. "Then I'll save the frown for the cave tonight." He often felt sad in her presence, having seen many of his friends meet the same fate from addiction. Of course, everyone on that mountain was playing with fire. Who could really define the line between drinking and drinking too much? Who among them didn't over-imbibe from time to time? Otis certainly had his days. In the end, though, there were some on the mountain who didn't wear the cloak of overindulgence well.

She smiled, bringing light to his dark comment. "I didn't know you had a cave." In a smoky voice, she asked, "Are you Batman?"

Everyone laughed, including Otis.

"I'm going to miss this mountain," he said.

"It will miss you, believe me." She kissed him on the cheek, leaving bright red lip prints, as the others at the table raised their glasses to the godfather of Red Mountain, or as they often referred to him, "the grapefather."

3

SAY YES MORE

S unk into a comfy chair near the fireplace in the dining room of Épiphanie, Brooks Baker pulled at the hairs on his four-day-old beard and took in the scene. The Red Garland Quintet played the perfect soundtrack to this band of misfits. The western wall was lined with leaded glass doors that opened into the night, letting the breeze creep in. Under a string of lights, he saw Otis hunkered down at a table on the crowded patio, surely discussing his philosophies of Red Mountain with the men surrounding him. Brooks chuckled when Carmen Forester sat on his mentor's lap, knowing the man was surely uncomfortable at having been put in that position.

Brooks had been reluctant about attending Margot's summer solstice party at Épiphanie. Though he enjoyed the get-togethers and the animated inhabitants of Red Mountain always shedding their social reservations in new and interesting ways, he'd turned inward since the demise of his relationship with Abby Sinclaire.

He'd thrown himself into his winemaking and when he wasn't working, he'd either jump on his Triumph motorcycle and ride, or go home to hide, eating whatever microwave meal was on special while taking in one of the movies everyone couldn't believe he hadn't seen yet. Because of his abnormal childhood, he constantly heard such comments as, "You haven't seen *Star Wars*?" and "How have you *not* seen *The Godfather*?" He remembered Abby nearly having a heart attack when he admitted he'd never even *heard* of *Pretty Woman*.

Tonight was different than the usual get-togethers, though, because people very special to him were leaving the mountain tomorrow.

Back inside, seated on mismatched chairs at the end of one of the long tables made of reclaimed wood, were his almost-sister Emilia and her boyfriend Jasper, heavily involved in a game of chess. Several others had formed cliques at these long tables that lined the center of the room. The eight seats at the bar on the other side were occupied by a particularly rowdy set of guests, who were knocking back a round of tequila shots.

Brooks admired what Margot had done with her inn and with this evening in particular. He loved her attention to detail and her taste: the wooden beams running along the high ceilings, the burning beeswax candles and the vibrant centerpieces decorating the tables, the polished silverware and sparkling stemware, the lavish crystal chandeliers dimmed way down, and antique sconces illuminating giant paintings of French landscapes in vintage gold-gilded frames.

He returned his gaze to the woman in the wheelchair sitting next to him. Her short silver hair almost hid the tiny diamond earrings hanging from her ears. The first two buttons of her white blouse were undone, exposing a quarter-sized scar from a bullet wound. Also exposed was a silver necklace, a gift from one of the many friends who'd visited her since the day she'd been shot. A silver medallion hung at the end with one word etched into it: *Faith*.

"I can't believe you guys are leaving tomorrow," he said. "This time tomorrow night, Otis Till will be in Bora Bora. I can't imagine him in a bathing suit sitting on a beach, trying to read a book. That man probably has the finest farmer's tan on the west coast."

Joan Tobey offered a tight-lipped smile and then said, "I should make him pack a Speedo."

"Oh, my, that's a vision I'd kind of like to see. Well, on second thought, no, not really. Maybe from a distance? If you pull this off and actually get Otis into a Speedo, you'll have to send me a photo."

"If it happens, you know I will. But don't hold your breath."

Joan sipped the glass of sauvignon blanc she'd been nursing, keeping it mostly on the table next to her. As always, she spoke to him as if he were the only person on earth, her eyes and ears never leaving him, nonplussed by the bustle around them. She was a woman who made every person around her feel important to her.

Brooks said, "Leaving the mountain right now may be the greatest challenge he's ever faced. Don't be surprised if he tries to ferment coconuts while you're in Bora Bora."

"He's a horse with blinders on, isn't he?" She shifted in her wheelchair. "It's going to be good for him. For both of us."

"Is he packing wine? I bet he'll try to get on every wine list from here to Hanoi."

"I'm sure he'll have bottles rolled up in his clothes."

"As the commander of the legions of Red Mountain, he'd better. Just keep telling him I have things under control. He has to let go. Elijah and I are more scared to let him down than he is of something bad happening. We'll take care of his babies."

"He knows that, sweetie. It's his history that plagues him. He's had some bad luck in his life."

Brooks nodded. "Otis either bowls gutter balls or strikes. Nothing in between."

"A man of extremes." Joan shrugged and resumed people watching.

Comfortable in the silence between them, Brooks sat back to take in the scene as well. By now, Carmen had hopped off Otis's lap and was rubbing her husband Jake's shoulders. Jasper was laughing hysterically at something Emilia had said. The group at the bar was getting louder and louder.

After watching the crowd for a while, Brooks said, "I get the feeling the universe tests you just as much as it does Otis."

"You ever hear that Carlos Castaneda quote about warriors? He wrote, 'The basic difference between an ordinary man and a warrior is that a warrior takes everything as a challenge while an ordinary man takes everything as a blessing or a curse.' The day Henry Davidson shot me was the toughest test of my life, and there are times when I want to kick and scream, 'Why me? Why me!' But on the good days, I see the challenge and not the curse. I just need more of those good days."

"Damn that man for shooting you."

Joan shifted again. "I've thought about Henry more than I should. Perhaps Henry's destiny was to be there on that day and pull that trigger. To deliver to me my ultimate test. Sounds silly. But who knows?"

"Well, I hope he's being tested in prison." Brooks didn't want to say what he really hoped. Not in the presence of a lady. "And may he never get out."

"If he does, he'll be an old, old man. He's lost everything. His freedom, his wife, his family, his friends." Joan reached for her glass.

As his drinking companion sipped the wine, Brooks saw her hand quiver. Her hand and the glass shook until she returned it to the table.

The bullet had shattered Joan's right clavicle and cut through her vertebral artery before settling into her shoulder. The paramedics had stopped the bleeding in the ambulance but not before she'd suffered significant blood loss. The resulting lack of oxygen flowing to her brain led to minor brain damage. The doctors called it global cerebral ischemia. She'd gone into a coma for four days before finally weakly opening her eyes, and she'd been suffering from and fighting the symptoms ever since.

In the months following Joan's trauma, Brooks had helped wherever he could. He'd spent most of his free time working in Otis's vineyard and winery, but had also taken Joan to a few doctor and rehab appointments. The two had gotten to know each other much better on the long drives and in the waiting rooms, and what Brooks had never suspected but later realized was that Joan was helping him too. Giving him courage, showing him how to fight to recover from his own battle.

She knew many of his secrets, so she wasn't out of line when she reached over and patted his knee. "Why are you troubled today, my dear?" She gazed around his head with her green eyes, and he knew she was reading his aura. "I see a man still desperately looking for something. For love. For success. For acceptance. Perhaps more than anything, you're still running from your past, trying so hard to separate yourself from anything outside the norm, terrified that you or those around you might screw up this new world you've built."

As usual, Joan was spot-on, and Brooks nodded, welcoming her insight.

She continued, "Your new world will never be normal, not in the way you want. It's good to set the bar high, Brooks. It's good that you have so much drive. But you shouldn't set the bar *too* high. Not for yourself *or* the ones you love."

"That's funny, my mom told me the same thing."

"Always listen to your mother."

"So where do I go from here?" he asked. "What's the recipe? You know what happened with Abby. I think I'm coming around a bend, but I still don't feel right."

"You need to say 'yes' more, Brooks Baker."

He tilted his head, looking for her meaning. "What?"

"Say 'yes.' That's your homework. Every chance you get, say 'yes.' Don't think about the consequences; don't think about what else you have going on, what else you'd rather do. If someone asks you something, say 'yes.' If you ask yourself something, say 'yes.'"

Abby had brought a part of that person out of him, that extroverted, loving, open-to-anything Brooks. It had felt so good. But the fall was much harder. She'd thrown it all away, betrayal and a hard, bone-breaking fall.

"Say 'yes' more," he repeated, glancing around the room, processing the idea.

Brooks noticed a pretty young Mexican woman with long dark hair dressed in a lavender housekeeper's uniform coming from the swinging kitchen doors. He hadn't seen her before and took an interest. He thought she might only be a few years younger than him. When you're single on Red Mountain, it's exciting to see new faces.

Heck, when you live on Red Mountain, it's exciting to see a new face. It comes with the territory of the middle-of-nowhere lifestyle.

The woman turned in his direction, and he saw that something was wrong with the left side of her face—some kind of deformity or scarring. He didn't want to stare, so turned away.

As the woman passed by, Joan said, "Adriana, have you met Brooks?"

Adriana stopped and turned toward them with a smile.

Brooks looked up at her chestnut-brown eyes, trying to ignore what he now could see were scars. He smiled back.

Adriana glanced at him briefly and then replied to Joan, "No, I haven't." She returned her eyes to Brooks and said quietly, "Of course, I know *of* you, and I know your brother."

"Oh, cool," Brooks said feeling caught off guard by her scars, but also those disarming eyes. He gathered himself, desperate not to make her feel uncomfortable. "It's good to meet you."

"You too," she said. "May I take your plate?"

Brooks nodded, and she reached past him and collected his empty plate. He took a longer look at her face. There were several pink scars running in different directions, the most evident being a thick slice that ran from the side of her nose to her upper lip. Brooks thought she might have been in a car accident. He could smell her light flowery perfume and noticed her ring finger was bare.

He asked, "So how long have you been working here?"

"Only a few days."

"Welcome to the mountain."

"Oh, I don't live on the mountain. Closer to Prosser."

Brooks could hear a shy insecurity in her voice as her sentences trailed off, perhaps stemming from her appearance. Attempting to draw a smile, he said, "This place, she'll start to pull you in. Before you know it, you'll be a Red Mountainite. You'll be desperate to find a place to live here."

She smiled genuinely, and it was a grand reward for Brooks. She said, "We'll see, I guess. Does that mean I have to start drinking wine?"

"One million percent yes."

She smiled more confidently. "Well, in the meantime, I better get back to work."

"I hope to see you again," Brooks said.

After he watched Adriana walk away, Brooks told Joan, "She has beautiful eyes."

"She's single," Joan said. "And she's your age. You should ask her out."

Brooks nodded. Maybe he would.

Joan touched his arm. "We all have our scars, don't we?"

4

THE CASE OF THE MISSING PURPLE STALLION

A driana Hernandez announced, "Coming through," as she
pushed open the doors into the bright white kitchen of
Épiphanie.

A woman in a white chef coat was standing at one end of the long
custom-oak island pulling Saran Wrap over leftovers. On the opposite end of the rectangular room, a woman wearing a ponytail washed
dishes in one of the two farm sinks situated below windows that
faced out to the garden.

Balancing a tall stack of dirty dishes bound for the free sink,
Adriana crossed the marble floor, dodging, for no reason in particular, the silver fleur-de-lis patterns marking the occasional tile. She
passed in between the island with its fat, sturdy legs and the open
shelving lining the subway-tile walls on her left. The higher shelves
exhibited Margot's favorite and most worn cookbooks, the ones that
had made the cut to travel from Vermont to Red Mountain. The other
shelves displayed large glass containers of a wide variety of flours,
rice, and beans.

Adriana barely noticed the two ladies arguing across the room
about how organic soap was a waste of money. She had just gotten a
little injection of confidence, a rare dose for this over-worked single

mother, or as she called herself, a mombie. Her life was so complicated—taking care of her sick mother, raising her son alone, running from an evil man—that she had lost her connection with femininity. The circumstances of her life had severed every iota of that sexy *mujer* who used to strut through West Los Angeles turning men's heads. Those who knew her at this moment would never believe she was capable of such a "strut." She hadn't even kissed a man since her ex-husband, a relationship that had ended with a well-planned escape.

Brooks Baker's eyes had met hers with thirst. She, of course, had no time to entertain such feelings, but it felt good that at least someone could still see her inner woman. Maybe he was just being nice. She'd experienced plenty of pity since the day she'd walked out of the hospital with those scars a few years ago, though his interest in her hadn't felt superficial.

Adriana gently set her stack of plates down in the free sink. She let her mind wander as she scraped the food leavings into a metal bowl for the chickens. She wasn't ready to ask herself how many more years it would be before she could entertain love again. Even if someone did find her attractive enough to marry, would she ever be ready? That's what an abusive marriage and being solely responsible for her beautiful son had done to her. The idea of going on a date seemed absurd at this point, and actually having to share a bathroom and television with another man sounded awful. Adriana envisioned this beast snoring all night, beard hairs in the sink, endless sports on TV with a bunch of stupid men kicking a ball back and forth. Truthfully, she wasn't sure if she wanted to be touched again.

Acknowledging an urge to make sure her son, who was with his grandmother, was okay, Adriana sidestepped to the counter where her phone was plugged in under a line of copper pots and bunches of dried herbs hanging from a hammered-steel bar. As she navigated the display, a commotion erupted out in the dining room. Leaving her phone on the table, Adriana darted through the swinging doors to investigate.

Carmen Forester was on her knees retching in the middle of the room, a pool of vomit surrounding her. Twenty people had stopped their conversations at the tables, at the bar, and around the fireplace to stare in shock. Adriana ran back into the kitchen and found an empty mop bucket on the floor. Returning, she slid the bucket under Carmen. "Here you go, Mrs. Forester."

Adriana knew Carmen as everyone knew her. She was Jake Forester's wife and a model known throughout the world. Hers was a face Adriana had seen in magazine ads and even on billboards all her life. She had never actually seen Carmen in person until tonight, but recognized her immediately when the regal woman had pranced in earlier. Now the woman was face down in a bucket, a poster girl for life's cruelty.

After several more heaves, Carmen glanced up at Adriana and muttered a thanks. The woman's eyes were bloodshot, and her smoky eyeliner had melted down her cheeks. Her mouth was dirty from puking. A couple of days earlier, while they were cleaning together, Margot had mentioned Carmen's overindulging tendencies. At that moment, Adriana recognized the sadness and alcoholism, both of which she knew all too well.

Adriana noticed Carmen's skirt had risen up in the back, exposing the flesh of her bottom. Aware of the eyes on them, she pulled the skirt down and gathered Carmen's hair as the woman began another round of puking.

When Carmen finished, Adriana whispered, "Can I help you get to a chair? It's going to get on your clothes."

Carmen nodded and took Adriana's hand.

Brooks appeared and helped Adriana lift Carmen up and guide her to the closest chair.

Adriana asked, "Will you keep an eye on her? I'll get a mop."

"Of course," he replied, taking a knee next to Carmen.

Adriana rushed into the kitchen for a mop and another bucket. When she returned, Brooks was still focused on Carmen and hadn't noticed Margot's wiry-haired mutt delighting in the mess. The dog was licking the edges. Some guests were laughing while others seemed to be avoiding looking at all.

"No!" Adriana yelled, running to the dog. "*Sal de aqui!* Get out of here." She shooed him away with her hands.

The dog got the picture and went on to find more trouble, something he was quite good at doing.

Adriana mopped up the mess as the party slowly returned to normal. She felt others looking at her but pushed away the feelings of inferiority.

Margot appeared and took the mop from Adriana, saying, "I don't pay you enough for this, but thank you so much."

"It's fine. We all have bad nights."

Margot touched her arm. "You're too good to me."

Adriana looked at the floor and shook her head.

Margot said, "I'll get this if you can just keep the dirty dishes flowing to the sink."

"Of course," Adriana said, already searching for empty plates.

As she dashed back and forth between the dining room and kitchen several more times, Adriana felt a sense of damaged pride. All those eyes looking down at her as she'd cleaned up Carmen's mess extracted awful feelings. And just the fact that she felt inferior made her even more ashamed.

She couldn't help thinking of her mother, who had cleaned hotel rooms and houses all her life. Her mother had always been proud of her own profession, even when Adriana was a snot-nosed teenager who said on multiple occasions that she'd never clean houses, insinuating plainly that was she too good for such a menial job. Instead of letting the insults affect her negatively, her mother would sit Adriana down and explain why she felt such pride in cleaning houses, to even have a job at all. She'd tell her daughter how so many of her destitute friends back in Akumal didn't have a job at all, and how lucky she was to have started with the Marriott so many years ago. Her mother would also remind Adriana of the Gospel of John, when Jesus washed his disciples' feet before the Last Supper. What a blessing it was to make someone else's life a little bit better every day. Adriana desperately wanted to find such rock-solid dignity in her new profession.

After several trips, Adriana finally caught up with her work. Other than a couple of abandoned wine glasses and a lone fork, she couldn't find any other dirty dishes. As she searched the room one more time, weaving through the people who'd returned to their animated conversations as if nothing had happened a little while ago, Adriana heard someone clinking a glass. She turned to find her boss requesting everyone's attention. Adriana found a position near the kitchen doors to listen.

Margot moved toward the back windows, tapping a knife to crystal until she owned the room. As she thanked everyone for coming, she looked very comfortable speaking in public, as an ex-Broadway singer would be.

Margot said to the quieted room, "I don't want to pull you away too long, but it's important to think of why we're here. The sun reached its highest altitude today. What does that mean for us? That we must all be little suns shining brightly on this planet. We've all had so much pain and suffering in our lives, but we're here now, and I've never seen a community more like family. Together, we can make Red Mountain shine."

She pointed toward her son Jasper and his girlfriend Emilia, who were holding each other as they listened intently. "Especially you two. As you leave us tomorrow, remember today. Remember Red Mountain. Remember that no matter where you go, you represent this place." Margot's eyes watered. Locking her gaze with Jasper's, she added, "Don't forget your mama. No one could ever prepare a mom for this day."

Her shaggy-haired son looked at her through his glasses and mouthed, "Never."

Glancing from Jasper to Emilia, Margot said, "I'm so proud of you both."

Jasper blew her a kiss, and Margot caught it and stuck it in her pocket.

Adriana couldn't imagine saying goodbye to her young son. She hadn't even found the courage to make him sleep in his own bed since they'd left California. Fortunately, she had more than ten years until saying goodbye would undoubtedly become a reality.

Margot wiped her eyes. "The vines outside have given us little green berries. Today marks the day when those berries start to ripen toward their full potential. I know we've all been indulging and letting go. When we wake up tomorrow with headaches and dry mouths and sweaty brows, let's remember today. Let's all focus on reaching *our* full potential. If not for us as individuals, let's do it for Red Mountain. I don't know about you, but this place means nearly everything to me. The real me was born here, and I hope to spend the rest of my life giving back to her."

It was about then that Adriana noticed Philippe plop down on the floor next to her. Close enough to almost be hit by the swinging doors. She tried to quietly shoo him away to save him from getting hurt, but the dog didn't budge. She bent down to give him a push and gasped when she saw what he was holding in his mouth.

It was long.

Purple.

Silicone.

"Philippe," she whispered, bending down. "*Dios mio.*" She reached for the vibrator.

Philippe growled.

She'd grown up around dogs and had been married to one, so she wasn't intimidated. She gripped the vibrator and tugged.

Philippe wasn't having it. He tugged back, growling through clenched teeth.

Adriana whispered his name again with more authority and tightened her grip on the prize.

Philippe rose on all fours and pulled harder.

Adriana reached for his collar with her free hand, but the dog dodged her with a step to the side.

"You crazy dog," she quietly spat at him.

She heard her name. And again. "Is Adriana out there?" called Margot.

Adriana froze. *No. No. Please don't let this happen.*

Margot continued, "If you don't know this woman, she's been

working for me only a little while and is already running the place. She's my savior. Where are you, Adriana?"

Adriana couldn't move, a fawn in headlights.

"There she is!" Margot exclaimed as she pointed toward her housekeeper.

Everyone followed Margot's finger to the corner of the room near the entrance to the kitchen.

At that moment, the dog let go of the vibrator and Adriana fell backward. No one cared that she hit her head. No one cared that she was seeing stars. The only thing anyone could have possibly noticed was Adriana on the floor with a large purple vibrator covered in dog slobber in her upraised hand. And somehow, as if God had decided this humiliation wasn't enough, the vibrator had switched on and was pulsing with gusto. The open-mouthed crowd was so quiet you could hear every throb.

Adriana's face flushed red, and she simply closed her eyes and wished herself to another place.

Then the room erupted in laughter.

After what felt like a lifetime of public shaming, the aftershocks of laughter still shaking the room, Adriana found the courage to open her eyes. Brooks was standing over her, offering his hand. She shook her head, refusing any more of the spotlight.

He read her gesture and turned to address the rest of the room. "Okay, everyone, that's enough. Give the poor girl a break."

The last of the laughter died as Brooks knelt beside her and held out an open hand. "Want me to take that?"

Adriana placed the vibrator in his hand.

He set it on the ground and said, "You don't need to explain. Seriously."

Adriana pushed herself up to a sitting position and rubbed at the back of her head. "That's the most embarrassing moment in my entire life."

"We've all had them. Really, don't worry about it."

"It's not what you think. I...I... It's not *mine*."

The ping of a knife once again striking a wine glass saved Adriana from trying to say anything more. The crowd quieted as a blushing Margot raised her glass higher in the air. She said, "Well, maybe now's a good time to tell the story of how I spent all day looking for my purple vibrator."

The guests shook the inn with laughter and cheers.

With a slight smile, Adriana looked at Brooks and shook her head, wondering what she'd gotten into with this place.

Brooks cracked a grin and offered his hand. "Like I said, welcome to Red Mountain."

5

THE EMPTY NEST AND OTHER MOTHERLY BURDENS

As she had foreseen, like a mystic stroking her crystal ball, Margot did indeed wake with a dry mouth and an aching head. Philippe had just passed gas, which only exacerbated the present moment of agony.

Then it hit her.

Jasper was leaving.

The sudden sobriety of an empty nest was like a long fall into an icy sea.

Margot had tried to prepare herself for this day. She'd been working to rebuild her own life for a long while, separating her identity from her child as Joan had taught her. Still, Margot's masterpiece was going away. They would never again live under the same roof. Judging by his success in the music world already, he'd never again live on Red Mountain. Jasper was big-city stuff now. He'd already cut a record with Jake Forester that was making its way around the world.

The lonely mommy dressed and applied her makeup, only the necessities, then stood by Jasper's door for a while. She knew she'd better let him sleep. He had a big day ahead, a flight across the country and moving into a new dorm. She wanted to go with him but leaving the inn right now would be entrepreneurial suicide. All eight guestrooms were occupied; enough said.

Adriana was good, but she hadn't been there long, and Margot knew that she, herself, still had so much to learn. Every day brought new obstacles. Besides, she cared too much about overseeing every single detail to trust someone else to run things. These days, one bad online review could crush her business. There was no way she'd be leaving Red Mountain until the anticipated slower business days of winter.

She ambled over to Épiphanie with Philippe at her side and turned on the lights in the foyer. The chandeliers in the high ceilings came alive, casting warm reflections of soft light over Jasper's Steinway. Her cheek quivered as she fought off the sadness. How many years had his music filled her soul?

Entering the dining room, she was able to find a smile. With the help of a few kind guests, she and Adriana had cleaned until three in the morning, and though there was plenty of work still to do, no one would ever have known she'd hosted the mountain's entire population last night.

Through the swinging doors and into the kitchen, she filled a kettle with water and set it on the gas stove. Breakfast typically began at seven and ended at nine to give her guests a little flexibility. She always asked the day before if they had a preference, but she never made them set a time in stone. When you're on vacation, the last thing you want is a rigid schedule. But today, she'd pushed back breakfast to eight, knowing she would need an extra hour of sleep.

Every morning for a week now, a neatly dressed Harry Bellflour would descend the stairs at precisely eight o'clock and follow the same routine. He sat in the same chair at the end of one of the long wooden tables, where the morning sun would spray a ray of light on the wooden floor and slice a line over one of his polished leather shoes. He'd cross his legs, begin reading his iPad, and wait for Margot to bring a glass carafe of freshly-roasted coffee.

Today was no exception. By the time the water had boiled, he'd arrived. Bellflour was dressed in a pressed blue button-down shirt, khaki chinos, and loafers. His short gray hair was combed with discipline to the left. He wore a massive gold watch so large it looked as if he'd plucked it off a wall and attached a band. A gold chain hung around his neck and fell into a thick patch of gray chest hair. He was a stout man, overweight but built like a bull. He had a deep orange-hued tan that looked like it came more from the salon than the beach.

"How are you today?" Margot asked, putting on her happy face as she finished her table settings.

As a cello eased into a Mixolydian melody from French composer Debussy, Bellflour peered up from his iPad and pulled the metal-framed glasses off his face, revealing hefty bags under each eye. Fine blue veins ran along the surface of his broad red nose, evidence of a lifetime spent overindulging. He eventually nodded.

"Any fun plans for today?" Piercing his armor had become a game for her, and she needed the distraction today especially.

"A little of this, a little of that," he said, putting his glasses back on and returning to the iPad. His subtle way of saying, "I don't feel like talking."

Like always, his vague response implied he had something to hide. Hence why Margot called him the mystery guest. Still, she wasn't done; still being slightly drunk lifted her inhibitions and fueled her sassy persistence. "How'd you sleep?"

Without looking back up, he muttered, "Fine. Fine."

"Missed you at the party last night."

"Yeah, I have a big day today. Needed some rest."

"Oh, gosh, I hope we didn't keep you up."

Bellflour actually grunted.

Margot forced herself to suppress a laugh, deciding she was possibly fighting a losing battle. She simply added, "Your coffee's almost ready."

Returning to the kitchen to finish preparing breakfast, she couldn't stop wondering about this man. Everything about him was secretive. He'd originally booked three nights, but each morning he'd added another. She'd promised him the room was his for as long as he needed it. Every time she asked him about future plans, he'd say, "Nope, not sure how many more nights. Thank you for being flexible."

A busy man. That was what came across when he spoke. A man involved heavily with whatever it was that made him money. If she had to guess, she'd say he worked at "The Area," which was local speak for the Hanford nuclear site down the road. The only problem was that he didn't appear to have a scientist "vibe" about him. He appeared to be more salesman than scientist, the kind of guy you might find sitting in first class on a Monday morning with a bourbon in hand, en route to peddle his wares. But with his stoic personality, she wondered how effective he could actually be as a salesman.

Margot had learned over the course of his stay that he was a white wine guy. Though he only wanted his room cleaned every few days, when she did get in there, she'd find five or six empty bottles lined along the window sill. Apparently, he liked to drink alone.

She returned with a carafe of a washed Ethiopian brew roasted by her current obsession, Methodical Coffee, located in Greenville, South Carolina. She'd been collecting coffee mugs ever since she'd moved to Washington, preparing for the opening of the inn, and for her own pleasure, she always chose one that fit her guest. With her humor lurking in the background, the white mug she chose for Mr. Bellflour today said: *Please close your mouth. And walk away.*

Setting the mug in front of her guest, she filled it and asked, "Are you planning to stay a few more days?"

He took a sip of black coffee and then harrumphed. "Most likely."

"Where are you from in California?" She had asked him the same question the morning before, and he'd sidestepped.

"The Bay Area."

"I love it there."

His eyes went back to the iPad, and he obviously and desperately pretended he couldn't hear her.

Okay, I guess we're done. She wished she had an *I love California* mug but suspected he didn't know much about love at all.

Margot prepared frittatas with the party leftovers and gorgeous bowls of fruit family-style, delivering the dishes to her guests as they slowly trickled down, wobbly and groggy-eyed. She hadn't let the night before affect her efforts. The presentation was exceptional, verified by the gasps at the tables. As with everything she did for the inn, she'd taken each minute detail seriously. For example, her fruit was perfectly ripe. Margot's pet peeve was sitting down to breakfast at a lovely hotel only to find hard or flavorless melon, so she would forgo fruit before putting unripe crap on her guests' plates.

Jasper found his mom tidying up in the kitchen. She dried her hands on a nearby towel as she turned to him. He was standing on the other side of the island. His hair was all over the place. There was a pimple on his nose. He wore a white T-shirt and sweatpants. He usually stumbled out of bed and into the shower, then put considerable time and thought into his hair and outfit before coming down the stairs. He'd woken up and walked straight over to the inn to find his mom, knowing how hard today would be for her. Of course, he wasn't hungover. He drank carefully, always mindful of keeping his brain in good shape for the piano. The only thing he put before his piano was his mom, and that's why today was going to be so tough.

He gave a small wave. "Hi, Mom."

Oh, the pride and pain, all mixed into one. The premature loneliness pulsed through her body, but she wanted to exude excitement; she wanted to send him off into the world without any reservations. They looked at each other, exploring each other's eyes. Margot admired him so much. Despite his parents' divorce and being the new kid in school and getting picked on for his smaller size and artistic demeanor, he'd persevered. Now, he was hours away from boarding a plane to attend one of the top music colleges in the world. Yes, he'd be the new kid again, but his artistic sensibility would finally be embraced. Hot off the release of the album with Jake Forester, Jasper would already be a celebrity there.

She couldn't hide it for another minute. She erupted into tears with a loud wail. She covered her mouth but anything short of a pillow over her face couldn't stifle the gushing emotions. The tears spilled out from points of sadness and happiness and pride and despair and fear and hope, all coming out in a jumble. It didn't help that, along with the full moon, her own red moon had risen, further igniting her emotions.

Jasper crossed the room and walked into her open arms. They embraced.

"Today's a happy day," she said.

"I can tell, Mom."

"You knew I had to do this."

"I just hope you don't forget about me."

She pushed him away. "I know you're joking." She looked him up and down, absorbing the being she'd created. He was indeed ready for the world. She'd put every minute of her life into him for eighteen years. Now it was his time to fly.

She rested her hand on the oak island she'd just wiped clean. "How do you feel? You're not going to see Emilia for a while."

"I'm going to miss both the women in my life, but I'm not leaving forever." He began stretching his fingers back one by one, a new habit he often indulged in. "Think about it this way. When you see me next time, after a little break, the reunion will be that much sweeter."

Margot smiled, loving how her son always said things beyond his age. "And Emilia? Are you guys going to make it?" She had tried not to pry the past few days but knew how hard leaving his girlfriend would be.

"I really hope so. A summer in Europe will be good for her."

"Are you sad you're not going?"

"Of course. If I could travel with a grand piano, I'd be in, but I can't leave my instrument for that long. Not right now. And I'm not going to backpack a keyboard around. I can't slow down. She and I will be together again soon. NYU isn't that far from Boston. A quick train ride."

"That's true." Margot so hoped he didn't get his heart broken one day soon.

"I'm not stupid. I know most high school couples don't last." He shrugged. "Maybe we're different. I know I'll never do any better. It just depends on whether she meets some French hunk who romances her on the Seine."

"I'm sure they'll try, but none of them will compare."

"Thanks, Mom," he said skeptically. "She's still above my pay grade. It's been a great year so far, but she deserves royalty."

God, she loved how he talked with such maturity. Margot sipped her African coffee and tried to back off the protective role, an effort that would be forever ongoing. "I will agree that high school relationships rarely last through college. You're right, but I'll not agree she's out of your league. Yes, she's beautiful. So what? She's lucky to have you. If she does meet some French douchebag who puts daisies in her hair and dines her along the Champs-Élysées or serenades her at the top of the Eiffel tower and she falls in love, it will be a brief affair. All the romance of Europe trapped into one man half as good as you are. Sometimes what happens is they meet someone else, and then they come running back. The question is whether you'll still be waiting for her. Either way, you and I both know the two of you aren't over."

Jasper cracked a grin. "I have to say, that was maybe the most grown-up you've ever treated me. What happened to your protection mechanism?"

"I've been working on it."

"I can tell. Mom, I know the world's a tough place. Dad taught me that. Truthfully, I want Emilia to be happy. I know everyone says that, but I mean it. I want her to go find what she's looking for. I want her to come into her own. She has so much potential, but the last year beat her down. It's time she takes care of *her*."

"At least she's not with Tex anymore. What's his story now, anyway? I haven't heard you say a word about him."

"He's backed off."

"He lost his girl to you and was thrown in jail for beating up Mr. Massey. Hopefully he's learning lessons."

"He's been cool lately. I'd guess he had a come-to-Jesus moment when there was some question about whether or not the Longhorns would rescind their offer to recruit him after graduation. But, lucky for him, they're going to let him play. I'm good with not seeing him again." He poured himself a cup of coffee from the glass carafe by the stove and changed the subject. "Did you extract any new clues from the Bellflour guy?"

Margot tilted her head and said victoriously, "Two things! He's from the Bay Area. And he's going to be here at least a few more days."

"Wow, he's really opening up." He sipped his coffee and said, "It's going to be all right. Boston's only three stops and a half a day away."

She smiled unconvincingly. "Was there somewhere farther you could have picked?"

"It's kind of a good school. My choice had nothing to do with you. I *could* have done Paris."

"If you'd have done Paris, I'd be closing up shop to follow you. Just remember who loves you. Your mom. And Emilia. You can love that piano all day long, but it's never going to love you back."

"I'm not sure I agree. That ivory touch, the way she responds when I tickle her...she's perhaps the greatest love of all." Never scared to break into song, he began singing Whitney Houston's "Greatest Love of All." He grabbed his mom's hand and pulled her into a dance. Not knowing the rest of the words, he hummed the melody as he wrapped his arms around her. Then he said with a chuckle, "I'll think of you every minute of every day. You are my greatest love of all."

She rolled her eyes and drenched his neck in tears. Days would be so empty without this being in her home, without hearing his angelic voice, without sharing the good times and the bad.

A single mom says goodbye to her son. And then she's without. Without.

6

THE MILE-HIGH CLUB

A gate agent with a wheelchair met Otis and Joan at LAX. Otis walked alongside as the agent pushed his wounded love toward their next plane. The craziness of travel spun around them. A family dressed in Hawaiian shirts and flip-flops rushed by, apparently chasing a tight connection. A group of kids stood by a Starbucks with their faces buried in their phones while sucking Frappuccinos through fat straws. A man wearing a Delta shirt pleaded with people to sign up for their American Express card. A voice from above was saying someone forgot his phone at security.

Though Papeete on the island of Tahiti was the destination on Aunt Morgan's list, Otis and Joan were only briefly stopping there before catching one more plane to Bora Bora, another island in French Polynesia. Otis figured Aunt Morgan wouldn't mind that much; he liked the hotels in Bora Bora better. Besides, he couldn't let her win everything.

"Are you hungry?" he asked Joan. "I smell bacon."

He leaned down to hear her answer. "I'm fine with what's on the plane. You can find something if you'd like."

Ever since his stroke last year, Otis had changed his diet in a big way. Joan had been his coach through it all, and somehow, some way, with her magic, he'd recovered completely. He hadn't experienced one setback; his palate and sense of smell were as strong as ever. Out of fear of returning to the place he'd been, he'd stuck with the diet, only cheating enough to keep his sanity. Even after a year of riding the healthy train, he still woke with one thing on his mind: thick cut bacon. In fact, if he were really on the kind of vacation where you set all your discipline aside and bathed in pure joy, he'd be flying first class to a bacon wonderland. He would glide through the grease of a bacon daydream, touching down on a crispy bacon landing strip. People would throw bacon confetti at the new arrivals as they climbed into the bacon mobile and headed toward their resort in Baconlandia. They'd sleep on bacon mattresses. They'd eat giant salads composed of tiny, nearly microscopic wedges of iceberg lettuce, a sprinkle of blue cheese, and a foot-high mound of thick cut bacon. Not thick cut like Oscar Mayer. We're talking Tulsa thick cut. With pints of Guinness! Rivers of Guinness! Taps spitting out Guinness!

"How much wine do you have in your bag?" he heard Joan ask, disturbing him from his daydream.

He leaned in, his chin touching her hair. "Huh?"

"Are you alive back there? I was asking how much wine you brought with you."

He burst into a laugh that rose from his gut.

"What's so funny?" Joan asked.

"I miss bacon, that's all."

It felt good to laugh. There hadn't been a lot of that lately. Not since Joan had been shot. Today, over seven months later, she still had a long way to go. She was improving, but her body and mind had weakened tremendously. What irony that she'd helped him cure the symptoms of his stroke only to later have one herself. It was almost as if she had sacrificed herself so that he could recover. Knowing her shamanistic ways, such a sacrifice was a possibility he couldn't rule out.

Joan had been the strongest and healthiest person Otis had ever met, mentally, physically, and spiritually. She was always pushing her brain to learn new things. She taught yoga; she meditated. She paddleboarded and rode Jet Skis and would do things most people her age would never consider. Then came that day and the bullet that changed their trajectory. She was fighting back with everything she had, but the road would be long, and many people never recovered from global cerebral ischemia.

She had a slight tremor in her hands and a weak grip, but the worst and most obvious effect was the damage to her stamina. Walking more than ten minutes was a great chore. Even simply putting up the dishes sapped her strength. When she began to tire, she'd stumble over words. Because of the toll on her body, her emotional stability also had suffered. Otis had never seen Joan lose her temper or snap at him prior to the incident, but now, on occasion after a hard day, she could lose control.

Watching her suffer the past few months had been more painful than anything Otis had ever been through, including losing his wife and two sons. Otis didn't want to accept the blame, but he couldn't help falling on the sword. It was, indeed, his fault that he'd started a war with his neighbor. It was his fault that he'd mishandled things that day. He'd taken the bait from Henry Davidson and jumped into an argument when he simply could have walked away.

So much for the bacon laughs. He'd returned to reality.

Boarding the plane to Papeete, Otis helped Joan to her seat and settled into the pod next to her. The flight attendant brought them pre-takeoff glasses of Champagne. He clinked glasses with Joan and toasted, "To Morgan. I miss the hell out of her. I slightly wish she were with us right now." Actually, her ashes were crammed into his checked bag with six bottles of wine, somewhere in the cargo hold, but that's not what he meant. "She'd probably be making out with the pilot." He waited to see if he sparked a laugh out of Joan.

Yes, he did.

And then, "May both of us handle our eighties with such grand vitality." He took a sip and squeezed Joan's hand.

It occurred to Otis how down and out he'd been. Not that his mood hadn't been as obvious as a Times Square billboard. Here Joan was, fighting to regain her general motor skills, and he'd been wallowing in his own mess. He needed to be stronger for her, and that would begin today. He couldn't deny that flying to paradise did in fact give him a taste of freedom.

"Honey," he said, "there's no place I'd rather be than with you. I love you dearly."

She touched her heart, a gesture she used often, meaning the same as his words.

He breathed a sigh of relief. "Well, we made it. Shall we see what's on the menu?"

"Ah, yes. Food. That's your real first love, isn't it?"

"I have a few loves, my dear. You're certainly number one, but wine and food are close, close seconds. That's why sitting at a dinner table across from you is my dream come true."

Thumbing through the menu, Otis found the wine list and decided on a Picpoul de Pinet to follow the bubbles. It would be a game-time decision between the filet and the bento box salmon. He'd do his best to shut out the little voice of discipline in his ear yapping about how the fish was healthier.

I'm on vacation, damn it.

"You want to die on vacation?"

What's a few days of eating something actually enjoyable!?

"You tell me, Otis. Remember your stroke?"

You're telling me eating one nice filet for once this damned year is going to break my whole body?

"It's a slippery slope."

That's how those conversations went. A battle until the end—the end being when the flight attendant appeared with her pen and paper just before takeoff. If he could drink enough bubbles, the voice of discipline would weaken.

Down the hatch! May I have another?

"Look." Joan pointed, reading his mind as she always did. "Mushroom risotto."

"Hmm. I guess I missed it! That's exactly what I want. A big gelatinous pile of white starch with fungus stirred in. Yum!"

"Hey, I'm not going to get in your way. If you feel the need to take an animal's life, do so."

"Oh, my Lord. You're sounding like Margot. That was the most passive aggressive attack on carnivorous temptation in the history of mankind. And you won."

"I'm not trying to win."

Attempting to lighten the mood, he said, "Actually, I'm a huge advocate for mushroom rights. Mushrooms have feelings too. I'm a member of the Mushroom Alliance."

She grasped the point, smiled, and let it go.

When the attendant did finally return, the battle among the voices in his head had peaked.

With a chipper voice, the woman in uniform asked, "What could I get you, sir?"

"I'll have the..." He looked at Joan. "Can I have the...?" He looked at his watch, stalling. Then in a surrender and acceptance of defeat as epic as Cornwallis at Yorktown, Otis conceded. "I'll have the mushroom risotto."

When Joan smiled, he wagged his finger at her. "You're not going to give me a hard time about the quantity of Guinness I will consume in Dublin. Promise me that. There are some things that might be considered more precious than life, and a pint of Guinness at a bar in Dublin is one of them."

In her best Irish accent, she said, "Don't warry. Oy'll drink a pint er two with ye fer shurr, laddie."

～

OTIS AND JOAN were an hour into their flight, both dining on the starchy fungus plate with movies paused on the screens in front of them. Until the food arrived, Otis was watching a war movie, Joan a foreign film with subtitles.

"Are you a member of the mile-high club?" Joan asked, diverting a chat about where to spread Morgan's ashes.

As the question set in, Otis did a double take and choked on his fungus. He grabbed the napkin off his lap and wiped his lips. Joan could speak so freely about sex, and though Otis wanted to be that open, it did not come naturally. "There's something about spreading my aunt's ashes and having sex in an airplane that don't belong in the same conversation."

"I'm not sure Morgan would agree."

"Fair point. No, I'm not a member. And I'm not sure I want to know about your own exploits."

"I wouldn't say either way, but if you don't want to become a club member, you'd better lock the bathroom door when you go in there."

"Joan," he said, stabbing his fork at a mushroom, "you're in no condition to make love in an airplane. And we're old. For God's sake, we're old. Those are the kinds of things you do when you're in your mid-twenties and don't have a care in the world."

"Seems to me, Otis, that the older you get, the fewer cares you should have. The only thing you should be worried about is whether or not you remembered your little blue pills."

He turned rosy red like jolly ol' Saint Nick. "Joan Tobey, I may have a heart attack on this plane. You're embarrassing me to no end." Moving in another direction, he asked, "How's your foreign film?"

She put her finger to her chin. "He says, changing the topic and turning down an open invitation to the mile-high club."

He continued to steer away from further sexual innuendos and said, "I don't do subtitles, and I try to avoid any movie someone refers to as a"—he made air quotes—"'film.'"

"So you've told me a million times, my love." She took a bite of bread.

"How are you feeling?"

"May I ask something of you? You've gone out of your way the past several months. It means so much to me, and your love shines on me like a bright star of hope. When I do get better, so much will be because of you." She turned closer toward him and squeezed his hand. "But you can't carry the guilt of what happened. It wasn't your fault. Henry Davidson is sick. You were trying to protect a dog. There's nothing you could have done to prevent what happened."

"I feel like we've had this conversation before."

"Many times. What if *you'd* been shot? Then what? What if *you'd* died? We wouldn't be on our way to an overwater bungalow in Bora Bora, would we? He missed my head. He missed my spine. I'm alive. A little weak, that's all. We're together. Let's bathe in the joy of our togetherness and let go of that awful day." She breathed slowly. "Let's not let Henry Davidson win."

"Easier said than done."

"Since when did *difficult* stop you? Your whole life is a story of overcoming."

"I've lived my whole life under a ladder. If surviving a long run of bad luck is overcoming, then you're right."

"I'd say you've done more than survive. How many times have you told me that the best wines come from vines that must fight with everything they have to survive?" She touched his face with her hand, her lips an inch from his. "You're the best wine I've ever tasted."

7

CARMEN'S INTERVENTION

With Advil and Gatorade smoothing out his hangover, Brooks stood behind the tasting bar addressing the full-time employees of Lacoda: the controller, the tasting room and hospitality staff, the assistant winemaker, the vineyard guys, and the cellar rats. The tasting room was steel, rusted iron, and concrete, except for the brick wall behind them. Created by a Seattle street artist, the abstractly painted wall offered the only bright colors in the room.

As they sat on stools along the bar, staring back at him, half of them sipping coffee from thermoses, Brooks wondered if they truly cared about wine as much as he did. Lacoda wasn't a massive operation—it produced around 5,000 cases a year—but it required a team running at high efficiency to make the kind of wine Brooks and the boss, Jake Forester, demanded.

"Do you know what wine means to me?" He met every one of their eyes before continuing. "Everything. Every. Thing. Wine is life. Wine is *my* life. What goes into the bottles back there is *all* I think about, *all* I breathe. This thing we're doing is not for a paycheck. This thing—all of us working together to bring this land to the people—is art. Do you understand me? If you don't enjoy your job, I need to know right now. If you're not ready to give me all you have, you need to go find another job. The only way our wine can be real is if we *all* put everything we have into it."

Brooks let that sink in for a moment. "I'm starting to feel like a babysitter. Yes, part of my job as winemaker is to manage you, and I'm happy to lead. But I can't have drama in here, and I can't have disrespect, not to other employees or the wine."

He picked up a corkscrew and toyed with it, thinking about what he was going to say next. "If someone has a major problem, you tell me and we'll fix it. But there will be no more laziness. When you have a break, you respect the time. When your break is over, you get your ass up and get back to why you're here. If you're on the bottling line, you don't disrespect the wine by grabbing a bottle and taking a sip." He eyed the cellar crew. "Yes, I see all. And you don't sneak beers. Not anymore. I'll tell you when you can drink. If we barbecue on Friday afternoon, you can have a couple of beers. But I see a beer in someone's hand at the wrong time, and I'm going to send you packing."

He laid down the corkscrew. "As far as the music back in the cellar goes? One day can be mariachi, the other is rock-and-roll. That's how we're going to do it. In the tasting room, nothing is more important than polished glasses. I will not have fans of our wine travel from their homes to this winery and sit down to enjoy what we're doing, only to be served vessels with lipstick stains around the rims. If you need to be here by nine o'clock, don't show up at eight fifty-nine. Don't test me. Show up ten minutes early. Show up an hour early. Take pride in what we're doing. It's important. Yeah, maybe it's just wine. We're not saving lives. But we're making art. To me, art is as important as saving lives.

"When people drink our wine, I want to see tears in their eyes. I want to see our wine go down their throats and spread through their veins, and I want to see Red Mountain glowing in their eyes." He stared down each employee one by one. "Can I make it any clearer than that?"

A collective shaking of heads.

He nodded. Glanced around the room. Then pounded his chest

with his fist. "Make me proud. Make your mothers proud. Make your fathers proud. Let's do something meaningful together." He waved his hands, shooing them. "Now, go, go, go. Go!"

As they dispersed, Jake texted him: *It's time.*

∾

BECAUSE OF THEIR NOTORIETY, a stone privacy wall wrapped around the Foresters' angular modern home. With the sand-colored stucco and desert landscaping, Brooks imagined it looked like a house you might find in Scottsdale or Palm Springs—two places he'd never been. He walked through the open gate, around the circular fountain, and found Emilia sitting on the front steps. She was flanked by two giant cacti rising out of well-manicured rock gardens.

The Foresters' two Weimaraners sat at her feet, and she was stroking their fur. They ran to Brooks.

As he let them sniff his hand, he said to her, "Good morning, kiddo."

"Morning." She'd shaved her head last fall, but her brown hair had already grown back down to her shoulders. She wore raggedy jeans with holes in the knees.

He called her his almost-sister, the Foresters being his only family for so long, so his heart ached as he thought about what she had to do today. Before she could leave on a plane to Paris, she had to send her mom to rehab. They'd been talking about the intervention for two weeks, so Carmen's behavior the night before had only verified their decision.

Emilia had endured a lot of pain the past year. She'd made a mistake and fallen for a teacher with whom she'd had some sort of relationship. No one knew the details, but everyone had suspicions, and that teacher had been fired and run out of the state. As anyone could imagine, especially for the daughter of celebrities, the following months had nearly broken her. But she'd endured. Ready to backpack Europe and then tackle NYU.

Brooks sat next to her on the same step. The cacti cast a shadow along their feet. "Is your mom up yet?"

She shook her head.

"I feel for you, Em. You don't deserve having to do this. You don't deserve this past year. You're eighteen. Life should be a playground."

"My life is anything but a playground. I just... I feel so bad for Mom. I know she has to go, but it sucks. Everybody knows her. Everyone's going to talk about her. I'm sure everyone on the whole mountain's already talking about her performance last night." As the dogs returned to her side, she said, "Our family's going back in the headlines. It never stops. If I hear one more person tell me how lucky I am, how they'd kill to have my parents, their fame, their money, I will go crazy. You know what I want? A life where no one takes pictures of us. Where we don't need a stupid gate and security cameras. Where people don't kiss your ass. Where people don't look at you, wondering what you can do for them. Where you can make friends without wondering if they have questionable motives. A life that wouldn't have led my poor mom to this."

Brooks wrapped his arm around her shoulders and continued to listen as his heart broke with each word. When she ran out of words, he asked, "Are you going to miss this place? It will be a big change."

"So much." She wiped her eyes. "It's not that big a deal, really. From Red Mountain, population one hundred, to three months of Europe, to a tiny dorm room in New York City. Itsy bitsy change."

"Only difference is you can't pee outside anymore."

She squinted her brow. "I don't pee outside."

"Huh? You missed out. I've turned into a borderline primate since moving out here. Do you think you'll return to the mountain of red?"

She breathed in the dry air. "I love this mountain. I love the people. Yeah, I could come back. I have to leave, though."

"Of course you do. It's a big world out there. You have to rule things out, experience it all, find your calling." He tapped her shoulder. "You know what I hope you do? Find your calling and bring it back here. Come back with a gift for all of us."

"I like that idea."

"What about Jasper? What's going to happen with you two?"

"I'm going to miss him every minute."

"Do you love him?"

"Yeah, and I don't want to lose him. But he's like my dad. Of course I had to fall in love with someone like my dad. No matter how much Jasper loves me or could ever love me, music is his first love."

"Maybe that's okay, Em. Maybe there's room for both. There are different kinds of loves out there. Your dad has a lot of love to give. Seems like Jasper does too."

Jake opened the modern metal-strapped door wearing his signature black jeans and boots.

Brooks turned from his seat on the steps, looking up at a man gearing up for one of the toughest moments of his life.

Jake said, "Hey, guys, are you ready? Carmen's about to come downstairs."

Brooks and Emilia stood and followed Jake inside. Brooks noticed Emilia's over-stuffed Osprey backpack next to a line of purple orchids in white square pots in the foyer. They entered the living room, and he exchanged quiet greetings with the others who were waiting while facing the fireplace with the giant flat-screen television hanging above. There was no fire in the fireplace and nothing displayed on the television screen, and Brooks imagined this silent awkwardness was much like the minutes in church waiting for the service to begin.

Carmen's oldest friend and her husband sat on the purple leather couch next to Abby, the Foresters' assistant and Brooks's ex-fiancée. Abby looked at Brooks through her tortoise-shell glasses and turned up one corner of her mouth. Brooks hadn't had a meaningful conversation with her in months. A big cloud of confusion still hovered between them. Luca, Emilia's younger brother, sat on the rug building a Lego robot, oblivious to the sadness around him. Brooks and Emilia sat down on the other couch and waited for Jake to bring his wife in—for the biggest surprise of her life.

Everyone twisted their heads as Carmen Forester, hair in a ponytail and still wearing her white robe and pink bedroom slippers, entered from the back side of the living room. Her bloodshot eyes

told a story of late-night partying and hangovers. Upon seeing everyone, she said, "You didn't tell me we had company, honey." She
cinched her robe tighter and covered up her cleavage. "Good morning, everyone."

She quickly sensed something was wrong when no one replied
with more than a curt wave and mumble. The reality of the scene
rose like a submarine out of the water. Her face—the face that had
graced hundreds of photo shoots in her career—morphed through
phases of shock, fear, and anger—and settled on understanding.
With a venom that everyone in that room knew well, she spat out,
"What is this?"

Jake stood up from a chair, approached his wife, and took her
hand. "You know what this is, baby."

Carmen pulled away from him.

Brooks felt their pain like it was his own, and he closed his eyes
and drew in a slow audible breath. He suppressed the tears that
threatened to escape and pushed back the lump of sadness stuck in
his throat.

Carmen cocked her head. "Don't you *dare* tell me you're trying to
do some kind of intervention."

"We'd like to talk to you for a little while," Jake said. "Please sit
down with me." He motioned to an empty chair next to the one
where'd he'd been sitting. He turned them both away from the television to face the others.

"Don't tell me to sit down! I'm not doing this right now."

"You're definitely doing this right now. Right now. The people
who love you most in this world are here for you, and we have some
things to say."

As Carmen and Jake stared each other down, Brooks saw the two
people who had given him a job and a chance diving into what might
be the rawest moment in their marriage. He saw a man so full of love
for his wife and family that he'd do anything to help her. He saw a
man who, despite years of tremendous success in so many fields, had
found humility in trying to save his partner, in trying to hold together
his family. And he saw the good part of Carmen, the person Jake had

married, the more conscious part of her, battling to control this addiction, wanting the help, pleading for it. Yet he saw the snake of the disease wrapped around her neck, choking her.

Carmen finally said, "Let me hop in the shower and pour a cup of coffee."

"I'll get you a cup. No shower. We're doing this now. Please."

"Mom," Emilia nearly begged, "*please*. Sit down."

Carmen heard the heartfelt plea loud and clear. After digesting the words, she nodded and found her seat. She grabbed a pillow and held it tightly as she fixed her eyes on a spot on the abstract-designed rug. A spot on which she'd keep her eyes glued for the next twenty minutes as the ones she loved and who loved her stripped her of her ego and revealed the shame of her addiction.

Jake brought her a cup of coffee. As she sipped, he said, "I'm going to drive you to a place outside of Seattle today. You have a disease. No one is judging you. All of us here have our own problems. It's just that we know exactly what yours is, and we know how to help you. This isn't fun for any of us, but I hope you can take it as a testament of how much we care about you."

He took a deep breath through his mouth and blew it out slowly, with intention. "I honestly don't know if you have a drinking problem or not. The pills, for sure. I pray that last night was the last time you take one. Today marks the day you wake up from this bad dream. I lost you three years ago to those damned pills, and today it stops." He scanned the room. "This is a wake-up call. I want everyone to say a few words."

Her eyes still down, Carmen said, "Let's skip all that. I know I have a problem. No need to strangle me with it."

"We're not trying to hurt you. We're going to tell you how much you mean to us, how much we need you back."

Carmen sighed and placed her hands over her face.

∾

AN HOUR LATER, Brooks drove Jasper and Emilia to the airport. They passed the incredibly busy Conoco at the bottom of the hill, drove around the traffic circle, and crossed under the highway. As Brooks turned left to join the fast-moving traffic of I-82, he saw a commercial *For Sale* sign—half the size of a billboard—to his right. Knowing the property would have suited a fast-food or hotel chain well, Brooks hoped, for the sake of the inhabitants of Red Mountain, that a buyer with vision and class would build something more worthy of the area's world-class wines.

Brooks tried to focus on his driving as these two kids, barely eighteen and holding hands in the backseat of his work truck, watched the mountain fade away and the miles stretch between them and their mothers. It was the first time either one had left their families for an extended period. Brooks could only hope they, together or apart, would find the good in the world.

After the tears had dried and they drew close to the airport exit, Emilia asked, "So, Brooks, what were you and Joan talking about last night? You were into something deep."

"She was giving me a little guidance."

"Like?"

"Say 'yes' more."

"I like that. Are you going to follow her advice?"

Brooks looked at her through the rearview mirror, eyebrows raised. "Yes."

Laughter filled the truck.

"Will you give me twenty dollars?" she asked.

Brooks tossed her his wallet. "Yes."

Another round of laughs.

"Will you..." She thought for a moment. "Will you take next week off work?"

Brooks didn't say anything.

"Gotcha," Emilia said.

"I'll think about it. Give me another one."

"Am I the most brilliant woman you've ever met?"

"Yes."

"This fits you well, Brooks." She turned to her boyfriend. "What else could we get out of him?"

"Let's see," Jasper said. "Can we stop for a cappuccino at Roasters?"

"Yes."

As Brooks drove east, he thought of the promise he'd made to Joan that he'd ask Adriana out. He didn't even want to *think* about it. Couldn't remember the last time he'd propositioned a woman. He'd intended to ask out Abby when they first started dating, but she'd been the one to initiate the relationship.

As fate would have it, Emilia asked, "Do you miss Abby?"

"That's not fair. Enough of this."

"Okay. Can I try one more?"

He lasered a warning with his eyes in the mirror. "Yes."

"Will you call Abby? Take her to lunch or something. Bury the hatchet. Will you just call her and take a step toward some sort of friendship at least? It's awkward for everyone right now."

Brooks found Emilia's eyes in that mirror. "Yes, I'll call her." *Why is everyone so concerned about my love life?*

8

FROM VIOLETA TO ADRIANA

Adriana Hernandez. That's what everyone called her now. It had taken a while to get used to her new first name. Last name, no problem. But to change the name her parents called her in the crib back in Akumal on the Yucatán Peninsula, that had required work. *Mucho trabajo*, as her father used to mumble with beer breath—his excuse for everything.

Adriana's son had finally stopped asking why people didn't call her Violeta anymore. Thank God, because she could never answer his question.

The memories of her eight years in Mexico were a blur of fighting, poverty, and unhappiness. Her mother, now known as Margarita, cleaned hotel rooms for the Marriott in Playa del Carmen while her father did nothing but hang around with a group of other bums in Akumal, watching *fútbol* and drinking cheap beer. For many years, he'd worked security for private investors who owned beachfront property along Highway 307, the four-lane road running from Cancun down toward Belize. He'd spent his days in a treetop bungalow watching for squatters attempting to run across the highway and climb the tall fences. All the sitting around had gotten the best of him, and he was soon packing his cooler with *cervezas* and passing out on the job. He was fired a few times before he finally decided their family of three could live off Margarita's wages.

When Adriana was six, the same age as her son now, they'd moved to Mexico City. Knowing he wouldn't want to go, Margarita had lied to her husband, saying Marriott was transferring her. In truth, the move was voluntary and a last-ditch effort to save her husband and marriage. None the wiser, he had reluctantly agreed.

The change hadn't done much for refreshing her parents' relationship, and it didn't take long for her father to find another set of bums to drink with. All Adriana could remember of him was an unshaven, abusive man in a dirty white T-shirt smelling of alcohol and constantly complaining or screaming about something, constantly walking out the door whenever her mother needed help.

When Margarita had woken Adriana up one morning to steal her away, she hadn't cried. Her father was a terrible, terrible man who'd been getting worse, his abuse turning more and more physical every day. As they had climbed on a private plane with her mom's new employers, a rich family from Los Angeles Margarita had befriended at the hotel, Adriana remembered smiling. She remembered seeing her mom's face, the thrill of finding a new life, the hope of leaving the violence they'd come to know in the past.

God works in mysterious ways. Adriana had relived her mother's life. It wasn't because of that move that she'd changed her name. They didn't have to bother changing their names when they moved to the United States. Her father was so lazy and uninvolved, he'd never come looking for them. He had no money. And more importantly, he had no love to give. What would be the point?

No. Adriana hadn't been forced to change her name until after she ran from Michael, her own poor choice of a husband. The judge had sent him to California State Prison in Lancaster to serve three-to-five for felony domestic battery. She, her mother, and Zack had left California. Violeta became Adriana, and her mother Eva became Margarita, but they hadn't changed Zack's first name. Adriana had hoped changing their last name would be enough. Honestly, she hoped just leaving the state would be enough.

As part of her plan to leave Michael, she'd spent many hours deciding where to go. Her first thought had been the East Coast, as far as she could go without leaving the country. But one day while she was walking Zack to Sunday school, she overheard a conversation, as if God himself were speaking to her, about eastern Washington's low cost of living and lack of traffic. She salivated at the idea of getting out of all that LA traffic.

Adriana didn't know much about Washington State but began her research. The Tri-Cities and the surrounding area enjoyed over three hundred days of sunshine a year. It had a large Mexican population, a decent school system, and a strong economy. And, indeed, very little traffic. When she saw the Google images of downtown Prosser with its old-west charm, she knew she'd found their next stop.

Adriana had found some happiness in their new home. There were even times when she no longer felt the need to look over her shoulder, as if the past ten years and her life with that man were all a bad dream. She rented a baby-blue doublewide in a little neighborhood of mostly trailers near Prosser. It came with furniture that looked like it belonged on the side of the road, but at the time, having something was better than nothing. One by one, she was replacing each piece as fast as she could afford it.

Excited to see her son, Adriana left work and drove west along the Yakima River on a winding two-lane road as rural Washington farmland unfolded before her. She walked into her doublewide. Her son was stretched out on the couch playing with his Etch-a-Sketch. He knew better than to have his shoes on the furniture, but knowing she had to pick her battles, she didn't correct him. Thank God she didn't see her ex-husband in Zack. At least not the parts that mattered. Adriana felt no anger or rage, and no resentment when she looked at her little boy. She felt pure pride and joy.

As proof of the resilience of children, Zack still loved his dad and asked about him often, even after the verbal and physical abuse they'd both been the victims of. Adriana had never figured out exactly what to tell Zack when they'd left, so she settled for putting it off, simply saying they'd reunite one day. The truth was more like—

hopefully—never. She hated how she could never be honest with Zack. According to her lawyer, Michael might get out of prison early, and Adriana was terrified he'd search for them. It wasn't fair. He'd been sentenced to three to five years but had a chance to walk after eighteen months. The man had beaten his wife and child! What was wrong with the legal system?

As it turned out, Adriana, Zack, and Margarita had settled in Prosser in time for Zack to start the second semester of kindergarten. He'd now just finished first grade. Though Adriana's mother was sick, she watched Zack when Adriana worked. As her mother's illness escalated, she'd have to figure out another daycare option for her son until school started.

"Hi, *mi amor!*"

"Mama!" Zack yelled, putting down his Etch-a-Sketch and running for her. His hair was cut very short, a #2 shave she'd done herself, and it spiked up around the ears. He had a beautiful smile with a gap between his front teeth. He wore his swimming goggles all the time, both in and out of the water. Adriana thought it was the cutest thing she'd ever seen, though she knew he used them to hide behind sometimes.

She swept him up in her arms and squeezed him like she was the one saying goodbye to her own college-bound son today. She kissed his neck. "How was your day?"

He looked at her through his goggles. "Tata drew me a dragon and made it breathe fire!"

"Really?" She wondered for the hundredth time how he had stumbled upon 'Tata' for his grandmother.

"And then I tried to draw one, but it's not as good as hers."

"Can I see?" she asked, putting him down.

He ran to the table and grabbed his notebook.

Adriana turned to Margarita, who was standing over the stove. She wore a wig of short black hair, having lost most of her white hair to the first round of chemotherapy. She'd steadily been dropping weight since the diagnosis, and loose skin fell from her neck. Her dresses were too big, but she refused to waste money on new ones, so

Adriana would tailor them as best she could. Before the disease had taken its grip, Margarita had looked ten years younger than she was. Now she looked ten years older.

"*Hola*, Mama." Though her mother could speak some English, their conversations were mostly in Spanish. "How are you today?"

"I'm great."

It was understood between them that nothing was okay, but they had to pretend sometimes.

After admiring her son's art, Adriana stepped into a kitchen clouded in chili powder and cumin aromas. She kissed her mother on the cheek and asked, "Have you taken your medicine?"

While working the spatula through a sizzling mixture of peppers and onions, Margarita said, "You don't need to manage my medicine."

"Why don't you lie down and let me finish dinner?"

"No, I'll finish."

"Take a break. Kick your feet up."

Margarita shook a spatula at Adriana. "I'm dying. Do you want me to die lying down or in the kitchen making your favorite tamales?"

"You're not dying."

"Of course I'm dying. And it's best you accept it. Do you think the doctor was joking?"

So much for pretending. Adriana said, "Doctors aren't always right."

Margarita had been diagnosed a month earlier with stage four pancreatic cancer. She was indeed dying, and it broke Adriana's heart a little bit more every day. She woke in the morning and enjoyed a few seconds of life's innocent bliss, only to be attacked with the fact that she was going to lose her mom soon.

"How's your new boss?"

"She's great. Her name's Margot. She's really, really funny. Treats me like a friend."

Her mom used the spatula to stir the sizzling onions and peppers. "She's working you to death. Come home at four in the morning. What kind of life is that?"

"She had a solstice party. I wanted to help. It's not always going to be like this. I just started."

Her mother nodded. Their relationship was one filled with love, but they were both strong Latina women, so their discussions could erupt into arguments if one word was uttered without caution. They always danced on the edge of the explosion, even though their loving bond could never be broken.

Adriana was in caretaker mode as she looked at the calendar on the counter. A painting of Jesus holding a lamb stared back at her as she fingered her way to the right date. "You have your appointment tomorrow. Do you think you can find a ride?"

"Yes. I already have one."

"Will they be able to tell you how the injections are working?"

"I hope so. Oh, I guess I should tell you I spoke with Graciella today."

"What, Mom?" Adriana's body tensed with fear. "I told you last time, you can't call her anymore. You can't call anyone back in LA." Adriana let out a puff of air and shook her head, once again frustrated at her mom's casual attitude regarding the risk of Michael finding them. "Do you think this is all a joke?"

Adriana could still see her ex's face so clearly. Michael was a *gringo* with a well-trimmed beard, a wide nose, and combed black hair that would sometimes get in the way of his handsome blue eyes. Her mother had once said he looked like a Baldwin brother. Those eyes and that man had spun a fairytale web that Adriana was quickly caught in. She was a high-school Spanish teacher in the Los Angeles suburbs. For extra money in the summer, she taught adult classes. Michael was the student who answered all her questions, even the ones she wasn't asking as a Spanish teacher. He didn't reveal the spider that he really was until the hard times arrived.

"I only talked to her for a few minutes," Margarita said. "I wanted to check on her. She was such a good friend to me!"

Adriana peeped into the living room, seeing that Zack was engrossed in his sketch. She looked back at her mom. Trying not to explode with rage, she said calmly, "We both agreed to walk away from our old life. I don't think you're taking this seriously. You know we can't look back."

"I can't cut Graciella out of my life. She knows about my cancer. I can't keep her in the dark." Margarita waved her hand in the air. "Michael's in prison. We couldn't be safer."

Adriana shook her head again. "Never underestimate that man. He'll kill us all if he finds us."

"I know, *mi hija*. I know."

Do you, Mama? Do you think you know what I went through because of how my father treated you? Michael was worse. So much worse.

9

DATING IN THE TECHNOLOGY AGE

After a day of taking care of guests and bearing the marks of a broken heart and a lack of sleep, Margot finally collapsed into her unmade four-poster bed. The last bits of the late-setting sun eased down the blinds. The nearby chair hosted a daunting pile of clean laundry waiting to be folded and returned to the closet and drawers.

Philippe jumped onto the bed, circled his spot on the duvet, and then settled in.

The Hallmark Channel was teasing the *Christmas in July* movies coming next month, but she barely paid attention. All she could think about, all she could hear, was an emptiness, a void. She felt hollow, as if her ribcage might collapse in on itself. Jasper had made it to his dorm in Boston. Save for Philippe, she was alone.

She wanted this for her son, all of it. She wanted the world for him. And he wasn't going to get anywhere hanging around the inn on Red Mountain. He might have stayed had she begged, but that's not what she wanted. She wanted Jasper to grow into the massive shoes of his destiny. As she'd always told him, he was meant for greatness. And she knew with all her aching heart, his story must continue in Boston, 2,918 miles away from his mother.

Of course, she'd been preparing for this moment for eighteen years, though it felt like she was a soldier seeing combat for the first time. You can drill all you want in boot camp, but the moment you're dropped off in live fire, you realize you can't ever fully prepare for the real thing.

One idea she'd committed to do once Jasper left was to find a partner. She felt the other side of her bed. The empty side. She'd only dated one man since leaving her husband. His name was Ron. Not too long ago, he'd been lying there next to her.

Ron was the contractor who'd stepped in and selflessly saved her from the evil contractor who'd been taking advantage of her. Only after Ron left town to care for his ailing mother recently did she realize she'd loved the thought of him more than the reality of him. He'd appeared at the right time, a vulnerable time for her, and been the first real gentleman to court her since the end of her marriage. She loved him for taking her on romantic trysts, treating her like a lady, helping her realize that she wasn't all washed up but still had lots of love to give.

But that wasn't exactly a love that's meant to last. He was a drifter, and he'd drifted into her life and given her a gift of a few great months. A couple of weeks after she'd opened the doors of her inn, Ron had walked into her kitchen to say goodbye. Just like that, gone in a week. Her last sight of him before he disappeared forever was a wave in her direction and a cloud of dust kicking up around his Harley.

Margot had cried in bed for two weeks while binging on extra-toasty Cheez-Its and Hallmark's *Spring Fever* lineup. She'd slipped right back into the hole she'd found comfort in after her son's father had crushed her. This time with Ron was a little different, though. She'd eventually pulled up her big girl panties, centered herself, and accepted that finding Mr. Right wouldn't be easy. In the dark caverns of her mind, in the places she tried to ignore, the idea that she'd never find anyone was ever present—ever stoking her fear that she might always be alone.

Margot had a new business to get off the ground, and as an

entrepreneur, she didn't have time to go trolling for men every night. And that's not how you want to find Mr. Right anyway. She'd prefer that Mr. Right simply knock on her door one day, but she was starting to accept that if she had any hope, she might need to employ modern technology. There was one answer to fast-forwarding the process: the internet. Algorithmic matching. She'd downloaded a couple of apps but was terrified of whom she might find out there in the desert of eastern Washington. There was no telling what could happen should she take that giant leap into online dating.

In a moment of clarity, before she slipped farther into the void, she decided now might be an opportune time to at least consider the leap. She couldn't find the belt on her robe, so it lay half open as she propped up three pillows and opened her laptop. She typed in a web address, looking around guiltily as if someone might be watching her. Judging her.

Match.com. Logging in, she saw that several men had reached out to her. She could only imagine how awful they might be. Even though her best friend Erica, who lived in Vermont, had met the second love of her life on *Match*, Margot had huge trepidations, partly because she was terrified of putting herself out there—afraid of who might find out—but also because she didn't think she'd be as lucky. Margot worried that the men she'd attract were the type that collected divorce papers like one collects stamps; the kind that mouth-breathed retched hot air when they slept, men with little cocktail sausage penises, unkempt feet, and backs carpeted with what looked like pubic hair. Not to mention the ones completely lacking ambition and chivalry.

Perhaps the toughest acceptance in diving into the online dating game was what she'd potentially be losing. Though Erica raved about the romance she'd found, Margot had always dreamed of an encounter and courtship less digital, one reminiscent of the fairy tales of her youth. What about a lost glass slipper, a charming prince, a chance encounter? How dare we feed those lies to our little girls? Before her ex-husband had plucked her from New York, Margot had played Kim in *Miss Saigon* and Belle in *Beauty and the Beast*. And so many more! Could she really find that kind of love through a dating algorithm? She was losing more and more hope each day that there even *was* such a thing as true love.

The voice in her head loved to repeat the same phrase over and over. *"You're not getting any younger."* Though Joan had taught her to control the inner blabbermouth, it was a skill that would require years to master. Considering the deep pool of negativity she'd just high-dived into, she was still clearly millennia away from her goal to find Mr. Right. *"You're not getting any younger,"* the voice kept saying. *"You're not getting any younger."*

"Shut up! Shut up! Shut up!" Margot yelled.

Her dog turned.

"Not you, baby," she said to him. "I'm not alone. I will always have you, Philippe."

Exhausted by all this nonsense running around in her brain, she rested her eyes on the smooth white ceiling. Why couldn't she push away these fears and respond to one of those idiots on *Match*. Why not give it a whirl? Why did she have to overthink it?

Margot went to the meditation altar in the corner of her room and sat cross-legged on a cushion. A short glass table held several Buddhas, her journal, and sticks of sage, palo santo, and incense. She lit the sage and began circling it around her body and head. The smoke transported her to a calm place. She breathed into all her lonely spots, filling them with self-love and hope. At the end of her prayer, she laid the sage on an abalone shell to let it burn out. She sang an *ohm* and settled into a very powerful meditation. It pulled her in quickly once her eyes closed, and then she was floating in space. All quiet. A canoe floating downriver.

A conduit for something more real.

Coming out of her trance, she began to wiggle her toes and fingers, and then slowly opened her eyes. Sad thoughts tried to return, but she let them drift away like clouds. Awakened and renewed, she reached into her journal and thumbed for a random page. In large red letters, her favorite Emerson quote was staring back at her.

To the dull mind all of nature is leaden.
To the illumined mind the whole world sparkles with light.

— RALPH WALDO EMERSON

She smiled, remembering how to tap into the more magical side of life. In truth, as Joan had taught her, life was defined by the lens through which we see. Adjust and clean the lens and let life sparkle vividly. Margot had summed up that idea as: *It's all in how you look at it.*

Returning to her original problem, she thought about *Match.* Through a cleaner lens, she began to see the potential. Perhaps, for the illumined mind, love existed in all sorts of places. All you had to do was open yourself up. That's probably what Joan would say if she weren't on a beach right now. It sounded like something Katherine, the woman with the outrageous black hat in *Under the Tuscan Sun*, would say in her British accent. Why not open every door? What if she were a few clicks away from finding the most romantic love she could ever imagine?

Like a soldier entering battle after a motivational speech from her commander, Margot rose from her cushion and marched back to her cozy bed. She had this *You Go Girl* strut, strengthened by her victory over the ugly voice inside. She opened up the laptop. Going one by one, she studied the profiles of each man who'd messaged her, trying desperately not to make harsh judgments based on their photos. No, she didn't have to find a Hollywood stud, some gorgeous hunk who could prance around Red Mountain and make flowers bloom with his abs.

She'd been around long enough and been brokenhearted enough to know that she wanted a gentleman. A man she could trust. A man who treated her like she was everything. A man who would open doors and send flowers and rub her shoulders after a hard day's work. Most importantly, a man who could be a role model for her son.

Her first option had a confident smile and a full head of hair, but his hobbies were "slaying salmon and shooting guns." Margot couldn't even stomp on a spider. She would spend ten minutes with paper and Tupperware saving any insects that invaded her house or inn, so "slaying salmon" was a deal breaker. The next guy was a bare-back rider, the eight-seconds type. She needed more of the eight-*minute* type! Besides, he'd messaged her saying, "You're smoking hot!" *Thanks, Mr. Rodeo Dude.* Margot went through the rest of the men and didn't see one that sparked her interest or even came close to who she was looking for.

She closed her computer. Not a gesture of giving up, more *the right man will come along. Don't close any doors. He might be on* Match *or even on* Tinder. *Be open, Margot. Be open.*

~

THE FOLLOWING MORNING, shortly after breakfast hours, the guests all departed Épiphanie, going their separate ways to begin the day's activities. One couple had driven to Walla Walla to taste wines and have lunch. Another was embarking on a jet boat tour of the Columbia that Margot had helped arrange. One man was going to try to sell a new kind of cork to the area winemakers. Harry Bellflour had driven off in his Lexus to do whatever it was he did.

Margot joined Adriana upstairs to clean the rooms. Per the usual, Mr. Bellflour had left the *I had wine last night. Leave me alone!* sign on his doorknob. In the room next to his, Margot walked Adriana through her cleaning routine, which she'd also printed out, lami-nated, and attached to the side of the cleaning cart.

As Margot folded several garments that the guests had left strung across the floor, she said, "How would you feel about working with me full time?"

Adriana stumbled and almost spilled the wastebasket she was emptying. "I would love that."

"Benefits too. You'd be my first full-time employee. We'd have to agree on a number, and I'm not rich. I spent a lot of money to get this place up and running. But I'd be good to you and give you raises when I can. I need someone to be my backup, and I think you're perfect. Even in the short time we've been working together, I've noticed your exceptional eye for detail and strong work ethic." Margot had also appreciated Adriana helping with Carmen during the party; it showed a caring side that Margot welcomed in her life.

Adriana's head was nodding as fast as Margot's lips opened and closed. "Yes, I'd love to work for you full time."

"I can't even tell you what you'd be doing. Not only cleaning. You might clean the rooms in the morning and help with ordering and deliveries another day. I can teach you a lot, if you're willing to learn. You might even find it interesting. You could help with marketing, with bookings. And if you like being outside, you can help with gardening and the chickens and things at the sanctuary. There's enough to do every minute of the day, if you're willing to be flexible."

"I would love the job. Thank you!"

"You don't even know how much I can pay you."

"I don't care. I know you'll be fair."

"Then it's yours. Congratulations. I didn't even ask, but can you cook?"

"Yes, of course. All Mexican women can cook! I might have to learn a few of your vegetarian tricks, but I definitely can cook."

The women talked more of what the job could potentially entail as they finished cleaning the room, following the routine exactly as Margot had written it out. She threw out a number, and Adriana formally accepted. Just like that, Épiphanie had grown. Margot bathed in the joy of giving someone a little boost. She showed Adriana how to clean the bathroom, how to fold the toilet paper into the shape of a rose, how to polish the sink and clawfoot tub, how to arrange her organic toiletries, how to freshen up the flowers on the balconies, and on and on, finishing with one final pass, looking for any less obvious needs.

It was in the next room when Margot—never one to let silence win but at least self-aware of it—asked, while cleaning a blemish off the window, "Have you ever tried *Tinder*?"

Adriana looked up from dusting. "No."

Through the glass and the railing of the balcony, Margot could see her hens bathing in the dust outside their unnecessarily lavish coop. "I'm thinking about giving it a try. I'm about to give up on *Match*. You know that one, right? Of the two, it seems less like a desperate attempt to drop your panties on the first date. But *you should see* the men who are after me. Yuck! Maybe *Tinder* is my next new best thing. Are you savvy to this stuff? You said you're divorced?"

"Yeah, about two years now."

"Have you dated since then?"

Adriana reached up to clean a cobweb spun along one of the wooden beams in the ceiling. "No. No way."

"Don't you ever get lonely?"

"Sometimes. I have my son and my mother, so my life is hectic. I don't have a lot of time for me."

"You and I are more alike than you probably know." Margot moved to the second window and sprayed her organic homemade glass cleaner onto a collection of fingerprints. Past the chicken coop, she noticed a couple of her speckled Roma tomatoes in the garden were reddening. "Suddenly, with Jasper gone, I have way too much time for me. I think I'm going to drive myself crazy. I wake up and want to hear voices."

Adriana returned the duster to the cleaning cart. "When my son goes to college, I'll have to check myself in somewhere. He's my every-thing. I can empathize with you."

"Trust me, you don't ever want that day to come." Margot bit her lip. "I'm fine by myself, really. I've been preparing for this moment forever. It's not like it's a surprise." She sighed. "Kids grow up and leave you. What goes up must come down. Right?"

Adriana, in a gesture that surprised Margot, touched her arm. "He will never forget you though. You're his mother."

Margot offered a half-hearted smile but wanted to collapse into a puddle of tears.

Steering away from the tender subject, Adriana said, "I'm sure the right men will come along for both of us."

Margot set her rag and cleaning solution on the desk next to the guest's closed laptop. The women faced each other, pausing from their chores. Margot said, "I hope you're right. Maybe using all this technology, *Tinder* and everything, will speed it up, though. I know it doesn't feel natural, but we do live in a new world. It's different from when I grew up."

Adriana crossed her arms. "I read about a man from Mexico City who met a girl on *Tinder*. When she wouldn't have sex with him, he murdered her and dissolved her body in muriatic acid in the bathtub."

Margot perked up. "Now, that's encouraging."

Adriana shrugged. "Do you wonder why I'm not dating?"

Margot wasn't asking when she said, "You're as scared as I am."

"You have no idea."

"When's the last time you dressed in sexy underwear thinking that a man might actually get as far as seeing them?"

"When I met my ex-husband."

"When was that?"

"My son is six. Before that."

"Adriana Hernandez. Sounds like the cobwebs on the ceiling aren't the only ones you need to be dusting off!"

Adriana turned away in embarrassment.

"You're too cute to keep them away forever. You deserve some fun."

Adriana blushed and retreated to the cart.

Margot worried that referencing Adriana's looks had hurt her feelings, or at least exposed some pain.

Adriana pulled the vacuum cleaner from the side. "Maybe one day." She unwrapped the cord and plugged it in, then turned it on, ending the conversation with the buzz of the machine.

Margot wasn't having it. She marched to the wall and ripped out the cord, instantly silencing the buzz. "One of us is going to find a man this year. I'm tired of all those people saying it comes when you least expect it. I've been least expecting it for years! They can all kiss my big butt. I'm taking hold of my destiny. Maybe you'll join me."

Adriana fingered the handle of the vacuum. "You first."

"Fine," Margot said. "Will you please help me find a man?" She sat on the bed and patted the spot next to her. "Our cleaning is paused."

Sharing her phone screen with her first full-time employee, Margot clicked the *Enable Discovery* button on *Tinder*. Suddenly a world of opportunity arose. Perhaps the gentleman of her dreams waited among the stack of serial killers and deadbeats.

First up, a man with dark Ray Bans stared at her. Margot said, "Can't see his eyes. That's freaky. That Bill, the lawyer, looks like he cooks meth for extra cash." She swiped left, eliminating his chances forever. "Next. James. 49. A scientist. Thanks to that story you told about the creep dissolving a girl in acid, I'm eliminating all scientists from the list of potentials. Swiping left!"

Adriana let out a high-pitched cackle.

Margot turned to her. "You have a real dark sense of humor, don't you?"

"It takes a lot to shock me."

"Me too." Margot returned to the screen and swiped left with more speed. "Nope, nope. Anderson, nope. Jim, nope. Not Matt. Oh, my God, I can't imagine finding a reason to swipe right."

Adriana pointed. "He's cute."

"Yes, he is," Margot said with calculation, looking at Kevin, the thirty-four-year-old engineer. "But he looks like he's fifteen."

"What's wrong with a younger man? For fun—"

"I'm too old to teach those young ones new tricks. I want an experienced man-stallion with rough hands and chiseled wisdom, the kind I can ride off into the sunset on...I mean with." Margot grinned at her own silliness. "Swiping left. Gone forever." Margot poked Adriana's leg. "What's your story? Your ex is terrible?"

"*El Diablo.*"

"Welcome to the club. Mine cheated on me and was caught on camera doing it. He was the mayor of Burlington, Vermont, and someone filmed him getting a blowjob from his secretary. Get this. Her name was Nadine. Nadine! Can you imagine? I found out about my husband's infidelity while watching the news and ironing one of his button-down shirts. What's your story? Couldn't be worse than that."

"I fell in love with a man who wasn't even there. I married a stranger. Tricked by love."

"And he cheated?"

Adriana nervously put a hand on her own cheek and quietly said, "He probably did."

Noticing Adriana's imbalance, Margot said, "I'm so sorry. It's really none of my business."

"It's okay. You're the kind of woman who's nice to talk to. You remind me of a friend back in California. A woman I really like."

Margot nodded, honored by the compliment. She also knew enough to realize she'd better stop prying; she'd struck some pain deep within her new employee. She eyed the screen again and swiped left to a few more wannabes. And then. There was a man. An extremely handsome man named Jerry. He was with his cute teenage daughter, holding skis at the top of a snowy mountain somewhere in the Cascades.

"Swipe right," Adriana said. "He could be your man-stallion."

Margot did just that. "Well, giddy up and yee-haw! Let me get my saddle. I'll run him around the corral a couple of times and see what happens."

"Make sure you wear your spurs. Every man needs a sharp kick in the side from time to time."

"Good point. I'll grab my whip too."

The women giggled like little girls laughing in grade school. Sometimes the friendship of two women can overcome the past.

10

A POLYNESIAN GOODBYE

Otis did something today he hadn't done for a long time; he slept in. He and Joan woke early, fell back asleep, and let the jetlag and exhaustion ease them in and out of more dreams. Their bare legs touched one another, the Bora Bora breeze softly blew through their overwater bungalow, and the song and smells of the Polynesian saltwater rose from below.

Not to say such a lazy morning was easy for him.

He hadn't slept in since Rebecca had died six years before. And even when she'd been alive, he'd only allowed the indulgence on a specific occasion. He and Rebecca would pick one Saturday a month and lie in bed until noon. It was a rule they'd created for themselves as part of their pursuit of emotional wellbeing. (And, frankly, it was her way to force him to stop farming and remember that he was a husband too.)

Back on Red Mountain, Otis always had something to do, a chore that couldn't wait another day. He ran a farm, so the list never dwindled. Feed the animals. Trim the sheep's hooves. Tend to that waterer the ducks had knocked over for the tenth time. Move the sheep to another pasture for grazing. Weed. Repair a fence. Repair a sprinkler or a cracked PVC pipe. Scrub the chicken poop off the patio. Hand pull the weeds in the garden. Not to mention the vineyard and the wine, the purpose of it all. He still had to take the grapes to bottle, an entirely new list of demands. Even with Elijah, Esteban, and Chaco, the work never ended.

Later, after drifting off again, he realized Joan had sneaked out of bed. He found her cross-legged by the small pool on their deck. Their one-bedroom bungalow was the last at the end of a long boardwalk, and the Pacific Ocean was all you could see. It was almost as if they were alone. Past two lounge chairs, a wooden staircase descended into the water where Otis had dipped his calloused feet upon arrival. On the other side of the pool, there was a circular loveseat shaded by a sea-blue umbrella. He intended to read an entire novel while relaxing in that chair.

Sensing his presence, Joan opened her eyes. "Good morning, my love." She reached for her toes, only getting to mid-shin.

Before she was shot, she could bend her body in ways Otis had never seen before. He'd often watch in awe as she practiced alone in his vineyard. Now, it was like she was starting over.

"I'm a little tight this morning," she whispered.

"Long plane ride. Oversleeping. That'll happen." Otis jammed his hands into his pockets and strolled to the edge of the deck, taking in the ocean, tasting the salt. "I could do this for a long time. Weeks even."

"Brooks said to make sure you weren't trying to ferment coconuts."

"I brought some vine cuttings. Later today, I think I'll hike up on that ridge above the hotel and see if there might be a slope for planting."

"You're joking."

"Maybe. But I do have lots of Red Mountain wine to share. Stuffed into my bag. Not just mine though. I brought some Canvasback, Hedges, Lacoda, Frichette, and Col Solare. I'm spreading the love, as the kids say these days." He turned with a guilty face, showing all his teeth. "And I may have shipped some bottles to a few of the other hotels."

She switched stretches. "Is that right?"

"It's what I do."

"Oh, I get it. It's adorable."

"Please remember that I prefer compliments that address my strength and power. Nothing close to 'adorable' or 'cute' appeals to me."

"You just fell further into my little bitty adorable basket. You're a soft, cuddly teddy bear."

He raised his arms and growled. "I'm a grizzly looking for my next meal."

~

OTIS PULLED out the small silver box carrying Morgan's ashes. At one time that box had carried his aunt's travel jewelry. He unclasped the latch and uncovered nine small Ziploc bags. He was glad to see TSA hadn't tampered with her remains. Back home on Red Mountain, he'd measured out ten bags with his scale at the winery. He'd thought it important that she be divided equally among her ten spots. The last bag was back home, and they'd spread that upon their return, the final ceremony. Today was the beginning.

At the restaurant, a woman with a purple orchid tucked behind her ear escorted Joan and Otis to a table under an umbrella of palm fronds that looked out over the beach and bungalows. Otis asked for a newspaper. They ate mangos and papayas and drank coffee, followed by mimosas. As was usual lately, Otis drank his mimosa like he'd been crawling through the desert for days. Joan drank hers with all the patience in the world, taking her tiny sips and closing her eyes and tasting every nuance of flavor. She didn't eat much, a result of that bullet. Her stomach was often queasy.

When the server brought the bill, Otis asked her to take a picture.

"Squeeze together," the server said.

"This one's just me," Otis said, holding up the front page of the *La Dépeche de Tahiti* toward the camera. I have to do this for...ah, long story."

The waitress shrugged and lined up his phone for the shot.

Otis smiled and extended his middle finger. The first photo of his journey to prove that he had accepted his aunt Morgan's quest. Morgan, to her credit, had correctly assumed that Otis wouldn't be easily swayed to leave his farm to make a pilgrimage around the world. Requiring a photo was Aunt Morgan's final way of making sure Otis took a break from his crusade for Red Mountain. She'd considered saving him from overworking and reminding him to have fun as part of her life's work.

Otis thanked the woman and looked at the shot. "There it is," he said to Joan. "Proof that I am able to leave Red Mountain."

"Did you have to stick out your finger?"

"You know Morgan would appreciate it."

"I'm not sure she'd appreciate it, but she'd expect it."

"Same thing. Shall we do this?"

Joan nodded, and Otis pushed her along the boardwalk to the beach. They left the wheelchair and strolled along the powdery sand past the sun worshippers and the beached catamarans and the massage hut. Joan used Otis's arm as a crutch. They stopped where a line of seashells met the water.

"This is it," Otis said.

"I think she'll be happy."

"She'll probably appear in the next few seconds and give me a hard time for spreading her ashes in Bora Bora as opposed to Papeete."

"It's a fair compromise," Joan said. "I thought about her all morning. What a lovely soul she was. I remember that day she approached me in the grocery store, determined to find you a woman."

"She was one of a kind," Otis said.

"I'd love to see her again."

"Oh, you will. I'm sure of it. Death can't stop her." He drew the bag of ashes from the box in his backpack and held it out before them. "This is what it all comes down to, isn't it? Ashes. More than eighty years on earth. All that happiness. All that sorrow. All that hard work. All those memories. All the lives she helped. It all comes down to some old grump sprinkling the last of her into the water. Like a herb into a pot of soup." He said "herb" with a hard "h," a habit he hadn't shaken since his early days in England.

They walked into the water, going ankle deep into the warmth. Tiny ripples of waves hit their legs and slid to shore.

"Do you want to say something?" he asked Joan.

Collecting her thoughts, she said, "Morgan, thank you for this man. Can you believe you got him all the way over here? If that was all you ever accomplished, you'd have done more than most. But that's only part of a long list of what you've done, from what Otis has told me. Your energy force was giant; giant and warm like the sun. I can only hope to find the end as gracefully as you did. You were so with it, so happy and active and sharp. Thanks for touching my life and bringing me to my destiny."

Otis choked up and his body wanted to cry. Even his hardened exterior and weak attempts at humor couldn't save him now. "She said it all, Morgan. You were more than that little body could ever contain. Never have I met a bigger pain in my arse, but I loved you with all that I have. Thank you for forcing me to leave the mountain. Sometimes I do indeed need a little nudge." He took Joan's hand. "And thank you for bringing me this one, this beauty to my life. I'm forever grateful. If you find any power out there beyond what I'm aware of, come back and heal her. Please."

He started to empty the bag, a slow pour of ashes into the saltwater. "Now go and enjoy your island vacation, and don't go thinking we're going to say all these nice things ten times in a row, every time we spread you. This one's special."

Otis caught Joan's grin at that one, and he smiled.

11

EXTINGUISHING OLD FLAMES

Brooks despised the bottling line. There weren't many things he hated, especially since he'd found some sense of peace in his thirties. Sure, in his teens and twenties, he'd hated the cops who always chased him. He'd hated his foster parents, who always wanted a piece of him. He'd hated his parents, who'd abandoned him. He'd hated all the kids who had it better than he did. But now, in his mid-thirties, despite being cheated on by his fiancée not too long ago, he was happy. Well, *happy* might be an ambitious word. He could count all the things he hated on the fingers of his two hands. Hitler. Crotch-rocket motorcycles. White supremacists. Most root vegetables. Pop music. Hollywood wines. Critter labels or any other wine labels that didn't tell you where the wine came from. And bottling lines. That was about it.

He'd gotten to know a few bottling lines over the years. Otis's geriatric piece of shit loved to break down. When Brooks had been working for Otis, the damned thing promised to shut down in the middle of a project every time. Otis and Brooks would spend the rest of the afternoon trying to figure it out. Sometimes, they'd have to hire a specialist from California to come for repairs.

Jake Forester had done quite the opposite of Otis. Knowing the horror stories of bottling lines, he had bought the best for Brooks, the Maserati of lines. It was still a pain in the ass. So that's where Brooks spent his morning. Once he saw the bottles were flowing again, filling properly and labeling well, he left his guys to it and headed back to his office on the second floor of the cellar. A giant glass window looked down at the action below. He'd thrown his laptop through that very window last fall, when his relationship with Abby had begun to wreck his whole life. He noticed the sticker was still on the new pane of glass, so he peeled it off on the way back to his desk.

As he sat, he heard someone at the door behind him and turned.

There she was. Abby.

It was in that office last harvest when he'd asked her out. Well, she'd actually asked him out after he'd been so passive-aggressive that she'd read the signs. Not that she needed permission. She was a strong-willed woman, a feminist of the highest order, certainly not one to follow the traditional rules of courtship. If she wanted to go out with him, she wasn't afraid to ask. She'd said something to the tune of, "If I wait for you to ask me, we'll never go out on a date." Brooks wasn't sure that was true. He'd have eventually gotten there. She'd just sped up the process. The process that would eventually lead to damnation.

"Good morning," Abby said, looking through her tortoise-shell glasses.

Through his eyes, she was still beautiful, and he hated that. He didn't want to find her attractive after what she'd done to him. She had light streaks in her brown hair that Brooks had always gathered in his hands when they'd watched TV together. She wore a black jumper and a white belt, an outfit she'd obviously claimed from Carmen's closet. Abby had been working for the Foresters for eight years, leaving her home in Las Vegas to follow the Foresters around the world. She helped with shopping, cooking, running errands, raising the children. Every designer in the world sent clothes to Carmen, and she'd often pass them along to Abby. As part of her war against the objectification of women, Abby typically only wore the more conservative of these. Still, in his eyes, there wasn't much Abby could do to dial down her beauty.

As he settled into his chair, Brooks offered her a weak greeting, which was the extent of their exchanges the past few months. It might have been best if one of them had left the mountain. But as Brooks had learned, you don't leave when you want to. And if you do leave, you realize you didn't want to. He had the perfect winemaking gig. He was following his passion. He was able to continue studying under Otis. And he was able to be near his newly found brother.

Abby zeroed in on his eyes.

Neither flinched.

If Brooks had been a gunslinger, he'd be eyeing her gun hand, waiting for the moment when he'd have to reach for his own six-shooter.

She had done her best to get him back, but he'd rejected the notion time and time again. She'd slept with Carmen. Yes, the same Carmen whose clothes she wore today. The woman married to Jake Forester. The woman currently kicking and screaming in rehab. Okay, the affair was early in the Abby and Brooks relationship—before their engagement—but Brooks couldn't get past it. He'd tried, but in the end, he'd come to the realization that he could never allow himself to open up to someone he couldn't trust. And he could never trust her again. Abby might not have even told him if she and Carmen hadn't been caught on camera.

Sometimes he wanted to be weak and take her back in his arms. If only for a night. For the memories. Making love with her was an unforgettably wild joy ride. They'd been one hell of a pair. She was his first love. She was his everything—for a moment.

Now, she was dangerously close to being added to his hate list. Maybe he'd consider trying to be friends someday. Like real friends, not like they were currently. Now, when they looked at each other, there were so many layers of pain and misunderstanding and anger, yet there was also hope that things could get better. She'd told him so many times that she'd take him back. He'd said no just as many times. Now they were here, a place uncomfortable and dangerous.

"So," she said and shrugged. "I enjoyed your article in *Rolling Stone.*"

He forced a smile, forgetting about the gun on his hip. "It *was* good, wasn't it?"

She leaned against the doorframe. "I remember that day. Sitting out in front of the winery. That writer was picking you apart."

"Like a vulture. I remember the pumpkin curry soup you made. That homemade roti bread."

She smiled. "You remember?"

He nodded hesitantly, scared of what these memories did to him. "I remember the native Chenin we drank too. That was a great lunch."

"Yeah."

The conversation trailed off, both of them daring to relive the memory.

"How's it feel to be famous like Jake?"

"I wouldn't put us in the same league."

"Jake says sales are through the roof since the article came out."

"They were through the roof the day he announced he was starting something." The only thing Brooks wanted to talk about less than their relationship was anything having to do with himself being famous. That magazine article had been good for the winery, but he was extraordinarily uncomfortable in the spotlight.

So he did what he did best. Turned the ship. "Any word from Carmen? I know she's only been there a couple of days." It had started as a true curiosity, a topic in which they both had a vested interest, what should be a simple question. He'd been scrambling for a new course but had turned them into even more dangerous water. He'd just cut to the bone. Right into the marrow of it all.

Abby nodded a few times, processing his question, probably deciding whether he was trying to start a fight or satisfy genuine interest.

"She's still in rehab. She's not happy, but she's there. Jake returns today."

"So you're on your own with Luca," he said.

"Yeah, but he's easy. He's signed up for a bunch of summer camps and other activities."

"I hate that's how Emilia had to go off to Europe."

"It's best this way. She's a tough girl. Last year was so terrible for her. She knows the ways of the world now. And it's not like this thing with her mom is new. We've all wanted her to clean up for a long time. Emilia always tried to take care of Jake, stand up for him. Now she knows Carmen is getting better, and Jake is safe while she's gone."

"She did always try to protect her dad, didn't she?"

"Not that he needs it. He's a strong man."

Brooks noticed a pen mark on his messy desk and tried to rub it away. Anything to calm him. "Yeah, he just has a weakness for that woman."

"He made a decision to love her, no matter what."

There it was! They were right back into dangerous territory. He'd let down his guard and Abby went for her own gun! Brooks thought she might be intimating that he, himself, should have stood by her no matter what. What the hell was he supposed to say now?

They returned the six-shooters to their holsters and tried again. A long stare. Where they could hear each other's breath. The ticking clock sounded like a man was in the corner hitting the wall with a sledgehammer every second. Bam! Bam! The buzz from the air rushing out of the vents hummed incessantly, like a bee around his ear.

Abby said, "I'm not trying to start anything. Don't look at me that way."

"How am I looking at you?"

"Like I'm a moment away from waging war."

"I know you're not."

She bit her lip. "We're going to be okay," she said, inviting herself in, walking toward his desk. "Not like we're going to get back together. We're just going to be okay. I'm not going to avoid you, Brooks."

Brooks knew this is when she would punch right into the heart of the matter. It's actually something he loved about her. He looked away as she moved in even closer, almost touching his desk with her waist.

She said, "I'm going to stop by and say hello. Every time I see you, I'm going to go out of my way to say 'hi.' Not to get you back. But to break this thing that keeps happening every time we see each other. It's too small a mountain. It's okay if there's some tension. Maybe you have a bit of Abby anger inside you. That's okay. Who could blame you? But we decided to stay, so we damn well better figure out how to make Red Mountain work for both of us."

"I'm not mad at you," he lied.

"That's good."

"I'm really not."

"I believe you. Sort of. Anyway, have a good day. Let's do this again tomorrow." She waved and slipped out the door.

Brooks returned his gaze to the window he'd replaced. He wasn't looking through the glass but at it, reminding himself of that day. When it all came crashing down. Maybe he really wasn't just mad at her. Maybe he was disappointed in her. Sometimes that can be worse than being mad.

12

WORKINGMOM'S DEAD

Adriana refused to open her eyes, trying desperately to avoid the first creeping thoughts of the day. She remembered a time when she'd woken with the energy of a million women inside her. She remembered that decayed idea of seizing the day. She missed that feeling, and every day, it shrunk more and more in the rearview.

She kept her eyes closed for as long as she could, shielding herself from reality, from the challenges that ate away at her. But then the one thing that mattered most and gave her the courage to keep going stirred next to her.

"Mommy!"

She finally opened her eyes and found Zack inching toward her, positioning himself on her chest.

"Mommy, do you ever wonder why Mickey is a mouse?"

She smelled the beautiful morning breath of a young child as he peered into her eyes. She smiled the first smile of the day as he touched her cheeks, pulling at them like Play-Doh, another toy in his universe. She ran her fingers through his hair. "*Buenos dias, mi amorcito.*"

"And why is Donald a duck?"

"That's a good question. They both begin with the same letters."

They were soon up and moving, and the madness of the morning routine and the countdown to getting out of the house began.

At the counter in the kitchen, Zack ate in a manner totally unaware of urgency. He would take a bite and then go grab a toy. Another bite and then find a crayon to color with. Another bite and then a spin on the stool. When he'd made it through most of his *chilaquiles*, Adriana wiped the red sauce from his cheeks, goggles, and ears.

Adriana said, "Please go brush your teeth. We're late."

Zack took another spin and then looked down through his goggles at his plate of breakfast enchiladas. "I'm not done!"

"We're late, sweetheart. Take a couple of more bites and then we have to go."

"*Si, madre.*"

Adriana's mother, not feeling well, was still in bed. At a recent visit, her doctor had delivered more bad news. Adriana peeked inside Margarita's bedroom just as her mother opened her eyes. Adriana blew her a kiss and returned to the kitchen to prepare Zack's lunch. She'd made an extra *quesadilla* the night before. She already felt like she was burdening her neighbor by asking her to watch Zack, so the least she could do was send him with food.

Zack stuffed a forkful of eggs into his mouth. "Don't forget the peppers, Mom!"

"How could I forget the peppers?" She shook her head. "You and your grandfather."

Zack had loved jalapeños since he was a baby. Margarita always joked that Adriana grew peppers in her breasts while she was nursing. In retort, Adriana would say her mom must grow peppers in her mouth, with all that fire coming out.

Adriana sliced some jalapeños and placed them into a plastic bag. "Okay, you're done. Go brush your teeth and go pee. I'm not going to tell you again."

"But—"

"Don't argue, please."

He squished his face, squinted his eyes, and kicked the wall underneath the counter. "I want to go play with my toys. I don't want to go to Lita's."

With all the calm she could muster, Adriana bent down, rested her elbows on the counter, and met his eyes. "I have a really big day at work. Remember I told you I was given a raise?"

"Yes, Mama."

"Do you think you should apologize for your little fit?"

He nodded his head and jumped off the stool. Rounding the counter, he ran to her, throwing his arms around her. "I'm sorry, Mama!"

She patted his head. "It's okay. Let's turn this day around." She looked down and saw that he'd left a lip-shaped mark of red sauce halfway down her lavender uniform. "Sweetie, look what happened. I have to wear this to work today."

"I'm sorry." He stood there, staring at her through his goggles.

How could she be upset? She took a rag from the sink and scrubbed. He watched her. Digging deep for more patience, she said, "I can't be late. Remember, you're the man of this house. I have to count on you. You're six years old now. Will you please go brush your teeth?"

"Mama?" he said, his mind elsewhere.

"What?"

"Can I watch cartoons for a little while?"

"Zack! Go brush your teeth!" She spun him by his shoulders and swatted him on the bottom. "Right now. It's time to go."

She shook her head as he ran into the bathroom. Finishing up with his lunch, she scrambled to find her car keys and then remembered she had wet clothes in the washer. She ran to the laundry room and moved the clothes to the dryer, careful not to dry any of her mother's dresses. When she returned to the living room, Zack was standing there naked.

"What are you doing?" she asked. "We have to go!"

"I can't find my green pants."

"I'm sorry, honey," she said, grasping for patience. "You can wear them tomorrow. They're wet."

"I'll wear them wet."

Frustrated beyond belief, Adriana turned to her mom's room and yelled, "I hope you're enjoying sleeping in!" Of course, her mother had cancer. Of course, her mother was doing so much to help. But Adriana yelled it anyway.

She helped Zack dress, finishing with his shoes. Getting him buckled up, she realized how badly she needed to clean her car. She sat in the driver's seat and looked at the rosary hanging from her rearview mirror. "You're testing me, aren't you?"

She backed out of the driveway but only drove fifty feet before slamming the brakes. Her head flew forward, and she turned to make sure Zack was okay. "Sorry, my love. I left your lunch inside."

She spat a long line of Spanish curses as she reversed all the way home.

~

"I'm so glad you're here, Adriana!" Margot was in the Épiphanie kitchen stirring something in a bowl. "Mr. Bellflour asked me to do a lunch for him and some of his clients. And I have a meeting at twelve. If I do most of the prep, will you serve them?"

"Sure. If you'd like, I can help cook."

"Where were you a month ago?"

Adriana asked what they were making as she washed her hands.

"A summer salad and a couple of *Cacio e Pepe* pies. It's a typical pasta dish from Italy." Like a seasoned painter moving back and forth from palette to canvas, Margot danced from the refrigerator to the sink to the cutting board and counter as she prepared.

Adriana found herself in awe watching Margot. The vibrancy of the vegetables she had procured dazzled Adriana. Margot washed her vegetables with pride and care, soaking them in white vinegar first, then inspecting every last piece before a final rinse. She wielded her sharp knife like an expert, slicing and dicing with the precision of a samurai. It was almost like she could do two or three things at once. By the time Adriana grated the Grana Padano and Pecorino cheeses, Margot had already finished preparing the salad, boiled the pasta, cleaned the dishes, and buttered the casserole dish. It was almost like she could do all these things at once.

As Margot dumped the eggs, milk, and cheese into a large bowl of spaghetti and black pepper, she said, "How did you get into cooking? I always identify a chef by whether or not they wash their hands, so a chef you are."

"It's funny you say that. My *abuelita*, my grandmother, she used to smack my hands with a wooden spoon if I forgot to wash my hands." Adriana had always been her grandmother's favorite and spent lots of time with her, learning the ways of Mexican cuisine. "I can still taste her *nopalitos*." Realizing very few people knew the term, Adriana said, "They're cactus pads she'd prepare with eggs, shrimp, and potatoes. It's a Yucatan thing." Her mouth watered. "She's the best cook I've ever known."

"Well, then, the next meal is yours. So…I…um…don't really have a meeting today," Margot confessed. "It's more of a date. That guy Jerry I met on *Tinder*. Just a day date. I don't even want to talk about it. I'm trying to stay positive."

"Perhaps he will be the one."

Margot nudged her. "As long as there are no bathtubs, it should be fine. We're meeting in a safe place."

When the pies had baked and cooled slightly, Margot sliced them into eighths, then offered a bite to Adriana. She closed her eyes and tasted the creamy, peppery noodles with the crispy cheese on top. It was one of the best things she'd ever had, so simple, yet so complex and perfect in flavor. With the pepper lingering in her mouth, Adriana said, "I would love to learn everything you know."

"Well," Margot said, "all you'll need is five minutes and a small sticky note."

∾

ADRIANA GREETED the guests at noon and led them to one of the long tables outside in the shade of a mature acacia tree. The clear day offered a stunning view of Mt. Adams to the west. A line of lavender bushes filled the air with their earthy, saccharine smell. Like in the front of the estate, roses grew everywhere.

Mr. Bellflour sat at the end of the table and turned on a charm Adriana and Margot had not yet seen. As the wine bottles emptied, the introvert he'd appeared to be melted away and was replaced with a giant laugh and endless stories, jokes, and questions. Adriana was reminded once again how alcohol can change people. The other five men at the table appeared to be mesmerized. At one point, after an exhausting diatribe on the instability of energy stocks, Bellflour began speaking about building a winery and hiring a crew to document the project. And then he was on to showing off his wine knowledge and talking about cult Napa cabernets. By the time Adriana returned to clear the dishes, her guests had indulged in more than a bottle each.

Mr. Bellflour said to Adriana, "Honey, I know you're going to ask about dessert. I can speak for all of us in saying that since the moment you graced our table, we've all been thinking sweet thoughts."

Adriana forced a smile as she stacked pasta bowls scraped clean on her tray. Some men laughed. She didn't bother looking around to see the reactions of the ones she didn't hear.

Bellflour cleared his throat. "Where did you say you were from again?"

Not wanting to make a spectacle—determined not to jeopardize her job—she said, "Phoenix." She was getting better and better at lying since she'd run from California.

"Are you married?"

She shook her head. "Can I bring you anything else?"

He twisted his body toward her and made a show of looking her up and down. "I can think of a lot of things."

Adriana sensed the momentary tension among the men before they all broke into laughter.

One of the men said to Bellflour, "That's what I like about you. Never afraid to speak your mind."

Bellflour said, "Oh, I'm just not scared of saying what we're all thinking."

"Leave the poor woman alone," one noble guy with a well-groomed beard said from his spot near the end of the table.

As she escaped with the stack of bowls balancing in her hands, one of the men whistled. A couple of others made equal sounds of disrespect. Her shoulders tensed, and a pain flared in her side. She had little patience for pigs, and if her job hadn't been so important to her family's survival, she would have given them a mouthful.

Adriana was certainly no stranger to fighting back. As that same man whistled again and the others grossly chuckled, the memory of her and Michael's last fight ripped through her mind with severe intensity. Zack had been four years old and watched it go down from the pool in the backyard of their home in West Hollywood. The thing was—and it almost seemed funny now—she couldn't even remember why her argument with Michael had started. Most of their fights began over such a little thing that she was often unable to put a finger on what had set them off. Nevertheless, once the escalation began, usually about the time she began to grit her teeth, Michael would clench his fists. That evening, as Zack played with his new water gun in the pool, Michael had attacked her. And as usual, she didn't cower. Especially the last few times, since she'd started secretly filming their fights—per the suggestion of her new lawyer. Though Michael always won in the end, she went for his face and mid-section with fury, and by the time he'd knocked her onto the pavers and she had nothing left, they were both bruised. When Zack had started shooting him with the water gun and Michael retaliated, the man had sealed his fate.

That was the last time he had hurt her, and the first and last he'd hurt Zack. Two days later, while Michael was at his office, Adriana and Zack had packed their bags and slipped away to freedom. She'd collected all the evidence she needed to not only gain full custody of Zack, but also to send Michael to prison. She'd been squirreling away money for months and had enough to run. As Adriana, her mother, and Zack had crossed the border leaving California, Michael had been arrested at his office.

Adriana swallowed the rage inside. She glanced back at Bellflour one more time, whispering, "*Métetelo por el culo...*"

13

FIRST DATES SUCK

Margot touched up her face in the parking lot of Madsen's, a new restaurant in Kennewick tucked into a strip mall in between a beauty salon and a shoe store. Her heart thumped like a techno kick drum as she attempted to steady her hands and apply a new organic lipstick—a dark shade of red called Posh Woman.

She'd heard mixed reviews of this place, but one thing she'd discovered was that good restaurants had a hard time gaining traction in eastern Washington. She was pulling for the owners, two friends who, according to the newspaper, had started six months ago on their own dream to bring fine dining to the Tri-Cities.

"Enough stalling," Margot said to herself. "Just get in there." Without another thought, she entered the crowded restaurant. Her kick drum heart drove a pounding in her wrists as forgotten and almost unfamiliar first-date jitters dizzied her mind and body.

Dodging the hostess's eyes, she fell into her habit of surveying the surroundings and pondering how she'd have designed the space differently. It was a simple build-out with a bar in the back. She'd have knocked down the back wall to expose the kitchen. Track lighting ran across the ceilings, spraying harsh light over the diners;

Margot would have installed industrial pendant lights and dimmed them down. The jazz they played wasn't loud enough. The blousy yellow and white tablecloths were unnecessary; for this particular space, she would have gone with the cleaner look of tablemats on bare wood.

And then she met eyes with him. Jerry Roberts offered a half-wave, probably looking for confirmation that she was his lunch date before he committed further. Aside from the charming eyes that had encouraged her to swipe right, he looked *nothing* like his picture. Old Jerry was definitely one of those lucky photogenic people who looked better in a photo than in person—or he was really good at manipulating images in Photoshop.

Margot's first instinct was to turn and run, but she said, "I'm meeting him," to the hostess and began her walk of trepidation. *I can't believe I'm doing this...*

Jerry wore a white button-down shirt and a blue blazer, which instantly reminded her of her ex-husband, the honorable jackass ex-mayor of Burlington. *Strike one against Mr. Roberts.* But unlike her ex, this guy looked like a slob. His button down was wrinkled, his blazer ill-fitting, and he wore no belt! Who does that?

He offered a Howdy Doody open-mouthed smile, revealing a rack of yellow teeth that reminded her of the row of yellowed ivory keys on an antique piano she'd once seen in Burlington. What little hair he did have, he'd combed over the front in a feeble and unsuccessful attempt to conceal a bald spot.

He gave her a two-handed shake and, in a scratchy soprano, said, "There you are. Good to finally meet you."

Escargot. That's the first word that came to mind as his hot breath hit her. Butter and garlic and snails.

He pulled out her chair, but there was nothing this man could do to redeem himself now.

"So here we are," she said, settling in.

"It's a little daunting, isn't it?" His mouth was still open. Gray hairs protruded from his nostrils like he'd shoved a sea urchin up his nose.

No wonder his mouth's still open. He probably can't breathe through his nose. Do men not groom anymore?

He scratched his head, and a blizzard of dandruff fell onto his blazer. Okay, maybe there wasn't a blizzard, maybe not even any dandruff. Margot couldn't be sure, but she suspected there was. Her imagination was now declaring war.

Jerry forged on with his high-pitched tone, a timbre Margot wasn't sure she could get used to. "I've been on more of these lately than I care to admit. Honestly, I'm running out of restaurants. The food's not even that good here but, what do you do? Is the Tri-Cities not the worst for dating?" He was making an impression; not a good one, but it was an impression.

Margot shrugged. "Apparently."

"Who knows? Maybe it's me. But everyone I've met is either looking to cheat on their spouse or recovering from a nasty divorce. Is normalcy too much to ask?" He grabbed a menu. "Anyway, do you know what you want to eat? I have to be out of here in an hour or my boss will kill me. We're approaching the end of fiscal. Have you been here before? I'd order the strip if I were you. The chicken's dry. Had it last time."

She started to answer, but he grabbed her menu—literally ripped it from her hands—and said, "Here, let me choose for you. I'll order you the strip. You want a potato with that? Yeah, have the potato. And I'd say a big cabernet would pair if you feel like a drink. Unless you're a Rombauer girl. God, I've met my share of Rombauer girls lately." Laying the menu down, he said, "So, what's your story?"

The urge to stand and run was so strong that Margot had to grip her hands together to find some control. She didn't want to hurt anyone's feelings, even this guy. Putting yourself out there to date again was tough enough. "Look," she started, "I'm not ready. You can mark me down as one of those crazy divorcees. I should say goodbye now before you order for us. I'm just not... I'm not there." And in an effort not to crush his spirit, she added, "It has nothing to do with you."

His shoulders dropped, and his eyes went past her to another table. With the slightest nod, he said, "Good luck to you."

Margot wished him the same as she hightailed it to the front door. Guilt filled her every step, but she knew she had to leave. Falling back against the seat of her Volvo, she screamed, "Why should I be surprised!?" Exploring the vulgar side of her vocabulary, she struck the steering wheel again and again, realizing too late that she was actually honking the horn! Flushing red, she looked into the restaurant to find half the patrons watching her through the window. Hopefully Jerry wasn't one of them.

She called Jasper on the way home.

"Mom!"

"Hey, sweetie." She fought to sound chipper. "You've been gone three days, and we've spoken twice! Is that what I have to look forward to?"

"I know. I'm so sorry. There's so much going on. I wish you were here to see it. My teachers are incredible. I've already met a bassist from Dallas who absolutely kills. We've been jamming together. He lives in my dorm. It's nonstop around here. I'm learning with every conversation. You can't go to the snack machine without running into a prodigy."

"You better not be eating out of a snack machine. I know I've taught you better than that."

"Actually, all I've eaten since I landed is processed food."

"Jasper. Hush your mouth." She changed the subject as she changed lanes. "How are you playing?"

"Better than ever. It's like when I started playing with Jake. My theory professor is almost like a god. I walk out of that class and run straight to my piano. How's the mountain?"

"Well, I just went on a really bad date." She gave him the lowdown.

Jasper wasn't like most children. Since the two of them had endured such pain together during the public execution of her marriage, they had confided in each other and become much more than mother and son. They'd formed their own little army against the world. He'd always supported her in the search for new love.

"Don't worry, Mom. Here's the thing. The pickings are slim around there. You're in the middle of nowhere. But more so, you're not *just* anyone. You're Margot Pierce. You deserve the best. Pairing you will be destiny's greatest achievement."

He spoke like such a poet sometimes. "You're a doll for saying that."

"It's your fault for being awesome."

She whispered, "Thanks," feeling the tear long before it hit her cheek. "You're making me cry."

"I'm telling the truth. You know it. Sorry, Mom, I have to go to class. Call you tomorrow?"

Despite that lonely tear working its way around the curve of her jaw, she felt encouraged. Jasper was often full of wisdom. Had she really expected to find the love of her life on her first date?

∼

Margot spent the rest of the drive to Red Mountain wondering about how many more of these dates she'd have endure before she was rewarded. Before she knew it, she was bumping along the dusty road past the inn and her house to the farm. The midday sun blared down, forcing her to shield her eyes as she looked through the windshield over the property.

An electric fence ran the ten-acre perimeter. Lines of portable fencing formed smaller rectangles and squares inside, allowing the workers to move the grazers from one patch of grass to the next. In the areas with shorter grass, spinning sprinklers showered water high into the air. A bright red barn with a steep roof stood tall in the middle. A month's worth of hay bales were stacked under a metal roof extending off one side.

Noticing the commotion of her passing car, a dog barked. The five pigs and a flock of ducks looked up from their mud bath. The sheep and goats hiding in the shade of the lean-tos turned. Their one Jersey cow raised her head out of a water tank. The two llamas with mouths full of hay slowed their chew. The animals kept their eyes on the Volvo, and only when she stepped out did they start running.

A smile rushed over her as she whispered, "My babies. It feels good to be loved."

Margot and Brooks's brother Shay had rescued each of these animals from unfortunate circumstances, mostly from neglect or unsuccessful slaughter. Since Jake and Jasper's benefit concert, they'd received calls from people all over the Pacific Northwest who had, or knew of, abused animals that needed a new home. They couldn't accept them all, so they provided a rehoming service as well.

Shay was inside the barn brushing Elvis, the blind horse he had rehabilitated. They waved at each other as Margot turned off the fence energizer, unfastened the gate, and cracked it open enough to sneak inside.

Cody, the Australian shepherd Otis had rescued from his neighbor last year, reached her first. Margot knelt and took his ears in her hands and massaged the top of his snout. As they met eyes, only inches apart, she said, "No escape today? Have we finally found all weak spots? Thank goodness the coyotes aren't as savvy as you."

Otis had taken Cody in after Joan was shot, but his Great Pyrenees hadn't wanted anything to do with another dog and attacked Cody twice. Otis had too much going on with Joan's health issues to spend any more effort on the two dogs, so Margot had offered to let Cody live at the sanctuary; they needed a guard dog anyway. Though Cody had proven to be an excellent defender most of the time, he possessed Houdini-like abilities at escaping the fence. And when he did, he always bee-lined it back to Otis's place. Even before Otis had saved the dog's life, those two had a connection that no fence, electric or barbed wire, could sever.

Scores of chickens and ducks followed the dog and then twenty-one goats and sheep came barreling toward the action. Singing greetings, Margot reached into a bin and pulled out a couple of handfuls of grain. The animals surrounded her, begging for a taste. One by one, she fed them, saying their names as they ate from her hand.

Shay eventually led Elvis over to Margot. "Another beautiful day," he said. With dirty jeans, beat-up boots, a rugged beard, and a straw hat, he looked more and more like a cowboy every day.

"Yes, it is." Margot petted Elvis's shoulder. "Hi, handsome."

Shay had rediscovered himself on Red Mountain. He'd been living in the darkness in Portland, an unhappy fry cook living with a bunch of other guys in a filthy apartment, when Brooks had showed up and offered him a job and a place to stay on Red Mountain. No one thought it was a good idea when Brooks brought his brother back and started introducing him to everyone, giving Shay the chance Otis had given Brooks. But so far, Shay had proved everyone wrong. He'd earned his stripes in the vineyard at Lacoda, working hard labor, happily doing anything anyone asked of him. When Jake Forester bought the animal sanctuary land and had gifted it to Margot, he'd also sent Shay down to help manage things. Shay had done an amazing job helping her realize her dream. They interacted daily, sometimes in passing, sometimes for hours, as they dealt with all the responsibilities that came with taking care of the animals.

Margot had a hard time imagining the Shay of a year ago, the one he himself had told her about—a guy wallowing in anger, looking for any reason to curse the world. According to Shay, his parents had put so much pressure on him to be perfect. After giving Brooks up for adoption, they only had one more child, Shay, and they'd worked so hard to raise him well, almost as if succeeding with Shay could bury the guilt they had for giving up Brooks. When Shay ended up in prison, his heartbroken parents gave up on him as well. Only last year did the four of them reconnect.

The Shay she'd gotten to know had a hard time wiping the smile from his face. She'd often catch him singing John Denver and Chris Ledoux songs, or whistling campfire songs, connecting more and more with the man he was becoming. By working outside, taking the focus off himself and putting it into the care of these animals, he'd found his calling. Margot saw in his face and smile a deep gratitude to the mountain and its inhabitants for assisting his pursuit.

She suspected Elvis was the one who really brought it all together for Shay. Elvis, a brown-and-white American paint horse, had arrived at the sanctuary shortly after they'd opened. Blind, underweight, and malnourished, Elvis had limped into the stables, barely holding onto life. An older woman in West Richland had lost a battle with arthritis and neglected the poor horse for way too long until her family had intervened. The man/animal connection was astounding. Shay brought Elvis back to life, rehabilitating his leg, fixing his diet, and giving the horse his youth back. Margot watched the lameness disappear and then Shay was riding him in the corral, and then riding this blind twenty-something-year-old horse to the top of Red Mountain! Anyone who saw Elvis in those first few weeks couldn't believe their eyes when Shay rode this proud steed up the steep rocky slope. After only a few months, Elvis held his head higher and his coat looked healthier. According to Shay, he rode smoother and with more trust.

Shay had taught Elvis how to run a till, and they'd taken up working the vine rows at Lacoda. Watching those two work the land was one of the most beautiful things Margot had ever seen. Seeing a horse that used to be broken smile with his whole body as though he'd found purpose again could melt even the most hardened of souls.

As the other animals returned to the shade, Shay said, "I think we found a home for Theo and Jackson," referring to two of their goats they'd found running down the highway a month before. "A couple called this morning."

"All these goodbyes are too much," she said.

"It'll be a great home. They seem like nice people." He knew what she meant, though, and asked, "Have you talked to Jasper?"

"Just did. He's really happy. Too happy."

"He's going to be missed around here." He ran his fingers through his beard. "How are you holding up?"

"Well, I'm not lying in bed cramming Doritos in my mouth, for whatever that's worth."

Letting go of Elvis's rope, he removed his hat and wiped his forehead. "Hey, it's the little victories that add up to winning the war." He looked down at Elvis's hooves for a moment and then finally looked up. "Can I ask you something, Margot? I've met somebody. Well, not met. I've known her for a while. But we're starting to kind of hit it off."

"Good for you."

"I guess. It's complicated. I'm not sure the whole mountain is going to be happy for me. One person in particular."

"Am I going to hear any details, Mr. Vague? Who is it?"

Shay spit tobacco juice to the ground and said his brother's name. "Brooks."

Margot threw her hand over her mouth to cover a gasp.

He looked down. "Yeah, I know."

"Couldn't you have picked someone else? Anyone else?"

Shay said, "You know what they say in Hawaii about dating? You don't lose your girlfriend, you lose your turn."

"Those islands are a lot bigger than this little mountain."

Elvis showed his teeth and neighed, and Margot combed his mane with her fingers. "So how did this come about?"

"Please keep this between us. I know I don't have to tell you, but…"

"Oh, I understand. Though I love gossip, I do my best not to spread it myself. Your secret is safe with me. But I encourage you to tell him before it goes too far."

"I wish there was an easier way."

"I guess the bigger question is…is she worth it?"

Shay met her eyes. "Without a doubt."

Moving on, they chatted business for a while: finding a new hay supplier; hiring a high school kid to help with some of the chores; replacing one of the energizers for the portable fence; figuring out a way to find the eggs the ducks were laying; and a slew of other topics.

When Margot returned to her car, she thought of her lunch date again. What a disaster. How could she possibly put herself through any more of those?

14

BORED IN BORA BORA

"Why is it so hard for me to be away from Red Mountain?" Otis asked Joan, giving up on reading *Tales from the South Pacific*. He slung the book across the wood floor, the thud barely satisfying his frustration.

A midmorning breeze drifted in through the open doors, tickling the white curtains that were drawn all the way open, making them dance like island ghosts. Otis felt groggy from the jetlag, and that's probably why he found little interest in reading, and instead kept staring at the bamboo ceiling in a particularly relaxed, reflective state. Before posing the question to Joan, he'd spent his time after breakfast searching for the answer within, wondering why the majority of the world dreamed of such a vacation, yet he somehow couldn't find the appeal. The damn ceiling certainly didn't have the answer.

"You really don't know?" Joan asked, putting down a novel set in Africa.

"Because I'm an old grouch who can't sit still." He tilted his head toward her. The white sheets covered her naked body up to the waist while the thin bedspread decorated in pink and red hibiscus had bunched up at their feet. Otis noticed her ribs were becoming more and more visible, a result of her muscle and weight loss.

He slipped out of bed and stretched his back. "I would have thought being with the love of my life in a tropical paradise would bring me pure satisfaction. Don't misunderstand, I love being with you. I just kind of love being with you more on Red Mountain than here." He pulled up his shorts. "What's wrong with me?"

"You know what humans have in common? Other than a need for oxygen."

"We all have to defecate," Otis said, reaching for his shirt.

She offered him a laugh, but only for a moment. "Yes. What else?"

Otis thought about it for a couple of minutes. "Food and water. The Beatles. Dirty politicians. Death. Taxes. Earth. The glory of pizza. Family dysfunction. But I have a feeling I'm missing your point."

"All true. How about something more meaningful? We all need purpose. We need to belong. We need a tribe. You, my lover, have your purpose. You and your other Red Mountainites. And you've left your tribe."

He sat in a chair by the bed, seeing the vineyards in his mind's eye like he might see an old friend or a fond memory. He was suddenly in a prop plane flying low over Red Mountain like some glorious Disney World virtual reality ride where he could see his mountain in all its grandeur. He could see the good people working the land, the ripening berries dangling from the vines. He felt an enveloping warmth no tropical climate could deliver. He could taste the desert air as it filled his lungs.

Otis licked his lips, smiling like he'd devoured a bacon milkshake, and said, "I do miss my mountain."

"Of course you do," she said, sitting up. "The mountain plays an important part in who you are as a person. Your life on the mountain is a part of your identity."

He rubbed his eyes. "So how do I find purpose in being here?"

She inched backward until she was resting against the headboard. "Perhaps it would be better to look at *yourself* as a soldier for your cause. How can you make yourself more effective? Yes, you could work tirelessly every day. But isn't it wise sometimes to step back? To recharge?"

That made sense. "You know, though," he started, waving his index finger, "you're my reason. I'd burn Red Mountain to the ground before I'd lose you."

She patted his face. "I know that, baby. Thankfully, no one's ever going to make you choose."

15

SAYING YES IS FOR THE BIRDS

I n the last days of June, Brooks grew weary of saying "yes." Sometimes, the exercise had indeed enriched his life. But there were a few times, like today, when he wanted to forget his little pact with Joan. Today, saying "yes" would bring great challenges.

The sun had not yet climbed over the back of Red Mountain, and the ridgeline glowed with the coming of morning. Brooks rode his Triumph Scrambler along his favorite dirt trail through the vineyards to work. He'd tried every little turn there was, and he had settled on one path lately. Over and over. Something about the turns appealed to him. Soon he'd know the feel well enough to close his eyes and let the mountain guide him.

Rain was in short supply this time of year, and the dust kicked up around him. The baby berries on the vines were green. Tractors came alive, the drivers getting ready for another long day. Starting in late May, most of the outdoor workers showed up before sunrise. That way they'd be on the highway driving home when the brunt of that afternoon sun raged over the southwest slope.

Brooks waved at a few of them as he took a right to run along Fritz Becker's vineyard. A gopher snake darted out of the way, slithering toward a pile of dirt. He noticed the drip, drip, drip of water from the black irrigation tubes onto the soil around each trunk. All the vine-yards were watering more than usual this year; it was going to be one of the hotter years on record. Thank goodness they now had access to water from the Yakima River. Before that, they'd had to rely on the aquifer alone. A year like this, the aquifer hundreds of feet below could soon run dry.

Lacoda was buried into the hill, and though it did look exquis-itely impressive with its stunning desert stone architecture, it wasn't until you walked through the front door that you realized how much care and money had been put into each stage of the building process. The building went several floors underground, creating what's called a gravity-flow winery, where gravity is used to move the grapes and juice from one stage to the next, a practice that offered a gentler hand in the berries' precious journey toward the bottle.

Parking his motorcycle in the side lot next to the other employees' vehicles, Brooks checked his phone to see the time. He'd just missed a call from his dad, who was also an early riser. Missing a call from his dad was new to him. Having a dad was new to him. In fact, his phone didn't say dad at all, only the man's name. Charles Wildridge had walked into his son's life the year before, and they'd whittled their way into some sort of relationship. Brooks was about to dive deep into work for the day, so he figured he'd better return the call now while he had time.

When his father picked up, Brooks asked, "Charles, how's it going?"

"Hey, son." Charles said the word proudly. "I figured you'd be up and moving."

"Yeah, Jake and I are spending the day together, tasting through everything."

"One of these days you have to let me taste through all the wines with you."

"Yeah, sure, next time you're up." His dad lived in California. There was that "yes" he kept using. If only he'd stopped there.

"Speaking of which, your mom and I were thinking about coming up next week. Just a few days. Celebrate your birthday. What do you think?"

This is where Brooks could have taken a politician's approach to Joan's "say yes" homework, spinning the words to fit how he wanted. Well, *yes,* it would be a problem. But Brooks knew better. *No,* in this case, was a *yes.*

As he paced in a circle, Brooks said, "No, that's fine. The more the merrier." What was he saying!? Did he just tell his parents they could visit? And stay in Brooks's house with Brooks and Shay? The last time hadn't gone so well. The house was already getting too small with Shay, let alone more family. They'd tried this family get-together before. Three times before, to be exact. The last time, three months ago. Brooks remembered every agonizing minute. The arguments, the awkward moments, the trying too hard, the moments that felt real but might not have been. The lies, the hiding. *Yes,* let's do that again.

"You sure?" his dad asked.

"Come on up!" Brooks faked enthusiasm, the exact inverse exploding between his temples.

"Great!" his dad said. "I'm thinking Monday. Only a few days. Can we stay with you?"

"Absolutely." *C'mon, what else you got?*

"Shay's in town, right?"

"Yes." *I'll do this all day. I'm a machine gun of yeses.*

"Maybe we could even swing the clubs while we're up there."

"Yeah, let me see how work goes. We're slammed right now with harvest coming." A moment of weakness almost won, but he gave it a second thought. *Keep saying "yes," Brooks.* "What the hell. I could figure playing nine at the least."

He finished the rest of the conversation without further torture. Let's be clear here, though. Brooks had a rough life growing up. Rough compared to most people he shared meals with now. As a youngster, when he closed his eyes at night, be it at one of the many foster homes or in a train car or in a cardboard box, he'd dreamed of a normal family. When his dad had entered his life last year, he had done some kicking and screaming inside his heart, but a big part of him felt whole in connecting with his lost family. They'd turned out to be normal enough, as families go. His dad was a bit of a hothead. His brother had traveled down his own dark path, running drugs and living on the streets, but he'd come around, almost astonishingly so. His mom had turned out to be the most damaged. She carried the weight of her lost sons around her neck like a heavy chain. Together, the four of them made the Wildridges. They were the new Brady Bunch; he could hear the new theme song playing in his head.

Leaving thoughts of family outside, Brooks went to work. With all the confusion on the outside of those doors, he found something that made sense in here. He walked through the empty tasting room and into the cellar. It was there that the fermentations began. He passed the steel tanks and barrels and walked into the lab, turning on the lights. The shelves on one wall displayed an ebulliometer, a refractometer, and a few other winemaking gadgets. A dozen hats from different wine equipment suppliers hung from hooks on the adjacent wall. The table in the center held nearly thirty different wine samples that his assistant Pak had collected the night before. Brooks looked at the labeling, making sure everything made sense.

Jake Forester walked in right behind him, saying, "Good morning." He wore his typical jeans, black T-shirt, and boots. "You ready to do this?"

"Totally ready. Couldn't sleep last night." Nearly every meaningful thing Brooks had done in the past year and a half had led to this moment. These wines had all gone through secondary fermentation by now and gotten a chance to settle in their aging vessels. He'd honed his skill of tasting a wine early into fermentation and guessing its future, but there was nothing compared to finally pouring into the glass something closer to a finished product. The wines would most likely see another year of aging, but today, Brooks and Jake would enjoy a solid glimpse of what Red Mountain had given them last year.

Of course, the two men continued to deal with some of last year's shocks on the mountain: their cheating partners; an assault with a gun on their dear friend, Joan; a new family for Brooks; and a heartbroken daughter for Jake. Last year had been a tough year for every-one. Hopefully, the mountain's gift from last year's vines would give them something to celebrate.

Jake said in his slow, mellow tone, "Everything comes down to this, doesn't it? It was a wild harvest, man."

Brooks nodded and almost said something but paused. "So what's going on with you? I've been listening to a lot of Pearl Jam, by the way. Do you keep up with them?"

Jake knew all those guys: Pearl Jam, Nirvana, Soundgarden, Alice in Chains. The ones that were still alive, at least. He'd been right in the middle of it when the Seattle grunge scene exploded. Brooks had met a few of the other musicians since he'd been working for Jake, but he'd never met Eddie Vedder. Considering everyone else on earth bugged Jake about music, Brooks tried not to go there. But he'd recently rediscovered Pearl Jam and was curious.

Jake smiled like the question had triggered a specific memory. "Yeah, I talked to Eddie last week. He keeps saying he's going to visit. He digs your wine, by the way."

"Yeah?" Everyone knew Eddie was a wine guy.

"That's what he says."

"How's Carm?"

"Ah, she's all right. She'd rather be back here." Jake began to inspect the samples.

"Yeah, I can imagine."

"She's in what they call the anger stage right now. I get her on the phone and she starts unleashing."

"What do you say?"

Jake shook his head and then stared down into his glass. "What do I say? I tell her to hang in there, which just upsets her more. In the end, I tell her she has to stay. She has to stick with the program. Then she hangs up on me."

Brooks set a hand on the counter. "When does she get to leave?"

"When she stops hanging up on me. I don't know. She can leave whenever she wants, but I hope she stays a few more weeks at least. It's only been a week now. She's still withdrawing."

"I'm sorry."

"All part of life, brother. She'll come out stronger. You know, she's a good woman. A lot of people on this mountain don't know that about her. She has a big heart, and she's a beautiful person. Inside, I mean." Jake threw his hand forward. "She'll be back. She's strong. We all lose our way from time to time."

"You're a good husband. I wish I could stand by someone like that."

"I'm trying to love harder and harder every day. It's not easy right now. We're going to have to cancel our European tour. The band is going to kill me, but I need to be around. Definitely not taking Carmen around Europe after all this."

Jake showed Brooks some pictures of Emilia in Copenhagen and said, "By the way, I have something for you." He disappeared and returned with a picture frame wrapped neatly in red gift paper. "For you."

"What is it?"

"Open it."

Brooks removed the paper and turned over the frame. It was the *Rolling Stone* article from two months before with a picture of Brooks riding his Triumph. "Thanks, man. That's kind of you."

"I know you don't like the praise, but hang it in your office. Remember what you've done here. Not that you need validation from some magazine, but still. What if you could talk to the twenty-year-old you and tell him you were going to be in *Rolling Stone* magazine?"

"The twenty-year-old me would have broken into a long laugh."

Jake hit him on the shoulder. "Yeah, well, who's laughing now?"

Brooks poured them both a syrah. "This is the block up by Sunset, the one we picked a little too early. Neutral barrel."

They both jammed their noses into the glass. Brooks let everything else go around him. Early picked syrah lacked some of the savage qualities he liked, but in turn, offered bright red fruits and fresh leather. He didn't detect any noticeable flaws. The wine didn't come off hot—meaning too obviously high in alcohol—which he wouldn't have expected from an early picked batch. Scientifically, the wine was flawless.

Almost too flawless, Brooks thought, smirking.

He didn't like his wines to be flawed, but he didn't mind a little less polish than some of his neighbors. He took a sip and ran it along his tongue, sucking in air, noticing how the acidity struck his tongue, then settled down in the mid-palate, allowing the fruit to show. He spat the wine into the sink and enjoyed the lingering finish.

Brooks modeled his tasting habits after those of Otis, who had taught him everything. He'd been brainwashed by the best, as Otis always told him. Brooks needed to analyze the wine for any flaws that could get out of hand, so he could make sure he was doing what he needed to do, but then he needed to step back and taste the wine more like a beginner. Almost how a child might.

Resetting his brain, tapping back into the less scientific, he took a few breaths and closed his eyes. He smelled again. This time, the wine transported him. He remembered strolling with Abby through that block during harvest. He remembered tasting those grapes with her. He could hear the magpies singing and feel the energy and health of the vines. They'd found a robin's nest with gorgeous turquoise eggs. He tried to ignore the fact that Abby had come to mind. It was their year, though. Of course this vintage would always be theirs.

He took a sip and let the wine dance in his mouth, arousing his senses. A chill ran through him. The lightness of the early picked fruit dazzled him, made him want to have another glass. He eventually spat the wine into the sink, coming back to reality.

He looked at Jake, having nearly forgotten he was there. They met eyes. Brooks wanted approval.

Jake cut a smile. "They all this good?"

"Let's hope so."

"God, I love syrah."

Brooks made circles with his glass, lifting up the nose. "The rest of the country needs to get on board."

"Well, you mentioning it in *Rolling Stone* won't hurt."

"It's coming. Syrah will be the variety on everyone's hit list soon. I feel it. Shit, the trade loves it. Eventually that will trickle down from the sommeliers and retailers. You ask anybody in the trade what their desert island wine is, they'll say Champagne. But if you ask for a red, most will tell you syrah."

Jake shook his head ever so slowly. "I hope Red Mountain syrah leads the way."

"Hey, did you see that piece of property on the highway went up for sale? That whole stretch."

"No," Jake said, perking up. "Hadn't seen it yet. Do they have water rights?"

"Not sure. I really hope some cheap-ass motel chain doesn't pick it up. That's the gateway to the mountain."

"Send me the info. Maybe we can steer the right investors. Does Otis know?"

"I haven't talked to him since he left," Brooks admitted. "He should know. You're right, we need to be the ones steering that development. I feel like the bloodsuckers are starting to look at our mountain, wondering how they can profit."

They spent the next few hours tasting what was an epic vintage of wine. Once again, Red Mountain had lived up to the hype.

Brooks was intent on fulfilling the promise he'd made to Joan. He'd thought about the notion often, though he'd done more pushing it off than anything. Rejection was what he feared most in this world. Any decent psychiatrist would point out his parentless childhood to be the reason. Still, awareness didn't necessarily solve the problem. He couldn't imagine being any more comfortable with rejection.

The idea of going out of his way to find Adriana today was a giant leap of faith. He'd have to go by Épiphanie and ask Margot how to get in touch with her. Then Margot would know what he was up to. One more person to witness the possible rejection. Then, *after* he found Adriana and half the world knew he was looking for her, he'd have to throw himself out there even more and ask her out. She might not even remember him. She might be totally caught off-guard. He thought he'd sensed a little connection when they met, but who knows? He knew nothing about her. Except that she was single.

But even if it worked out, even if she said "yes," he was afraid of the outcome. Look at what had happened with Abby. That feeling that everything was right in the world and you're moving a million miles an hour and no one can do wrong and then you slam into a wall. Whap! It all stops.

Was he really about to chase that again? He thought it comical that his "status" as head winemaker for Jake Forester, his "status" as the first winemaker to ever grace the pages of *Rolling Stone*, didn't do anything to aid his self-esteem in going to find her. He felt naked, afraid, and totally inadequate.

16

IT'S ALL IN THE TIMING

With grating trepidation, Adriana pushed open the door to Harry Bellflour's second-floor room at Épiphanie. After three days of no service, he had finally removed the *I had wine last night. Leave me alone!* sign from the door.

"Housekeeping," she announced, hoping she was alone.

Embracing the silence, she propped open the door with her cart and stepped inside. Turning on the lamps, she saw his room was in nearly perfect order, much like the last time she'd cleaned. He'd stripped the Parisian bed and left two sheets in the corner; the white duvet was folded in a square at the end of the bed. Unlike most rooms she cleaned, there were no clothes tossed about the hardwoods. A pair of tennis shoes rested neatly at the base of the bed. A suit jacket was draped over the French country chair.

Adriana opened the curtains that were bunched up on the wood floor to let the afternoon sunlight pour in. Stepping out to the balcony with the wrought iron railing, she collected five empty wine bottles. When she returned to the room, she felt a cold chill. She'd be so happy when he finally checked out. He was too close to the evil she already knew too well.

Her previous employer in Washington had taught Adriana the

importance of routine in cleaning—an exact list to follow—but it was Margot who'd taught Adriana the art of cleaning. Margot had stolen ideas from all the great hotels of the world and then honed her own regimen from there. The neatly typed, laminated instructions hung from the side of the cleaning cart.

Open the blinds. If necessary, strip the bed. Use the dirty fitted sheet to hold the top sheet. Walk it out of the room. Return and examine the duvet insert for stains. Fold the duvet and set aside on the chair. Make the bed using hospital corners on the ends. Fold the top sheet six inches back, ensuring crisp creases. Arrange and fluff the duvet and pillows. Finish with two pumps of lavender spray above the pillows. And on and on.

Considering they hadn't cleaned his room in several days, Adriana deemed it necessary to change the sheets. Once she'd finished with the bed, she continued with Margot's directions throughout the process.

Then there was someone behind her. She'd pulled out the hose and was vacuuming under the desk when she felt the disturbance. She switched off the machine and turned her head. Harry Bellflour walked in, dropping his briefcase by the door. He was breathing heavily from climbing the stairs.

"I'm just finishing up. So sorry."

Bellflour waved her off and walked into the room. "It's fine. Take your time."

Her heart rate accelerated. "Are you sure? I can come back." She hoped he'd tell her to leave.

He gestured toward the bed. "You're doing a fine job. That looks great. You're clearly as hardworking as you are beautiful."

He was scaring her now. Her heart frantically pumped blood, and her chest burned. She turned. "I'll get out of your way now."

He sat on the bed, eyes following her as she collected her things and prepared to leave the room. "How long have you been working here?"

She caught him looking at her legs and muttered, "Not long." She wrapped the cord around the vacuum like she was racing someone.

They were only a few feet away from each other. She could smell wine on his breath.

Bellflour slipped off his shoes, revealing light blue socks. "I don't mean to make you nervous."

"I'm not nervous. I'm just sorry I'm in your way. I'll come back." All she cared about was getting out of that room safely and not losing her job in the process.

Bellflour said calmly, "A woman like you could never be in my way."

Adriana faked a smile, but they both knew he'd crossed lines. She started toward the door with the vacuum cleaner, her terror now written all over her face and words. She turned back and said, "Let me know if you need anything else, okay?"

"Oh, I'm never satisfied." With a slightly open liver-lipped mouth, he gave a confident and disrespectful grin. Then he winked—a repulsive wink as intentionally dirty as it was excessively vulgar. There was no doubt what fueled his mind. The look that followed was one devoid of humanity, a gaping hollowness so purely black as to be demonic. A look Adriana had seen in her ex-husband a thousand times.

As Adriana turned away, he asked, "Would you care to share a glass with me?"

Without looking back, she said, "No, thank you. I have a lot of rooms to clean." She clumsily set the vacuum cleaner in the cart and pushed the cart into the hallway. She kicked the doorstop and the door swung closed behind her. She breathed in the relief of her escape.

As she rushed to push the cart into the closet, Adriana turned to ensure that Bellflour hadn't followed her. While repeatedly glancing back, she raced toward the stairway and descended the steps.

"Adriana," she heard a voice say from near the front door in the lobby downstairs.

She recognized Brooks Baker. "Yes?"

"Are you okay?" He pulled the entrance door closed.

"I am...yeah, I'm okay." She glanced back up the stairs. She could hear her own heartbeat, her fight-or-flight response set in high gear.

"You look scared."

"Ghosts," she said, searching for something to say. "It's a little too quiet up there." Scrambling for more explanation, she said, "I'm like my mother. Very superstitious. It gets the best of us sometimes."

Brooks stepped toward her. "Want me to go up there and fend them off?"

She forced a smile but wanted so desperately to run away. "I think I'm the only one who sees them."

"Well, we all have our ghosts. How are you otherwise?" he asked, putting a hand out, palm up. His words spurted out in shaky staccato blasts, the evidence of his unstable nerves.

She took a peaceful breath and tried to relax, tried to remove Harry Bellflour from her mind. "Do you mean have I recovered from the night of the purple vibrator?"

He smiled. "Well, I mean, in general. But that too. Have you recovered? I know it was embarrassing."

She wiped her forehead. "Thank goodness Margot accepted the blame. But I'm not sure I'll ever forget it. Thank you for coming to the rescue."

"You're welcome." He stabbed his hands into his pockets. "It wasn't anything out of the norm for this mountain."

"Playing tug-of-war with a vibrator and a dog?"

"Sure. That's a normal night around here."

"I haven't been here long enough to get a feel for the place," Adriana said, crossing her arms, wondering what he was doing here, hoping they could wrap up this conversation quickly. "Are you looking for Margot?"

"Actually, I was looking for you."

"Oh." A light bulb turned on. She hadn't been asked out in a long time, but she recognized the moment. She had a quick vision of a sweaty and shaky Rudy Miles asking her out for the senior prom in between classes, in front of her locker.

Brooks said, "I wanted to stop by..." He looked up into the air above her, looking for words. Collecting himself, he blurted out, "Would you go out with me? Maybe this weekend?"

Oh, don't do this right now. Oh, Dios. Without any intention of doing so, Adriana looked at him like she'd bitten into a lemon. "What?"

He deflated like a bike tire with a nail in it, his eyes looking down, his body shrugging. Finding another burst of confidence, he said, "Would you go out with me?"

"I'm sorry," she said, caught totally off-guard. "No, thank you."

"Oh." He looked at her, waiting for more.

She wished she'd said it wasn't the right time, but it was too late now.

He waited for more. Then, "Okay. If you ever change your mind..."

Adriana nodded, trying her best to make eye contact for a second, then looking left, a habit she'd gotten into since her face had been cut up. She felt terrible and could see the defeat as he turned toward the big wooden doors.

"Have a good day," he said, tugging one side open.

She tried to smile but didn't have it in her. He wasn't looking anyway.

He was gone. The latch snapped shut.

Adriana wanted to say she was sorry. Wanted to say something. Anything. After a few moments, she approached the door and looked out the long vertical window just in time to watch the Lacoda truck roll away.

~

"*QUE?*" her mom asked as she stirred her weekly batch of chicken and lime soup, a recipe from Margarita's grandmother. Smells of citrus, allspice, and cinnamon rose from the pot. "*Tu eres muy loca.*" (You're crazy.)

"I don't have time to go on dates," Adriana said, also in Spanish. She could see Zack was watching cartoons on the couch.

"What could be more important?" her mother asked. "What matters more than finding a man? A partner?"

"Taking care of my son and my mother."

"How are you going to care for your son without any money? Without a man in your life? I'm not going to be here forever."

"I'm doing fine."

"Not long ago you were living five blocks from Beverly Hills. And you weren't cleaning houses. You *had* a housekeeper. You were driving a BMW! Can you imagine how lucky you were? The rest of your family in Mexico would kill for that dream."

"Mama, *you* were a housekeeper."

"There's nothing wrong with being a housekeeper, but I want you to be able to give Zack what I couldn't give you."

Adriana stomped her foot and threw out her hands. "It's all stuff, Mama. Stuff can't make you happy. What? You want me to go back to that man?"

"Of course not!" Her mom jabbed her wooden spoon at Adriana with each syllable. "But I want you to find another."

"Maybe one day," Adriana said, collapsing on a stool, exhausted. "I can't even imagine sharing my space with a grown man again. It's not appealing."

Not getting Adriana's point, Margarita said, "You're not going to look young forever." There it was...the venom of her mother.

"Mama!" she screamed. "That's enough." Adriana turned to see if Zack had noticed them arguing, relieved to find he was lost in his show.

"It's true," her mother said. "No one will ask you out in five or ten years."

Adriana screamed quietly, "Mama, look at me!" She pointed to her face. "There's nothing young or beautiful about me anymore. Who would want me now? Who would want an ugly woman with a child anyway?"

"The right man will love..." She lowered her voice. "The right man will see past your scars. And he'll look at your son as the best part of you."

"I doubt that," Adriana whispered back.

Margarita stepped toward her and sighed. "You must open your-self up. If a man asks you out, say yes! Even if it's another *gringo*."

"I don't care about his skin."

"Well, Mexican lovers are better, but you need to take what you can get. Go find him and tell him you want a date."

"Absolutely not."

Margarita shook her hands in the air. "Go find him!"

Adriana ran out of words. She didn't bother telling her mom about Harry Bellflour.

Her mom kept going. "You're impossible. What? Are you worried you might have to make Zack sleep in his own bed for once?"

Adriana felt her Mayan blood begin to boil but held back. "Don't go there, Mama."

"He's six years old. How long is this going to go on?"

"He's been through a lot." Adriana shook her head, eyeing her son, who was oblivious to the argument. "I'm not discussing this right now."

"You're never discussing this. Are you going to move into his dorm room when he goes to college?"

"Go suck an egg, Mama!"

Margarita feigned spitting to the floor and then returned to her soup. "Impossible."

Adriana joined her son on the couch and laughed with him at his show. Margarita retired to her room. It took ten minutes for the women to calm down.

When they were back in the kitchen, Margarita said, "So what's he like?"

"He's very cute," Adriana said, letting the previous stuff go. "He's a winemaker. He's very nice. Kind of shy."

"What if you lost your chance?"

"Then it's not meant to be."

"Stop feeling sorry for yourself. Go out and find a man. Find a partner for this life. I couldn't have made it through half of what I've been through without your stepfather by my side."

Every time her mother brought him up, Adriana could see the pain of loss in her eyes. A few years after Margarita and Adriana had moved to Los Angeles, Margarita had met her second husband. He gave Margarita and Adriana a secure, stable life in California before dying of heart disease months before Adriana married Michael.

"He died a long time ago. You've done fine."

"I'm dying. I'm lonely, and I'm dying. I miss him every minute."

"Why would I want to put myself through that?"

"Because your stepfather put smiles on my face that I can still feel to this day. Smiles that you'll never know if you don't get back out there. When he and I met, we made the stars shine even brighter over the Hollywood Hills." Her mom closed her eyes, most likely seeing her husband's face. "Soon, I'll be joining him."

"Don't speak that way. You're such a drama queen."

Adriana read through the mail while her mom did the dishes. A few minutes later, she asked, "Will you please watch Zack for a little while? I need to take a bath and relax. Just a few minutes of me time."

"Yes," her mother said. "Please take a break."

Adriana thanked her and walked into her bedroom. After Adriana closed and locked the door, she sighed audibly. She kicked off her shoes and collapsed onto the bed. She just wanted to sleep. For a long time. For days. She needed a break. Curling up, she wrapped her arms around a pillow and squeezed tightly. She prayed to God for the strength to carry on, then wondered if He was even listening.

In a shoebox in the back of her closet, she pulled out the gun she'd bought shortly before she left Los Angeles. She touched the cold steel, thinking about the power, about the finality of the weapon. Wondering if she'd ever have to pull that trigger.

Wondering if he'd ever find them.

17

A BIGGER RABBIT TAKES THE CARROT

"What kind of name is Remi Valentine?" Margot wondered out loud, scrolling and clicking through *Match.com*. She was sitting in one of the mismatched chairs at one of the long tables in the dining room of Épiphanie, answering emails and placing food and wine orders. Her guests had left to explore the mountain, and the room was quiet and lonely.

He was handsome in his profile picture, sitting on a bench with his legs crossed. Not delicious but handsome. She could imagine kissing him. Bushy black eyebrows. Darker skin. He almost looked Greek from the photo. For a moment she imagined Remi as Princess Diana's Dodi Fayed. A total playboy who was so bad for her, but oh, so good.

"Are you my Dodi, Remi Valentine?" She read his profile, getting better and better at sorting out the awful ones. Her first relief was that his profile didn't contain any initial comments like, *Hey, ladies.* Or, *I'm looking for my partner in crime.* The clichés got old quickly. He actually wrote well and sounded interesting.

According to his profile, Remi was divorced and had a teenage daughter. Both of those were okay with Margot. Being divorced herself and at their age, how could she demand otherwise? He was 6'2" with an athletic build. He was a social drinker. No red flags yet.

She moved on to the *About me and who I'm looking for* sections and read:

I don't know what kind of woman I'm looking for. All that I do know is she's out there. I've spent my life looking for love in all the wrong places. I've spent most of my life misunderstanding love. Not the love that I have for my daughter. I do understand that love. I mean the kind of love that you share between partners. After a lifetime of doing it wrong, I finally know what love means. Love is something we do as an offering, expecting nothing in return. Love requires trust. Love takes everything you have. Love is NOT a lusty affair. Love is a commitment beyond any others, an action that takes every ounce of effort you have. I'm looking for a woman who will allow me to love her with everything I have.

In a sea of men looking to get laid, this guy said exactly what Margot had been thinking. All she wanted in life was to be loved that way. And to love that way.

∼

TWENTY-THREE WOMEN COLLECTED in the dining room of Épiphanie that evening for Margot's weekly cooking class. They were farmers and winemakers and wives of the same. There was a psychologist, a doctor, two lawyers, and several stay-at-home moms. Not that their jobs defined them. Margot tried to ask who they were, not what they did. But still, the women would typically say what they did. That was okay.

If someone had asked Margot who she was, she might have said an innkeeper. But the truth was that she was a lover of animals and music, a mother of one, a chef, and a dream chaser with a tarnished past. And if they kept prying, she'd say she was a lover without a lover.

Standing at the head of the table, Margot clinked her glass with a knife blade, silencing the crowd. She'd given these toasts so many times on Red Mountain and loved each one more and more. Perhaps it was her only chance to be on stage again, a chance to revisit those costumed days in New York. With each toast, she opened up more and more, knowing that vulnerability gave way to connection.

"Truth be told, I cook my feelings. I always have. But you don't have to be in a lovely, worry-free mood to cook well. At least I don't. In fact, I cook my best when I'm having a terrible day. And guess what? I just so happen to be at a low point. Why? I was born without a filter just like my mother, so I'd like to overshare. The truth is, I'm lonely. My son left to attend a school on the East Coast. I've been dreading his departure for a long time, but I had no idea how deep it would cut." Margot pretended to chop her arm off at the elbow.

"On top of that, you all know about my divorce, and you know I've done a pretty grand job growing past it, if I do say so myself. I'd like to think I've found a healthy space. That doesn't make being alone any easier. Throwing away all my romantic hopes, I have turned to technology to save the day. I've been dabbling with *Match* and *Tinder*."

One of the ladies said, "You're not the only one, sister."

The rest of the room nodded and laughed.

"Oh, great," said Margot. "So the slim pickings are even slimmer with all of you poaching my men. No wonder I can't find anybody." She clapped her hands together. "Sexual frustration and loneliness, that's what we're cooking tonight. I know I have you girls, and that's a wonderful thing, but no one in this room is going to give me an orgasm. Not unless you have something I don't know about under those dresses."

The room burst into laughter.

"Because we're all competing for the same rodeo clowns, and I want you all to be as fat as me, we're going to make the best fries, or *frites*, of your life. We'll make a homemade garlic aioli to dunk them in. And pair it with a grower's Champagne, a blanc de blanc, otherwise known as bubbling chardonnay, from Duval Leroy. After a naughty start, we'll try to behave with a Nicoise salad, using the first of the veggies from the garden and eggs from the pretty ladies out back.

"Those of you who've been coming for a long time know how

much I like purple. I have some small purple potatoes and purple *haricot verts*. That's green beans, by the way. Then we'll make a squash blossom and goat cheese galette, which is like a pastry pizza. The goat cheese comes from our goats down at the sanctuary."

After a sip of wine, she said, "Many people like to save the reds for meat. In a vegetarian establishment, that would keep us away from the reds of this beautiful mountain. I love reds with vegetables. We'll start with a delicious merlot from Charlie Hoppes at Fidelitas. I talked him into letting me buy some older wines, which we'll drink tonight. Then we'll cancel out all those healthy vegetables with a delicious desert. I wanted to pour Kiona's Ice Wine, which is a guilty pleasure of mine. We'll stew some raspberries and apricots and top them with a crème fraiche and nut crumb sprinkle. With a spoonful of local honey on top." She raised her glass. "Here's to a night of eating our feelings and hopefully manifesting a few of our desires along the way."

The ladies nodded in anticipation, and then Margot led them all into the kitchen to begin her class.

∾

LATER IN THE EVENING, Margot found Harry Bellflour smoking a cigar on the front steps of the inn. She hadn't seen him smoke before. "Hey there, Mr. Bellflour. How are you?"

He turned from his stargazing and said, "Big crowd tonight."

"Yeah, we do this every Sunday."

"You're not married?" he asked.

"Nope." She noticed an empty wine glass by his feet.

"Seems lonely out here. You don't ever feel a little scared?"

"Only when someone asks me if I feel a little scared."

He puffed. "I was just wondering if it gets lonely."

"We stay pretty busy."

"You're a good-looking woman. I imagine someone on this mountain has his eyes on you."

"Are you asking me out?"

"I've thought about it. What would you say?"

"I'd tell you I don't date guests."

"What if I said I'm checking out?"

"I'd tell you I need the business. It's nice to talk to you." She started toward her house across the yard.

18

THE HAWAIIAN SUN FALLS ON OTIS

O tis walked barefooted along the beach of the St. Regis in Princeville, Kauai, his phone in hand. The darkening sky burned pink and purple. Even though the property faced a protected lagoon, he could hear the roar of the waves from the surfer's break around the bend. Off behind him, a singer strummed his guitar on a stage by the pool. At the exact minute they'd agreed upon, he dialed Brooks.

"I was hoping you'd forget to call," his protégé said cheerfully.

"I wish that were a possibility. How are things going on the mountain?"

"The minute you left, things started falling apart. Your syrah vineyard somehow has the first reported case of Phylloxera in Washington State. Scientists are all over the vineyard right now, talking about shutting it down. Maybe even pulling the vines out."

"Right," Otis whispered, letting Brooks enjoy his little game. Everyone loved to pick on Otis.

"It's not good. Your wines all taste like vinegar. Strangely, a fault line has suddenly appeared on the northern edge of Red Mountain. They're saying it's the end for us."

"Are you enjoying yourself?"

"Tremendously. You've only been gone a few days. Everything is just fine. How's Bora Bora?"

"Hawaii now."

A seabird landed on piece of driftwood, eyed Otis, and flew off again.

"Poor thing. I hope you're drinking pineapple wine."

Otis updated him on Joan and then fired off a list of questions about the vineyard and the winery.

Brooks answered briefly, not allowing Otis to run through his large checklist without some resistance. "I have everything under control. Actually, Eli, Chaco, and Esteban have it under control. I went by there at lunch. Things are looking great. There is one thing though."

"What's that?" The philosophizing Stoic in Otis had been prepared for something.

"A piece of land popped up for sale directly across the highway from the Conoco. And it already sold."

"What? Who bought it?" Otis felt a vein rise on his forehead.

"No idea. Nobody knows yet. Someone was in the tasting room at Lacoda talking about it. Some real estate guy; I don't know."

"You didn't get the details?"

"I'm just hearing rumors."

The beauty of the Hawaiian night dissipated. "This isn't good."

"You can't assume that."

"Christ, I'm not happy about it. You should have told me sooner. That piece of land can break this mountain. I need to get back home."

Brooks laughed. "No, you don't. It's gone. There's nothing you can do about it now."

"Find out for sure if it's sold. Get details. Please. If there's something we can do to stop it from happening, let me know. You know how big a deal this is."

"Yes, I do. I'll look into it."

"Don't look into it," Otis said. "Put everything you have into finding out. Like, now. Find out who is buying that damned piece of land."

"Yes, sir."

Otis sighed. "Sorry, Brooks. I'm worried."

"Don't be. No one can ruin this mountain."

"Imagine if some crap chain gets ahold of it. What if Applebee's buys it? Comfort Inn?"

Brooks laughed. "Applebee's isn't going to buy it."

"You don't know. Our mountain is starting to attract people. People with money. Not everyone with money has vision. Don't forget that. We have to steer the vision."

"Calm down, Otis. I get it."

"I'll keep my phone on me the rest of today and tomorrow. Please call me back."

"Okay. Now go try and enjoy your island vacation."

"Call me back." Otis hung up, feeling helpless and afraid. When he returned to their room, he was so distracted he didn't notice how beautiful Joan looked in her green dress and purple and white Hawaiian lei. And he didn't even allow the slightest curl of his mouth when she raised her hand to present the gift of a brand new Speedo swimsuit for his upcoming beach days.

19

THE WHOLE FAMDAMILY UNDER ONE ROOF

A week after Adriana had rejected him, as June gave way to the hotter days of July, Brooks could feel harvest creeping up on them. He could already smell the fermentations of their year of work. He'd barely scrubbed last year's purple stains off his hands.

Two months and counting.

His parents were landing in a few minutes. He teetered back and forth on an emotional seesaw—one side trepidation, the other the excitement of a full house.

On his way to the airport, he eyed the piece of property that had gone under contract a week before. The plot line ran not forty yards off the highway to the south, abutting the frontage road. The land rose up to a plateau clearly visible from both sides of the highway. Cheat grass and shrubs, the kind of plant life that can survive in the desert, sprinkled the arid land.

Though this property wasn't part of the Red Mountain American Viticultural Area—or AVA, as most people called it—the land gave off an appearance of domination because of its clear view across the highway to the vines. The lack of slope didn't promise excellent grape growing and was more suitable to service the growing needs of the wine appellation. Like, as he and Otis mentioned, an Applebee's or Comfort Inn. Or, as these two men would prefer, a fine boutique hotel, or maybe a family-owned deli with stunning picnic lunches for visitors, the kind of deli that would offer homemade baguettes, cuts of charcuterie and cheese, and perhaps small picnic bottles of Red Mountain's finest. That kind of concept would be a beautiful step in the right direction.

The difference between a boutique inn similar to something you might find on Highway 29 in Napa and a large chain with an ugly billboard could not be overstated. The occupant would set the stage and anticipation for those visiting the area to taste the wines. No, the establishment would not affect the wines, but it would affect consumers' perceptions of quality. Often, perception is everything. He and Otis had exhausted this conversation on countless occasions.

He dialed Otis, hoping his mentor wouldn't answer, but he did. The old man was standing by his phone like the guardian of Red Mountain that he was.

"Aloha," Brooks said, trying to start off on the right foot.

"We're in Vietnam now."

Brooks was surprised at the crispness of the connection.

Otis jumped right into an interrogation. "Did you find out anything?"

"Oh, c'mon. You're in Vietnam, and you can't even take a second to tell me about it before you dive right into asking about Red Mountain? The most important question: did Joan get you into a Speedo yet?"

"The people are nice. The hotel is fine. Lots of motorcycles. Lots of noodles. And yes, she talked me into the damned Speedo." Brooks laughed as Otis continued, "Now what's going on with that piece of land?"

"Still nothing. Trust me, I'm working on it. I can't find any answers, Otis. I've spoken with the listing agent. She confirmed the property is under contract but won't tell me anything else. They're trying to keep it quiet. I've asked everyone I know on this mountain. No one knows anything."

"You keep things quiet when you know you're going to upset people. Who the hell could it be?"

Brooks said, "Even if we knew the buyer, there's nothing we can do."

"You never know."

"Otis, you've been my mentor for many years. You've taught me so much about not only wine, but also life. I know I don't have much to offer in return, but may I say one thing without you biting my head off?"

"For God's sake, spit it out, son."

"In the years to come, you're going to look back on this trip you're on, and I truly hope you can revisit the memory knowing that you had fun, that you gave everything you had into being there with Joan, enjoying it. Know what I mean?"

A long beat. Then, "This is me not biting your head off."

"Thank you for listening. What time is it over there?"

"We're just waking up. Seven or something."

"Are you spreading the Gospel of Red Mountain to all these foreigners you're encountering?"

"Every chance I get."

Brooks took the exit to 182, deflecting Otis's questions for a while before finally getting off the phone. Spending the next few days with his parents was much higher on his list of worries. As he had wondered aloud to Otis, what could they do about a property that's under contract?

Brooks stopped outside the baggage claim area of the Pasco airport, the kind of airport where you can still park at the curb without a man on a Segway telling you to move along. You could even leave your hazards on and go inside if you wanted to. The young woman in front of him jumped out of her car to hug a soldier returning home. Brooks's parents walked out next.

He embraced his mother first as she wished him a happy birthday. Mary Wildridge had long thick white hair and flowery blue eyes. Feather earrings fell from her ears.

"Thanks, Mom." He knew the word "Mom" meant a lot to her, so he forced it. Brooks had only met her for the first time last fall, so things were certainly new. For that matter, the "happy birthday" thing was something he would need to adjust to as well. He barely knew his birthday and certainly hadn't celebrated it growing up.

His and Mary's few times together were still moments of surface exploration. They'd met last year on the day Joan was shot, so with the tragedy thick in the air, they hadn't gotten much of a chance to connect. Charles and Mary had returned several times since, but the relationship was so new that they were still testing the waters, not yet opening up the way a family should.

As Brooks and Mary stepped away from each other, she offered a colorful smile that she'd not shared before, one deficient of skepticism. She was getting used to having her boys back.

He looked at his father. "Pop."

"Hey, son. Happy birthday." He liked the way his dad dressed. Always like he'd just walked off the eighteenth green. Charles wore a Dri-FIT St. Andrews golf shirt tucked into pleated khakis.

Brooks looked down at his shoes. "Did you get your penny loafers shined during your layover?"

"I did. In Seattle. Glad you noticed."

They went for a handshake that morphed into an awkward hug.

Brooks patted his dad on the back. "Good to see you again."

The drive home was uneventful. They hadn't seen each other in a few months, so there were plenty of questions and answers to keep them talking. His dad always liked to ask about landmarks. What orchard is that? What vineyard? That a new winery? It kept them busy.

They reached Brooks's home on Demoss Road. Bought after Jake had hired him, his ranch-style, three-bedroom, two-bath house symbolized a security that he'd spent his whole life never knowing. He'd slept in boxes and in train cars and under trees. To this day, he could sleep on the floor without any discomfort. For Brooks, having a home with a comfortable bed and a clean bathroom all to himself was beyond belief. The fact that he was able to buy this house on the river was still hard to grasp. It still would have looked like a bachelor pad with empty walls and cheap furniture had Abby not stepped in the year before to decorate.

They found Shay in the kitchen, fileting a pink fish. He had been living with Brooks for almost eight months now, and they'd built a solid relationship. Despite the missing years, they'd found a real connection, the kind they talk about in books and movies. How siblings can feel each other. Brooks had found that true time and time again. Still, it was now time for Shay to find another place to live. Two grown men in one house equaled a ticking time bomb.

Shay wore a red bandana around his head, keeping his curly hair away from his eyes. Brooks had rarely seen him without that bandana. His beard was shaved neatly under the jaw.

"Hello, everyone," Shay said, hugging his mother and shaking his dad's hand.

"What are you cooking?" Charles asked.

"Coho salmon. I figured you don't see much real salmon down there in Cali. I caught this with a friend on the Columbia during the spring run."

Brooks was quick to open a bottle of wine, and the four of them were quick to drink it. They went through two more bottles at dinner. None of them enjoyed silence at the table, so there were moments of desperate topics. It felt like they were all falling off a cliff and desperately reaching for a ledge to stop the fall.

That's not to say the entire experience was a torture chamber. Attempts at finding something together after the lost years would never be easy. They all wanted it, and that was a start. At least no one had gotten up and left. In fact, there were even times of laughter and genuine connection.

As the men started on their second helpings, Mary asked, "Shay, have you met any girls out here?"

He swallowed his fish and muttered, "Not really." He started to say more but shook his head, eyes to his plate.

"It's the tourists you have to go after," Charles said.

"I'll keep an eye open." Shay went back for another bite, his head down, clearly not interested in the conversation.

Brooks sensed some apprehension but wasn't sure why; his brother was usually happy to talk about women.

Charles continued, "I imagine a pretty young lady visiting the mountain, perhaps the sanctuary, could meet a strapping young man like you and never want to leave."

"Probably need to find my own place before I start the hunt." Another bite, head still down.

"Well, Shay," Charles started, picking something from his teeth, "I'm proud of you. We both are. I know you don't need to hear it. But I wanted to say it anyway." He looked at Mary, who nodded, and then, "We've always loved you. We've always been supportive. There was just a time when you made some decisions we didn't agree with." He raised his finger. "That *I* didn't agree with. I can't speak for your mother."

Brooks sat back and began playing with the napkin on his lap. They were starting to fly into dangerous airspace. These words weren't easy for Charles, and Brooks could tell his father was digging deep.

Their dad said, "I could have supported you more. I won't toss out any excuses. Life's just tricky. No matter what path you chose, I should have been your biggest fan." He reached to a higher octave for a moment with, "And I was, deep down. But maybe I had a different vision, a different idea of what you should be, what you should be doing. Something I had no right to expect of you. Or want for you. I see that now. Your mom has helped me see that."

For once, Brooks didn't know exactly what was going on in Shay's head. His brother hadn't looked up in what felt like hours.

"All I'm saying, son, is I'm sorry I made your path harder to walk over the years. Lord knows life's tough enough as it is without your dad breathing down your neck. I'm going to try harder. Your mom and I want you both back in a big way. We want to try to make up for lost time." Charles sipped his red and looked at his wife again. "And we have something we wanted to run by you."

Brooks and Shay both popped their heads up at the same time.

The air raid sirens began to ring. Brooks braced himself. *Where the hell is this going?*

"Your mom and I having been thinking about moving up here."

Brooks's mouth fell open like someone had crammed a ping-pong ball down his throat. He looked at his brother, who was showing similar symptoms, a giraffe neck and dropped jaw.

Mary appropriately jumped in, speaking more than she had the entire night. "I know there's trepidation for you both. It's okay to say 'no.' It's okay to say 'it's a bad idea.' We certainly wouldn't judge you or take offense. It's a big step. We've only been together as a foursome a handful of times. We don't know how it could end. But let me say this. I have a hole in my heart." She grabbed Charles' hand. "We've lived a great life, and there have been smiles and laughter and love. We've done fun things, and your dad has been a great husband to me. But I don't feel whole. A piece of me has been missing since we said goodbye to you, Brooks. When we lost Shay, the hole in my heart grew. You boys mean so much to me."

Her eyes became wet, and she took a moment to compose herself. Shaking her head, a moment from breaking down, she said, "I don't want to be a burden. Charles doesn't either. What we want is to pursue a life as a family together. Forget the past and go on as a team. We want to help you both any way we can, be that with children you may have down the line or whatever. We want to be close, and we want to be a part of what you're doing."

Brooks did the only thing he could do. Despite the grand fear of his own, despite the dragons breaching the moat and breathing fire onto the wall he tended to keep high, he stood up and walked around the table. He placed his hands on his mother's shoulders from behind and reached down and kissed the top of her head. "We would love to have you on this mountain. Nothing would make me happier."

At that moment, their mom released a waterfall of tears, and then everyone's eyes turned red and wet. This family of four, this newfound pack, was going to jump off another cliff together.

Fueled by the unknown, they drank another bottle of wine. After

Mary retired to bed, the three men watched *Sports Center* and sipped Scotch.

On a whim, Shay said, "We should go jump into the river."

Charles said, "You boys go for it. I need to hit the sack."

The brothers met in the grass of the backyard, shirtless and in shorts. Tom Sawyer and Huckleberry Finn. The crickets made their music, bowing the higher frets of their violins as the Yakima River eased on by.

Shay patted Brooks on the back. "That went pretty well, didn't it?" They were both inebriated, the potion of family get-togethers running through them.

"What just happened?"

"I think our dad is having a midlife crisis."

"Midlife?" Brooks waved his hand in the air. "He's way past that. Did he really say they're moving here?"

"That's what I heard."

"Are you cool with it?"

"Shit, Brooks. The mountain can't get any smaller."

"Famous last words."

Brooks faked a smile, showing his teeth. "We're getting the band back together."

"It just... I don't know. I don't even know what to say. I feel my shoulders tightening up just thinking about it."

"You sure that's not your nuts? That water is going to be cold."

"Race ya." With that, Shay pushed Brooks and started running toward their swimming hole, a spot with a sandy bottom, marked by a leaning oak.

Brooks ran after him and couldn't help but smile. Maybe everything would be okay. So this is what having family is like.

As they neared the river, the moonlight and stars lit up his brother's back. There were fingernail marks running both ways away from his spine. Brooks had seen those marks before, in the mirror, not too long ago. His heart skipped a beat.

20

RAISING HIM ALONE

I t didn't take long for Margarita to bring up Adriana's dating problems to the posse of women standing in their neighbor's kitchen. As they'd walked over earlier, Adriana had specifically asked that her mom keep her mouth shut. Her mom had nodded and said, "Of course."

And Adriana had known it was a lie.

Adriana diced tomatoes and watched Zack through the window. With goggles covering his eyes and a beaming smile lighting up his face, he bounced on the trampoline with the other children. She didn't like that trampoline. It never failed that one of the children would end up hurt by the end of the day. The oblivious men stood around the grill drinking Coronas and grilling chicken and pork. Mariachi music thumped loudly from the stand-up speakers in the open garage.

Roberto and Lita had been kind and generous from the moment Adriana and her family had moved in next door. Lita was the one who cared for Zack from time to time when Margarita had doctors' appointments. The couple had parties every Sunday, hosting their extended family and several neighborhood families. They kept the large backyard filled with toys, a trampoline, a grill, and a playset.

And there was typically a piñata waiting for the kids to enjoy after the meal.

Adriana was always too exhausted to go, but she never turned them down. It was all for Zack. She wanted him to get as much time as he could with other children. Especially other Mexican children. She felt great pride in her Mexican blood; loved the people, the culture, and the food; and never wanted Zack to forget his origins.

The five women, gobbling up the gossip, spoke mostly in Spanish as they wielded their knives and spoons and spatulas, preparing their part of the meal.

The one reason Adriana hadn't stabbed her mom in the arm for mentioning that she'd turned down Brooks was that Margarita hadn't been doing well. The second round of chemo was taking everything out of her. She sat on a stool doing her best not to let anyone else know. All six women knew she had cancer. It was hard to hide. But she still wore her wig and her makeup and dressed her best every Sunday. She still jumped in and led much of the conversation.

"I told her she was crazy," Margarita said, throwing up her hands, embracing the dramatic. "He's a winemaker. She says he's good-looking. What's she waiting on?"

"Mama!" Adriana said. "This is no one else's business." She side-eyed the other women, daring them to join her mother's side.

"It's everyone's business," Margarita said. "A man—a very *successful* man—is pursuing you. You say no because you have a son? That's why you say *yes!*"

"Yes, yes!" said Lita, halfway through crumbling a block of cotija cheese. She was a large woman with a chubby face and a warm disposition. Always entertained by Margarita's passion, she offered a wide-eyed grin as her puffy cheeks reddened. "Your mother could be right. If I were single and had a body like yours, oh, *Dios mio*, I'd spend half my day with a man on top of me! I'd have a good grip on his hair with both of my hands and keep shoving him down until he was done!"

A collective gasp filled the kitchen. Adriana thought Lita sounded a lot like Margot. The Mexican version. She had a bright, infectious smile that made it impossible for anyone in the room not to smile with her. Even Adriana.

Shaking her head, attempting to shuck her little smirk, Adriana said soberly, "Does it look like I have time to date?"

Margarita sat up straighter on her stool. "For the right man, you will find the time."

Lita said, "Adriana, perhaps you should try a *gringo*. You'll have to teach him how to move his hips, though." A round of laughter circled the kitchen.

Another woman chimed in. "Let's hope you know how to fake orgasms!"

Adriana wasn't laughing anymore. In fact, she was a minute away from swinging that blade. Those women didn't know about her past. They didn't know what she'd been through. They had no idea she'd been married to a *gringo* in Los Angeles. "Let's talk about something else. I'll date someone eventually."

Margarita wasn't done throwing jabs. "After your *panocha* has dried up. Who is going to want you then?"

"Mama! Not every man is obsessed with *la panocha*."

"You're wrong about that!"

"Stop, Mama! This is embarrassing."

Lita wrapped her arm around Adriana. "Don't be embarrassed. We're all friends here."

"My mother is impossible!"

"I'll be dead soon, and you'll miss me giving you a hard time."

Adriana threw up her hands, seconds away from throwing a plate. "Why! Why do you have to talk about dying?"

"Because I'm dying!"

All the women went silent, the breath escaping them.

Adriana said, "You're the only woman I know who would give me a guilt trip based on your demise."

Her mother smiled, ignoring the uncomfortable air the way a dying woman might. "I want to see my little girl fall in love. Real love. Before something happens to me. It's my last wish."

"That's not fair." Adriana no longer cared that the other women were listening.

"Perhaps not."

Adriana eyed her mother, wanting to say more but careful to avoid the past. The slices across her face tingled, taking her back to her old life. Violeta. Her ex. Los Angeles.

"We all know the truth," her mother said. "To reach your heart, he has to go through that little boy out there."

The buzz of a fly near the refrigerator was the only sound in that room for a moment.

Adriana looked out the window again. Zack and another boy were tossing a ball back and forth on the trampoline. Her son was so happy. Her mom finally had said something truthful.

"Don't worry, *mi hija*. A man will come to you soon." Margarita cupped her hands together. "He will take your heart and hold it in his hand. He'll love you like you need to be loved. He'll be a father for your son. He'll be everything you need. But you must let him in. That's what I'm trying to say."

"I will let him in for that, Mama, but I will not let him in just because it's your wish. I'll know when the right man comes."

Her mom raised her eyebrow. "Will you?"

"I can take care of myself. I'm not desperate. I'm not lonely. I don't even have time for a man." Her last words tumbled out with a tear, a lonely tear broadcasting to the world.

No one could possibly understand.

∼

ALMOST TWENTY PEOPLE lined up to attack the buffet. Making Zack's plate first, Adriana pulled steaming handmade corn tortillas out of the warmer and stacked them with *pollo,* shredded *queso,* sour cream, Lita's delicious guacamole, and three forkfuls of jalapeños.

She handed him his plate and reached to remove his goggles.

"No, Mama!"

"You can't eat with goggles on."

"Yes, I can."

Adriana knew she had to pick her battles. "Fine."

Roberto wasn't quite as overweight as his wife Lita, but he still had a belly that hung over his western belt. He patted Zack on the head and said in a strong Mexican accent. "You like the peppers, yeah?"

Zack looked down at his food, not answering.

Roberto touched the boy's head again. "I do too."

Zack didn't acknowledge him.

Roberto walked toward the buffet and stood in line.

Adriana started to say something. She wanted to kneel down and put her face to her son's face and tell him not to be shy around other men. It wasn't only Roberto. Zack often curled up into a ball, reverting to a boy half his age, whenever a man spoke to him. What was she to do? She wanted so much for Zack. She wanted him to live the American dream. She wanted him to embrace his Mexican heritage. She wanted him to live in a world without racism. She wanted him to find a job that would make him happy and proud. To find a woman who would love him and give him healthy children. As that thought rushed in, she realized just how much she was like her own mother.

As Zack turned toward the kids' table where the other kids were fighting over who got to hit the piñata first, Adriana frowned. She wanted to shield him from all the pain. The divorce. The lies. The abuse. The stealing. She wanted so badly for him to somehow avoid all the bad things she'd encountered in this world.

And of course, she wanted him to have a dad.

21

I JUST DIED IN YOUR ARMS TONIGHT

R ecovering from last week's date with Jerry, which ranked as the worst she'd ever been on, Margot began engaging online in some banter and even flirted with several men. But when they asked to meet in person, she turned them all down, except for one.

Today, Margot would meet Remi Valentine. Though she was attempting to temper expectations, something felt right about this guy, and she couldn't deny the flutter in her stomach. Remi had been the one to take the first step, and he'd done it well. He'd asked for her number, and they'd texted about little things. He'd flirted beautifully without crossing lines, drawing out little giggles from Margot that would revisit her all day. When he asked her out, she'd taken her time to respond. It wasn't easy, but she felt like she was playing the game well. After an agonizing wait, she finally texted: *Let's do it.*

They met for lunch at a Mexican restaurant in Benton City. His idea, not hers. The last guy had chosen something fancy, and *that* hadn't worked out. Maybe Remi had the right idea. A casual and quick spot where either party could hit the road running if it went awry.

Benton City was as small-town as eastern Washington got. Hardworking people who woke long before the sun rose to work the land. There were more tractors and beat-up old trucks than anything else running up and down the one road in and out of town. It was the closest town to Red Mountain, so Benton City claimed the Red Mountain wine-growing area.

As Margot and many of the other huge proponents of Red Mountain would tell you, Benton City needed to do more to help elevate the area. They needed to support the Red Mountain AVA interests. There was a great deal of money sitting on the table if Red Mountain and Benton City could work together. Margot had heard that a huge plot of land on the other side of the highway—the gateway to Red Mountain—had gone up for sale and sold before the city could do anything about it. No one knew who was involved, but everyone knew the leaders of Benton City had dragged their feet when they could have done something to protect the land. That was a scary thing.

Why was it so hard for the Benton City Council to work with the leaders of Red Mountain? Not just the Red Mountain Alliance leaders, but all the thought leaders involved. Why? Because everyone was so different. Margot had learned quickly that even the small population of Red Mountain, who all shared a love of wine, had so many different visions and desires that it was nearly impossible to get on the same page on anything, even recycling! Bring in the wants and needs of the citizens of Benton City, who didn't necessarily share a love of wine, and the complications swelled. Though wine growing was arguably the most beneficial for tourists, grapes were only one of many different crops growing in the area.

Margot parked along the road that went through town. There were a couple of local watering holes, a hardware store, a post office, a coffee stand, and a Mexican restaurant. Margot froze at the door. This was brutal. Another first date, like she was in her twenties again.

"Here we go," she said, taking the brave steps inside.

Mariachi music danced from the speakers. Sombreros hung on walls covered in colorful murals.

He was easy to find. Remi Valentine stood from a booth and

smiled. He held a Boston Terrier in his hands. An Elizabethan cone wrapped around the dog's head, the kind that protects a dog from chewing at a wound. He wore a red *Service Dog* vest. Margot's eyes bounced back and forth between Remi and the dog. What a curious sight to see.

"Hello, Margot," Remi said.

His eyes made you want to run to him, wrap your arms around him. His broad jaws and broad cheeks exuded manhood. He actually looked better than his profile photo! His crisp white shirt was unbuttoned enough to reveal a hairy chest, and Margot immediately thought he looked sexy, like foreign sexy. She took special notice of the light blue laces of his fancy Oxfords. His smile whispered kindness and wisdom and warmth. He reached out his hand, and she noticed his hairy arms, something she had always liked.

"Hi, good to meet you." She offered a smile and then looked at the dog. "Poor thing, what's wrong with him? What's his name?"

"This is Henri." He pronounced the name: *On-ree.* "He hurt his leg on the farm, just a little cut."

Margot frowned at the bandage on his back leg and then perked up. "I have a dog with a French name too!" She went to pet him and stopped, thinking of the vest. "Oh, can I pet him?"

"Yes, of course." Then he whispered, "He's not really a service dog. I mean, he is. He's registered, but I only registered him so he could travel with me. He's my best friend."

This notion cut right through Margot's ears to her heart. "That's adorable." She wrapped her hands around Henri's squishy face. "You're adorable; yes, you are. I have a terrier too. At least part terrier." When she'd gushed enough, Margot looked back at Remi. "Sorry, I'm kind of a dog freak."

"That makes two of us."

They sat across from each other in the booth. Henri cuddled up to his owner. Margot was reminded of her love/hate relationship with chips and salsa as a rawboned Mexican man delivered them to the blue tile table. She loved chips and salsa with all her heart but hated how weak they made her feel. Never could she cut herself off at three or four. It was always a crack-like addiction that turned into a blood-bath with salsa all over her shirt and crime scene investigators rolling out their yellow tape. She decided not to touch them.

As Margot sipped her water, Remi led them into their first conversation. "I have never met someone online before. I'm nervous."

"Me too."

Remi smiled. He had polished white teeth and a fine posture. "We'll laugh about it later, I think. It's like high school all over again."

"That's exactly what I was just thinking!"

His smile stretched even wider. "If you can look past my borderline unhealthy relationship with my little buddy here and the fact that I ride motorcycles, it's all clear sailing."

"Let's just say your dog has boosted your appeal in a big way."

Remi looked at Henri. "What would I do without you, buddy?"

Margot said, "And as far as motorcycles go, I apparently have a thing for motorcycle men." She shook her head. "Maybe that means I like bad boys? This is a new thing for me."

He leaned and whispered, "I hate to disappoint you, but I'm a long way from being a bad boy. I'm riding an old BMW, and my darling little Henri rides in the sidecar. Wearing *doggles*. In other words, I'm no Hells Angel."

"Hold on," Margot said smiling, feeling the hilarity in her gut. "Let's back up. Doggles?"

"You know, goggles for dogs." He turned to Henri. "Look at those big beautiful eyes." He petted the terrier's head. "We have to protect those gems, don't we, buddy?"

She didn't know whether to burst into laughter or jump over the table and squeeze that adorable dog with everything she had. "I could just eat you, little guy."

"Yeah, he doesn't do well with helmets, but he has his doggles and scarf. Like any Renaissance dog." Remi was smiling now too.

Margot broke into a laugh that left her with wet eyes.

The ice having been shattered completely, the two slipped into comfortable conversation as they ordered and waited on their food. He asked about her first date as a teenager, and as she told him, she noticed how Remi listened. Not a distraction in the world. Her words were all that mattered. It gave her a much-needed boost of confidence.

After telling her story, Margot dabbed her mouth with her napkin. "On a side note, the guy found me on Facebook recently. He's working on an oil rig in the Gulf of Mexico." She shrugged. "Aren't you always curious what your exes are up to?"

"Of course."

"I want them all to be pumping gas or...I don't know, on their fourteenth divorce, heavy alcoholics, wishing they'd held onto me. No, just kidding. Just the ones who broke my heart."

She was thankful to see him laughing. Her unfiltered mouth could often get her into trouble. "For the record, I'm kidding about my exes. Mostly kidding. I hope they're all happy and healthy and all that. Maybe just a light divorce, a tiny little car wreck."

He laughed even harder! A handsome man was one thing. Caring, honest, sweet...all great. But a man who found her funny held the key to her heart. They laughed and laughed and asked questions and told each other stories and enthusiastically bounced through topics like they'd both been starving for conversation for months.

When the conversation turned to music, Remi asked, "What's your favorite song?"

"'I Just Died in Your Arms Tonight.' You know. Cutting Crew."

"*That* is a good answer." He sat up straighter. "I'm a yacht rock guy."

"Yacht rock? What in the world is yacht rock?"

"Oh, it's only the best music in the world. Music you play while you're on your yacht, of course."

"You have a yacht?"

"Maybe. But that's beside the point. Yacht rock is kind of soft rock from the seventies and early eighties. Anything Michael McDonald ever touched or even thought about is yacht rock. Steely Dan. Doobie Brothers. Toto. Hall and Oates."

"I love yacht rock," she said. "I had no idea it was a thing."

"Oh, it's a thing. I'm the spokesperson."

"I really love Toto," Margot admitted. In a fearless burst, she broke into their most famous song "Africa," loud enough to hit the high notes but without drawing every eye and ear in the restaurant. She even did her best to imitate the synthesizers before finishing the chorus.

"Oh, wow." He clapped. "You're brilliant." Remi had a giant smile as he said, "I could listen to you sing all day."

She thanked him, and he poked and pried until she confessed her past on and off Broadway. She blushed when he asked her, "What's an amazing girl like you doing in a little town like this?"

What every single girl is doing. Looking for love.

The conversation didn't stop. She didn't notice until the server brought their lunch, but she'd shredded through the basket of chips and salsa and felt full already. At least her attack on the appetizer wasn't premeditated. Roll out the crime scene tape!

"I'm having way too much fun," she said, as the server cleared their table.

"Me too!" He was really excited.

"We should end this right now."

He tilted his head.

"Not in a bad way," she said. "But I think if we end right now, it will officially be the best date I've ever had. A Mexican restaurant in Benton City. Who would have thought?"

Remi held up his pointer. "How about this? I pay the bill, say goodbye, and walk out? Then I'll text you and ask if you want to go on another date. You write back 'yes,' I'll come back in, and we'll hang out some more."

"Let's do it."

Remi looked at her and bowed. "Margot, it was truly a pleasure to meet you. I'd like to do this again."

"I would too."

He smiled and stood, collecting Henri in his arms.

She noticed he had this almost Steely-Dan, yacht-rock strut as he walked away that made her smile. He was so smooth and easy.

Closer to the door, he waved one last time.

Margot smiled until it hurt like the corners of her mouth had wrapped around her ears. She checked her phone, read his text, and responded "yes."

He returned and sat, placing Henri next to him. "It's good to see you again."

"You too."

"How are things?"

"I just had the best date of my life."

~

MARGOT WAS MOSTLY on top of the world for the rest of the day. *Mostly*. She hadn't felt such a high from dating in decades. But when she thought about the last man to sweep her off her feet, her ex-husband, the fear that Remi Valentine wasn't as great a man as he appeared terrified her. She couldn't go through another bad breakup. She just wasn't sure if she had the strength for another long recovery.

22

EGG COFFEE

O tis proved to be the worst world traveler on earth. Being in Vietnam while that piece of property on the highway was being transferred to an unnamed entity was about as close to dipping his feet in the fires of hell as he could bear. Satan was lashing Otis's back at every turn. Obsessed with the potential outcomes of that sale, he did his best to be there with Joan.

Following the advice of the concierge after requesting off-the-beaten-path ideas, Otis and Joan found themselves at the crowded Giang Café on Nguyen Huu Huan Street. They sat in short chairs at a table outside in the humid air under an umbrella. The waiter brought two cups of cà phê trứng, or egg coffee. From the moment the concierge had mentioned the idea of a famous café serving egg coffee, Joan had demanded they make it happen. Reluctant, for no reason beyond grumpiness, Otis acquiesced.

They both stared at the concoction. Otis thought it looked like a normal latte. But as they'd read, it was much more. The recipe, which had been created because of a shortage of milk in the 1940s, included coffee powder, condensed milk, egg yolk, butter, and cheese. The trend had taken off and spread to other cafes in Hanoi, but Joan and Otis had found the original.

Otis raised his cup. "To being adventurous."

"All the way to the end," Joan agreed.

Otis noted the eggnog-like texture first. Much creamier than the velvetiest of steamed milk. Then came the flavors. The strong coffee had a savory element. It didn't taste egg-y, like he'd expected, but between the egg and butter, faint elements of a breakfast plate teased his palate.

"It's extraordinary," Otis said. "I'm taken aback."

She said, "This man and his son have been making these for thirty years. The dad is not much different than you, is he? This is the Till Vineyards of Vietnam."

Otis's eyes drifted up, missing his sons.

"I'm sorry, darling," Joan said. "I know."

"You know what?"

"That it makes you sad to think about your sons. To think about the future of Till Vineyards. To think they won't be a part of it." She was right.

Otis and his wife Rebecca had lost their first son to a fishing accident on the Snake River. A few years later, Rebecca and their second son slid off an icy road into the Yakima River and both drowned.

Otis said, "My boys weren't farmers. They had bigger things to do. They always respected what I did, but they never caught the bug themselves. I never wanted to push them. It's a tough life, being a farmer. It's not for everyone."

"No, it's not." She sighed. "I'm sorry I never met your sons, but I'm quite sure they not only respected you, but looked up to you. You would have been great at whatever field you chose. You inspire those around you. You inspire me."

"I do?" Otis was trying to make light of the suddenly dark road they'd traveled down. "Exactly how do I inspire you, Joan Tobey?" He took another sip of his egg coffee.

Joan smiled, appreciating the challenge of the question. "Well, there are times where I lose my momentum. I wake up and wonder what it's all for. I lose my own sense of purpose. For you, your mission is always clear. That farm, Till Vineyards, that is your art, and when you wake up, that farm gets you out of bed. That's why your wines are out of this world. Because you are on an unstoppable mission to make honest wine and spread the goodness of Red Mountain. Even if you doubt yourself, you never doubt your mission. You couldn't if you wanted to. Until your last breath and most likely beyond that, you will be a soldier to your mission. That's how you inspire me. I've never seen anyone want something as badly as you do."

"You really love me, don't you? Sometimes I feel like you are a princess in the forest who has found a bird with a broken wing—named Otis—and you're nursing him back to health. I have a hard time believing that someone of your greatness could ever give me a second look."

"You know why you and I are made for each other?"

"Why?" he said cocking his head, excited to hear her response.

"Because sometimes I feel like I'm the wounded bird in your story."

23

THE SCRATCH MARKS BROTHERS

Brooks knew the truth. Even in the haze of alcohol consumption the night before, as he and Shay were jumping into the water, he knew.

Shortly after he awoke, he found his dad sitting on the back porch reading the news on his iPad. The rest of the family still slept. Brooks raised his cup of coffee and said, "Morning," putting his free hand on his dad's shoulder. Maybe the first time he'd ever done that, he was most likely making the connection because he was hungover and slightly detached from his rational side.

"Good morning, son." Charles set down his iPad.

"Sleep well?"

"We both did. Your mom's still out."

Brooks took a sip and looked out to the slow-moving river. The river ran faster than it had the night before and looked dirtier too. Browner and debris-laden. A gaggle of geese floated on the other side. A tree trunk had caught on a rock and was collecting other floating debris. A man in a wide-brimmed hat kayaked downstream, staying with the faster water in the middle. Brooks waved. His mind wasn't with the man, though.

Brooks could still see his brother running toward the water. He could still see the scratches from where Abby had wrapped her arms around his brother and dug into his skin with her nails. He cracked a grin and shook his head. The older he got, the more he felt like he was living a life like Otis, the kind where black cats crossed his path and mirrors broke. Brooks was certainly always one Jenga block away from a hard crash.

"After sleeping on it," Charles said, "how do you feel about us moving up here?"

Brooks closed his eyes and tried not to say something without really being sure of his words. These kinds of conversations could go badly quickly. He didn't want that. He turned to his dad. "It would be good for all of us. We've made it this far. Why not?"

"There might be some hard times. Believe it or not, I do have a less charming side." His dad couldn't help but grin at that one.

Brooks tilted his head down. "That makes two of us. Will you miss it down there? California is different from Washington."

"We have some friends we'll miss. The truth is, the thing we've been missing most is up here. Family. You guys. We've watched all our friends raise their kids, and then their grandkids show up. We want that. Grandkids or not. We feel like being around you and your brother will be more satisfying than anything we can do in California. A few hours a week selling wine in a tasting room. A decent golf course. Family. That's all I need. We can get used to this mountain. The smallness of it."

Brooks raised his eyebrows. "The smallness of Red Mountain. I'm not sure you ever get used to the smallness of it. You grow accustomed to it. It's like getting summer feet. At first you walk around barefooted, and every step burns and stings and aches. Then, after a summer, your feet are callused, and you can walk on anything. That's how it is here. You'll get your Red Mountain feet. Nothing much will shock you anymore." As Brooks was saying the words, he knew them to be true. He wasn't that shocked about Shay. Hurt, yes. Broken, yes. Disturbed, yes. Sad. *Yes.*

Shocked. No.

Charles said, "If you help me find a job in a tasting room around here, I bet I can sell more wine than anybody in this state."

"I believe that. I'm sure I can find you a job. What about Mom? Is she going to get bored?"

"Nah. You see her now. Her color has returned. She has her sons back. She's always wanted to be a part of something like this. She loves getting outside, having a garden, cooking. Entertaining. Shay told her about Margot's Sunday night cooking classes. She'll fit right in, trust me." He asked, "You're not going anywhere, are you?"

"I can't make any promises. This mountain is the answer to every question I have. Every important one, that is. I'm a part of something here that I've never known before. But like bad medicine, this mountain sometimes tries to reject me. It may win out one day."

"I hope not."

"If the mountain runs me out, there's nothing I can do."

"Of course." His dad lowered his head. "We're not asking you to sign a contract to stay for a period of time. Your—and your brother's—happiness is most important. Even having a few months with family would be worth the move. Who knows? Maybe we'll keep following you two. I can see you maybe leaving the mountain someday, but it seems like you and your brother have really connected, and I have a feeling you won't let that relationship go easily."

Brooks's imagination went to work. He saw a flash of Abby naked. He saw her kissing his brother. He saw her ripping his brother's clothes off, throwing him against the wall, tearing at his skin. He opened his mouth to speak but closed it again.

The tears were coming.

$$\sim$$

BROOKS FOUND Shay running the horse and plow through the Marsanne vineyard at Lacoda. Shay followed a few feet behind Elvis, holding the till as the metal shanks dug into the sandy soil. A long set of leather reins ran from the horse to around Shay's neck. As he and the blind horse reached the end of a row, Shay would work the reins to communicate directions.

Shay had his shirt off. Brooks noticed a much harder body than the one Shay had brought to Red Mountain. Perhaps he noticed it only to further drive into his head that scene with Abby that he couldn't unsee. When Shay turned, Brooks saw the scratch marks again, ensuring him that the night before hadn't just been a bad dream.

Brooks wanted to witness the beauty of a man plowing a vineyard. He'd fought for so long to convince Jake Forester to bring in the animals. The chickens were easy. The sheep and goats and horses, though, had taken convincing. This was Brooks's dream. He'd taken what Otis had taught him and pushed it further. Now his own blood ran a plow with a rescued blind horse. This was the essence of Red Mountain.

As the first winery running a horse plow here, there was much to learn. At times, he wondered if it would even make a difference. Brooks could only guess its effectiveness after geeking out on how other vineyards in other parts of the world had benefited. Having Elvis till the land would certainly limit tractor passes, which meant less soil compaction. Brooks believed in the power and potency of the microbial life hidden in the topsoil. Even in the sandy low-nutrient soils of Red Mountain, life could be found. A tractor with its combustion engine pounding the surface year after year was sure to disturb and, in effect, declare war on that topsoil.

If there was one thing he believed affected the wines more than anything, as Otis had taught him, it was the health of the soil. Yes, you wanted the vines to struggle, to suffer, and to fight to find water. But you didn't want those vines to be denied vitality. The more the roots could be free to soak up the surroundings, the better. Elvis was giving back to the land, not taking from it. Elvis was making those vines happy, a synergy a Monsanto corn farmer could never understand.

None of that mattered to Brooks today. All he could think of were those scratches.

Shay saw Brooks coming and tugged on the reins. "Ho," he said. "Ho." Elvis stopped, and Shay set down the till and pulled the reins from his neck. "Hey, bro." He removed the bandana from his head and wiped the dirt from his face.

"You're getting the hang of that thing."

"Yeah. Elvis and I are connecting. What's going on with you? You seem disturbed today."

"Wrong side of the bed." Brooks was suddenly finding it hard to bring up what he'd intended.

Shay ran a hand through his hair. "I hate to hit you on an off day, but I wanted to ask you something."

Every time someone came to Brooks with a question lately, he thought of Joan. He thought of how he'd have to say "yes," no matter what. He'd done pretty well until now.

"I'm just going to say it," Shay continued, scraping the sweat from his eyes with his bandana. "Don't know how else. What would you think about me and Abby?"

There it was. And Brooks responded, "It would be the same as a fucking dagger jabbed into my rib cage by the brother I saved from frying rotten fish in a shitty restaurant in a shithole part of Portland." No, he didn't say that, but it's the first thing that popped into his mind. Those words had been bubbling up in his throat, waiting for release. In fact, Brooks didn't answer quickly at all. He felt a tension run through his body, then asked casually, "What about it?"

"How would you feel about us getting together? I don't know what's on the horizon. We're feeling things out right now."

"Feeling things out," Brooks whispered. "Feeling things out."

"I don't know what to do. That's why I'm coming to you. You brought me here. I'm not here to hurt you. Abby and I...we've hung out a couple of times, and it seems to be going in a direction I didn't expect. You made it clear to both of us that you have no interest in continuing with her, but I'm not going to step on your broken heart either. I want your permission; otherwise, I'll stand down."

It was hard for Brooks to think as his heart flooded his body with blood. "So? So what are you asking me?"

"You know what I'm asking. Can I pursue something with Abby?"

He could hear Joan's words. *"Say 'yes' more."* Doing his best not to reveal this feeling of giving up that was permeating his mind, Brooks said, "Yeah, go ahead."

"You sure? You don't seem sure?"

"I don't own her."

"That's not why I'm asking. I know you don't *own* her. But I know there's history."

"That's what it is. History. I can let it go."

"You sure?" Shay asked, lowering his chin. Elvis stomped the ground behind him.

"Yeah, I'm sure. Go for it. I'll deal with it. I'll get over it."

"Bro."

"Don't *bro* me. Stop talking about it and let me deal. Keep asking, and I'll find a way to say 'no.'"

"Okay." Shay spat tobacco on the ground. "Why don't you think about it? And get back to me."

"I don't want to think about it."

"She tried with you. Over and over."

"Shay. I made the decision. If I have some kind of lingering crap to deal with, that's none of your or Abby's concern. If this world has taught me anything, it's how to survive. If it works out, maybe I'll even find a way to be happy for ya."

"Thank you, brother. Thank you."

Brooks nodded and turned. He dropped his eyes to the ground and watched every step he took. A foot into the dust, the Red Mountain dust. Step. Step. The earth shaking below him. Long, lonely steps. The runaway running again.

He dodged a pile of coyote scat, stepped on an ant hill. The tears rose like lava, rising from the burning inside. The dust clouded around his ankles, and he kept walking, kept moving. Anywhere but here.

Anywhere but here.

24

IN HIDING

Adriana woke Zack early to go fishing. His father had always promised to take Zack on a fishing trip but had never delivered. Though Adriana had no idea what she was doing, she wanted to give her son this gift. She typically had to drag the boy out of bed, but today, with the promise of fishing, he sprang out from underneath the covers like they were going to Chuck E. Cheese's.

They parked in a gravel lot next to a boat launch near the Benton City bridge. Though the light of day had arrived, a fog not yet burned off by the sun hovered over the Yakima River. In the coolness of the desert morning, it was almost impossible to imagine the coming afternoon heat.

Zack darted out of the car and nearly broke the rod as he yanked it from the backseat.

Adriana ran around to his side of the car to help him, saying, "*Tranquillo*, my love." The day before, she'd arrived home with a Mickey Mouse rod and reel and a small tackle box from Wal-Mart, and in doing so, committed to an extra hour of bedtime stories in order to get her overly excited son to close his eyes.

Between the advice from the man behind the counter and some

lessons on *YouTube*, Adriana felt prepared for their adventure, but they spent the first thirty minutes untangling the line from several annoying and obstructive trees. For once, Zack's goggles came to good use, as the green worm at the end of the line—though sans hook—had turned into an assault weapon, ripping through the air in unpredictable zigzag patterns around their heads. A mysterious bird cackled from the other side of the river, almost as if laughing at their comical attempts.

When Zack finally landed the lure into the water, Adriana possibly woke most of Benton City with her prideful yelp. "There you go, *mi hijo!*" She clapped and cheered and then sneered in the direction of the critical bird.

"And then watch what you do, Mama. Are you watching?"

"Yes, of course."

"You see this? You turn it really fast and then the fish bites." He reeled in his lure as fast as his little arms could manage. The lure danced along the water on its return.

"I think you might want to go a little slower. I'm not sure the fish are that fast."

"Oh, yeah, they are. Fish can sometimes fly. I've seen it."

"You have?"

"We have to stop talking," he said with the confidence of a seasoned fisherman. "I have to focus."

"Okay, you focus."

She cleared the way as he wielded the rod and reel, and yet again succeeded in his cast, the green worm dropping twenty feet out into the water. She couldn't help but smile as she watched her boy slowly becoming a man.

It was all right there, everything she was.

When it was time to go, Zack begrudgingly climbed back into the backseat. "I'm never going to catch a fish," he said, reaching for his buckle. "Why didn't they bite?"

"It takes practice. You'll catch a fish soon."

"Mama?"

"Yes?" she asked, reversing out of the space.

"Can we adopt a pet? A rabbit or a dog or a snake or something."

"Maybe one day. Definitely not a snake though. That's the scariest idea I've ever heard, *mi amor*."

"I want a friend to play with."

"You have friends. You played all day with our neighbors."

"Yeah, but they're not really my friends. They're not my age. I don't have any friends here."

Adriana thought about his first year of school here; it hadn't gone so well. Because of what they'd been through with Michael and her mother's sickness, Adriana wasn't at her most outgoing and had done a terrible job at organizing playdates. Zack kept mentioning a boy that he liked, but Adriana failed to encourage their friendship outside of school. It turned out okay, because during the last week of school, Zack came home asking what a taco-burger was, saying his "friend" had called him one. Though she knew the term was a reference to being mixed race, she'd shrugged her shoulders and lied, saying, "I don't know...just a silly name." She knew then that her hope for Zack to never know racism was futile.

Glancing at him in the rearview mirror, she said, "Sweetie, I have a feeling you're going to find a good friend soon. It takes time."

He was looking out the window, his bottom lip turned out. "Sometimes I want to go back to California. Dad was my friend. I had Richard and Simon. Why can't we go back?"

"Because we're on an adventure, little man. It's you and me and Tata on a huge adventure. We're your friends for now."

"I need friends my age."

"I know you do." And then she said *sotto voce*, "Me too."

Tata was on the couch watching one of her *novellas* when they arrived home. She paused her show. "Did you catch a fish?"

Zack shook his head.

Adriana said, "He's sad, says he doesn't have any friends."

"Oh, come here, my love." Tata hugged him and kissed him over and over, saying, "That's nothing to worry about. You have a whole life to find friends. When you're back in school, you'll find someone."

Adriana asked Zack to go clean his room and he obeyed. Once he was out of earshot, she said to her mom, "He was so fun to watch, but, once we returned to the car, he snapped. Brought up this friends thing. Breaks my heart."

"God has a plan for him. Zack will find his way. I've been around a long time. I know these things."

But Adriana wondered, not for the first time, *What if I can't give him what he needs?*

~

AT ÉPIPHANIE, Adriana slipped into the kitchen, avoiding the guests eating breakfast. She dreaded another encounter with Harry Bell-flour. Margot was slicing oranges and grapefruit on the butcher block. Waves of something yummy and sweet rose from the oven.

"Good morning!" Margot almost sang, running her butcher knife through the middle of an orange with an easy stroke.

"Good morning," Adriana replied dutifully, unable to match Margot's enthusiasm.

Margot set down the knife and turned. "I see a frown on your face."

"No, no. Everything is fine."

Margot tapped the butcher block with mild frustration. "What's going on with you? Don't you know by now you can't internalize around here?"

Adriana audibly exhaled. "My son told me he has no friends. He says he wants a pet because he's lonely. He says we left all his friends in California. It's a terrible thing to hear from a six-year-old."

"Oh, dear." Margot crossed her arms, and her eyes wandered. "You are barking up the right tree. Honey, moving is hard. When we arrived, Jasper went through horrors. Kids were sticking notes on his back, throwing him to the ground, picking fights. Then, everything started to work out. He met Jake, and a few months later they made a record. He met Jake's daughter, and they're in love. Zack is going to be fine. What he's going through will build character."

"What he's going through isn't fair for a young boy."

"It really isn't." Margot set down the knife and took Adriana's hand. "If there's anything I can do to help, I'm here for you. Beyond the fact that you're saving my life right now, I'm your friend. I'm serious. If there's something I can do to help, you tell me."

"Thank you, Margot. We'll be fine. I've walked rocky roads before."

"You're a strong woman. I know you'll be okay, and I'm sure Zack has those same genes."

If Margot only knew—Adriana didn't always have such strength. She had so many weaknesses and fears. She was scared to go into that dining room and see Mr. Bellflour. Even more scared to report his approaches. She'd finally found a job she loved. She couldn't risk losing it over an offensive man's grotesque advances.

That's why she mustered the courage to say, "I should go check on the guests."

Margot waved her hand. "Oh, they're fine. They can wait a minute. May I be selfish and talk about me for a second?"

Adriana didn't mind. "Please." Then it occurred to her. "Remi?"

"Yes, Remi. Yes, yes, yes."

Adriana couldn't believe how fast and easily she and Margot had become friends. She had experienced the ups and downs of being Mexican in a mostly white community. Almost naively, Margot wasn't one to even notice skin color or financial differences.

"What if I told you I think he's the one?"

"I'd tell you that you're crazy. You've known him for how long? Have you forgotten about your last marriage?" There's no one else Adriana would feel comfortable saying that to, but Margot was different.

"I have certainly *not* forgotten about my last marriage. This man is different. First of all, he's delicious. The second I saw him, I felt like... Oh, God, I don't know...like Little Caesar's pizza. Hot and ready! You know what I mean? Hot and ready!"

Adriana threw her hand to her mouth and her eyes bulged.

Margot shrugged. "What can I say?"

Forgetting the predator in the dining room, Adriana couldn't help from erupting into a laugh. A laugh like she hadn't shared with anyone in as long as she could remember.

"So, Remi. Remi Valentine. We had a lovely first date." Margot gave her the details. "He's taking me out again in two days."

"I'm very happy for you."

"I honestly feel like a little girl." She raised her hand to her chest and closed her eyes. Coming back to reality, Margot clapped her hands together. "Okay, we should feed everyone now."

Bursting through the swinging doors with fresh fruit and hot sticky buns, Margot and Adriana put on their smiles and went to work. It was only a moment later that Adriana realized Harry Bellflour was the least of her troubles. Sitting opposite of Bellflour was a man she knew from her old life.

Adriana lost her balance. The tray tilted; the fruit bowl slid to the edge. Just in time, she was able to collect herself enough to keep the tray from falling. It was her survivalist instinct that composed her. She grabbed the tray with both hands and dashed back into the kitchen.

Margot followed her in. "What happened?"

"I'm sorry." Adriana set down the tray, just shy of gasping for air. "I can't go out there."

"What? Why?"

She crossed her arms and shook her head. "There's a man I know. He knows my ex. I have to leave."

Michael had built a house for the man several years ago, and upon completion, he and Adriana had gone to the housewarming, where they'd met and shared a brief conversation. She was having a hard time thinking, but it had to have been before she got her scars. Everything had changed after that day. She'd stopped going out, stopped talking to friends. The way people skeptically looked at her when she told them how it happened drove her deeper and deeper into her shell. No, this had to be before. Maybe he wouldn't recognize her.

Margot said, "Calm down. You're safe in here. Did he see you?"

"I don't think so." Adriana raised her hand to her thumping heart. "I'm scared."

"Which man is it?"

"The short man in the baseball cap."

"I wouldn't worry about it."

Adriana closed her eyes for a moment. "My ex is a bad man, Margot. A very bad man."

"Why don't you go home for the day? Everyone in the hotel except Bellflour is checking out. Go home. Be with your family. Let's talk on the phone later."

"I'm scared to walk back out there."

"I'll go distract the table. No big deal. Give me two minutes and then slip out."

Adriana nodded. "I'm so sorry, Margot. This job means a lot to me. I don't want to bring all my baggage here."

"You forget who you're talking to." Margot touched her arm. "We have plenty of room for all your baggage. Don't worry about your job. Just go take care of your family. This man will be gone soon, and you'll be safe."

Adriana nodded and met Margot's eyes. "Thank you."

Two minutes later, Adriana made her move. Hearing Margot tell a story in a remarkably animated fashion, she gently pushed open the swinging doors. A squeak in the right door hinge startled her, and though it couldn't have been that loud, it was an alien scream to her ears. But it was too late to turn back now.

Thankfully the table full of guests was on the other end of the dining room, so she hoped they hadn't heard the door squeak. With a hand discreetly covering her face, she marched with determination toward the lobby. When she saw the wooden doors just past the piano, she breathed a sigh of relief...

...until a voice chased after her. "Excuse me," he said.

Adriana's joints locked. She didn't know whether to make a run for it or play it off, but she knew it was him. He'd recognized her. Breathing in, she scrambled to decide her next move.

"Don't I know you?" he asked.

Adriana turned to address the man coming into the lobby. He was short and had squinty eyes. She remembered his features so well, how his cheeks and eyebrows were pushing at each other, the whites of his eyes barely visible. And she watched with familiarity as he processed the scarring on her face. Everyone had similar reactions, first the shock, then pity, then the desperate scramble to pretend like they didn't notice.

Once he'd gotten to the "I didn't notice" stage, he clicked his fingers and said, "Starts with a 'V.' Vick... no... Violet. That's it. No, Violeta! Right? Michael's wife. What are you doing all the way up here?"

"Not sure who you're talking about," Adriana said, firm on her decision to lie. If he'd never seen the scars before, there's no way he could be sure she was the same person. "You must have me confused with someone else."

The guy nodded. "Strange. You look a lot like someone back in Cali."

Adriana shook her head. Felt a pounding in her chest. Did her best to hide it. "Guess I just have one of those faces."

He let out a skeptical grunt and then said, "Sorry to bother you." The man didn't look convinced as he pivoted and made his way back to the dining room.

∽

MARGOT CALLED her five minutes later. "I'm so sorry. There was nothing I could do."

"It's okay," Adriana said, driving away from Red Mountain.

"He obviously recognized you. Are you okay?"

"Yeah, I think so. Did he say anything when he returned to the table?"

"Not a thing."

Adriana nodded slightly. Part of her wanted to drive straight to the house, grab her mother and Zack, and hit the road. If it were only that easy. Just as she began to imagine yet another escape, another name change, Lita called.

Her mom had collapsed on the way to the mailbox.

25

THE TREELESS MOUNTAIN

After agonizing days of waiting, Remi asked her out again.

Margot hated everything she had to wear. Her hair grew in places that had no business sprouting. And speaking of hair, her long blond hair looked like a garden for split ends. Her hands and feet looked like she'd been living in the woods for months. A disaster, a complete mess.

After a brief phone call with Joan, who was in Vietnam, Margot found Adriana cleaning one of the rooms. "Adriana, I have to step out for the day. I have a date and not a thing to wear. And I need a mani-pedi and haircut. The whole shebang. Can you please stay a little late today and make sure all the guests are happy?"

"Of course."

After her long day of appointments and shopping, Margot returned to her house and drew a bath. In the old days, she would close her eyes in the clawfoot tub and imagine killing her own ex-husband, the man in Vermont. She'd moved on from that though, thanks to Joan.

Today, as she soaked in the tub, she looked at her body. She touched her breasts. She tried to ignore her sags and said, "Any man

would be lucky to touch me. Any man would be lucky to love me."
She wanted so much to believe what she was saying.

Throwing on a robe, she sipped on a glass of merlot and applied
her makeup. She chose her favorite lace underwear, then began the
long process of trying on the dresses she'd bought. She hated all of
them. After eight outfits, she returned to the first dress, a long yellow
one. She liked how her rose lipstick met the yellow.

The woman in the mirror looked nervous, unaccustomed to this
kind of feeling. Her dates with Ron had come easily. This one, with
Remi, came with jitters she'd not known in many, many years. She
forced a smile. "I love you, Margot Pierce. You're so worthy of a good
man. He's lucky to take you out. Any good man can see that."

Remi arrived with a lily in his hand, wearing black jeans, a blue
shirt, and a tailored linen sport coat with a white handkerchief
peeking out of the pocket. His initials were embroidered in small
lettering on the collar of his shirt. His hair was short and trimmed
neatly, as if he might have left the barber only this afternoon. His red
suede shoes looked brand new. Margot thought he looked European,
like a gentleman you might see sitting at the bar in La Tour d'Argent
in Paris, waiting for his lady. He was freshly shaven, and when he
wrapped his arm around her waist and kissed her cheek, she smelled
menthol. Margot sensed a great deal of confidence, but when she
heard him speak, she noticed his own nerves pulling at him. It made
her feel comfortable.

He handed her the white lily and looked her up and down. He
started to speak and then shook his head. He looked at her again,
gazing into her eyes. "You take my breath away." He wasn't following
protocol, saying what he was supposed to say. He meant it.

Though she buried her nose in the flower, she couldn't hide her
smile. She was already in love with him, and she knew he was falling
for her as well. They were like an antique fork and spoon from a
silver set separated years before, finally reuniting. They knew each
other. They'd already spent a life or more together. How could it be
so easy?

Margot complimented his ensemble and said, "I'm glad to see you. Thank you for the lily."

She placed the flower in a vase and followed him to his truck, a thirty-year old diesel. He opened the door for her and held her hand as she climbed up. Classical music sounded from the radio, fighting over the loudness of the engine. He crossed Sunset Road and drove the vineyard paths, taking lefts and rights, getting lost in the vines. They made small talk as she saw a side of Red Mountain she hadn't seen before. The sun fell in front of them, and the puffy clouds lit up in pastel.

He stopped in the gravel by a wooden gazebo in the middle of a vineyard. "This place belongs to a friend of mine. I've always wanted to have dinner here."

"Oh, we're eating here?"

"I made a picnic. Hope you don't mind."

"Not at all." *Hot and ready!*

He helped her out and grabbed a picnic basket out of the back. With music from the truck still playing through the open windows, they sat on either side of the table in the middle of the gazebo. He opened the basket, the kind you might find from Orvis or L.L. Bean. The basket had a leather strap holding a bottle of wine and a small insert for a corkscrew. Another strap held fine china plates and a compartment held stemware.

Remi undid the buckle on the strap holding the bottle of wine. He held it out in front of her and said, "You said you like merlot, right?"

Margot saw the red circle and text on the label, and her mouth fell agape. "How do you know about this bottle of wine?"

"I'm a big Charlie Hoppes fan. Love Fidélitas."

"You're never going to believe this," Margot said. "That's the bottle that brought me to Red Mountain."

Remi smiled. "You're kidding."

Margot tilted her head skeptically. "Did you plan this?"

Remi shook his head and looked at the label. "Not at all. What's so special about this bottle?"

Margot couldn't believe it. The memories of her last Christmas in

Burlington hit her with a waves of emotions. "It's a long story, and one I'm not ready to tell. I'm not ready to give away how much of a loon I am." Margot brushed her hands across the air in a sweeping motion. "Not a big deal, just ex-husband yuckiness. Let's just say I was at rock bottom when this wine came into my life. It was a different vintage, but still. A bottle of Fidelitas merlot is what introduced me to Red Mountain." What she didn't tell Remi was that the woman who'd slept with her husband was who had given her that bottle.

"I'm ready for the story when you are," Remi said as he cut the black foil with the blade on the corkscrew. "Don't worry, there's nothing in your past that's going to scare me off."

Margot nodded. "Thanks. Still, let me keep showing you my good side for a while. The skeletons will sneak out of the closet soon enough."

Remi smiled and that was the end of the discussion.

He had prepared a French grated carrot salad, warm potato salad with arugula, and a Mediterranean cannellini bean salad with haricot verts and fresh tomatoes. He pulled out a baguette and admitted to driving to Walla Walla that morning to buy the bread from his favorite bakery. He placed several cheeses on a cutting board and stuck a gorgeous knife with an ornately carved wooden handle into the middle of an Amish Swiss.

They drank the bottle of wine and fell into conversation as if they'd been starving to share words for decades. She told him more about her inn and the animals and about her son, while he focused more on being humorous and discussing lighter topics like his favorite restaurants and neighborhoods in Seattle. He didn't like discussing his past, but that was okay. Who did? In fact, Margot thought it was nice that they hadn't fallen into an uncomfortable interrogation like many did in their first dates. There was something so nice about having fun and not worrying about the details. They'd come soon enough.

After they'd explored the facts of each other, the talk grew more lighthearted. They dined and talked of Red Mountain and cheese and wine. After dinner, he led her outside the gazebo, and they stood facing west in the gravel at the edge of a vineyard block. The vineyards rolled down the gentle slope west toward the Yakima River. As the sun dropped, the lights of Benton City began to shimmer. Beyond and to the right, Rattlesnake Mountain stared back at them. It looked like Red Mountain's big brother.

"They say that's the highest treeless mountain in the country," he said.

"I've heard that. And an elk reserve. I've seen the elk herds on the other side of the mountain."

"Really?" Remi asked.

"Yes," she said. "They're breathtaking."

He asked, "Is there really not a single tree on that mountain?"

"I've never seen one."

"What if we planned a secret mission to plant a tree at the top?"

"That would be absurd."

He looked down, defeated. "I know."

She winked. "Absurd. Exhilarating. Amazing. I'd love to join your mission."

He smiled with renewed confidence. "Do you have any Navy SEAL training?"

"Who told you?"

He gave a light chortle.

"No, I'm serious. Who told you?" She grinned.

Remi said, "We'd need a helicopter or plane. I'd want several back-up extraction areas. We may need a medic and a support team. A demolitions expert. Do you have comms experience?"

Margot raised her hands, palms up. "Communications? Who doesn't?"

"Good. I'll man the shovel."

They met each other's eyes, and she saw the twinkle in his irises from the moonlight. She thought he might kiss her as he turned more toward her.

He leaned in, but stopped inches from her face. He asked, "What kind of tree? That's the question."

She smiled and said quietly. "Something that doesn't need a lot of water." In her mind, though, she was screaming, *Kiss me! Kiss me!*

He didn't break his gaze. "I think a fir will do."

She couldn't handle the overwhelming energy and turned away. With her eyes back on Rattlesnake Mountain, she said, "If we actually go on this mission, it might go up high on the list as one of the silliest, most wonderful things I've done since college. Or before."

"I just want to know what you did in college that would top it."

She grinned, weighing whether to tell him. "I streaked through campus for animal rights. During the day. During class change. That was probably the craziest thing I've ever done."

Remi raised a finger. "Not if we accomplish Mission Rattlesnake."

"Very true."

"This topic is to be continued," Remi said. "So, when will you sing for me again?"

"Soon enough." The truth was she didn't like singing as much as she used to. At least not performing. It made her sad...that feeling of what could have been.

He changed gears. "When am I going to meet Elvis?"

Margot bit her lip. "Meeting my animals is like meeting my son. You're not quite there yet. Don't beat yourself up, though. You're close." She pinched her fingers together. "You're just not quite there."

"I'm not discouraged."

"Don't be. Tonight you might get a kiss. Tomorrow you might get to pet my horse."

"When you say it that way, it makes me wonder what follows petting your horse."

"You get to tickle my turkey." She winked.

"You have a turkey?"

"Of course I have a turkey."

"And if you're really good, I'll let you shear my sheep."

"Please sign me up for all of the above." He turned more toward her. "Unless I'm reading the traffic lights wrong, I think you just gave me permission to kiss you."

Margot smiled.

That's all Remi needed. He moved in. They touched lips. It felt new and familiar at the same time. Her heart opened. He took her into his arms. She felt like she'd come home after being gone a long, long time.

They returned to the gazebo and spent another hour enjoying each other's company before he dropped her off. It took all the discipline she could muster not to invite him in, but she knew a relationship like this couldn't dare be rushed. After he was gone, Margot cuddled up with Philippe on the couch in the living room and told her dog all about her wonderful date.

The good times only lasted so long. She thought she'd better check the inn before going to bed. Bellflour was in his spot on the front steps smoking another cigar.

As she approached, she watched him tug on that cigar and the red flame light up the rest of his face. There was something about this man, not necessarily evil, but he didn't make you feel good inside. It was as if he could suck all the good energy from a room as easily as he could suck the tobacco smoke from that cigar. How had she not noticed it at first? He exuded bad vibes.

"I knew you'd come to me eventually," he said, reaching for a half-full lowball glass of a brown liquor.

She shot her eyes at him. "What did you say?"

"I think it's about time you and I spend the night together. Could be worth both our whiles." He was stumbling over his words.

She threw out a hand. "There's no possibility on earth that I would sleep with you. In fact, I'd like you to leave in the morning. I appreciate your business, but it's time you pack your bags. I will not be spoken to that way." And as an afterthought, she said, "You can check out by nine. No breakfast."

He slapped his leg. "Now, hold on. Can't a woman take a joke?"

"I love jokes." She spun her finger in the air. "This here...your behavior, nothing funny about it. Be gone by nine, thanks." With that, she turned and stomped toward her house, furious that he'd dared get in the way of her perfect evening.

No way she'd let a man talk like that to her. Not anymore.

Fueled with anger, she marched into her house and slammed the door. As she checked the locks and turned off all the lights, she couldn't help but think about her ex-husband back in Vermont, the man who'd shown her the dark side of life. Frustrated beyond belief, she climbed the stairs shaking her fist and wondering, *Why are men so awful sometimes?*

After a hot bath, she wrapped her hair in a towel and pulled on her nightgown. Approaching her bed, she dropped to her knees and prayed that Remi Valentine wasn't too good to be true. There had to be some good ones out there somewhere.

26

THE RED MOUNTAIN MISSIONARY

O tis was standing in the lobby of their hotel in Hanoi. Thankfully, it was not the Hilton, which was Otis's inappropriate Vietnam War joke referring to the Hỏa Lò Prison, where the North Vietnamese had held American prisoners of war. The POWs had called it the Hanoi Hilton. He intended on repeating the joke until Joan laughed.

Otis had convinced the hotel staff to let him do a tasting of Red Mountain wines. At great expense, he'd shipped a case to every hotel on their journey, and he'd been giving them out to the sommeliers, other guests they'd met, and even to bellmen as a tip. These weren't just his wines; he'd shipped a variety of all his favorites from the mountain. Otis stood behind a wooden table near the piano. A small line of tourists stood behind the Vietnamese man.

"Step right up," Otis said, waving his hand with pride.

The people shuffled toward him.

He filled the small wine glasses the hotel had provided and passed them along. "This is a syrah from Red Mountain, a tiny wine-growing region in Washington State." He added, "Not Washington, DC, Washington State! The home of Amazon, Microsoft, Starbucks.

But don't think of the rain of Seattle. Think high desert. We only get a few inches of precipitation a year. We make better wine than California for half the price." Otis realized many of these people couldn't understand a word. In an attempt to simplify, he said slowly, "If you remember one thing, remember the words 'Red Mountain.' That's really all that matters. You are now tasting the magic elixir of Red Mountain."

Otis searched for approval from the tiny Vietnamese man who'd taken a sip. "What do you think?"

The man nodded.

Otis had no idea if the man understood him. It didn't matter. Otis knew this is how you break into new markets and spread the Gospel of Red Mountain. One mouth at a time.

He'd drawn quite the crowd by the time Joan exited the elevator and entered the lobby. When he realized she wasn't sitting in her wheelchair, Otis accidentally overpoured the glass of a kind American woman. The woman barely dodged the syrah that threatened to stain her dress. "That's enough," she yelled.

"I'm so sorry," Otis said. "Forgive me. Enjoy the wine, I'll be right back." He left the bottle on the table and moved through the crowd to help Joan.

Once he reached her, he put his hand under her free arm and asked, "Are you sure you want to do this? You're scaring me."

"Do what? The cane?"

"Yes, exactly."

"I have to break free from that chair at some point. Might as well be today. It's okay. You can let go."

He dipped his chin. "Are you sure?"

"I've got this," she said. "No big deal."

He let go of her arm and faced her. Holding back tears, he said, "You're the strongest person I've ever met in my life. You're a damn hell of a fighter."

She smiled "Don't exaggerate. And aren't you supposed to be a tough guy?"

Otis smiled back and whispered, "I don't deserve you, but I'll take you. I'll take every bit of you for as long as you'll have me."

She patted him on the cheek. "I'm all yours, my love."

27

THAT WHICH YOU CAN'T UNSEE

L eafhoppers were tearing through one of the cabernet vineyards. The pests had gone after the canopy, the once-green leaves turning white. If nothing was done, the grapes would soon shrivel undeveloped.

Brooks tore a leaf off a vine and examined it, watching the tiny white bugs scatter. He'd already released legions of lacewings and ladybugs to go after them, but these bastards were relentless.

Years ago, Otis had told him of a technique to rid the plants of the "the little shits." As with all of his mentor's techniques, the idea was unorthodox and way out there, but always worth a shot. And more times than not, effective. The particular trick he had in mind involved placing sheets of flypaper on the vineyard posts. Once the flypaper had collected enough leafhoppers—it usually only took a day or two —you burn that flypaper, stir the ashes into water, and spray it back into the vineyards. The leafhoppers would sense their own dead around them and stay away. Because the spray was harmless, he could even use Elvis to carry the sprayers, eliminating the risk of a tractor pass.

Brooks went through the vines peeling the backs off the flypaper and hanging the sheets. The mid-July sun baked his arms, and sweat seeped out of his tattoos.

Completing his task, he hopped on his bike to go grab lunch. Riding along Sunset Road, he noticed a figure riding a horse along a gravel road through the vines to the east. It wasn't too far from Margot's inn, so he assumed it was Shay and Elvis. But as he rode closer and was able to make out the rider, he realized it wasn't Shay. It was Abby. They passed within a hundred yards of each other, and Brooks lifted a hand in a weak wave. Abby, on the horse, and Shay, walking closely behind, waved back.

"You're kidding me," Brooks spat, gassing his Triumph, the purr turning more into a roar. He cranked the music on his bike, and Kurt Cobain wailed into his ears.

That's when the tears finally came, rushing out like something inside him was chasing them down his cheeks. It didn't stop with the tears. He cried. He cried almost as loud as his motorcycle purred and Cobain sang.

He crossed into Kiona and cut through the Horse Heaven Hills, riding south. He hauled ass, ripping past the wheat fields and grapevines, passing in the other lane anything in his way. Nirvana songs came and went, and he felt Cobain's pain. The first fifteen minutes of his ride were sadness and anger, not allowing any reasoning.

Eventually, as his bike rides did, this one allowed him to find enough calm to know that he couldn't blame Abby and Shay. He, himself, had ended it with Abby. She'd tried time and time again to convince him to forgive her and to allow her back into his life, and he'd shut her out. He'd also told his brother it was okay.

So, what the hell was the problem? He didn't want her. Or did he?

The cheating was one thing; this was worse. He tried so hard to ignore visions of those two together, but it was all he could see.

Brooks stopped in the middle of nowhere and hopped off his bike. He wiped his eyes and twisted his head around. A house and grain silo stood in the distance. Other than that, miles and miles of grapes and grain.

He kicked a rock across the road. *What's wrong with me?*

After a few minutes of staring off to nowhere, Brooks climbed back on his bike to head home. Riding along the Yakima River, he noticed a tall man hopping off an old BMW with a sidecar. Brooks slammed the brakes and pulled into the man's driveway. He hadn't seen a bike like that, let alone a sidecar, in a long time.

"That's a beautiful bike."

Both riders removed their helmets. "Thank you. Yours too."

This guy didn't live too far from Brooks, but they'd never met. He'd of course noticed the tractor shed and the Airstream, but he'd never seen that bike before. Fruit and nut trees covered the land. Outside of the RV, under a purple awning, were a grill and seating area, the chairs positioned toward the river. A cluster of tall acacia trees provided additional shade.

"Can I look?" Brooks asked.

"Yeah, c'mon."

Brooks hopped off his bike. "A '55 or something?"

"'53 R67/3."

Brooks circled the bike and checked out the Steib sidecar. All of a sudden a little dog wearing an Elizabethan cone poked his head out. "Who's that?"

"That's Henri."

Brooks gave the dog some attention. The men shook hands and introduced themselves. The guy's name was Remi. Maybe ten years older than Brooks. Dark skin, thick black hair. Broad shoulders. Tall. A couple of inches taller than Brooks.

"I have two in the shed you should see too, if you're into bikes." Remi picked his dog out of the sidecar and set him on the ground.

"Love to. I thought my brother and I were the only bike guys on the mountain."

"Not by a long shot. This area has some of the best riding in the country. I think the word's getting out." Remi led him to the shed and entered a code on the keypad for the shed door.

The door lifted and revealed two more BMWs from post-war Berlin. The two men walked around the bikes for almost half an hour, exhausting a discussion on motorcycles, exploring topics only bike guys could. As their conversation wound down, Brooks walked to the back corner of the work shed and pointed at two glass carboys with something fermenting inside. "What do you have there?"

Remi followed him. "This is my first attempt at mead."

"No kidding? With honey?"

"Yep. Local honey, water, and yeast. I'll bottle it in a couple of days. Hopefully it doesn't kill anyone."

Brooks was having one of those rare moments where you meet someone, and you instantly know you're meant to be friends. Needless to say, he hadn't experienced many of those. Something about Remi Valentine made him yearn for friendship.

Remi offered him a beer, and they sat in chairs facing the river.

Brooks asked, "What are you doing here on Red Mountain?"

"Having a midlife crisis. Running from my old world." Remi's dog chewed on a wine cork at his feet, growling occasionally as if the cork were biting back. "I've only been here a year or so, but Red Mountain has grabbed me in a big way. I almost feel like it pulled me back from the ledge."

"You're not the only one this mountain has saved."

"I'm telling you. I feel like I owe it something now." Remi smiled. "How about you?"

"Otis Till brought me here. I studied under him and now make wine at Lacoda."

"Oh, you're Brooks Baker! I know you. Or *of* you. I love your wine." Remi placed his hands on his hips. "Yours was the first Red Mountain wine I ever tried."

"You make wine too?" Brooks asked, shying away from the flattery.

"No, no, not yet." Remi talked about his mead and how he wanted to make cider from his apples. He pointed to a stack of cinder blocks and told Brooks he was building a sweat lodge. "I'm basically a washed-up suit and tie trying to connect with the outdoors again. A few months ago, I couldn't have even replaced a sprinkler. But I've gotten my garden and my trees figured out for the most part. All organic. I have a consultant at Bleyhl's helping me with the details. I tell you, farming organically isn't easy. You guys are conscious farmers, right?"

"Yeah. You know, in the great vineyards of Europe, they don't call it organic. They just farm their vineyards like they're feeding their children. I don't have kids, but I wouldn't feed my kids pesticides."

Remi nodded in agreement and pointed farther south on his property. "I planted those vines in May. All syrah. I'm hoping to harvest enough fruit to play with next year. Might buy a half ton this year to start."

"Give me a few turns on your bikes sometimes, and I'd be happy to help however I can."

"That's kind of you."

"I mean it. You know Till Vineyards? Otis Till?"

"Sure. I haven't met him, but I know of him. Love his wines."

"He took the time to teach me. For no reason other than to help. I like to pass that kindness forward when I can."

Remi thanked him for offering to help and said, "Some guys were in the Cougar Café, down at the Conoco, talking about Otis just yesterday. I was eating a sandwich and couldn't help overhearing their conversation. They were saying that he's so anti-modern that, one year in Sonoma in the nineties, he picked his cabernet vineyard in late July. Late July! These guys were in awe, talking about him like he was some mythical character. Is that really true? Can you even pick red wines in July?"

Brooks crossed his legs. "Otis swears by that story. Says it was the hottest year he'd ever seen, and he refused to let his cabernet turn into chocolate syrup. He is one of those guys who puts poetry first. In some ways, he doesn't even care if the wine tastes good. He just wants to do right by his vineyard. That's it. As long as the wine tastes true, then he's done his job."

"And he thinks high alcohol is bad?"

"He wouldn't dare generalize. To do so would go to war with Spain and the hot parts of Italy, among others. But he thinks picking late in order to produce high-alcohol wines, just to have the biggest wines on the block, is a sin worthy of tarring and feathering."

After processing that thought, Remi asked, "What's your story? You married?"

"Long story, but no, not married. Came close." He wanted to say, "Now my brother has her." But he didn't. Instead, he said, "How about you?"

"Long story too. I was thrown out. Deservedly so. I'm still licking my wounds." Remi seemed to visit some past pain as he cast his eyes toward the moving water.

"You and me both. Women never stop tearing your heart out."

"Every day. Gouging it."

When Brooks finished his beer, he stood and shook Remi's hand. "Let me know how I can help you around here. It's a lot to learn."

"Never ends, does it?"

"Otis says it ends when they bury you."

"Let's hope that's a long way out."

"Take care, Remi." With that, Brooks jumped back on his bike and rode the rest of the way along the river to his house, where he made his fifth peanut butter and jelly sandwich of the week.

28

DEATH DON'T HAVE NO MERCY

A driana removed her mother from life support in the early hours of July 11. Margarita had spent the past few days in the hospital fading away, the cancer claiming the last of her.

Though she'd been dying for a long time, it still didn't soften the blow. Adriana needed her mother; they'd been through so much together. Including Zack, it had been the three of them against the world. Now, it was two. Two desperate souls clinging to the memories of Tata.

Drowning in exhaustion, Adriana left the hospital. She'd stayed up for two nights straight, save a couple of hours drifting off in the recliner next to her mother. The room was so small she'd had to step out every time the nurses returned.

Tears had flowed steadily as she battled with the life-support decision. She had known the answer from the moment the doctor confronted her in the hallway—she and Margarita had already exhausted the topic—but she still had to process sentencing her mom to death.

She was the one pulling the plug. The executioner. Of her own mother.

Now, she somehow had to teach her son about death and tell him that he'd never see Tata again.

She found him at the breakfast table at Lita's house, waving a piece of bacon drenched in syrup like a wand from Harry Potter. The moment she saw him, she burst into tears. It wasn't fair that this beautiful little boy had to live this life of running from his father and losing his grandmother and being raised in a town where they knew no one.

She took him in her arms, pulling him away from his bacon and pancakes.

"Hi, Mommy. How's Tata?"

Adriana squeezed him even tighter, kissing his head. She sat him on the couch and petted his face. "She's gone. Tata has gone to heaven."

"What?" he asked.

At that moment, Adriana wished she'd prepared him. She wished she'd given him a chance to say goodbye. Instead, she'd hidden Tata's dying, almost like ignorance would soften the pain. She'd kept a lot of things from him. Her son didn't know that she'd been recognized by an acquaintance of his father, that they might have to hit the road again. He didn't know that she'd been battling the decision to leave Red Mountain alongside the decision to keep her mother on life support. He didn't even know they were on the run in the first place. Perhaps his ignorance was a blessing.

As he looked at her with both parts curiosity and perplexity in his eyes, she told him, "Your grandmother died, my love." She cupped his cheek and whispered, "She's gone to heaven."

"When is she coming home?"

How do you answer such a question from a six-year-old?

29

THEY'RE PUTTING UP BILLBOARDS

On July 16, almost a month into their trip, Joan and Otis arrived in Dublin. As they left their bed and breakfast, a charming spot one block from the River Liffey, Otis straightened his tweed cap and said, while clapping his hands, "Well, when in Rome. Point me to the nearest Guinness."

"It's ten a.m." They'd left her wheelchair in the room, and Joan was putting along rather well, using her cane and Otis's arm for support. Despite some serious jetlag from crossing into Europe from Asia, these world travelers were beginning to settle into this new lifestyle. And Otis saw strong determination in his lover's eyes.

"Then we're already one behind. We'll order two each to catch up."

She scanned the street. "I don't see anyone else drinking."

"They're all in the pubs!"

Soon they were strolling hand in hand down narrow cobblestone streets through the heart of Dublin. They peeked through the windows of art galleries, antique stores, and old bookshops that were propping open their doors for the start of a new day. They sat on a park bench and listened to a man picking a jig on a four-string banjo.

After an hour, they *finally* walked into a pub named Paddy's, where men screamed at a football match displayed on several flat-screen TVs along the crumbling brick wall. A chalkboard announced a Jameson whiskey special.

Otis and Joan posted up on leather stools at the bar, and he finally ordered his Guinness. They watched the bartender start the perfect eight-minute pour, pulling back the tall black handle. Not soon enough, the barman stamped a four-leaf clover in the frothy heads and slid them to Joan and Otis.

"My gods," Otis said, licking his lips. "I've been waiting this whole trip to drink this beer."

As he reached out for the glass, his phone rang. He stopped his hand just as his fingers felt the chill of the glass. "Let me answer this. I know it's Brooks. Something's up." He dug into his pants pocket and answered, "You have no idea your timing."

"Why?" Brooks asked.

"You should see the cold, creamy black beer I'm admiring. My first Guinness in Ireland. You know, you can't get these anywhere else on earth. The rest, even in England, don't hold a candle to a Dublin Guinness. And here you are about to ruin it, aren't you?"

With a sigh, Brooks said, "I hate to. Want to call me back?"

Otis's heart sank. "My dear boy, four-leaf clovers have nothing to do with luck in my world. I'm ready for the worst of it." He shook his head, knowing he couldn't hold onto the beauty of the day any longer. Something was coming.

"Looks like Drink Flamingo is coming to Washington. Billboards are popping up all over the highway."

He walked outside. "What do you mean, like near us?"

"Everywhere from Walla Walla to Seattle. Actually, they look like those old Guinness ads. *Drink Flamingo. Make life fly.* Or, *Drink Flamingo. Pink Looks Good on You.* They're all over social media."

"What the shit is this?" Otis asked.

The Drink Flamingo wine boxes, the ones stacked at the end of store aisles across the country, flashed in his mind. His jaw tensed, and his tongue retreated like he'd drunk turpentine as he visualized their logo, a pink flamingo soaring past overly ripe vines with giant purple clusters. Each variety or blend had a bird name, like Wayward Egret, One-Eyed Heron, Prickly Pigeon, Vulture Canyon. A Lodi zinfandel named Peacock's Crown was as popular as Coke. Anyone who'd ever shopped in the past two years couldn't help but notice these atrocious boxes of rat juice with their despicable names.

With acid bubbling up through his esophagus, he said, "Those bastards should stay in California." The obvious hit him. "Do you... do you think they could be gunning for that piece of property on Red Mountain? You think they already bought it?"

"No way to know, Otis. We can't speculate. Washington is a big state. They could be going to Walla Walla. We just know by the billboards that it's not Woodinville."

Otis couldn't help but crack a grin. He eyed his dry stout through the window. Joan had turned her attention to the game. "This is honestly funny. I can't think of a winery I'd want less in Washington. If they're coming to Red Mountain, I might just have to burn the whole damned mountain down. I wouldn't wish a bottle of that Drink Flamingo spit for Hitler. You know you've bloody ruined my day. A bloody box wine of Red Mountain. Oh, Christ." Otis slung his cap to the ground.

"Hey," Brooks said, "millennials are embracing alternative packaging."

"Maybe so, but they're drinking cat piss! Fine, reinvent box wine. But not with bulk Lodi juice thick in mega purple, organophosphates, and powdered oak. I wonder what else can go wrong while I'm gone."

"How much longer do you guys have?"

"Three weeks. We have Iceland, Africa, then shoot over to South America before heading home."

"Don't let this ruin your trip. How's Joan?"

"She's turned a corner. I don't even know what happened, but she's doing great. We're having a lovely time." Otis rolled his eyes, picturing a Drink Flamingo box with the words *Red Mountain* plastered on the side. With great exaggeration, he pronounced, "We're having such a great time."

"Don't let this knock you down."

"By God, man. We need to erect a wall around Red Mountain and start defending it. I'm trying not to jump to conclusions. Find out more. Find out where they're going. Someone has to know."

"I have a feeling we'll know soon enough."

"I'm afraid you're right," Otis agreed. "Keep me posted."

"Yes, sir."

After saying goodbye, Otis stomped back inside and sat back down at the bar, his untouched Guinness waiting for him.

Joan asked, "What's new?"

Otis shook his head in disgust. "You know that box wine, Drink Flamingo, from California? In Lodi?"

"Doesn't everyone?"

"They're coming to Red Mountain. Well, we don't know for sure, but there's a good possibility. Knowing the world I live in, they're already there, plotting, no doubt."

She touched his shoulder. "So, are we going to toast, or are you going to sit there and let your beer get warm? Toughen up, Otis. Your mountain is still standing."

Otis raised the glass toward his love and then glanced at the bartender. "Let's get another on the way, kind sir. It's going to be a long day." He turned up his black beer, a drip rolling down his chin.

What do you do when it all comes crashing down?

30

BACK ON THE TRACKS (STILL RUNNING OFF THE RAILS)

Three days after burying Margarita, Adriana and Zack moved into Jasper's old room in Margot's house. Margot was determined to do anything she could for Adriana, this single mom fighting so hard to survive.

Though the tragedy with Margarita slowed Margot's relationship with Remi, the interruption didn't last long. They couldn't get enough of each other. They talked and texted and emailed. He sent flowers. To be funny, he sent her a coffee mug with the Navy SEAL Trident on it and underneath it read: *The only easy day was yesterday.* She added it to her growing collection of mugs in the inn.

Finally, they were able to see each other again when Margot invited him for lunch. She'd combed through cookbooks for hours before deciding on what would be the first meal she would ever serve him. At first, she thought she'd go complicated, show off her skills. She overthought it, though, and her instincts told her to settle down, to go simple. To follow the season.

Stopping by the farmers' market in the morning, she was thrilled to find the first of the summer peaches. Back home, she roughly chopped two ripe peaches and mixed them with two of her home-grown heirloom tomatoes and a jalapeño pepper, all chopped as well.

She poured in a splash of organic, single-orchard olive oil from Lazio, Italy, and sprinkled some pink salt and freshly ground pepper. After a gentle stir, she set it aside to marinate and then prepared the rest of the meal: crispy black bean cakes, a perfect sunny-side up egg from her feathered Broadway ladies outside, and some sautéed dandelion greens from the garden.

It was too hot to eat outside, so they ate in the dining room. She paired her spicy peach and tomato salad with a split of riesling from a nearby winery and added a chilled, light-bodied Red Mountain sangiovese for the rest of the meal. If his moans were any indication, her meal was a success. Their conversation felt absolutely relaxed and comfortable. Remi had a way about him, a beautiful blend of humor and depth. He insisted on doing the dishes and then asked her to introduce him to her animals.

Margot held his hand as they walked the road from the inn to the sanctuary. She liked the way his hand felt. She liked the hair on his arms and on the backs of his hands. She even liked the hair on the backs of his fingers. Everything about him was so manly. And yet, like little Henri who was running around with Philippe, he had a gentle side that made her feel comfortable. Trusting.

"How's Jasper?" he asked, wiping the sweat from his brow. "Have you spoken with him?"

"We talk a lot. Oh, my gosh. I call him way too much."

"There's no such thing."

"That's what he tells me. I think he's being sincere. He's doing what he does. Playing that piano. Learning. Dreaming of ivory keys and large crowds. Probably teaching more than learning. He's really happy. He misses the mountain and Emilia, but he's where he's supposed to be."

Halfway to the gate leading into the sanctuary, Margot felt a sense of pride as she pointed out a rectangular wooden sign above the gate with *Épiphanie Sanctuary* etched into it that Shay had recently mounted for her.

"What a great name," Remi said, "and what a woman you are. Chasing your dreams like this. It's not easy to start over, yet you've done it beautifully. This new chapter in your life is so inspiring to me."

"Thanks." Margot smiled at his compliment but could feel the fear in her heart. She hadn't explored Remi's past too much, but she was extremely curious. It was time she ensure that he wasn't too good to be true. *Before* he got to tickle her turkey. "Tell me about your daughter. Your life. You're so secretive."

He sighed. "It breaks my heart thinking about it."

"Then we don't have to," she said, waving at a group of vineyard workers taking a water break.

"Oh, no. I need to. I want to. It's hard, but I want to. I want you to know more. I think I told you Carly's going to be a senior in high school next year. She and her mother are in San Francisco. Amber, my ex, chased another guy down there. Disgusted with me for tearing up the family, Carly happily followed. She's looking at schools, wants to go to UCLA. Her mom just tells me stuff via email."

"We can talk about this next time." Margot felt slightly uncomfortable and now didn't want to know more.

"No, really, it's okay. It just reminds me how much of a...a...a jerk I was." He shook his head. "I brought this on myself. She'll forgive me one day. We'll reconnect. I just hurt her at a time when she was already fragile. Being a teenager is tough enough without going through a divorce. I still write and call. One day she'll respond. Until then, I can't and don't blame her. She's sixteen and has plenty of other things to deal with." Looking away, he wiped his eye.

She squeezed his hand, sure he'd just hidden a tear. "I'm sure she misses you."

The animals noticed Margot coming. Not many things could brighten her day as easily as seeing her animal family running toward her. The ducks and chickens and pigs, the cow and horse and llama, all moving toward her like an army of love. The turkey trailed behind but waddled with absolute determination. She opened the gate and the couple slipped through. He laughed as she grabbed a handful of grain and the animals fought for her attention, the sheep and goats the most aggressive.

Gushing over all her animals, she lifted up a baby goat and held him close to her heart. "This is Papa. He's kind of my favorite. Don't tell the others."

Remi touched the goat. "Hey, Papa. Why do you call him that?"

"Because he's always humping everything. He wants so badly to be a papa."

He smiled. "You're just awesome. Look at you. You're a dream come true."

"This is my dream come true." She squeezed Papa to her heart. Letting him go, she knelt to say hi to her turkey. "This is Precious," she said, petting the bright red caruncles running along the top of the turkey's head.

Precious flapped her wings and stretched out her tail feathers.

After a few more minutes, the animals lost interest in their human friends and returned to their favorite shady spots. Margot and Remi walked along the gravel road back to her place.

Halfway back, he glanced at his watch. "You know, I was thinking about our mission to plant a tree on Rattlesnake."

"I was just laughing about that this morning," Margot admitted.

"I think we should do it."

"You're not allowed to go up there. It's a reserve."

"I didn't realize you were such a rule follower."

Margot frowned and chastised Remi with, "I didn't realize you were such a bad boy." Then, with a conspiratorial grin, she asked, "How would we get up there?"

He slowed and raised his fingers to his lips. "Listen."

"What?"

"Just listen."

"I am listening. I hear birds and tractors."

"Shhh."

He wrapped his arm around her waist in silence.

Margot had no idea what she was listening for, but she loved being so near to him.

Remi looked at his watch again. "What do you think the best way to get to Rattlesnake would be? How would a Navy SEAL do it?"

As Margot shook her head, a sound like the static from an old radio pulsed in the air. They both turned toward the north. He touched his ear. "There it is. Right on time."

Margot couldn't pinpoint the location of the sound. "What?"

"How would a SEAL get to the top of Rattlesnake? Humor me."

The static grew louder and morphed into a tractor purr and then...

"No," she whispered, spinning her head around, looking. "You didn't."

He flicked his eyebrows. "I might have."

She hit his arm. "I know that's not a helicopter."

"I wouldn't be so sure."

She hit him again. "Stop it."

A big grin from Remi.

"You hired a helicopter?" She hit and kissed him and spun around, asking, "Where is it?"

The helicopter soon rose over the top of Red Mountain, the *chop chop* reverberating through the vineyards. Margot was reminded of the giant wind fans that spun in the spring to protect the vines from a late frost.

"This must have cost a fortune," she said, taking his hand. "You're crazy."

He shrugged, and she watched in awe as a white helicopter soared over the mountain, moving southwest, directly toward Épiphanie. By now, some of her guests had exited the inn and watched from the patio and grass. The vineyard workers blocked the sun from their eyes as they gazed northeast. Adriana and Zack were near the garden with their eyes turned toward the sky.

Looking back at the helicopter, Margot smiled. She couldn't believe what was happening. Couldn't believe this man.

They exchanged waves with the pilot as he landed on the gravel road, the words on the side of the bird clear now: Desert Sky Rides.

Margot turned her wave to everyone watching—the guests and neighbors. She beamed with pride, beamed with...love and pride, and she felt like she could burst. As she only could have imagined happening in a movie, Remi grabbed her hand and they ran with their heads low to the helicopter door. He opened it and helped her up, the action so smooth it is was clear this one wasn't his first helicopter ride.

Who is this man?

The roar of the engine and the spinning rotor blades were so loud that she couldn't hear the door shut. They sat in the two seats behind the pilot, who turned from his controls and gave a quick thumbs-up. She saw herself in the mirrors of his Ray-Bans. They fastened seatbelts and fitted their headphones over their ears.

The pilot flipped a few switches, pulled back on the throttle, said, "Welcome aboard," and they were off.

Remi turned to Margot and spoke into the microphone extending from one ear of the headset. Coming in loud and clear, he said, "The hardest part was finding a tree that would stand a chance up there."

"I can't believe you did this. I...I just... I—"

"The things a man will do to impress a woman."

"This is pretty good."

He bathed her with a loving look. "I'm just getting started."

They rose over Épiphanie, the people below shrinking.

Margot waved at Shay, who was sitting on Elvis. Even the sheep and goats watched the metal bird rise into the sky.

"What's the verdict?" she asked, her focus back to the mission. "What kind of tree?"

He pointed behind them. She hadn't noticed the shovel and the small tree in a black plastic pot behind her on the metal floor. "An acacia. A shoestring acacia."

"You are winning my heart, Remi Valentine." A beat. "We need water to set the roots."

He pointed to a case of bottled water.

"Evian?" she said. "You couldn't find anything fancier?"

It was impossible not to glue herself to the window as they rose over Red Mountain and saw what all those vines and all those vineyard blocks looked like from the air. There was that Irish checkerboard, filled with people now all lifting their heads upward. She could see the entire growing region from the window, and she couldn't believe how much was going on down there. The people, the stories, the wines, the collective energy.

They flew over the Yakima River and cut over the eastern side of Benton City, and she saw the giant water tower passing on the left. They flew by grain fields and hayfields, cow pastures, and farms. A variety of farms unfolded over the landscape. As the pilot straightened toward their destination, Margot and Remi looked past him through the cockpit windshield.

There it was.

Rattlesnake Mountain stood two and a half times taller than Red Mountain. But, unlike Red Mountain, there was nothing on it—nothing manmade, at least—only true eastern Washington scabland, painted with scrub brush, cheat grass, and chunks of granite. And somewhere, that elusive herd of elk.

As they climbed with the slope, the pilot said, "Wait until I'm on the ground to unbuckle. Then you'll have about twenty minutes. No more. In and out."

Remi clapped his hands together. "In and out, Cobra Leader. Twenty and counting, then wheels up."

Margot looked at Remi like he was crazy.

He shrugged. "What? Isn't that what they'd say? So, who's digging?"

Margot pointed at him, wagging her index. "My digging stops at trowels. My man does the shoveling."

They landed two-thirds of the way up the mountain with a jarring bump. When the pilot made a circular signal with his index finger, the passengers unbuckled and shuffled out with their contraband and shovel.

With the blades still spinning, the chop echoing down the mountain, Remi and Margot found a prime spot amid lichen-covered granite and army green shrub brush. The wind howled in gusts. Stabbing the spade of the shovel into ground, he located a soft spot in the soil and began to dig. The shovel looked small in his hands and his biceps swelled with each thrust.

Her smile had been stretched for so long that it just might get stuck if she didn't calm herself down. Rattlesnake Mountain would no longer be the highest treeless mountain in the country. She could actually edit its Wikipedia entry on that fact.

Hurrying to the beat of the pilot's countdown, he breathed heavily as he reached below two feet. "We're getting close!" he yelled over the helicopter.

Margot wrestled the tree from the plastic pot and lifted it in her right hand. "Ready?" she yelled.

"I think so!" He reached over and kissed her lips. He whispered into her ear, "This is the coolest thing I've ever done."

She raised the tree to shoulder height, as if exhibiting this grand planting to spectators. And then she dropped the roots into the hole, her smile stretching to the back of her head. He came in behind her, emptied most of the water bottles around the root ball, and pushed the loose soil back into the hole. He poured the last bottle around the trunk.

Mission accomplished.

31

DRINK FLAMINGO. DRINK INSIDE THE BOX

A day after ruining Otis's perfect Guinness, Brooks still hadn't gotten to the bottom of what could be a potential Drink Flamingo disaster. He knew as well as Otis what this potential intrusion could mean for Red Mountain. It was tantamount to Napa Valley finding out Coca-Cola was going to build its next plant on Highway 29. Still, Brooks knew he couldn't jump to conclusions. At this point, the idea of Drink Flamingo coming to the mountain was nothing more than speculation.

Red Mountain was powerful in its own right; he needn't discount the power of this place. Fast food chains could be scattered up and down Sunset Road, and those Red Mountain wines would continue to be worthy of nobility. The harvest was still on track to be superb. The little berries were ripening at a nice consistent pace. Though the first two weeks of July had been brutally hot and demanded heavy watering, it sounded like good luck was coming. According to forecasts, they could expect some cooler weather sneaking in around mid-September, which would slow things down. No problem on Red Mountain. As Otis liked to say, he'd never met a grape on the mountain that didn't ripen to perfection by the end of the year.

Brooks had beat the vineyard workers in to work today, arriving shortly after five a.m., so he didn't feel guilty sneaking out early. He wanted to reach Margot's place before Adriana left. Something kept telling him not to give up.

He parked in the waning shade of a group of cypress trees outside Épiphanie. He could taste the bitterness of fear and rejection creeping up his throat as he walked to the big wooden doors. He pushed one open, suddenly hoping she wasn't there, that maybe she'd gone home and he could try again another day—maybe on a day where he had a little more confidence.

The bell sounded when he opened the door, and Philippe came running and barking.

Margot soon poked her head from around a corner, drying her hands. "Hi, Brooks! To what do I owe the pleasure? It's not often we have celebrities stop by."

"Who, me?"

"Of course, you. If only I had a dollar for every time I've heard your story in *Rolling Stone* mentioned in my dining room, I'd be rich. All the girls want to sneak a peek at you. I can't keep your wines in stock."

"I'm just taking Jake's spotlight for a little while. A spoke in the wheel of his story."

"That's not what I hear." She shook his hand. "What can I do for you?"

Brooks looked away but finally found Margot's eyes. "I was looking for Adriana."

"I didn't realize you two were friends."

"I'm working on it."

Margot raised her eyebrows. "Good for you. She's one of a kind. I guess you heard what happened?"

He cocked his head left. "No."

"Her mother passed away last week."

Brooks said, "That's awful. I had no idea."

"Adriana's doing okay. They knew it was coming. More than anything it's Zack I worry about. Have you met him yet?"

"Who's Zack?"

"Her son."

"No, I don't really even know her." He shrugged. "I've only spoken to her a couple of times."

"She's out in the garden if you'd like to see her."

"No, no. Can't imagine she wants to see anyone right now." *What terrible timing.*

"Brooks Baker, if you're interested in Adriana, go say hello. I'm not going to let you leave my property until you do. A handsome man like you will brighten her day."

Brooks smiled. "I can't argue with that."

Margot gestured toward the dining room. "You can go out the back there."

Brooks walked through the inn and through the back door. Once he reached the patio, he saw Adriana, wearing a wide-brimmed straw hat, harvesting something in the garden. Zack was playing in the dirt on the far side; it looked like he had a trowel in his hand. Brooks took in a big breath, searched for confidence, and then approached her.

"Adriana," he said, noticing a basket half-full of vibrant red strawberries.

She turned and smiled. "Hi."

Brooks couldn't tell if she was happy to see him; it wasn't the most welcoming greeting. Considering her circumstances, maybe that's all she had in her. She did smile, at least. He wanted this encounter to go well, but his nerves forced him to speak with unnecessary loudness as he said, "Those look delicious. That is a gorgeous red color." His voice cracked on the last word.

She ignored his awkwardness and said, "They are. Try one." She carefully stepped out of the strawberry patch.

He met her on the edge and reached in for a couple of beauties. He ate them one at a time. "Unbelievable. I could eat that whole basket."

"I know. They're so good, but you can't eat all the fruits of my labor. My back is on fire from all this bending over."

"I wouldn't dare." His grin faded. "Margot told me about your mom. I'm sorry. Is there anything I can do to help?"

"No, thank you. We're getting by."

"I can't imagine." He clasped his hands behind his back.

Where does one steer a conversation from there? Brooks breathed in the warm air and looked at her son. "How's he taking it?"

"He hasn't said a word in a week. She was his everything."

"Mind if I go say hello to him?"

With her consent, Brooks found Zack digging like a dog, burying some action figures in the soil.

"How's it going?" Brooks asked, squatting down.

Zack wore swimming goggles over his eyes, and didn't look up.

"My name's Brooks. What's yours?"

Zack stopped digging and turned to him with a penetrating, almost intimidating, stare. He returned to digging.

"I know your mom a little bit. She said your grandma passed away. I'm sorry to hear that."

The boy didn't say anything.

"I never had a grandma. Wish I had."

Zack stopped and looked at him again, this time with less intimidation.

"You wondering why I never had a grandma? I was kind of an orphan, like Oliver Twist. You know who that is? I didn't have parents growing up. I didn't have parents *or* grandparents. But I heard about them. I always wished. I can't imagine how you feel right now. It's really sad."

Zack said, "Yeah. You never knew your mommy and daddy?"

"It's funny that you ask that. I do now. I met them for the first time last year. But my grandparents had already passed away. I've only seen pictures of them."

"That's sad."

"Tell me about it. So what's with the goggles? You going swimming later?"

"No. I don't know how to swim yet." Then he answered with a defeated tone, "I just like wearing them."

"Well, nobody is going to poke your eye out."

"That's kind of why I wear them. And just in case I have to go swimming. Or if we have one of those...those dust devils where the sand turns into a hurricane thing. You know?" Suddenly the boy was bursting with words.

"A dust devil, yeah. I know them."

"They're pretty cool."

"I think so too. In fact, we had one last year hit Red Mountain. You couldn't see three feet in front of you. It was crazy. People were running into each other."

"Was anyone hurt?"

"No, I don't think so. But it was scary. I was driving down the road and had to slam on the brakes."

Zack said, "We just moved in with Ms. Pierce. Maybe another one will come soon. I'm not scared."

"You moved in with Margot? That's cool. So you're a Red Mountain transplant now." Brooks remembered that he had predicted Adriana would get pulled into the mountain. "Do you like wine?"

"Um, I'm six. What kid likes wine when they're six?"

"Good point. I know it would taste yucky to you, but it's fun to smell. You wouldn't believe all the different scents you can pick up from a glass of Red Mountain wine. Cinnamon. Vanilla. Blueberries."

"Like cereal."

Brooks smiled. "I suppose so. What cereal do you like?"

"Fruit Loops."

"Fruit Loops? Don't tell me you eat Fruit Loops! I'm a Cap'n Crunch guy."

"Yuck!"

Brooks and Zack were both laughing when Adriana walked up. "What are you two giggling about?"

"He likes Cap'n Crunch," Zack said.

"Cap'n Crunch?" Adriana looked at Brooks. "What kind of man likes Cap'n Crunch?"

Brooks jabbed a thumb at his own chest. "This man right here."

Zack laughed out loud.

"Wait a minute," Adriana said to her son. "You've barely said a word to me since Tata died, but you're talking to this stranger? Didn't I teach you anything about stranger danger?"

"He's not a stranger, Mom. His name's Brooks. He's an orphan. Like Oliver Twist."

Brooks raised his eyebrows and nodded. "That's me. Oliver Twist." He set his hand on his head. "Without the funny hat."

The three of them shared a laugh; Adriana had a strong cackle that Brooks found appealing, if not for any other reason than it was nice to see her happy.

"Hey, Zack. Now that you're a Red Mountain kid, you have to meet my friend, Luca. He's a little bit older than you, but not much. I think you'd like him. I'll talk to him. Maybe bring him over sometime."

"Yeah, that's cool."

Brooks talked about the Foresters' son Luca for a little while and then, "All right, well, I'd better get going. Talk to you later."

"Bye, Brooks." Zack waved at him, and a piece of Brooks's heart broke.

Adriana followed him back toward the inn. When they were out of Zack's earshot, she said, "This isn't fair."

"What isn't fair?"

"You go to Zack to get to me."

Brooks, obviously taken aback, turned to her and stopped. "That's not what I was doing!"

Adriana said, "Sure. Uh huh. I really can't imagine dating a biker."

Hearing her even mention the idea of dating gave him a shot of courage. "You can't stereotype all bikers. I'm not a *biker*. I ride bikes. That's it. The riding is amazing around here. Lots of guys ride."

"Your arms are covered in tats. Your closet is probably half leather. I'd say you're a biker."

"I'm whatever you want me to be. How about that?"

She rolled her eyes.

Brook almost brought up how he'd read her future and knew she'd move to the mountain, but he bit his tongue at the last moment. Perhaps it was too soon after her mother's death. He tried a different direction and said, "Has he really not spoken since your mom died?"

"Hasn't said a word. Now he won't shut up. What's that all about?"

"Probably speaks to my own development. I'm still a kid at heart."

She smiled, and he realized he'd barely even noticed the scars today. They were, of course, blatantly obvious, but they no longer caused him any sense of discomfort or insecurity when he looked at her. In fact, as they smiled at each other, he saw the beautiful woman that she was, and he wanted desperately to kiss her one day.

Apparently, she didn't feel the same way. She asked, "So does this mean I have to agree to go out with you now? You and your tats and your motorcycle and your leather."

"No."

"Good," she said with a large dose of relief.

He was nearly offended until he saw the smirk on her face. Almost forty years on this planet, and he still couldn't understand women. Was she indicating that he might have a chance? Should he ask her out again? He certainly wasn't seeing green lights, so he said, "I'm really sorry about your mom, Adriana. Let me know if I can help. With Zack or anything."

"Thank you, I appreciate that. We'll survive." As he turned to leave, she asked, "What are all those marks on your arm?"

"Oh, things that happened a million years ago. Rebellion in ink." Brooks decided to stay a little longer and asked, "What's Zack doing all summer?"

"I haven't figured that out. He's hanging around here for now." Adriana stayed on course. "Are you ashamed of your ink?"

"No. They're reminders of my past. I mentioned the Foresters. Maybe he can hang out with Luca some."

Adriana shrugged. "Maybe. I have to return to the garden. Thanks for talking to Zack. That was weird. He doesn't talk to men."

"He's a great kid. I had fun."

Adriana smiled, turned, and walked away.

32

THE SILENCE OF LOSS

In the days following her mother's death, Adriana had hid her breakdowns—every last tear—from Zack. Other than briefly responding to her questions, he'd barely spoken. The only connection he'd made was with Margot's dog Philippe. Adriana missed his enthusiastic and somewhat embellished stories, his wild claims, and even his television commentary. So, to bring him back to normal, she felt like she had to show him nothing but strength.

Never-ending questions had tortured her mind. How could God be so cruel? Why would a six-year-old have to experience such loss? Why would God allow a child to know such ugly things? Why would God take away her mom when she needed her most?

Adriana hadn't prepared Zack like she should have, and she regretted that. Instead of explaining cancer and explaining death, she'd chosen to let him live his life not knowing why Tata tired so easily. Why she moved so slowly sometimes. Why she took so many naps. And then, all of a sudden, Adriana had to sit him down and tell him he'd never see Tata again. Maybe he'd heard them talk a few times about her sickness. But he was six. He hadn't understood she was going away forever.

Forever.

How could Adriana blame him for not talking? At least she'd been able to process her loss over time. With Zack, she'd dumped the news on him like a bucket of ice water.

When Margot had asked her if they wanted to move into Jasper's old room, Adriana was overwhelmed with reservations. She hated getting help from others; it made her feel weak. But letting Margot come to the rescue was different. There was this feeling of camaraderie, these two women fighting together to survive. Adriana had a lot to consider. Living with Margot would save her rent money, travel expenses, and travel time. It would allow her to have Zack with her all day and night. She'd be available twenty-four hours a day if Margot needed her at Épiphanie. And Margot had expressed how lonely she'd been since Jasper moved out. This could be a win-win for both women.

Fast forward a few days, and here she and Zack were, sitting with her boss at a table set with fine china in one of the most beautiful homes she'd ever seen. The house she and Michael had had in Los Angeles was large and very fine, so much more than Adriana ever could have imagined, but it had never felt like a home, and it most certainly had never been cared for with such an eye for detail.

Being here, Adriana felt a simmering hope inside. Margot's generosity made her believe that despite her and Zack's loss, they might just be okay. It had now been two weeks since the man with the squinty eyes recognized her. He'd checked out of the inn that very day, and she hadn't seen him since. Adriana was starting to think she'd pulled it off, that he'd gone on about his life without giving the encounter a second thought. Not that she was worried Michael would suddenly show up—he was still in prison for the time being. But on their last phone call, her lawyer had said Michael was coming up for parole and had a good chance of getting out.

As Zack tore into a second helping of eggplant Parmesan and red sauce dripped down his face, Adriana asked, "She's a great chef, isn't she?"

Her son offered a slight nod, avoiding eye contact. His goggles were raised to his forehead, and red pressure marks circled his eyes.

She hurt seeing the smallness of him, this shrinking inside, like he was losing the little bit of security that he had.

Adriana said, "Now you like eggplant?"

He muttered, "Yes, ma'am," and went back to his food.

"Please talk to me, sweetie. I don't understand why you could barely stop with Brooks but won't talk to me. You turned into a chatterbox, and now you're frozen again." She turned to Margot. "Forgive me. This is not your burden."

"Burden. Ha! You're my gift. You both are. Zack, I think it's perfectly fine if you want to be quiet for a little while. I remember when I lost my grandmother... I was devastated." Margot sipped her red wine and then turned to Adriana. "As far as you two burdening me, come on. Finally, this house has some life back in it. You have no idea how welcome you are. After Jasper left, I felt like I was living in this giant lonely castle, just hoping I might find even a bug that would say hello."

Adriana touched Zack's shoulder. "Would you like to be excused?"

Nodding again, he pushed away from the table and headed toward their room upstairs.

When he was gone, Adriana poured more Coke into her glass and said, "I don't understand why he talked with Brooks. He's always shy around men."

"Sometimes we find connections in the strangest of places. Brooks has a nice way about him. Zack probably felt comfortable."

"More comfortable than with his own mom?"

"Don't worry. He'll be talking your ear off again in no time. I promise." Margot raised her eyebrows. "How does it feel to know Brooks Baker likes you, by the way?"

Adriana blew out hot air. "I don't think of men like that anymore. I don't know how I feel. Appreciative. He's nice. He's fine."

"Um, nice. Fine. More like, *fiiiine*. A big "G" for gorgeous. Trusting. Kind. Warm. Successful. What did you two talk about?"

"He talked to Zack most of the time, but he asked me out."

"What?"

"I told him no."

"Why in the world would you turn down a date with Brooks Baker?"

"I'm not sure I need a man in my life anymore. They're so... I don't know. They get in the way. Not everyone is like Remi Valentine. Not every man picks you up in a helicopter."

"It's taken me many years to strike gold, darling. Don't give up yet."

"Brooks asked me out the day that Harry Bellflour came on to me."

"Ah, yes, the secret you kept for more than a week." Margot shook her clenched fist. "If you would have told me what that man had said to you, I would have kicked him out that day! You would have saved me from going through the same thing myself."

"I know, and I'm sorry. I was so afraid I'd lose my job."

"I understand. Hopefully now, you know you can trust me." Margot sipped her wine and pushed her plate away. "By the way, I finally looked up Harry Bellflour. He's part of a California winery called Drink Flamingo. They make boxed wine. It's all over the place. According to billboards on the highway, they're opening somewhere in Washington State. We can only assume he was here to check out Red Mountain. That's the rumor. Ugh, I can't imagine having him as a neighbor."

"Oh, my God," Adriana said, "please don't let that happen. I never want to see him again."

"You and me both."

Adriana drank her Coke and wondered aloud, "What's so special about this mountain anyway? I can't believe how into wine everyone is here, like it's a religion."

"Wine is different from Coke, my dear. Wine has a soul, and you can capture it in a bottle and send it out into the world." Margot stood, retrieved a stem, and poured Adriana a glass. "There's this cerebral thing that needs to happen. You have to sense the land and the people and everything they've done to bring this bottle to you."

The only wine Adriana had ever tasted was the sweet wine on

Sunday mornings; it never appealed to her otherwise. Michael some-times drank red wine when he wasn't drinking liquor, but she'd never been interested. Adriana stuck her nose in the glass. "Smells nice."

"Don't smell it. Feel it." Margot touched her own chest. "Feel the romance. Art is always more special when you know where it origi-nated. Do you know what I mean? Taste the wine like you're kissing Brooks for the first time."

Adriana's face flushed red. "I think I'm going to take baby steps."

"With Brooks or the wine?"

The women smiled and clinked glasses.

Despite all the bad, Adriana felt like everything would be all right. Like losing her mom wasn't going to be the end. Death was a part of life. With or without cancer, her mom was going to die. Adriana had to hold on to her own faith, not cast it aside when life became tough.

She knew that if she could change her mindset, she and Zack would have a fighting chance at finding their way to happiness and security.

33

THE REALITY OF FAIRY TALES

To Margot's delight, Remi and Henri stopped by the next morning before she headed to the inn to feed her guests. They sat on the back patio watching the dogs play like littermates in the grass. The sun was peeking over the mountain, casting warm morning rays over the vineyards.

Margot named the chickens pecking at a pile of leftovers from the night before. "The brown one is Mary Poppins. Then that fluffy one, the silkie, her name's Anita. From *West Side Story,* of course. Sassy little Anita. That black-and-white beauty is Eliza Doolittle from *My Fair Lady.*"

From there they talked more about her Broadway years and then she pried more into Remi's past. In the early hours of the morning, Margot had woken terrified of being heartbroken again. She'd dreamed of this beautiful life with Remi. They married and moved in together. Jasper thought he was the greatest stepfather on earth. Remi's daughter came back, and the four of them got along famously. Margot got everything she wanted. Life was perfect.

And then her dream ended when Remi sat her down to tell her that he'd found someone else. Just like that, the dream became a nightmare, and that's when her eyes sprang open, fear setting the mood for the day.

"I'd like to ask you something," Margot said. "Will you tell me about your ex-wife? What happened to you two? What happened in your marriage that led to divorce?" Margot had a strange and urgent need to know. "I know I'm prying. Forgive me."

Remi nodded, as if he'd known he would have to go there. "We met in the air. She was a Delta flight attendant based out of Atlanta, and I was on her flight from Atlanta to San Francisco. We hit it off." He smiled in a way that made Margot uncomfortable, like he enjoyed the memory of that day up in the air a little too much. "But she wouldn't give me her number, said she didn't date Diamonds, meaning Diamond status. We ran into each other at a ramen shop the next day. She gave in, and we dated long distance for a while. I took long layovers in Atlanta when I could. Our relationship heated up, and I asked her to marry me."

"While you were living where?"

"I'd been in Seattle forever, grew up there, as you know. We got engaged, and she eventually moved in with me. Everything was good for a while. At least I thought so. My workaholic ways started to eat at her, especially once we had Carly. I had too much going on at work, developing properties all over the country. Shopping malls, hospitals, apartments, hotels." Remi raised his hands. "A cell phone in one, a large cup of coffee in the other, juggling the world. I didn't realize until it was too late that I was giving my family the least of my attention. She tried to talk to me toward the end...tried to point out how overworked I was, but I...I wasn't there."

Remi kept going and going and going. He even said a few things that made Margot think he'd forgotten *she* was there. At one point, he said he'd made "the biggest mistake of his life."

Margot's uneasiness grew. Nothing quite obvious at first—a far-off shooting star you're not quite sure you saw. When he palmed his forehead like a football and took a moment to compose himself, the truth revealed itself. His ex was still breaking his heart. Was he still in love with her? What if everything Margot and Remi had was a façade?

Margot was barely listening as Remi looked back up toward the dogs and continued what she now considered a confession. He might as well have said he wanted his old life back.

"One deal after the next and as soon as I'd have everything under control, something would come up. Even when I was back in Seattle, I was sleeping at my office a lot. Forgetting important days: Valentine's, anniversaries. I can hardly believe I even missed Amber's birthday one year. Totally forgot. Was just immersed." He shook his head. "She was nice about it. Little did I know what I was doing to my marriage." And on and on.

Margot felt like they'd been on a canoe cruising downstream the past few weeks, and suddenly little tiny leaks were springing up. She didn't want to know *this* much. All the giggles and shivers and giant smiles the past weeks. All the opening of doors and hand-holding and romantic flirts. They didn't make sense anymore.

Margot didn't need to go down this road. She'd only somewhat recovered from her divorce, a battle that had taken years. She absolutely could not let this relationship blossom any longer, because it had become all too evident that Remi was going to pull the plug one day. It might not be for another year or two. Who knew? But she now saw that the two of them weren't going to last a lifetime, and that's the only kind of relationship she was interested in.

Finding some hidden strength, Margot lifted her hand up. "Remi. Please stop."

He zipped it.

"Do you hear yourself? You still love her."

He turned his head to the right and cut his eyes toward her. "My ex-wife?" Like she'd said something so absurd, something impossible.

"You don't see it, do you?" She'd known he was too good to be true.

"I'm floored right now. Where are you going with this?"

"Remi. You are the finest man I've met in a long, long time. I care about you deeply. But you're not ready. You have things going on. It couldn't be clearer to me. I love, love, love how it was going, but really, this doesn't feel right." Margot could sense the protection mechanism deep inside her coming alive, forcing her to walk away before something inevitable and awful happened down the line.

"Stop it." He set his coffee down and reached out to her. "Stop."

"We can't do this. You're not here. Not totally. And I need you to be." She couldn't imagine going through more heartbreak. Maybe she wasn't ready either.

"I don't love her. I mean, I love her as in she and I spent many years together and brought our daughter into the world. But I don't love Amber like I used to. I don't love her romantically—"

"Either way, I can't be the conduit for your recovery, and it's suddenly feeling that way." He tried to interrupt, but she continued. "You can't even talk about her without tears. Look at you, Remi. You're not ready to start dating." She wasn't even sure of her own words, but she felt like some wise hidden part of her had stumbled upon a truth that would eventually tear her apart.

"Don't say it," Remi pleaded.

Their eyes searched each other's.

She could see past the brown around his pupils and into the arena of his mind. He was even sadder than before. He was looking for a lifeline.

Then tears pricked his eyes, a rising pond of sadness. "Don't. Don't say it."

"I can't be with you anymore. Maybe one day, but not now, not this year. Not while she lingers." Saying those words hurt so badly, but Margot also felt a strength, like she'd finally been able to protect herself.

"She doesn't linger. Can't a man be sad for destroying his marriage—for tearing his family apart?"

"There's nothing wrong with being sad. We all must process the past. But you have some things to work out before you start a new relationship. Whether or not you want to admit it, she does linger—"

"She doesn't—"

In a sharp stern voice, Margot said, "Remi."

"Margot, I love you. How could I possibly love her when I love you?"

He hadn't told her that before. "I need you to go find where she stands in your world. Go deal with that. I understand. I know. But us? No. Not right now."

They hugged.

Margot bit her upper lip and stifled her own breakdown. Here's one of those times you hate so much in life. When one of you in one of the few great relationships you had calls it quits. Maybe the honeymoon was over too soon, or one of you grew out of the other. Maybe one of you found someone better. Maybe the relationship had just run its course. But those times when you hug for the last time, and you both know it's the end and squeeze a little tighter and take it in. Take it in like crazy.

Margot eventually patted Remi's back and pushed him away. He called for his dog, and Margot walked them to his truck. He drove ever so slowly out of that driveway, creeping away from her.

Crashing down. And all alone again.

34

JAKE FORESTER, DON'T YOU DARE

I t could never happen this way. Not on a TV show. Not in a book. Not even in a Hallmark *Hall of Shamer*.

But it's what happened. Period. Truth is indeed stranger than fiction.

Later that day, Margot was in the dining room telling a couple of guests, "You must go have a glass or two at Anelare on the other side of the highway. They're lovely people with delicious wines and have a stunning view of the mountain," when Jake Forester walked in and said, "Look at you."

The guests Margot was talking to did what looked like a synchronized double take when they saw Jake. A couple having coffee and researching their trip turned their heads. "Is that? No. Yeah."

For Margot, when a man like Jake Forester says with a certain amount of zest, "Look at you," it stops her heart. Especially in her current state. Margot heard, "Damn, girl!"

Margot muttered, "Excuse me," to her guests and went to greet him. Her legs felt wobbly. She said, "Hey there, Jake."

"You really look good, Margot."

She raised her knuckles to her chin. "I do, don't I? How are you?"

"I'm great." He threw up a hand. "Medium happy to be alive."

Escaping the prying eyes, she led him back toward the foyer near the piano. "Medium?"

"I miss my girls."

"I bet you do. How's Carmen?"

"All of a sudden she's a different person. Completely sober. Coming home soon."

"That's great to hear." Suddenly it occurred to her. "What are you doing here, by the way?"

He stifled a George Clooney grin and threw up his hands. "I came to borrow some sugar."

"What?"

"Yeah, I'm baking with Luca and realized I was out. Thought the best baker on the mountain might have some."

"You're kidding me. What world do I live in that Jake Forester comes by my house to borrow sugar?" She recalled their brief one-time sexual encounter of a year ago during a difficult emotional time for both of them—an encounter that Carmen later knew about. Margot added, "And to think not too long ago you were looking for sugar of a different kind."

He scratched his two-day-old beard. "You make me think sweet thoughts, I guess."

"You dog." She winked.

He smiled beautifully and shook his head, then exhaled.

"Jake Forester, are you sure it's just sugar you're looking for?"

"*Now* I'm not so sure."

They both laughed.

"Hey, your wife is the one who said she likes to share. No need to feel guilty. You can flirt with me all day long."

"Well, seriously, you do look good, Margot. I miss seeing you around."

"Not bad for losing the love of my life this morning."

His face flushed with concern. "No."

"Uh, yes." She gave him a vague rundown, aware of the occasional mumble giving away her current state.

"I just realized," he said. "You're drunk, aren't you?"

"What are you talking about?"

"I smell alcohol."

"I'm not drunk. I've had a couple. A couple meaning a few. A few meaning... Okay, fine. Maybe I *am* drunk."

"Well, good for you. Day drinks can fix a lot of things."

"I have a lot of things that need fixing."

They met eyes and shared a moment. A scary one.

She raised a hand. "Well, on that note, let me retrieve your sugar. Two cups?"

"Yeah, that'll do."

Margot covered her mouth to burp as she turned in the direction of the kitchen. She smiled when she heard Jake sit at the piano bench and tinker around with some jazz chords. Her mind drifted to thoughts of Jasper.

～

WHEN MARGOT SOBERED up that afternoon back at her house, her world crumbled. The crying came in giant wails that the guests could probably hear in the inn. Her tears splattered onto Philippe and the cooking magazine she'd been reading.

Soon, Margot 2.0 completely folded, collapsing into the couch, pulling the throw over her head, hiding from it all, digressing to Margot 1.0 and then 0.5 and then 0.4 and then she held at about 0.2, just short of checking herself into the hospital. Much lower and she'd burn the place down.

Margot 0.2 needed someone to talk to. She called her best friend Erica back in Vermont. "I'm falling apart," Margot admitted.

"Oh, gosh," Erica said. "What now?"

"I hate internet dating, and I hate all men. I don't even know why I'm talking to you. You found your perfect man on *Match,* and it's all happily ever after. Easy peasy, lemon squeezy. I find my perfect man and realize he's still in love with his ex-wife!"

"No."

"Yes." Margot told Erica what had happened.

Margot and Erica never held back when speaking to each other. Today was no different. Erica asked, "Aren't you blowing things a little out of proportion? Seriously, he was just telling you about his past, which you asked about. He still sounds okay to me."

"Oh, does he, Erica? Didn't you see what happened to me in Burlington? There's no way I can go down this road any farther unless I know for sure he's not going anywhere. I can barely handle the breakup now. Imagine if we dated another six months before it happened. I'd jump off the closest bridge."

"You know I don't like you talking like that," Erica said. "Pull it together, honey. He's either right for you or he's not, but stop putting your life on the line. Stop searching for Mr. Forever and just find someone to hold for a while."

"I don't want someone to hold for a while!"

"I know," Erica said. "I know."

The two women talked for more than an hour, but Margot was still craving compassion by the time they hung up. There was only one other person she could call. Sitting up on the couch, she dialed Joan. When she picked up, Margot said, "I don't even know where you are, but I know it's late. I'm so sorry. I just need you."

"Are you okay?" Joan asked.

"No, I'm not. Remi and I broke up."

"Oh, dear."

Margot put her hand on Philippe, who was curled up on the couch next to her. "I'm just miserable." She talked for fifteen minutes straight and eventually admitted, "I just don't think I can do this."

Joan replied, "Are you kidding me? If anyone can, it's you."

"I'm caving in, Joan. I feel empty inside."

"Do something for me," Joan said. "Close your eyes."

"Right now?"

"Yes, right now. Put me on speaker, and then sit back and close your eyes."

Margot turned on the speaker and placed the phone on the coffee table. She sat back, closed her eyes, and said, "Okay, I'm here."

Joan said in the most calming voice Margot had ever heard, "Take a few breaths." After a minute or so, Joan said, "I want you to visualize yourself standing on the top of a mountain with your arms in the air. Not Red Mountain. Think Everest."

"What would I be doing on the top of Everest?"

"You've just climbed it. See yourself in cold weather gear with crampons on your feet. Picture a specific color jacket. Picture your stocking cap. You've just defeated one of the tallest mountains in the world."

Despite the doubt running through her, Margot followed Joan's instructions. Soon Margot could see herself on top of that mountain. As she pictured herself in a red jacket and white hat, the image grew more crisp. She was standing in the snow at the peak with her arms high in the air. "I got it," Margot said, noticing how much better she was feeling. Maybe it was just the distraction that was working.

"That's how I see you," Joan said. "When I think of you and your search for awakening over the past year, this is the Margot that I see."

Margot instantly burst into tears. "You're lying."

"I don't lie. Lock this image in, don't forget her. The coming days might be awful, but when it gets too hard to handle, close your eyes and find this woman standing on the mountain. That's the real Margot. She can handle anything."

Margot nodded. "I know she can."

Joan showered her with more encouragement.

After talking ten more minutes, Margot asked, "Where are you, by the way?"

"Iceland."

"I'm so sorry to wake you up."

"That's what friends are for."

The two friends chatted for a while about less painful things, and by the time they hung up, Margot felt so much better. For a moment, she tasted the strength of that woman on the mountain.

But it didn't take long for Margot to lose the connection with her inner warrior. Without a friend on the line and without Remi sitting next to her, the loneliness of her living room consumed the light Joan had shared with her. Margot came to the conclusion that getting over

Remi would take more than a few quiet moments visualizing. Maybe the woman on that mountain was the real Margot, but Everest was a long way away from Red Mountain. Maybe tomorrow she'd try to reconnect.

Margot stood and walked into the kitchen. She poured a generous glass of merlot. She moved the glass containers of flour and sugar from the open shelf to the island. She grabbed chocolate chips, a dozen eggs, and a stick of Amish butter out of the fridge. Through clenched teeth, she said, "I'm going to eat anything I want. Fuck it." She turned the oven to 350 degrees. Slipping on an apron, she returned to the container of flour, reaching in with her hands. Then she dragged her index and middle fingers across both her cheeks— the culinary war paint of her mental breakdown.

As she waited for the cookies to bake, their healing hedonistic scent filling the kitchen, she paced. Then as the cookies began to rise, she was stomping back and forth on the tile, saying, "Fuck it! Fuck it! Fuck it all!"

35

UNFORTUNATE TIMING

G rocery bags in hand, Adriana and Zack climbed the front steps of Margot's house—their new home. They'd been living there ten days, and though the sadness of Margarita's death bogged down their every breath, Adriana and Zack felt blessed to be taken care of by such a nice woman in such an amazing home. Margot had spoiled them both to no end, and it was impossible not to feel God's compassion working through her.

There was also that sense of female power the two women had found together. They had already fallen into the same monthly cycle, having linked up shortly after Adriana started working there. Today was one of those days on which ovulation had set her emotions on fire. Her mother's death tore at her like the Chupacabra tearing at flesh. And she couldn't let go of her mom's wish that she find a man. Adriana had this very real fear that her mom would return from the dead to make sure her wish was granted. Why does every woman think she needs a man to survive? Why can't people mind their own business?

So, when Adriana opened the door with Zack a few feet behind her, she was totally fired and thinking to herself, *I can do it on my own. I don't need anyone else. I don't want a man!*

There Margot was, looking like she'd gotten in a fight with a bag of flour, pumping her fist in the air and screaming obscenities.

"*Mi Dios!*" Adriana said, quickly covering her mouth in shock.

From the kitchen, Margot twisted her head in painful surprise. "Oh, my God, I'm so sorry." She set her hands on her head. "I'm...I'm losing it, Adriana. I'm just losing it. There! I said it." Margot dropped her eyes to Zack. "Honey, close your ears. And your eyes."

Mother and son entered slowly, testing the waters. Adriana smelled something sweet baking in the oven. "Maybe we should come back later?" she suggested, hovering with extreme trepidation near the entrance, by the potted plants.

Margot rushed toward them, waving her hand and saying, "Come in, come in. I forgot for a moment I have roommates. Please come in! Just ignore my breakdown."

"Don't worry about it," Adriana said, setting down her bags. "Seriously, breakups are awful."

"I think I've finally lost it, really. Like, totally. Losing. My. Mind. Right. Now." Margot looked at Zack again and whispered, "Don't ever grow up. It's so much easier when you're young."

He shyly fingered the goggles dangling from his jean pockets and said, "Okay."

Adriana asked him, "Have you ever heard Mommy go a little crazy?" He nodded eagerly, and she asked, "How many times?"

"One million probably," he said, stringing together his longest phrase of the day.

The women smiled at each other, and Adriana asked, "Really, should we come back later?"

Margot waved her off. "No! It's your home." Pretending like *all that* hadn't just happened, she put on a smile and asked with a Julia-Child-like exuberance, "Did you two have a nice day?"

∿

BOTH WOMEN TUCKED Zack in that evening. Though he was still short on words, he kept calling them back to read another story until he eventually fell asleep.

They decided to get drunk. Or Adriana decided to. Margot was already lubricated. According to her, she'd been hungover in the afternoon from her morning indulgences and went right back to the bottle for happy hour.

Sitting in the cozy chairs facing the fireplace, a small table with a bottle of white standing between them, the two women embarked on their journey.

Margot filled their glasses almost to the rim. "I put fries in the oven, and I'm going to spread Beecher's Marco Polo cheese all over them and serve them with a side of sriracha ranch. Then, if I feel like it, I'm going to follow that with a giant bowl of ice cream and a stack of coconut chocolate chip cookies on top. Don't even think of trying to be all skinny around here right now. I want to see you stuffing that perfect figure of yours with everything in my kitchen, matching me bite for bite."

"We could be a reality show, the two of us falling into rhythm together."

"Poor Zack," Margot said.

It wasn't long until they were into the second bottle of white wine and laughing and saying things they'd surely regret in the morning. Adriana felt so good! She had no idea wine had this kind of power. She didn't have a care in the world. For a while, at least.

After they'd laughed themselves into exhaustion, in what Adriana interpreted as a dangerously bold move, Margot inquired about Adriana's face. She explored the topic gently, but clearly the alcohol had given her the guts to address what Adriana knew to many was the elephant in the room. Adriana told her the same story she'd told everyone else.

Margot replied like most. She shook her head and said, "You poor thing. How unfortunate."

Adriana thanked her, her buzz turning more into dizziness with each minute. "I'd better check on Zack."

"Oh, let him be. Honey, you really need to give him some space. You're as bad as I am with Jasper."

Adriana didn't like the comment but bit her tongue. She knew she needed to give Margot some slack, considering the circumstances. She negotiated the stairs and found Zack's right leg dangling off the bed. A drunk smile came over her. How could kids sleep in such strange positions? She carefully straightened him, pulled the covers over, and turned off his nightlight. Leaving the love of her life, she worked her way back down the stairs holding on to the railing like she was descending a glacier.

Back in her chair by the fireplace, as Margot poured more wine, the comment about Zack began to fester in Adriana's mind. Margot had lost her happy buzz and was now starting to wax on about Remi, how she'd just known he was too good to be true. But Adriana was barely listening and finally found the ovaries to ask, "What did you mean, I'm as bad as you are? Earlier. You said I need to give Zack some space?"

Margot stopped mid-rant. "Oh, no big deal. Just saying you and I are helicopter parents. You sleep with him every night. You probably still wipe his butt. We need to both let our boys grow up."

"My son is six. Yours is eighteen. There's a *huge* difference."

"Whoa, sweetie. Please. I didn't mean anything by it."

"I hope not." It was the first time they'd ever clashed.

"I meant nothing by it. I'm just drunk."

"I think it's time for me to go to bed."

Margot whispered an apology as Adriana excused herself.

36

DRINK FLAMINGO. YOU'LL DIE FOREVER

The grapes swelled and sweetened as the first days of August arrived. Harvest was around the corner. The winemakers and vineyard workers were already saying goodbye to their families, already seeing purple, tasting purple. They were spending as much time as they could with family, because by the end of August, when the white grapes ripened, these men and women would go to twelve-hour workdays, seven days a week. Very soon, the reason they were on Red Mountain turning those grapes into wine would be upon them.

So it was that the grapefather of Red Mountain returned to his land. Even as the plane flew over the eastern Washington State scabland, Otis Till felt home. He felt needed again. He felt reconnected with all that he held dear.

Margot met them at baggage claim, and Joan and Margot did most of the chatting while Otis tasted the desert air of his home and prepared for his reentry into battle. He focused on what needed to be done and how in God's name he was going to prioritize it all. He trusted his guys. He trusted Brooks. But no one could run his farm like he could. There would be messes to clean up, fences to mend. There would be rows of grapes with too much or too little canopy.

Knowing Brooks, there was more bad news he'd held back. Of course, Brooks sure as hell hadn't held back the dagger that stabbed him with the disastrous news of that piece of land along the highway being purchased.

When they reached the gravel drive of Till Vineyards, they passed Henry Davidson's doublewide trailer. He and Joan both looked over at the place where the man who shot Joan had lived. The yard had been cleaned up. Otis saw the pole sticking out of the ground where Cody used to be chained. There was a *For Sale* sign out front. The Davidsons had been living there longer than Otis, but they were finally leaving and it was a good thing. Henry would be behind bars for ten more years, and the rest of his family would soon leave this place for good.

Otis glanced at Joan.

She just nodded.

Time moved on. Red Mountain was growing up, shedding some bad parts.

Of course, when Otis returned his eyes to the *For Sale* sign, he wondered what they were asking. Added that to the list. Perhaps he'd buy it if he could. But in the end, he couldn't buy everything that came up for sale. He couldn't protect every square foot, all the time. Maybe that's the one truth he'd accepted in the past few days of worry. He had to trust that this mountain would take care of itself.

Then he heard barking and saw his big white mammoth of a dog running up the hill. Jonathan was stopped by the fence below the house but barked and jumped relentlessly.

"Will you let me out?" Otis asked Margot.

She slowed the Volvo to a stop and he climbed out, his knees popping and his back aching. He hadn't exercised since they'd left. He didn't do gyms. The farm was his gym, and he'd been gone a long time.

"Hey, ol' boy," he said, walking toward the dog he often called the Great White Beast.

Jonathan jumped higher and barked louder, pushing at the fence, desperate to reconnect with his master. Otis slipped through the gate, and Jonathan jumped on him, dusty paws to his shoulders and slobbery licks to his face.

"I missed you too, chap. It's been way too long." He took a knee before Jonathan toppled him. After enduring the onslaught, Otis rubbed his face. "Did you hold down the fort? I sure missed the hell out of you."

After their conversation, Otis stood and eyed the property. A couple hundred yards down the slope, Otis saw his Southdown sheep working a section of tall grass. They were confined by a five-foot-tall portable netting charged by a nearby solar energizer. "Hey down there!" he yelled. "I'll be to you soon enough."

He made his way to the closest row of vines; Jonathan followed. It was the cabernet sauvignon planted seven years ago. The clusters looked good. Healthy, but not too tight. Too tight meant mildew. He plucked one of the grapes and stuck it in his mouth. The beauty of the grape's flavor nearly made him cry.

The red grapes were still a couple of months out, so the strong acid made his mouth pucker. But the complexity and power, that Red Mountain signature, was already there. He could pick these particular grapes out of a long lineup.

Otis spat the pomace—also known as the leftovers—to the ground, knelt, and lowered his face. He kissed the dusty soil and said, "I'm home."

Rising, he thought *now* was as good a time as any to fulfill his promise to Aunt Morgan. He walked down to the house and found the two women unloading the car. He said, "It's time to spread the last of Morgan's ashes. Margot, would you like to join us?"

"I'd be honored," she replied.

Otis retrieved the last bag of ashes from his office. They meandered up the hill, Joan wielding her cane with more and more strength. Otis was proud to see his vines looking so healthy and well taken care of. He led them to the row where Morgan had caught Otis howling a year before. He laughed to himself—he would never forget that moment. Morgan had died right after finishing a painting depicting that exact scene. Now anyone entering his living room could see what she saw that night, Otis, stark naked, singing with the wild dogs.

"She liked this spot," he said. "She'd appreciate the memory."

They stood in a triangle, and Otis held out the bag. "All right, you crazy woman. You're now spread across this whole world. With any luck and a little water, maybe you'll start sprouting again. I wouldn't put it past you." He brought the bag to his chest and pressed it against his heart. "We love you, Morgan. Don't be a stranger."

Otis opened the bag and dumped the ashes. He didn't want to say it out loud, but he felt like he'd let Morgan down in a way. He should have enjoyed the trip more. He should have been able to let go of the mountain, of all the worry. All Otis could do now was keep trying and growing. Knowing Morgan, one way or another, she'd find ways to keep reminding Otis he was indeed a work in progress.

The ashes drifted and settled, and the memory of her was as strong as ever. He removed his tweed cap and said, "Until we see each other on the other side." Joan and Margot each said their piece, and they all returned to the house with wet eyes.

As Margot left, Brooks pulled up on his Triumph motorcycle. A round of hugs ensued, and Brooks said, "I have really bad news."

"That's all you have lately." Otis already knew something was coming. Like someone whose knees hurt when the rains came, he'd felt a dark storm brewing. He said, "Drink Flamingo?"

Brooks nodded. "The press release just came out on *Wine Business*. They're coming to Red Mountain."

What do you do when it all comes crashing down?

37

SHE'S KIND OF INTO HIM

After delivering the bad news to Otis, Brooks left in the Lacoda work truck to go see Adriana. It turned out he pulled onto Sunset Road at the most perfectly wrong time. This small mountain almost never failed to put you right where you didn't want to be. Abby was passing along in her SUV. He waved but kept going.

She stopped and held her hand out the window, flashing her brake lights. He saw her do this in the rearview mirror and felt his right foot stutter between the gas and brakes. *Stop or go. Stop or go. Pretend I don't see, or...?*

He stopped and put his truck in reverse. Sunset Road was quiet today, and as long as he didn't hit a tractor, he was safe. He reversed almost one-hundred feet and pulled onto the shoulder. The ex-lovers met in between their vehicles. Their sunglasses hid their eyes.

"Shay told you." She wasn't asking.

"Yep. Congratulations."

"Do you mean that?"

"Shit, Abby. What do you want me to say? I'm ecstatic for you guys. Everybody deserves love."

"Please help me understand how you could possibly care?"

"What is that supposed to mean? Of course I care. I'm happy for you. I mean, I'm trying to be happy for you. Did you think I'd process the news with glee? Hooray, my ex-fiancé is getting along well with my brother!"

"I figured you and I had established our place. You either want me or you don't. And you don't."

"That doesn't change the fact that less than a year ago we were on our way to spending the rest of our lives together." He laughed. "I mean, come on. Carmen? And now Shay? You're working your way through this mountain, aren't you?"

"Don't be a jerk."

He dropped his chin. "Am I wrong?"

"I know how it sounds. I can imagine how it feels. But what do you want me to do? Sit around and cry for the rest of my life? Or what? You want me to leave this place? You told me not to."

He kicked the dirt and waved toward a passing car. "No, I don't want you to leave."

She pulled off her designer shades, no doubt hand-me-downs from Carmen. "Shay's a good guy, Brooks. He's nice to me. He likes me. I'm happy."

He gathered a handful of his own hair and tugged. "I know."

They both crossed their arms at the same time and stared into each other's eyes for a while. A tractor kicked on in the distance. A dog barked. They kept staring.

Finally, Brooks said, "Where's Luca today?"

She put her shades back on. "Summer camp."

"I have a kid I'd like him to meet. Have you met Adriana yet? The woman working for Margot?"

"The one with the vibrator?"

"That's the one." They were both relieved to be on another topic. "She just lost her mom, and she and her six-year-old boy have moved in with Margot. He's going through a hard time. I was thinking we could get him and Luca together sometime."

"Yeah, of course. Anytime." Abby changed her tone. "Are we going to get through this, Brooks?"

"One way or another." Brooks scratched his head. "I'll see you around, all right?"

She nodded, and they both attempted smiles.

Back in his truck, he watched her pull away. "What am I supposed to do!?" he yelled. "I don't know!" He couldn't ignore the rage inside. Angry at Abby for even considering a connection with Shay. And Shay for daring to date his ex-fiancé. Brooks felt like Abby wasn't allowed to simply move on and fall in love. Especially not with his brother. No, Abby wasn't done paying for her sins.

Brooks tried to shake off the encounter as he drove the rest of the way to Épiphanie. Stepping into the inn amid the chamber music and shimmering chandeliers and candles, Brooks mentally prepared himself to see Adriana. He'd bought a gift for Zack the day before, so he did have an excuse to get him through the door.

Brooks didn't see anyone around but heard a vacuum cleaner above and figured Adriana might be running it. He climbed the stairs and found Zack playing with a couple of toy cars in the hallway. He knelt next to him and rubbed his head. "What kind of cars do you have there? One looks like a Jeep."

Zack looked up at him. And then back down.

"I used to have Hot Wheels growing up," Brooks said. "Do they still make those? My favorite one was a Camaro. Red with white stripes. You should have seen how fast it would roll. All the girls would turn their heads."

Zack glanced at him and then returned to the cars, pushing them back and forth along the floor, mouthing engine sounds.

Brooks rubbed his head again. "Your mom in there cleaning?" He looked toward the open door of a guest room.

Zack didn't respond.

"Hey, I got you something. You might already have one, but I remember thinking when I reached your age it was time to start carrying around some money." Brooks drew a wallet out of his pocket. It was blue and had one of the new *Star Wars* characters on it. "I'm assuming you like *Star Wars*."

"For me?"

"Oh, now you're talking? Yeah, it's for you."

Zack snatched the wallet and opened it up.

"I just so happened to have met two world travelers who gave me some foreign currency. Money, I mean. I put it all in there for you."

"Really?" Zack pulled out the wad of cash.

Brooks felt the joy of lifting this young kid up out of his desolate mood as he pointed. "That's a dollar. And that's a euro. I don't know what that one is, but I bet it's Vietnamese. Looks Asian. See that guy with the long beard? Is he Irish or Asian?"

"Um, Asian?"

"Yeah, I think so. That must be a Vietnamese dong."

Zack smiled. "Dong?"

"Not that kind of dong. You're just like me. Nothing funnier than farts and dongs."

Zack let out a laugh.

"Oh, boy. Your mom's going to kill me. A dong is what the Vietnamese call their money. Please don't get me in trouble."

Adriana came out of the room to find them smiling at each other.

Zack held up his wad of cash and the wallet. "He gave me a wallet and all this money."

"He did?" Adriana twisted her mouth and looked at Brooks.

"I hope that's okay. Thought he'd like it. My friend Otis just returned from traveling, and I told him I knew someone who could put that money to good use."

"Yes, it's okay. I just want to know why Zack is so talkative when you're around." She looked at her son. "Zack?"

Zack shrugged as he explored the wallet.

"Hey, I talked to Abby, who takes care of Luca. Remember I told you about him? He's a little bit older than you. He's nine. If your mom approves, Abby said you could come over and hang sometime."

Zack nodded as Brooks looked back at Adriana for permission.

"He can do that sometime. Not today, but sometime."

Leaving Zack to his wallet, Brooks and Adriana walked down the hall, past a series of photographs featuring animals from the sanctuary that decorated the walls. "He's a really great kid. Is he talking more?"

"Not much, but a little."

"And how are you?" he asked. "I guess that's not much of a question. Are you getting by?"

"Yeah. It's hard." She motioned to her son. "Even harder on him."

"Well, let's get Zack together with Luca. I really think they'd like each other."

"Maybe. I don't like leaving him right now. He's in a lot of pain."

"Ball's in your court. I don't want to get in the way. Can I ask you something else?"

She looked at him like she already knew exactly where he was going.

Now or never, Brooks. "Will you go out with me? I don't think I'm going to stop asking until you say yes."

She looked down and turned away.

He'd never met a woman who played her cards so close to her chest. He waited. He waited like he was on a boat waiting for the water to rise in the locks. "Your poker face is the best in the business. Are you a gambler?"

"Do you talk a lot when you're nervous?"

His mouth opened. "Uh. Ah." Finally, he spat out, "I am indeed nervous. And you're taking advantage of me right now. You're torturing me."

She smiled in total enjoyment.

"Okay, beyond waterboarding. They should send you down to Guantanamo. A few minutes with you, and even the most hardened of terrorists would tell their secrets."

"If you'll stop talking for a minute and let me speak."

Brooks made a motion of zipping his mouth.

Adriana opened hers and then closed it again. She smiled, then opened and closed her mouth again.

He dropped his shoulders, playing the victim. He had a feeling he finally had her. "C'mon."

Suddenly her grin faded, and she put a hand on her cheek,

covering her scars. "You don't want to go out with me. You don't even know me."

"How am I going to get to know you if you won't give me the time of day?"

"You can't just get on my son's good side and then expect me to go out with you. That's not fair."

"I like your son. I didn't bring him that wallet to—"

"It's fine. I'm giving you a hard time. Yes, I'd like to go out with you, but I don't have a babysitter."

"Bring Zack. Let's go bowling. All three of us. Tomorrow night."

As she nodded, he asked, "You know what they say is the most important thing about making a sale?"

"What's that?"

"Know when to shut up. I'm shutting up now. Be back at seven, tomorrow night. Goodbye."

Before she could respond, he was high-fiving Zack and descending the stairs. A rejuvenating smile forced its way to the surface. He felt something in his heart that hadn't stirred in a while. Maybe there *was* someone out there in this world meant for him.

38

SINGLE MOM, SING IT

L ater, in her bedroom, Adriana dug her toes into the oriental rug as she stood looking at herself in the mirror on the door. Mariah Carey sang "Always Be My Baby" from her phone speaker sitting on the French chest of drawers. She could hear Zack humming in the bathtub.

The scars weren't getting any prettier. Her mother and a few others had encouraged her to continue with more surgeries, but Adriana didn't want to end up looking like Michael Jackson. What she'd later learned about herself was that her scars protected her. She could focus on raising Zack without any distractions.

What did Brooks even see in her, anyway? She wondered what was in it for him. Even if he was sincerely interested, why? And was she ready to go down this road? She couldn't imagine showering and shaving and trying on outfits. Doing herself up like the days back in Los Angeles. If you didn't count her ex, she hadn't been on a date in a decade. It made her pulse pound, but she wasn't sure that was a good thing. She was nervous, yes, but not like she had flutters of excitement. She was nervous because she knew how much pain a new relationship could bring. Not only to her but to her son. She couldn't bear to let Zack suffer because of her loneliness.

Putting on a robe, she sat on the bed and listened to Mariah sing. She collapsed backward into her impossibly comfy bed—the down duvet, the cloudlike mattress—and closed her eyes, escaping. Those precious moments when Zack was safe and close by and she could just let go. Mariah was always there for her. Oh, what a world it was for a single mother.

"Moooooommmmm!" Zack screamed, and she could hear water splashing onto the tile floor, like he might be climbing out.

"Yes, my love," she said, speaking over Mariah.

"I'm done!" he yelled.

And there it was. A few peaceful moments with Mariah and now back to her life's work. She poked her head into the bathroom, and Zack looked at her through his goggles, bubbles dripping down his arms and chest.

"Mom, d'ya know Luca? The kid Brooks talked about?"

"Yes, I do." She didn't want to talk about this right now.

"Can I go hang out with him?"

"I think so. Sometime soon."

"Like tomorrow?"

"Honey, I want to meet his family first. These things take time."

He dropped his head. "I'll never have any friends."

Adriana felt his sadness in her chest. "*Mi amor*, there are things you can't understand. We're finding our place right now. I'm still sad about Tata. Let me process losing my mom. I don't know how long we're going to be here. I don't know anything right now."

"I want to stay here forever."

"I know you do. Give me a few days to work things out. Let me work on a playdate, okay?"

If she could only explain why she was so protective. Maybe when he was older. For now, she wanted him to live in this bubble while he was young. He didn't need to know what a bad man his dad was. She wanted him to bathe in the beauty of this world before he saw the potential of drowning in the ugliness of it.

39

PUT YOUR HAIR UP

For Margot, the three weeks after Remi were a slow burn toward something all too familiar. When her ex had cheated so publicly and destroyed her marriage and her life, she'd had a complete meltdown. Then there was Ron and now Remi. She was becoming a professional at dealing with heartache. This time, she was actually aware of herself and how the days had unfolded. In other words, she'd watched it all go down like a curious spectator.

She could see herself lying in bed, watching her sappy stories with flowing tears, spooning heaps of pistachio gelato into her mouth, her waistline stretching by the minute. She could see the thoughts of hopelessness running around her mind, *you're not getting any younger* echoing incessantly. Margot could see she was overworking. She could see that she was a long way from being in the moment. Shay would ask her a question about the sanctuary, and she'd look off into space. He'd ask again, and she'd say, "Huh?" Same thing with Adriana and Zack. She'd tell them goodbye without even looking up, not even realizing they were gone until a long time afterward.

Here was the stupid part. Some people got depressed and weren't able to eat. Oh, not Margot. She ate her feelings. When she was down and out, the first thing to go was her discipline. The little voice that often chirped healthy advice from her shoulder would take a vacation, and she'd succumb to temptation without any reservations.

But! Over the past year, she'd learned to tame her cravings. To accept it as a good feeling. A feeling of being healthier. She'd learned to focus on eating less, eating only what her body needed. She'd learned that just because something looked delicious didn't mean she needed to stick it in her mouth. She'd learned that some foods were a gateway drug, and she just had to say no. The Nancy Reagan diet, she called it.

Fries, for example. She couldn't have just one. If she opened the door to a French fry, she guaranteed herself a feeding that wouldn't stop until every last fry within a mile had been consumed. Same with gelato. Same with cupcakes. Especially mini-cupcakes, which she had mastered in the kitchen. Doughnuts. Especially mini-donuts, which she had also mastered. Something about the minis of deserts was so much more appealing. And you could eat more of them, which of course destroyed the point.

Since her fall, she'd started on that list of weaknesses and couldn't stop. In fact, if something on the list came to mind, she said, "Fuck it." If *you're not getting any younger* was the chant from the inner voice, *fuck it* was the motto.

She either worked her face off, totally distracting herself. Or, she indulged in anything she could think of to numb it all. Drink. Eat. Work. Bathe. Drink. Eat. Sleep. Drink. Eat. Bathe. Drink. Eat. And every once in a while, stalk Remi's ex on social media.

Right now, hours after driving Joan and Otis home, she witnessed herself lying in the tub drinking a dirty martini out of a plastic cup. Merlot didn't cut it anymore. Her iPad on the counter played a *Summer Nights* movie on Hallmark. The remnants of a slice of cake sat on a plate next to the sink like the leftovers of battle. Five towels lay bunched up in the corner. The trashcan overflowed with wadded up toilet paper. A half-smoked joint lay on the soap shelf. Not having smoked in a long time, her attempt at rolling had resulted in a joint that would indeed smoke, but only after twenty minutes of trying to light it. In the end, she'd gotten high from the rising smoke and not the poorly rolled joint.

After a long soak, she dried off and stepped on the scale. The digital number that appeared took her breath away. *How is this even possible?* As her stomach twisted in disgust, she closed her eyes and blew out a slow breath. "That's it," she muttered, clenching her teeth. She picked up the scale, cranked open the window that overlooked her garden, and without another thought, tossed the scale into the air and watched it fall. The scale smacked the ground and broke into pieces, bringing her a small amount of satisfaction.

Margot found Adriana and Zack cuddled up with Philippe watching a cartoon in the living room. Having just taken a bath himself, Zack wore Pokémon pajamas and his wet hair was combed back. The umpteen bouquets of flowers Remi had sent in the past weeks decorated the tall, skinny glass table by the window and the floor around it. Margot hadn't found the courage to throw them away yet.

"Hi, guys," Margot said, knowing she'd turned into the worst of roommates.

"We can turn something adult-friendly on if you want," Adriana said. "We don't want to take your TV."

Margot shook her head. "It's perfectly okay. I'm going back upstairs."

Adriana left Zack on the couch and approached cautiously as Margot made herself another martini. "Is there anything I can do for you? I hate watching you go through this."

Margot apologized for the fifth time today and then said, "I can't imagine how horrible I am to live with."

Adriana crossed her arms, coming into the kitchen. "I've been in your position. I understand. I just wish there were something I could do."

"I need a little more time."

"Has he texted you again?"

"Not today. I think he's finally starting to get the message."

As all good friends do, Joan soon knocked on the door and

ambled in with her cane, arriving exactly when Margot needed her most.

Margot tried on a smile and grasped blindly for some enthusiasm, straightening her robe. "What are you doing here? You're supposed to be sleeping! Aren't you jet-lagged?"

Joan reached out for a hug.

After their embrace, Margot said, "You're not supposed to see me like this."

"That's exactly why I'm not sleeping," Joan said. "Oh, darling. This guy has really torn your heart out, hasn't he?"

After saying hello, Adriana returned to the couch with Zack, and Margot and Joan moved into the kitchen.

Suddenly, weeks of pain erupted from inside Margot, and she collapsed into Joan's arms. "I needed you."

Joan patted her. "I'm here."

"But you have your own problems."

"Of course I do." Joan let go of her. "And maybe I need you to help me!"

"I'm here for you," Margot promised. "Not that that's saying much."

Joan said, "A friend of mine emailed me a picture of a bumper sticker yesterday. I think it might be perfect for us. *Put your hair up in a bun, drink some coffee, and handle it.*"

Margot smiled. "That's funny."

"I think it's time we both do just that."

"Should I put the water on? It's late to have coffee."

"How about we have tea, and tomorrow we'll have coffee."

Margot wiped her eyes. "Yes, let's do that."

"Good. You and I are going to take the world by the tail. Let's go climb our Everest."

That's what you say when you've hit the bottom, but do you really know when you've hit the bottom?

40

WTFLAMINGO!

Otis had enjoyed strolling around in flip-flops and swim trunks in the beach towns, and he adored St. George's Basilica in Prague, and the little wine bar they'd found in Cape Town, and the Guinness in Dublin—despite the circumstances—but it felt good to be back on the farm in his Carhartt pants and Red Wing work boots. It felt good to be sweaty, dirty, and achy.

After fixing a broken pipe in his cab vineyard, Otis stepped into the cold of the cellar to taste his lone barrel of wine from last harvest.

A few days before shooting Joan, Henry Davidson had broken into the cellar and emptied all of Otis's wine. This Minnesota oak barrel was all he had left. It was a blend of everything red he grew. Sangiovese, syrah, cabernet sauvignon, merlot, cabernet franc. He and his guys had collected the last bits of the wine that hadn't been dumped onto the concrete floor and flowed down the drain. Of course, people wrote every day begging for a bottle. They called it the "Lost Vintage" in the trade publications. Word of his loss of wine had spread throughout the wine world, and he'd been hearing for months from winemakers expressing their sympathy. He'd also heard from the people in his wine club and collectors around the world.

They wanted that wine!

He stuck his wine thief into the barrel and drew out a small amount, transferring it to a glass. He swirled the vibrant red, then jammed his nose in. He smiled, and his laugh echoed in the dark cellar. What a wine it was! A field blend that captured a year he'd never forget. One of the finest harvests of his life. Hot, yes, but those cool nights Washington State was known for had come to the rescue.

For Otis, the vintage in his glass was the year he'd met Joan. The year he finally could move on from his beloved Rebecca. He could smell Rainier cherries and mint. He could smell cigars. Not cigars in a humidor. He smelled fresh leaves in a cigar factory. And he also picked up these gorgeous smoky and gamey qualities that delivered the savory essence ever-present in Red Mountain wines.

He tasted the wine. Didn't even think of spitting. He couldn't ever spit this wine. It meant too much. There was too little. A round, velvety structure gave way to an angular acidity that wet his mouth and begged for another sip. He obeyed and enjoyed the wine as it hit his palate again, exploding with the flavors of Red Mountain, the wild tertiary notes coming alive. He shook his head with pride as he finished the glass.

He hadn't slept much since they'd arrived home yesterday. It wasn't *exactly* because of this Drink Flamingo thing. Well, it mostly was, but not because he was worried. The feeling that stole his sleep was a dire need to grow better grapes, to make better wine.

Of course, when he thought *better*, he meant *truer*. He didn't believe in better wines. Only wines truer to the *terroir*. And *terroir* had become such an all-encompassing word for him. Where the French might sum it up as slope, climate, and soil, he included anything and everything that could impact the wine. Even if the impact was passive or metaphorical.

He believed that people had a great deal to do with the wines they farmed. If you hire and work with good people, then the wines become truer. He thought of Esteban and Chaco and Brooks and Eli. He was proud their footsteps graced his vineyards.

Lately, because of Joan, Otis had started to sneak thoughts of how spirituality affected the wine. He thought about the energy force.

How could he make that force thrive? What else could he do to bring out the depths of Red Mountain?

He left the cellar with a mild mid-morning wine buzz and breathed in the air as he gazed up to the top of the mountain. "I missed you."

Walking through a vineyard row back to the house, he reached both arms out and dragged his fingers along the canopy and grapes. He felt a deep sense of belonging.

Back home. To be back home.

He found Joan practicing yoga on the back deck, immediately noticing the strength she'd found. "You look flexible today," he said, reaching down and kissing her as she came up from a downward dog.

"I feel good," she said. "You look happy, my dear. I take it the mountain has welcomed you back with open arms."

"Oh, you're so right."

She smiled. "Will you join me? Grab your mat."

"I already did my rounds before you woke up."

"Oh, you already practiced yoga today?"

"Around four this morning. Did a few downward dogs, upward cats, upside down chickens."

"You'd be surprised what a practice would do for you. I didn't buy you that mat so it would stay rolled up in the closet."

"One day, my dear. One day." *When hell freezes over,* he thought sinisterly.

Back inside, he parked at the kitchen table and opened up his laptop to address the business side of wine. The emails and texts flooded in. There was a common theme among the messages as he scanned the most recent.

Drink Flamingo had given its first interview.

He fumbled to click the link from *Wine Business*, the main news feed of the wine trade, and pressed play on the video interview. For the next ten minutes, Harry Bellflour, one of the owners of Drink Flamingo, described his and his partners' plans for Red Mountain. He went from sitting straight up to slumping back in his chair as this son of a bitch talked about their plans to destroy everything Otis had put into this place.

Drink Flamingo wasn't only building a winery on that optimum plateau on the highway, they were making it a destination. They planned to build a compound that would draw people from all around the Pacific Northwest and even farther. They were going to build a water park! Several flamingo-shaped swimming pools. A lazy river. A flamingo-themed motel. And if you didn't want to stay in the motel, there would be RV hookups. This Harry Bellflour didn't even talk about the vines and wines for the first five minutes. All he talked about was this glorified shithole of a tourist attraction. He said they'd have a petting zoo and an arcade and a fast food burger joint. They'd have a carousel and other rides. "A real family destination," this pompous ass said.

When Bellflour *finally* reached the topic of wine, he said, "We want to make Red Mountain wines accessible. We're going to put 'em in a box just like we do down in Lodi. It will be our first premium offering." He ended the interview by offering one of their catchy slogans. "Drink Flamingo. It's what your beak seeks."

Otis was fuming by the time Joan walked in balancing on her cane.

"What are you doing, honey?" A light sheen of sweat painted her face.

"They've done it. They've figured out how to ruin this mountain."

"Who has done what?"

He told her about the interview.

She moved closer to him, leaning on her cane. "You're *letting* them win."

"They've won. There's no *letting* them do anything." He blew out all his air and dropped his head. "After everything we've done to protect this place, all gone. Just like that."

She set her hand on his shoulder. "They'll never win."

Otis felt like crying. He patted her hand and stood. "I'm going for a walk. Don't worry, I just need to blow off some steam."

Joan smiled and said, "I understand."

With every step, he grew more enraged. How could this be happening? He looked out over his vineyard and beyond, thinking how majestic of a place he'd discovered. He thought of how the one thing that had never been victim to his bad luck was Red Mountain itself. Until now.

He aimlessly stumbled down the hill, and Jonathan came running. "They're coming for us, Jonathan. These Drink Flamingo flakes are coming for Red Mountain."

The sheep farther down offered a collective *bah*. Chaco had moved them the day before, and the long white electrified ribbons marking the boundaries held the animals in a tight square of barely touched tall grass. Plenty of food to eat for more than a week.

The fury left him dazed, and Otis almost lost his footing before finally reaching the sheep. He didn't bother turning off the energizer. He touched the white ribbon. The shock jolted him awake as he hollered up into the air. He grabbed the fence again, with both hands this time, and felt the power of 5000 volts surging through him.

With his teeth chattering and body jittering, he looked up at the sky and started howling. "*Ahhhwooo! Ahhhwooo!*"

The sheep watched from nearby, chewing on their cud. Jonathan sat on his haunches, his tongue dangling, spanking the air, and the poor animals had to be wondering what the hell was going on with their fearless leader.

41

BOWLING FOR LOVE AND OTHER THINGS

Brooks and Remi sat outside Remi's RV in folding chairs, talking bikes and watching the river run. Steely Dan's *Pretzel Logic* played from a speaker on the table. Even though Brooks lived right down the road, he still found himself in awe of the diversity of Red Mountain. So strange to drive down in elevation from the wine-growing area to the perimeter, where you left the treeless desert and dropped into a lusher landscape full of richer soil with tall healthy nut trees, and the wide river with its contribution of humidity, and to see all the birds. At Lacoda there were magpies, chukar, red-winged blackbirds, hawks, and maybe an occasional eagle, but down here, ducks and geese and even seabirds circled the water. A whole other world. He wondered which varieties of grapes might do well in this area. Something more like grenache or gamay. Maybe vermentino or ribolla gialla.

"So you finally got your date," Remi said to Brooks. "Are you nervous?" Henri sat on his master's lap snoring, Remi stroking him like a villain in a Bond movie.

Brooks eyed the geese along the water's edge. "Yeah, I'm nervous."

"That's a good thing. Means you like her."

"I do. I'm just getting to know her, but something about her moves me. She's spicy. So spicy, man. A little guarded too, but I think that will go away. Maybe she had some bad things go down in the past."

"Don't we all have a past chasing us? Like a dog after a cat. Right, Henri?"

"No doubt. How's your love life?"

Remi smiled the smile of a sad man, then told him the details.

A few months ago, Shay might have told Brooks the latest about Margot's life, but they weren't talking at the moment. Even though Shay still lived with him—spending some nights there—they'd been avoiding each other as best they could for more than a month.

Remi squashed the smile. "I'm broken. I haven't given up, but I'm broken, brother. Maybe she's right. I'm still carrying some baggage. But not like she thinks. I don't love my ex, and I don't want her back. I just want my daughter back. Thinking about my ex just makes that worse. Doesn't make me want her back."

"Did you tell Margot that?"

"We're not talking at all." He continued to stroke Henri.

"Don't give up. That's what you told me."

"Yeah, I know. I'm not giving up. Not yet. I just want some time with her, but I'm borderline stalking her. I've sent her flowers and chocolate every other day."

Brooks smiled. "Yeah, maybe you need to back off. That's a little aggressive. You still have to play the game, you know?"

"At my age, I don't know how much game I have left."

"Be patient. That's all the game you need." Steely Dan switched to Hall and Oates as Remi said, "She has a birthday coming up in three weeks. I was thinking about doing something big for her. Even if she doesn't want me back, she deserves a party. I was thinking I could fly Jasper home. He and Jake could play a few tunes. I don't know. She's such a good woman. I feel like she's always doing stuff for other people...and all the animals. Somebody needs to do something special for her."

Brooks sat back, legs crossed. He was still shocked by how different the plant and animal life were down here. If he turned and looked back up over Demoss Road toward the top of Red

Mountain, he could see the vineyards begin. He could see the lush landscape turn to the arid brown; the only green came from the canopies of grape leaves. Maybe a coastal Italian varieties would grow well here.

"I haven't met Jake. You think you could talk to him about this birthday thing?"

"Yeah. I'm sure he'd be in if you can get Jasper back home."

After exhausting more chat about bikes, women, and farming, Brooks excused himself. "I need to get cleaned up."

"Good luck tonight," Remi said.

The two men shook hands, and Brooks went home to take a shower.

When Brooks arrived at Margot's house, he heard Adriana yelling at Zack through the door, "It's time to go! Where are your shoes?"

When she finally opened the door, his mouth fell open. He'd never seen her wearing anything other than her housekeeper uniform. Tonight, she was wearing dark jeans and a revealing lacey top. Gold hoops hung from her ears and she'd curled her hair.

"You look great," he said, a little afraid of how she'd handle compliments and almost thinking she might hit him.

"Thank you. We're having a little trouble getting dressed today." She twisted her head. "We're waiting, Zack."

"Coming!"

On the drive, Brooks's nerves kicked into full gear. If Zack—his goggles strapped tightly around his eyes—hadn't been in the back-seat laughing and asking questions and talking, that cab would have been dead silent.

Brooks couldn't tell what Adriana was thinking. She was quiet, but he thought that maybe she was often a little quiet. He had a para-lyzing fear that if he attempted to make conversation, his voice would crack. Or he might give away his nerves. Or he might say something so utterly stupid that she would just ask him to turn around and take them back home. What could he say that was interesting enough to pierce the silence?

He focused on Zack.

The boy said, "This is a super rad truck. I'm going to buy an even bigger one when I'm older. Have you seen those monster trucks?"

"Of course I have."

"Yeah, I want to go to the Monster Jam. You can see all the trucks in Seattle in the arena. Mom says she'll take me someday."

Adriana whispered, "You really have a way with him."

"You know why? Because the inner me is about seven years old. Like Tom Hanks in *Big*."

"So this is more of a play date than a date."

"That's—no. Not fair." Of course he knew she was joking. He loved this woman's fire.

As they entered Atomic Bowl in Richland, a place that also hosted a comedy club and gambling, Brooks asked, "How many times have you been bowling, Zack?"

The boy took in the sights, the video games flashing their lights, popcorn popping behind the glass, the sound of balls striking pins. "My mom takes me sometimes."

Brooks shook his head. "The first time I bowled was three years ago, believe it or not."

It didn't take them long to claim their balls and find a lane, each of them wearing the ridiculous shoes that can instantly humble even the most egotistical ass. Bad disco played in sync with the fake crystal balls turning on the ceiling.

Brooks entered their names on the computer, but he didn't enter their real names. And he didn't bother telling Adriana or Zack until they noticed them on the large screen above their heads.

"Zack Attack!" the boy yelled, cracking up. "I like that."

"I thought you would. How about your mom's name?"

Adriana placed her hands on her hips as she read it out loud. "*Mujer Mysteriosa*. Really?"

"What does that mean, Mom?"

"It means a woman with secrets." She winked at him.

"What secrets do you have, Mom?"

"If I told you, I wouldn't be mysterious, would I?"

Adriana looked back at the screen. "And you're just Brooks."

"Yeah, I'm just Brooks."

She wagged her finger at him. "I don't think I'm the only one with secrets."

"Who's first?" Zack asked.

"You are, champ!" Brooks said. "Can I give you any pointers?"

The boy stuck his fingers into the holes and lifted the ball into the air. "I've been bowling longer than you have."

Adriana burst into laughter.

"Oh, snap," Brooks said. "In boxing, they call that witty retort a knock-out punch." He rubbed Zack's head. "I'm down for the count."

With a great smile, Zack approached the lane and sent the ball rolling towards the pins.

As more and more pins fell, Adriana opened up, and Brooks felt optimistic. Each time Zack took his turn, Brooks and Adriana tested the waters of their relationship, feeling things out, learning little bits and pieces about each other. At times, he thought she might be interested. Other times, he worried she'd gone out with him out of some sense of duty.

After the first game, Brooks bought them Cokes and nachos— with extra jalapeños for Zack. While Zack was taking a turn, Adriana snatched a nacho out of Brook's hand.

"How dare you," he said. "I will defend my chip to the death."

She met his eyes, stuck the chip in her mouth, and began to chew. Slowly. Deliberately.

Damn it, he liked this feeling. He liked her.

He went for another chip, and she stole that one too. She ate faster this time.

"Who do you think you are?" he asked.

She lowered her chin and gave him an eyeful of attitude. Her Latino spiciness blew his hair back.

He grabbed the container of nachos and made a dash for it, settling on the opposite section of circular seating. As she chased after him, he wrapped his arm around her and their cheeks brushed. For a moment he saw something come alive inside of her, and he felt like she liked him, but as fast as the push of a button, she stiffened and retreated. He wanted more of that coming alive, but it was gone. Then Zack busted in between them and stole the nachos, and the tension dissipated.

When Brooks dropped them off, he hoped so badly they could do it again.

42

THE DAY OF THE DEAD

As they entered Margot's house, Adriana said to Zack, "You have to brush your teeth, honey. Every single night. Why do we still argue about this?"

"I don't like it."

"Nobody does, but it's much better than your teeth falling out. Please, Zack. Just trust me."

"Yes, Mommy," he said, dropping his head.

She put her hand on his shoulder. "That's better."

Margot was sitting at the dining room table flipping through a cookbook. She stopped and turned her head. "How was it?"

"Fun!" Zack said. "I beat everybody!"

Margot clapped her hands. "I'm not surprised."

Zack went upstairs to get ready for bed, and Adriana walked into the kitchen to get them two glasses of water.

Margot closed her cookbook and asked, "And how was Brooks?"

"We had fun."

"Just fun?"

Adriana reached into the cabinet for the glasses. "I don't know, it was good."

Margot left the table and approached the counter. "Look at you. Are you in love?"

Adriana rolled her eyes and set the glasses on the counter. Looking at Margot, she said, "No."

Margot dipped her chin. "You have feelings for him, that's for sure."

Adriana covered her face and turned away.

"Don't you?" Margot said.

"Maybe." Adriana felt like she was being cornered and turned further away.

"Okay, okay," Margot said. "I'll leave you alone." Margot returned to the table, and Adriana resumed her task.

Waters in hand, Adriana bid Margot goodnight and climbed the stairs. In bed, she read Zack two books, and he eventually closed his eyes and drifted off. Adriana wasn't too far behind.

A nightmare ripped her from her rest. Even as she jumped out of bed with a scream that she feared might wake Zack, her eyes wide open and sweat soaking her Lakers T-shirt, she could still see Michael raising his hand, threatening to strike. She hadn't dreamed about him in a long time, but his impending hearing was dredging up old emotions. For most of the early morning, she lay on her back, staring at the ceiling and listening to a lone owl coo outside, wishing away her ex-husband's memory.

Her wandering mind eventually came to Brooks. She didn't know what to do about him. She didn't know how he fit into the picture. Was he really a good thing for Zack? Was he a good thing for her?

It was obvious Brooks had brought something good out in her son, but what if she peeled back his layers and found something off? Let's be honest, what if he was just looking for a tumble in the sack?

"Mommy," Zack said.

"Hey, honey," she said, touching his head. "Go back to sleep. It's only four o'clock."

"I was thinking about Tata."

"Oh, baby. I think about her a lot too."

"I miss her so much," he said in a voice younger than his years.

Adriana pulled him into her arms. "Me too."

"Will she really come back on the Day of the Dead?"

"Of course she will. But we'll have to create an altar for her. Maybe on a table. We'll light candles. We'll have some pictures of her. And maybe some of her favorite things."

"What are her favorite things?"

"You were her favorite thing."

"So I have to sit on a table?"

Adriana smiled. "We could set a picture of you on a table, so you don't have to sit up there all day. You can draw something for her. She loved flowers. We'll have to buy lots of flowers."

"And she loved food!" He was wide awake now.

"That's right, she did love food."

Oh, that memory struck a chord, and Adriana's eyes watered as she thought of some of the old Mayan dishes her mother had mastered: her maize soup, her street tamales, her chocolate sorbet. She bit her lip, trying hard not to collapse into sadness. She couldn't dare let her son see her cry anymore.

He sensed it and turned to her, sitting up. "Are you sad too?"

"Of course I am, baby," she said, a tear rolling down her cheek.

"I don't like people dying, Mommy."

Adriana wrapped her arms even tighter around him. "No one does, *mi amor*. No one."

43

THE AERIAL YOGA VIRGIN AND THE LADY'S NIGHT SURPRISE GUEST

Margot didn't climb out of her hole with ease. Though she'd acknowledged the hole she'd fallen into and made the decision she wanted out, she was still very much angry at the world three weeks after she and Remi had come to an end. Even with Joan back home, Margot felt lost.

But! There was a *but*! She did indeed want out. *That*, she was sure of. It had been several weeks of spinning around the toilet bowl, and it hadn't been fun. Why did wallowing in self-pity look so much more entertaining on television? Diane Lane did it so much more gracefully.

Margot had cried oceans. She hadn't exercised once. She often didn't even apply makeup. She'd even presented breakfast to her guests in her robe one morning.

Fuck it!

Right now, she felt like an ugly, swollen heifer so far gone from the person she'd become. So going to yoga with Joan this morning was not just a challenge. It wasn't like a normal person deciding to exercise. Going to yoga was her Mount Everest. She was afraid. Afraid to look into the studio mirror and see what she'd become.

Margot had been smoking a lot of marijuana too, given that recreational use was now legal in Washington. And she wasn't just drinking wine any longer. She would start with liquor and then ease into white wine, each night going to bed with a very heavy buzz and waking up every single morning with a tremendous headache, thinking that all she wanted to do was go back to sleep. The only thing that kept her from drinking was eating desserts. Anything that would distract her from her inner feelings.

While they drove into Richland in Joan's electric car, Jasper called Margot to tell her he was coming back to Red Mountain. He said he had a few days of quiet before the school year began, and he missed his mom.

"What! Yes! Please! You have to! You'd better be careful. I might not let you leave again."

Margot didn't just walk into that yoga studio, she prowled into it, ready for anything. Jasper coming home had wiped the lenses of her life clean.

Have a cup of coffee, put your hair up in a bun, and handle it.

Everyone in the lobby surrounded Joan. As she balanced on her cane, they lined up to hug her and tell her how much they'd missed her. Margot slipped into the studio to stretch and was taken aback by what she saw. While she was away in her weeks of collapse, the studio had installed aerial swings from the rafters. She'd read about them in one of the blogs she followed. All the excitement of Jasper's homecoming tightened into a ball of stress. *I know they're not going to make me hang in that thing.*

The wavy blond teacher entered, set her water bottle down at the front, and introduced herself. She had abs and biceps that Margot could only dream of. A flower-patterned tattoo decorated her right arm.

"Is this an aerial class?" Margot asked, wondering where to unroll her mat.

"Yeah! I guess you haven't been here for a while."

"It's been a couple of months, sad to say." *Look at me. Can't you tell?*

"We're incorporating it into every class." The teacher touched her shoulder. "Don't worry. It's not threatening at all. Set your mat down near one. I'll walk you through it when the time comes."

"I'm afraid of heights."

The woman smiled. "You'll be three feet off the ground at most. Don't worry. Trust me."

Once Joan broke free of her followers, she walked into the studio and placed her mat next to Margot. "You look ready to go."

"You didn't tell me this was aerial."

Joan grinned. "I assumed you knew."

"Does it look like I've been frequenting this place?"

After a brief meditation, the teacher led the class in a series of animal calls. Before she knew it, Margot was crawling around on all fours making bear sounds. The slithering around like a snake and hissing was when Margot started to die laughing.

"Yes, laugh!" the blond teacher said. "Please."

Margot looked over at Joan slithering next to her. "If a video of this surfaced, it would be the end."

Joan stopped slithering and met Margot's eyes. Margot anticipated some words of encouragement. Instead, Joan scrunched her eyebrows and nose, showed her teeth, and hissed.

Margot fell into even deeper laughter and by then, as often happened when she was in attendance, the whole class was trying to hold in their own laughter, as was evidenced by the cracking grins and occasional outbursts. She knew the others were laughing more at her than with her, but that was okay.

When the time came to climb into the swings, the teacher helped Joan up first. Joan still moved very slowly, but she was nevertheless fearless in getting upside down. Leaving Joan swinging, her head a foot above the ground, the teacher approached Margot.

"You can skip me. I'm thinking I'll try next time."

"Nonsense. You can *do* this. It's really fun."

"I'm sure, but seriously, I haven't worked out in," she lowered her voice, as if she held the secret location of the Holy Grail, "in a long time."

The teacher looked around. "Class, let's give Margot some encouragement. Clap your hands if you think Margot can do this."

By then, all twelve students were upside down in their swings. The clapping began and then Joan started chanting, "Margot! Margot!" Then the whole class was upside down chanting, "Margot! Margot!"

The teacher quieted them down. "Thank you, everyone. What do you think, Margot?"

Touched by these strangers, feeling like she was in the front row with a bunch of Evangelists, Margot said with clenched fists, "Some women fear the fire. Some simply become it. Let's do this."

The class roared and clapped, and Margot ate up the attention. There were very few places where she could find such joy and inspiration while also being so exposed. Having Joan as her neighbor on the mat helped tremendously.

Thankfully, everyone went back to what they were doing as the teacher guided Margot. She started by sitting on the swing, then gently falling backward with a firm grip on the straps. The teacher guided Margot as she prayed that she wouldn't hurt herself.

And then she did it. Her legs lifted, and she wrapped them around the higher part of the swing, and in a somewhat graceful motion, her body turned upside down and her hair tickled the floor below. For the first time, she analyzed the bar carrying her. It looked very sturdy. They'd spray-foamed it before hanging the swings, most likely to provide some cushion to the thick straps.

The teacher bent down and turned her head toward Margot. "Not so bad. Right? I told you that you could do it."

Blood rushed to Margot's head. "I love this. I'm so in love."

Margot met eyes with Joan for a moment and then focused on herself. She closed her eyes, and the teacher guided them through a meditation. A few minutes in, as Margot bathed in the bliss of her daring and the teacher talked about being the watcher, watching thoughts go by, Margot thought she felt something falling onto her body.

The high she'd been feeling went away, and she sprinted back to reality. She raised her head and looked. Something fell toward her, and she closed her eyes to avoid it. She heard a small, light object hit the floor next to her. And then again. Like it was raining. Looking again, she saw that the spray foam had cracked where her swing was attached.

A wave of embarrassment rushed over her. "Are you effing kidding me?" she whispered. She looked around. *Did anyone else notice?*

The cracking grew louder and the pieces larger as they fell toward her. She bit her tongue, still trying not to attract attention. As she tried to figure out what was coming down from above, a giant piece, the size of her hand, hit her on the forehead with a *whack* sound that no one could have missed.

It was foam, so there wasn't any pain, but the shock was overwhelming. Fearing that the beam might be weakening too, Margot unwrapped her legs from the straps and began to sit up. In doing so, she created so much momentum that she swung up and flung out of her seat face forward. Her knees smacked the floor as she caught herself with her hands. That's when she heard her pants split. The string of curse words that flowed out of her mouth surely set records for any yoga studio on earth.

The other yogis unraveled from their swings and circled Margot. The teacher and Joan were there first, asking her if she was okay, petting her with more words of encouragement.

There Margot was, flat on her back, two red knees, a rip in her pants, spray foam all in her hair, and a face flushed so red it looked like she'd lost her top at her own wedding.

When Margot told this story that night to her cooking group of twenty-plus, the laughter nearly shook Épiphanie to the ground. It was cathartic to tell the story and draw so many laughs, but she still felt sad, fat, and worthless inside. Yes, Jasper was coming home, but what a sad wreck she'd become.

At the end of the evening, after the ladies had left, Remi was standing by his motorcycle in the circle drive, his helmet in his right hand.

"No," she said.

Remi stepped toward her.

"Go home, Remi. I'm not doing this. Please go home."

He didn't argue, and he didn't see her crying as he sped away.

44

TO TWIST OR BREAK HIS ARM

Armed with Joan's wisdom in confronting *without* confrontation, Otis left Red Mountain and crossed over into Kiona for a morning visit with Harry Bellflour. It wasn't hard to find the home of his nemesis. Everyone knew Bellflour had paid cash for "that big monstrosity" on the other side of the highway. You couldn't do much in Benton County without everyone knowing.

The house Bellflour had bought stood halfway up one of the Horse Heaven Hills, overlooking the future site of Drink Flamingo like a watchtower from which a king could lord over his kingdom. Otis drove his truck under the highway into Kiona, the tiny, unincorporated community next to Benton City. So small, the easiest way to tally the population was to drive around for a few minutes counting houses and cars. Immediately on the left, he saw the property that had weighed so heavily on his mind lately.

Otis couldn't help but imagine the future—a rickety amusement park with RVs everywhere. He saw tall blue waterslides and giant neon signs. He saw a line backed up on the highway for all the wrong reasons. They wouldn't be here for the wine. They'd be here so the kids could pet the zebra while adults in tank tops got drunk on strawberry spritzers! He shielded his eyes with his left hand, wishing it away.

Passing the road to Anelare Winery and coming around another bend, he soon saw Bellflour's wood-framed house, boasting a giant deck that reached out on stilts over a wide patch of shortly-cut, uber-green grass currently being showered by a line of pop-up sprinklers. Otis had no idea whether or not the man was there, but he might as well find out. He cut right, and his truck spat rocks on the dirt road as it wound up the hill. A giant apple orchard with ripening red and green apples filled the acre in the back. The orchard looked perfect, too perfect, and Otis could only imagine the amount of chemicals that had been sprayed over the past couple of months. He found the paved driveway and drove halfway down before noticing a gold Lexus.

No running from me now.

Otis parked next to the Lexus. Resisting the urge to drag a key along the car's side, Otis approached the front door and ran the obnoxiously loud doorbell.

Harry Bellflour, dressed in business casual attire, opened the door.

Otis immediately noticed the gold on Harry's wrists and neck. The man had a deep tan, and Otis didn't think that tan came from working outside. Holding a phone to his ear, Bellflour stuck his fat index finger in the air, indicating for Otis to wait. Back to his call, he motioned Otis to enter.

Otis took in the surroundings of the foyer: the moving boxes stacked neatly along the wall, the steep wooden staircase, the blank walls.

Bellflour said into the phone, "Yeah, yeah, I got you. But we're putting all our eggs into one basket. Let me bounce that off the other brass. I want the film crew up here before we break ground."

As Otis listened, he thought about how nice it was not to work in a world of corporate clichés.

The man finally hung up. Putting his phone in a belt holster, he said, "I'm sorry to keep you waiting."

Otis stood with his arms crossed. "You know who I am?"

"I wouldn't be here right now had it not been for you. I've thought a lot about this moment. What you'd think of me. I'm assuming you're not my biggest fan." Bellflour, a tad bit taller, dipped his head and met Otis's eyes.

Otis let a puff of air out through his nostrils and pressed his lips together. *You have no idea.*

Bellflour nodded. "Yeah, I figured. I can't imagine I'm a part of what you hoped for this place."

Otis shook his head. "It's not just me. I don't understand why you'd choose this place. We're in the middle of nowhere."

The fool threw up his hands. "Disney World was in the middle of nowhere when they first broke ground. Anyone with eyes can see Red Mountain's momentum. The way I see it, we're making a safe bet on the future." Bellflour motioned him into the next room. "Let's sit down and talk. Can I offer you some lemonade?"

"No, thanks." Otis wouldn't drink the man's Pappy Van Winkle if he offered it.

He led Otis into the living room, which featured giant windows overlooking Red Mountain. Otis sat down on a leather chair facing the windows and waited for Bellflour to pour himself a lemonade from the bar.

Bellflour sat down in the matching leather chair next to Otis, breathing heavily as he enjoyed his first sip. "You probably haven't realized it yet, but you and I want the same thing."

"What's that, Harry?" Otis's gaze found Till Vineyards through those windows.

Bellflour sipped and took his time answering. "To make a difference."

Otis smiled open-mouthed. "That's a vague aspiration. Any bonehead can make a difference. Not all differences are good ones."

"I guess you're right. It's more than that. We both want to do something big. And good."

"I guess 'good' is a relative term."

"You think I'm ruining your mountain?"

"I don't think you're ruining my mountain. No human can do that. It's not *my* mountain anyway. But I think your idea is a big fat hairy mole on the face of something beautiful. I think you need to cast aside your wants and those of your financial partners for a minute and consider those of us who have been here a long time."

"I wouldn't be a solid businessman if I did that, would I? What do you want me to do, Otis? You're going to have lines out the door of your tasting rooms. You won't be able to make enough wine."

"You ever been to Burgundy, Bellflour?"

"Of course."

"Were there lines out the doors? No. You had to make an appointment. Nobody here wants a line of bachelorette-party folk with wine stains all over their dresses stumbling into tasting rooms with their glasses stuck out in the air."

"No one ever told me you were a snob. Now that's the difference between you and me. I think everyone is entitled to enjoy the wine experience. I bring wine to the people."

"You have me wrong. I think everyone is entitled to wine, as long as they're pursuing it for the right reasons, of course. They can go down to Mardi Gras if they want to get hammered on Budweiser. The vignerons of Red Mountain want to be respected like any other artists. We don't want a damned amusement park with a bunch of rednecks—" Otis stopped himself. Joan would be shaking her finger by now.

Calmer, he said, "I'm not explaining myself correctly. The people of Red Mountain...look at us. There's no judging here. We welcome people who share a similar mindset. This thing you're doing." He shook his head, already knowing he was wasting his words. "This water park and motel...the whole family-friendly RV park. It's not what we want here. We want boutique hotels with fifteen-table restaurants serving dirt-to-plate, not a cheap motel with a burger joint attached to it. Why can't you go down to Walla Walla with this thing?"

"You didn't come here thinking you were going to change my mind, did you?"

"I thought I'd give you a chance."

"A chance or what? What are you going to do? We've bought the land. I bought this house." He pointed down at the land. "You might as well accept it. You don't own Red Mountain. We can do with it what we please."

"You don't have a damned clue about wine, do you? What a shame."

"Oh, I 'get' wine. You might be some famous farmer, and you might even be considered the godfather of this place. But I've poured wine in more mouths in the past two months than you will in your whole life."

"You call the shit you're putting in those boxes wine?"

"You're damned right, I do."

Otis nodded his head, gritting his teeth. "I'll tell you one thing, Bellflour."

"What's that?"

"You build your place. Go pair your box wines with funnel cakes and push pops, and God knows what else. Throw up your signs. Destroy the poetry of this place. Do whatever you need to do. This mountain will get you." Otis twisted his head toward him. "Bet your ass that's true. You being here is not a good thing, and she knows it."

Bellflour laughed. "Oh, the mountain is a *she* now?"

"She's always been a *she*, you moron." Otis felt the cords of muscle in his neck straining. "Haven't you had the wines? Haven't you walked the vines? How do you *not* know that? And since you're here to suck off the teat of what all of us have built, she'll get you. In the end, she'll get you."

"You know, they always said you were the visionary. But no one told me you'd gone senile. Time to step aside and let people with a larger vision intervene, old man. You've done what you could."

Otis stood. "I'm not done with you, Bellflour."

"I hope not. We're going to be neighbors a looooong time."

Otis muttered, "Go to hell, you clueless windbag." He left Bell-flour in the living room and marched out the front door, leaving it wide open.

45

ADRIANA IS NOT MY NAME!

driana finally had some time to herself. Brooks had taken
Zack and Luca fishing, the boys' first playdate together, and
she had the day off. She should be going to the spa or
sitting out in the sun enjoying a book. There had actually been a time
when she read. Hard to believe now, but she used to be caught up on
all the latest bestsellers. She should be cooking. Or sleeping. Sleeping
is exactly what she needed most.

But she couldn't stop her leg from shaking. What if Zack was
snagged by a hook? He was wearing his goggles less and less. What if
he fell in the water? What if he and Luca didn't get along? What if
Luca was mean to him?

The truth was she hadn't done anything but worry since the
moment Brooks stopped by to pick up Zack. She'd met Luca. He was
a nice boy and immediately was kind to Zack. Why did she have to
keep worrying? Why couldn't she let go?

Only after an hour of wasted time did she settle into some
novellas on the television. Watching Mexican soap operas reminded
her of her mom and was perhaps the best way to take her mind off
things. As Adriana's worries weakened, as she settled into the couch

with a blanket, as Esperanza was about to find out that Horacio was sleeping with her neighbor, Zack ran through the door.

"Mom! Mom!"

She turned off the television and ran to her son, first looking for bruises or blood or tears. But he wore a smile that blew her mind. No goggles. He ran to her, and she plucked him up into the air. "Did you have fun?"

She noticed Brooks and Luca following him in.

Zack held up three fingers. "We caught three fish!"

"Three!" Adriana said, looking over at Brooks and Luca.

"Well, three if you're counting minnows," Brooks replied.

Stepping greatly out of her comfort zone, Adriana asked Brooks if he'd like to sit on the back porch and drink a Coke while they let the boys play. Since the moment Adriana had agreed to move in, Margot had filled her house and backyard with toys. Amazon brought something new for Zack almost daily, and Margot had convinced him to start calling her Auntie Margot.

Luca and Zack ran straight for the oversized Jenga blocks resting on a tree stump. As the boys took turns, Adriana brought out two bottled Mexican Cokes, the ones without high-fructose corn syrup. Margot refused to buy the others. Adriana handed one to Brooks. "Thanks for that today. He really needs some guy time."

"We're buds. I'm happy to do it."

Adriana let out a breath of air and shook her head. She needed to cut to the chase. "You've been amazing for him. He wasn't even talking, and you're bringing out his words. He's actually walking around without his goggles. I don't understand that. And it confuses me. I don't know whether I like you for that or because of our connection. That's messing me up."

Brooks nodded his head. "Who cares how it starts? Whatever the reason, we're connecting and we should explore it."

Adriana felt compelled to go further. Was she going to spend the rest of her life telling everyone lies? Brooks had shown enough effort and caring and commitment that he deserved some truth. She felt like she could trust him, and trust was something she was short on these days. Other than Zack, she had absolutely no one. She'd left everyone else back in California. Maybe she did have some room in her heart.

"I'm just... You don't know what you're getting into."

"Tell me then."

"I have things in my past that you couldn't imagine. Things that will scare you off."

Brooks nodded, his eyes on the boys and the tower. Zack pulled a block that left the tower on the verge of collapse. "Adriana. You can't run forever. I don't know what you're running from, but I know you're running. At some point, you're going to have to trust someone again."

"I'm going to be running the rest of my life. That's the thing you don't understand."

"Then tell me. Help me understand."

It was Luca's turn to extract a Jenga block now. Zack jumped up and down, so excited about the climaxing finale of the game. As Adriana mulled over her thoughts, she watched Luca reach for a block toward the bottom. He tugged, then let go, and the tower wiggled. He tugged again, pulled ever so slightly. Freeing the block, he held it up high. "I did it!"

That's when the tower crashed down on his head.

Pain pressed at her temples as Adriana finally admitted, "My husband is looking for us. My ex. He's a bad man. Looks like he's getting out of prison in a few days, and I know he will come looking for us."

"What?" Brooks said. He'd expected something shocking but not that.

"Adriana isn't even my name," she said.

"What?"

Adriana dropped her head. "There's so much you don't know."

Crashing down...

MARGOT 3.0

"I have a confession to make," a nude Margot said to the hopefully nonjudgmental mirror attached to the inside of her bedroom armoire. She wagged her finger. "I am lonely. Soooooo lonely. And I'm sad and fat and out of shape." She eyed herself up and down. "I've totally let myself go." She closed her eyes for a moment. "Today, that all ends. No more walking around braless in sweats. No more chipped toenail polish." She clapped her hands. "Today, I am stronger than ever before. No, not Margot 2.0. I'm coming back better than ever." She jabbed her chest with her index finger. "This girl right here—she's Margot 3.0."

She'd known when she woke today she had a choice to make. Keep on falling or finally get a grip. Today was get-a-grip day.

Margot 3.0.

This new Margot could laugh all day long at aerial yoga mishaps. She could laugh at herself while loving herself at the same time. She could handle the loneliness. She could handle bad news. Challenges are only opportunities for growth. Margot 3.0 has discipline. She has fire. She has courage and love.

Time to start thinking about herself! Time to find that inner woman who moved across the country and chased a dream while being a single mom! And dealing with a cheating ex. Time to reconnect!

Margot 3.0 wore a dress she'd found in Seattle a few months ago, a dress similar to the white A-line Frances had worn in *Under the Tuscan Sun*, the one accompanied by a black belt and strappy heels. Margot looked pretty darn good in it. If she could return to her October weight, it would fit perfectly.

By the time she sat down in the dining room, she'd developed a confidence that pushed out a confident grin, like she had everything under control. That's when Jasper called. She sipped her coffee as he told her he wasn't coming.

"I understand, sweetie," she said, knowing his studies were more important. Her bottom lip quivered as she fought off the crying.

Before they could talk much more, he said, "I have to run."

"Go get 'em, tiger."

"Love you, Mom!"

Keep on kicking me, she thought, hanging up. She wanted to scream, but instead, composed herself. Margot 3.0 could handle it. She had to laugh. What else could she do? Her laugh turned to a powerful cackle, and she forgot about her roommates until Adriana and Zack appeared out of nowhere. She'd been so lost in her outburst that she hadn't heard them descend the stairs.

"What's gotten into you?" Adriana asked.

"Oh, my gosh." She covered her mouth. "I was just...just laughing at life. When you look at it a certain way, all you *can* do is laugh."

"Good for you, Margot. I like to hear you laughing. You look lovely!"

Margot stood from the table and straightened out her dress. "I do, don't I?" She spun around. "Zack, Adriana. I'd like to introduce you to Margot 3.0." She stuck out her hand, shaking Zack's first. "I know you think Auntie Margot is crazy, Zack. But I'm... Well, I am. But I'm a good crazy. I'm sorry I've been such a bad roommate. Today, I'm turning it all around."

She took Adriana's hand. "I'm Margot 3.0. Good to meet you.

Please forget any previous versions you may have encountered." In a whisper, "That wasn't really me."

Adriana smiled. "It's good to meet you, 3.0."

"This B-I-T-C-H is back," she said.

"Hey," Zack said. "I can spell."

Margot 3.0 rolled her eyes. "Oh, my gosh. I'm that terrible aunt who always says inappropriate things. Ignore me, Zack. Just ignore me. At least I'm not sitting outside sucking down Pall Mall 100s and appletinis. Anyway, I'm going to head next door to the inn. You guys enjoy your breakfast."

With her coffee in hand, Margot dashed out the front door, ready to take on the world. There, at the bottom step, stood Remi Valentine.

"Hey," he said. He was carrying a bouquet of yellow roses.

"No," Margot replied, quickly. Not even thinking.

"I just—"

"Stop."

Remi wore khaki shorts, a white button-down shirt with rolled-up sleeves, and blue suede shoes. She watched his shoulders sink, his chin lower, his body shrink. He was giving up.

"Margot, you have to give me a—"

"I said *stop*!" she yelled. "Shut your mouth."

He closed his mouth this time, not a chance he'd say another word.

Meeting his eyes, she glared. Her head spun; emotions exploded like fireworks. She wanted to slap him. She marched down the steps and cocked her right arm, ready to go.

Margot tossed her coffee mug to the ground and reached around the back of his neck. Remi flinched. She grabbed him and pulled his head to hers and put her lips to his. His eyes exploded as she thrust herself onto him, pushing her tongue into his mouth, grabbing his rear end with her left hand.

"What are you—?"

"I said shut up."

He dropped the yellow roses, and she felt them land on her strappy heels and slide to the ground. She bit his lip, gently at first, and then harder. Her heart raced as she kissed his cheek and then tugged at his ear with her lips. "I want you. Right now, I want you. Don't say another word."

She felt his nod against her cheek.

Margot was so hot by that moment that she nearly dropped her dress right there at the bottom of the steps. Grabbing Remi's crotch, feeling him in her hands, she whispered, "I'll be right back. I hope you don't have plans today."

He shook his head like a little boy. "No."

She smacked his ass. "I said not to talk! Stay right here."

Margot ran up the steps and opened the front door. "Adriana, I need you to take care of breakfast."

Adriana was pouring cereal into a bowl for Zack. She set down the box. "I can do that. No problem."

Returning to Remi, she took his hand. "Follow me."

He did as he was told, and when they entered through the wooden doors of Épiphanie, she marched to the reception area, checked her books, and grabbed a room key. Then it was up the stairs and barely into room 2C when Margot pushed Remi against the closing door and returned to his lips.

Oh, he was a good kisser. His lips were welcoming, his breath like a man from an Old Spice commercial.

"I love this dress," he whispered. "But I'm going to rip it off."

"Don't rip my dress!" she said, slapping him. "I thought I told you not to talk." She turned away from him. "Unzip."

The buzz of the zipper tickled her ears as he undressed her, and she shimmied out of the last of it. He kissed her neck. Her back.

The chills rushed over her.

Her thighs kicked and heaved. She reached around and grabbed him, taking in the hardness of him, missing him.

"I want you, Remi," she whispered. "Make love to me."

∽

"AM I ALLOWED TO TALK YET?" Remi asked.

They'd opened the windows, letting out some of the steam that had built up over the past hour. One white sheet covered the lower halves of their bodies. The comforter had been thrown to the floor a while ago. The TV played an old *Law and Order* episode. Margot would have smoked a cigarette if she'd had one.

She put her hands behind her head. Damn right, she'd shaved her pits! "You've earned a few words."

He didn't say anything.

"Well?" she said. "Cat got your tongue?"

"How do I even begin?"

She watched his hairy chest rise and fall. "I'd start by telling me you don't still love your ex-wife."

"I *don't*. Period. You're right, there's some stuff there, but not what you're thinking. If I think about my ex, it's because I'm thinking about my daughter. I'm thinking about the pain I caused my family. I wouldn't take Amber back. We're not meant to be. That damage is done. Yes, she kicked me out of the house, and I was an asshole. That ship has sailed." He shook his head. "All that pain you might see, whatever you saw that day, has to do with my daughter."

Margot nodded slowly, taking it in. Coming to the realization in its entirety for the first time, she said, "If I'm being honest, I think I was looking for a way to end our relationship. The way you spoke about your wife wasn't *that* bad; it was maybe all I needed. I was looking for a weakness."

"Why would you do that, Margot?"

"Because I'm terrified you'll break my heart one day." Her eyes watered. "I can't survive that again."

He rolled over and moved closer to her. "I love you. I love you like I've never loved another woman. You'll need a restraining order against me if you want me to stop, because I'm not stopping. You're my destiny, Margot Pierce. You're my everything. I knew it at that Mexican restaurant. I've known it every day since. I'll never leave you. I'll never cheat on you. I'm yours forever."

She burst into tears, and he showered her with a hug that made her feel so safe inside. So safe. After he'd turned her tears to laughter, she said, "Did you know I'd take you back? Even when I wasn't answering your calls?"

"I don't know a lot of things, Margot. I've messed up in life. But I still value the magic of us humans being on this round ball. I still believe in miracles. I've been at my place waiting for you, convinced there was more of us to come. And if there weren't more, then there was no magic left in this entire world. I refuse to believe that." He turned to his side and pushed a strand of hair from her eyes. "I need you back. I want to show you the kind of love you deserve. I want to show you a love you've never known."

She licked her lips. "That wasn't too bad, what you just did a little while ago. Were you ever going to stop sending flowers? That florist must love you."

"She was starting to think I was a stalker."

"Me too," she said.

"So what's next? Will you take me back?"

Margot looked away for a moment. How could she say no? She loved him. "You always know what to say, Remi. You'd better be sincere. I can't handle more heartbreak."

"I'll never break your heart. You're my everything."

"Still, I need something in return other than flowers and chocolate, which by the way haven't helped my waistline. You know what I've always dreamed? That my man would watch Hallmark movies with me. Once a week."

"Though you did kind of let me off the hook earlier, I'd love to watch a Hallmark movie with you once a week. That's not a punishment, that's a gift."

She grinned. "You're going to regret this promise."

"I would have agreed to watching one *every* day. Anything for you. Anything to share your space. So we're a thing again?"

Margot let out a big breath. "Yes. Yes, we are."

A little later, after *Law and Order* ended and they were drifting in and out of sleep, Remi asked, "Will you sing something for me?"

"Right now?"

"Why not? There's nothing I want more."

She started to protest and then thought, *Why not? What would Margot 3.0 do?*

Collecting herself, noticing some nervous jitters but not letting them affect her performance, she closed her eyes and sang one of her favorites from *Les Miserables*, "On My Own."

When she finished the song, she found him wiping his eyes. "I could listen to you sing all day every day."

"Thanks," she whispered, feeling his love like a hot bath on a cold day, the kind of bath, of course, in which she wasn't murdering her ex with kitchen utensils.

THE GUARDIANS OF RED MOUNTAIN IS BORN

After sharing a French press of coffee and a bowl of fruit, Otis and Joan weaved through the vines, taking in the morning air with Jonathan tailing closely behind. No sounds but the birds calling. Joan had one arm in Otis's, the other working her cane. She was doing better. They'd walked longer than they had since the bullet, twice as long as in Dublin.

"What were you doing that day in the doctor's office?" Otis asked, the caffeine kicking in. "I mean the day I asked you out. The day we ran into each other last year."

"What made you think of that?"

"I woke up thinking that something was happening with you. Like something was wrong that you were hiding."

"Why would I do that?"

"Because you're that kind of woman. You wouldn't want to burden me."

She stopped him and touched his face. "Other than what you see here, nothing is wrong with me. I was just getting a checkup. And, of course, fulfilling my destiny by connecting our dots."

He chuckled. "I like that. Sometimes I think you already know what's going to happen."

"That wouldn't be much fun, would it?"

"Might make things easier."

"Yeah, but the mystery is the best part. The tension of the unknown, that mysterious light we're chasing, slowly revealing itself only to go dark again, forcing us to stumble, to squint, to look a little harder."

"And then it appears again."

"That's the light I like. That light that turns on after it's been dark for almost too long."

He turned to his faithful companion, the Great White Beast. "What do you think of that, Jonathan? Can you believe we found this woman?" He grabbed the dog's muzzle and looked him in the eyes. "Can you believe she found two mutts like us?"

Joan turned her face up to the sky. "*Ahhh-wooo!*"

Otis looked at her like she was crazy.

Jonathan barked.

She howled again and looked at Otis, then at Jonathan. "You think you're the only dogs on this mountain?"

Otis grinned. "You're coming back, aren't you, my love?"

"One day at a time."

Otis stood. "You know what I like about you? I have conversations with different people, and there's a certain plane that we speak on." He flattened his hand and held it, palm down, near his chest level. "We hover in this area. Maybe a few ticks up or down, but we're not too far from here. When I'm on your plane, its way up here." He raised his flattened hand above his head. "We talk in ways that bend my mind."

"I don't want to be stuck on that plane."

"Oh, I don't think we're stuck. We're only getting started. I'm just in awe of your mind, my love. That's what I'm trying to say."

"What if we had a completely simple—not shallow—but simple conversation? Maybe you're right. Maybe we don't have enough of those."

"I don't even know what that would look like with you."

She stopped and looked around. "If we were going to have the exact opposite of the previous conversation, what would it be?"

They both looked to the sky for answers.

He threw up his hands. "I have one. What kind of chewing gum is your favorite? What flavor? Not that I've ever seen you chew gum."

"Now, that's a question. I'm a peppermint girl. I loved the peppermint ice cream my dad used to make in the summers. With one of those ice cream makers you crank and have to use rock salt. You remember?"

"Nope, you can't go deep. Just give me the flavor, don't start revisiting your pigtailed, lollipop youth."

~

LATER, Otis hiked up to the winery. Jake and Brooks sat at a table in the Till Vineyards tasting room. Because Otis always sold out of his wine, he didn't need a tasting room and only opened upon appointment. Today, it would become their battle station. After shaking hands, Otis sat and looked at the two men. An unlit nub of a candle stuffed into the top of a wine bottle stood in the middle; the beeswax had dripped to the wood.

"This is us," Otis said, moving the candle out of the way. "The Guardians of Red Mountain." Otis looked at his two *compadres*, both covered in tattoos.

"Gotta start somewhere," Brooks said, eyeing both of them.

Otis rested his elbows on the table, one fist into the other hand. "Well, Jake. I hate to put you on the spot, but you're the one with the power. Can you stop this thing?"

Jake, in a tight black T-shirt and leather bracelets covering both of his wrists, scratched the back of his head and spoke in his typical laid-back fashion. "I'm happy to do anything I can. Still kicking myself for not jumping on the property earlier."

"You and me both," Otis admitted.

"How could we have known?"

Oh, Otis could have known. This is the way his world works.

Jake asked, "You met with Bellflour?"

"He's a lost cause. That guy is a bulldog clamped down on trousers. Nothing will break that bite. I spoke with a lawyer friend in my wine club. From a legal standpoint, there's not much we can do. An appeal would have to be filed within thirty days of the closing. But we don't have much to appeal. Bellflour did his homework. The closest I've gotten is looking into sewage rights. His development is beyond septic abilities, which means he's going to have to pay for one hell of a long pipe. But he has the rights. He already cleared it with the city." Otis removed his cap and scratched his head. "I only see one way out of this thing. A smear campaign."

"I've thought the same thing," Jake said. "It would bring negative attention to the mountain though. We don't want that elitism factor. We want to welcome people. That's our whole thing here. No judgment. We have to ask ourselves who we are, who we want to be."

"Let's ask that question after we get rid of this guy," Otis said. "There's nothing wrong with acceptance, but we still have to define the experience here. Do we want this second-rate Bozo circus to be the first thing people see when they visit the mountain?"

Jake spoke again. "I see a few ways. We can buy him out. We pay him whatever it takes, which I'm not opposed to. Or we can run a campaign where the whole community chases him out. *Or.* We can appeal to him. We go to his heart."

"I'm telling you, Jake. There's no going to this guy's heart. I sat with the man. He's a shark."

"Let me meet with him. What if we could all help each other? There has to be some sort of agreement."

"He gets off on this sort of thing. And he's so damned rich, I'm not sure you could ever buy him out." Otis sighed. "I'm not saying we should give up. Maybe you can talk to him. I think I've burned my bridge."

Brooks took the floor. "Jake, you can take this to the media. I know you don't like using your fame, but it could work."

Otis agreed. "The more you can do with your PR power, the better. And you too, Brooks. You're the new *Rolling Stone* kid. There is one more option," Otis said. "Not exactly a smear campaign. We can blackmail him. We hire people to go after him. Frame him if we have to. We force him to move elsewhere."

"That's a dark path to go down," Brooks said, "but I'm not totally opposed to the idea. What do you think, Jake?"

"Very dark idea."

Otis said, "I thrive in the dark, boys. We're the Guardians of Red Mountain. There's nothing I wouldn't do to protect this place." He slammed his fist onto the table. "Nothing!"

48

THE LAST STAND

"The Guardians of Red Mountain Raise Their Wall" was the headline in the *Tri-City Herald* article displayed on Brooks's laptop the next morning. He was sitting on the couch in his boxer briefs, drinking coffee. Shay had been staying at Abby's lately, so the house was quiet.

No, it wasn't Brooks or Otis who had reached the media. Only one guy on Red Mountain could command the attention they needed, convince the journalists to make room above the digital curl. That was the power of Jake Forester. It took only a few phone calls, and he was on the front page in less than twenty-four hours.

Jake's quotes were scattered about the article. The rock star passively attacked the Benton City Council for allowing Drink Flamingo to throw anchor. "He's not what we want here. When I think of Red Mountain, I think of words like *art, passion, dedication, terroir.* That's not what Harry Bellflour is bringing. He's going to cast a giant shadow over Red Mountain. He's not even here for the vines." Farther on in the article, another Jake quote: "We don't want to exclude. We're not in that business. We don't want to be snobs, but we have to stand up when we know something isn't good for our community. He could go two exits down, and they'd probably love to have him. It's just not what we want here."

Bellflour's retorts were littered throughout the article as well. "There's plenty of room for all of us. Don't these people realize how much money and jobs we're going to bring?" Then later, "There's nothing stopping us now. They can try all they want. That piece of land is ours, and this project is happening. I'd suggest they make peace with us and we all learn to get along. This is wine, after all, not religion."

Brooks pushed away his computer in disgust. It was almost a comical farce, this mountain rising culturally, this wine place offering juice unlike any others. Nothing could stop this uprising. It could only get better. And yet, something had suddenly gotten in the way.

He felt helpless. Otis had always believed this mountain could protect its own, but Brooks could see even Otis's resolve weakening. Brooks knew as well as anyone: life isn't a poem. Sure he'd seen the poetic virtues of this place, but in the end, no place and no one is protected forever.

49

HE'S ALWAYS ON MY MIND

"This is Luca's house?" Zack yelled, poking his head up from the backseat, checking out the house through his goggles. "It's a mansion."

"Not bad, right?" Brooks said. "Good place to spend a Saturday."

"Are you kidding me!? Holy hell!"

"Zack!" Adriana scolded, feeling the tightness in her jaw. "What have I said about that word?" She was already on edge. It wasn't just her mother's death. It wasn't just leaving Zack for the first time since then. Earlier that morning, her lawyer back in California had called. He was the only one from her old life who knew their location. He confirmed that Michael's parole hearing would come up in three days, and it was highly likely Michael would be set free.

Adriana had been thinking of an exit strategy long before hearing this news though. She'd been thinking about leaving ever since they'd moved to Washington, and even more so after she'd run into the man who recognized her at Épiphanie. She knew that the moment she decided to run from Michael, she'd be running for a long time.

Even if she took Brooks out of the equation, leaving the mountain wasn't as easy as she'd imagined. It's not like Adriana had inherited any money from her mother. In fact, she still owed money. Dying is expensive. Not only did she have to pay for the funeral, but since Margarita had refused cremation, Adriana also had to buy a cemetery plot in Prosser, which ended up having many unforeseen costs: the casket, a grave liner, the fee for the perpetual care of the land, the grave being dug, the headstone. Even after you're dead, they go after you and your loved ones.

On top of that, Margot provided quality healthcare benefits. When she and Zack did finally leave, she would have to find a job immediately. She didn't even know where she was going. After a grueling winter in Washington, though, Florida sounded tempting. She'd spent hours looking at pictures of Miami and Ft. Lauderdale, dreaming of a tropical life. But she needed cash to move, and she barely had enough to buy Zack a new backpack for school. They'd depleted everything she'd saved in anticipation of their escape from Michael. What if her car couldn't make the more than 3,000-mile trip? Where would they shower and sleep along the way? She couldn't even afford cheap motels. Sure, she could put it all on a credit card, but she'd just gotten out of debt and didn't want to go through that again.

Perhaps more than anything, though, the reason she wasn't ready to leave was because of this amazing man sitting next to her. She couldn't believe this thought was surfacing. *If* he really liked her, and *if* he was really over Abby, and *if* he truly wanted a relationship, one that included Zack, then maybe Brooks Baker was the real thing.

After Zack apologized for his potty mouth, Brooks said, "Hey, dude, I think you ought to leave your goggles here."

Adriana speared Brooks with her eyes.

He looked at her, ignored the look, and returned his attention to Zack. "Want to leave 'em here in my truck?"

Zack tugged off his goggles. "Yeah, okay."

Adriana's mouth dropped. Just like that. Before she could process what had happened, Zack had left them in the center console and jumped out of the truck. "How did you just do that?" she asked.

"He's growing out of them."

She took his hand. "Thanks." Brooks blushed, and she asked with a smile, "Are you turning red?"

"When you warm up to me, it kind of messes me up."

She rolled her eyes. "You're a cheese ball."

He patted the steering wheel. "There's the turning back to ice. I had you for a moment." He pointed to the front door of the Foresters' house. "There they are."

Luca came running, Abby following closely behind. Adriana looked Abby up and down, taking in the tortoiseshell glasses, the long brown hair, and the blond highlights. She wore a loose denim jumper. She was cute and well dressed. Brooks had told Adriana the story. At least, Brooks's side of the story.

The boys ran inside. Doing her best to avoid measuring herself against Abby, Adriana shook the woman's hand. She couldn't help but look at Abby's ring finger, the one that had worn Brooks's ring at one time. She said, "You're so kind to do this."

"Oh, gosh. Luca had a blast fishing. He gets bored out here." Abby spun her head. "Look around. We're in the middle of nowhere. Most of his friends are thirty minutes away. We can do this as much as you like!"

"That's really sweet of you. Brooks has told me a lot about you."

"Is that right?" Abby asked, turning to Brooks. "Don't believe any of it."

Adriana suddenly felt like a third wheel.

Brooks slashed through the silence, a machete in the jungle. "Would you mind showing Adriana around a little bit? She hasn't left Zack on his own in a while."

"Oh, no, that's okay," Adriana said. "I'm sure he'll be fine." But Adriana wasn't sure; she was terrified.

"Of course!" Abby said. She linked arms with Adriana, the kind gesture both awkward and touching. Abby gave her a tour of the house while Brooks watched the kids. As they reached the pool area, Adriana eyed the clean blue water and said, "Zack's not the best swimmer. I'd rather he not swim today."

"No problem. We have plenty to do. I'll keep an eye on them. You guys just enjoy your day."

The throaty charge of an electric guitar sounded from the building on the other side of the pool. Abby said, "That's Jake's studio. I'm assuming you know he's a musician?"

"Yeah, I grew up in Los Angeles. He's huge there. I saw him play one time."

"Oh, cool. He's a super nice guy."

And forgiving, Adriana wanted to say. She couldn't believe the smallness of this mountain. Abby, Jake, Carmen, Brooks. All of it going down right here.

Brooks joined them out front as the boys played with fake swords and pretended a dragon was climbing over the wall surrounding the house. Adriana could see the battle taking place inside of Brooks, the emotions she and Abby evoked in him.

He stabbed his hands into his pockets and said to the two women staring at him, "Well, let's, uh, we better hit the road."

Abby opened her arms to Adriana. "Give me a hug."

"Do I look like I need one?"

"A little."

The two women embraced, tension and kindness tugging at one another. Adriana wasn't used to people being so nice. Those who'd been the nicest to her always turned out to be the evilest in the end.

Adriana and Brooks said goodbye and climbed into Brooks's truck.

"I finally have you alone," Brooks said, driving away.

"Do you miss her?" Adriana asked, the skeptic coming alive inside.

Brooks pushed the gas pedal a little harder. He shook his head and stuck out his bottom lip a hair. "I want *you*, Adriana. She's a million years ago."

"No ex is that far gone."

"Isn't yours?" He slowed the truck to a stop on the side of Sunset. "I like you. Why is that so hard for you to comprehend?" He leaned in and touched her chin.

She flinched, and he let go.

A whisper. "I'm not going to hurt you."

"I know."

A car passed by; she barely heard it.

He tried again and guided her toward a kiss. She was shaking. So many years. So many years since someone had touched her. He let go again and sat back in the driver's seat. "We can wait, Adriana."

"I don't want to wait, it's just difficult."

"It shouldn't be difficult."

Her shoulders dropped. "Try again, please. Kiss me."

～

THEY SPENT the late morning sitting at the wrought-iron table in Brooks's backyard, both chairs facing the river.

"What was life like growing up without parents?" she asked. "I can't imagine."

"I don't know what to compare it to, but I always had this lonely feeling that never went away. I remember watching families. Always studying families. Watching the way the dad would pick up his son and hold him high with pride. I'd see these happy faces and want to reach out and jump into their world."

"Sounds sad."

"My life wasn't always sad." He smiled at a memory returning. "I remember this one kid. I was fourteen or fifteen. You don't even think about birthdays when you're a runaway. His name was Rick. We spent a year together, running from things. We used to jump on trains and ride for days, watching it all go by. We jumped off the train in Canada one time. We'd just sneaked over the Washington border, hiding in a car carrying gravel. We stopped in some no-name town in Canada, found a diner, and had a bite to eat.

"When we left the diner, Rick dangled a set of keys at me. He'd stolen them from the biker at the table next to us. Rick knew how to ride motorcycles. He pointed, we climbed on, and we were off. I rode on the back as we explored western Canada for months. No one ever caught us. We'd sleep around a fire in the wilderness at night, freezing our asses off. When we climbed on that bike though, it all made sense. I'm telling you. It was...there was nothing better."

"That's how you got into bikes?"

"Yeah, Rick taught me how to ride on that trip, and something clicked." Brooks pushed away a rush of emotion. "I miss that guy."

"Where is he?"

"Who knows? We had some good times together though, sitting around those fires, pulling on whiskey or vodka, smoking cigarettes. That beautiful Harley standing not too far away, waiting to carry us farther down the line. Then one day we were done. It was time for a change. He went one way, I went the other."

"And now you've found your family, and they're moving into your house."

"Hold on. They're going to move in for a few weeks until they find something, but only a few weeks." He pointed out a school of carp feeding along the bank and then, "I'm getting hungry myself. I'd offer to cook, but my food would scare you off."

"You can't cook? How can a winemaker not cook?"

"That's what everyone asks."

"What would you cook for me?"

"Oh, wow. I'd go back and forth between a serious grilled cheese —really serious—and pasta. Of course, I'd doctor both up. Throw some garlic salt in there, a little hot sauce."

"I don't know if I can date a man who can't cook for me."

"Oh, c'mon. With Uber Eats and Domino's online ordering? Who needs to cook anymore?"

"Does anyone deliver this far out to the middle of nowhere? Margot says she can't get anything."

He smiled. "Fair point. Not at all. Not even Domino's."

"So?"

He threw his hands up. "So, I got nothin'."

She shook her head with disappointment.

"But I'll..." He took a breath. "I'll learn?" She nodded approval as he kept going. "You know what? I'm going to cook you the meal of your life. Not today, but soon." He rubbed his hands together. "I have to brush up on a few things. You know, like cutting, flipping, sprinkling."

"Sprinkling?"

He shrugged and kept going. "I'm going to prepare a meal that will make your jaw drop. Not like, 'Oh, my God, he just poisoned me.' I'm going to surprise you with some serious mastery. This whole cooking thing can't be that hard."

Their conversations weaved in and out with escalating comfort, and though they didn't officially acknowledge it, Brooks started to feel like they were indeed a couple. He had so much more to learn about her, but he could see himself with this girl. He could see a time in the near future when she fully opened up to him.

As that comforting thought floated through his mind, she said seriously, "I'm wondering something. Why haven't you ever asked about my face?"

Brooks was caught off guard and took some time to answer. "I figured you'd share when you were ready. I don't feel like it's essential to getting to know you. Is it?"

"It's a part of me."

"No more than my tattoos are a part of me."

Adriana nodded and touched the left side of her face. "This doesn't define who I am, but it's a pretty big part of me. I'm not sure your tattoos are comparable."

"Of course. I don't mean to belittle it." He realized he should be quiet now.

"I know," she said, making him feel better. She ran a finger along the most prominent of the scars, the one that ran down to her lip. A tear followed her finger tip. She wiped it away and admitted, "I've never told anyone the truth. Not even my mother."

Brooks smiled from his heart, encouraging her to feel safe. This was her way of telling him how much she liked him. Adriana might not be capable of some things in a relationship. She might not be ready to dive into the physical side, as much as he might be. She might not be ready to vocalize exactly how she felt about him. But she was sitting there facing him while also facing one of the most painful struggles in her life, and she wanted him to know, maybe even help her carry the burden of it.

Adriana told him the story. Her words tore him down emotionally, but he fought off crying, because he wanted to show how strong he could be for her. When she finished, Brooks knew he would be honored and privileged to help carry that heavy weight. He would be there for her and do everything he could to help her get back on top.

Adriana slumped back in her chair and closed her eyes. She looked exhausted from reliving the memory, but she also looked totally relaxed. The faintest Buddha-like grin graced her lips. He'd never seen a more beautiful woman in his life, and he wanted to tell her so. At the same time, it didn't seem right. It felt terribly superficial to break it all down to appearance. Her beauty was such a small part of what made her special to him. Her strength is what lifted him to his feet and led him around the table. He put his arms around her and kissed her. He kissed her scars and ears, her lips and eyes. She cried, and he kept kissing her, and then she stopped crying and kissed him back.

The rest of the day went by in a flash. He drove her to a dive pizza place in Benton City and then they went to do some wine tasting, visiting their neighbors on Red Mountain. He taught her how to taste and spit. Though she would often retract into her shell, she also opened up and laughed and even initiated a public kiss before they finally returned to the Foresters' to pick up Zack.

I USED TO BE THAT GUY

"I'm dating a man who lives in a trailer," Margot said, driving her Volvo down the mountain to Remi's place. It would be her first time seeing the property. She said again to herself, "I'm dating a man who lives in a trailer." She smiled. "I'm in love with a man who lives in a trailer."

She'd been down Demoss Road many times and had a very good idea of where he lived, but she'd avoided the river altogether since their breakup. Now, as she drove along the water, she couldn't wait to see him. After only a mile, she found McDreamy. Hard to miss the Airstream and work shed on a four-acre gentleman's farm.

Remi walked up from the giant, slightly overgrown garden, holding a wooden harvest basket bursting with vegetables. Margot thought he was the most handsome man she'd ever seen. Henri chased after him. Remi smiled, his white teeth glistening.

"Here you are," he said.

"Here I am."

When he was close enough, he wrapped his arm around her waist and kissed her. "You didn't turn around and leave when you saw the trailer."

"Honestly, it's kind of sexy."

"There is an element of romance to it, isn't there?" He held up his basket. "I thought we'd eat from the garden."

They toured the property first, and he pointed out his different crops in the vegetable garden. They strolled along the river, getting lost in the English pecan trees and watching a line of ducklings follow their mother in the water. The couple moved up through the old concord vines and the orchard. Returning to his living space, he showed her his bikes in the shop. "You'll take a ride with me, won't you?"

"I most certainly will not. I'm terrified of those things."

"I'm a good, safe driver. Never say never."

Then they were in the Airstream. He gave her a tour. She was surprised how nice it was inside—like a modern apartment. Judging by the smell and polish, Remi had obviously bought the trailer brand new. Panoramic windows let plenty of light in. Some yacht rock played in the background. He'd picked some poppies to display on the counter. His bed was neatly made. The only untidy area was the table and sitting area, which was covered in two laptops, a printer, and stacks of what looked like work papers. The kitchen was surprisingly well-appointed and even adorable, and Margot imagined preparing a meal in there one day. She saw herself popping out the door of the trailer in a yellow apron, saying, "Darling, dinner's ready." Remi had built a perfectly wonderful life down here by the river.

Back outside, they sat in a double rocking chair facing the river, clearly the spot where Remi had spent most of his time since he'd moved to Red Mountain. An awning above provided shade. A well-used grill emitted heat waves of charcoal. Margot felt giddy. She grabbed his hand as they gently rocked back and forth.

She nestled more into him. "You have no idea what I've been through to find you."

"Was it worth it?"

"We'll know soon, won't we?"

"I already know it was worth it to find you. I want you to be my girl. I want us to be exclusive. I don't want you out there searching anymore. I like you so much."

"I'll be your girl." She smiled and felt naked and lovely and exposed. Chills ran through her.

A little later, Remi asked, "So what's the latest with this Bellflour guy?"

Margot sighed. "It's not looking good. A year from now, when you Google 'box wine and cheap motels,' Red Mountain will be the first result."

"Who Googles box wine and cheap motels?"

"Hopefully, no one."

"Will it be bad for Épiphanie?"

"I don't think so. Bad for the mountain, yes. Not much different from putting up a fast food place in the middle of the vineyards. But there will still be people who want luxury. If they destroy the romance of the mountain, I'm in trouble."

"I have a few ideas about how we might be able to stop this guy."

"What do you know about such things?" Margot asked.

"Well, I haven't been here that long. On the mountain, I mean. But it's my home too. I feel compelled to protect it."

Margot said, "There's only what, two weeks left to appeal the zoning? And no one can come up with a good reason anyway. After that, construction begins."

"I have a couple of ideas up my sleeve."

"Who are you, Remi Valentine? You have a whole world up your sleeve, don't you?"

He sipped his rosé and admitted, "I hate to say it, but I used to be that guy."

"What guy?"

"Harry Bellflour. I used to be a Bellflour. I used to develop properties that weren't necessarily in the public's best interest. All I saw were dollar signs." He raised his finger. "I'm not that way anymore, but there was a time. Bellflour and I are veterans of the same game. But I bite a little harder. At least I used to."

"So what are you doing in a trailer, Mr. Big Shot? Do I even know you?"

"I think you know that already. I'm trying to separate from the part of me that I don't want to be anymore. Trying to reset. You know the best part of me. I have a past that I'm ashamed of, that's for sure. But if this guy wants to bring the game to Red Mountain, I'll happily leave the sidelines and take him on."

"What *could* you do exactly?"

"There are many options. It depends on what kinds of skeletons he has in his closet."

"He's certainly a dirtbag." She told him about what had happened with Adriana and her, and he listened intently.

"Now I want to get him even more."

51

DANGEROUS MOTORCYCLES AND MEN

A few hours after he said goodbye to Adriana and Zack, Brooks lay in bed, flipping channels on the television and revisiting the day. There was something unique about this woman. She had a strength that he admired, and she was warm, too. No matter how hard she might try in the future, she'd never be able to mask her sweetness again.

The ringing phone from his pants pocket on the floor startled him. He might have ignored it, letting the emergencies of his wine life wait until tomorrow, but something told him he'd better answer the call. When he saw *Jake* on the display, he had no doubt.

Brooks grabbed the phone, sitting straight up, and answered. Before he could say hello, an out-of-breath Jake said, "Brooks, your brother and Abby, they were in an accident and were transported to the hospital in Richland. The bike slid across the highway. That's all I know."

Before Jake had even finished talking, Brooks was running for his shoes.

After helping Joan the past few months, Brooks knew the hospital in Richland all too well. He sped into town, parked his bike in the closest lot, and ran through the sliding doors of the emergency room.

Every day that path was hardened by the sad souls hoping today wasn't the day they'd have to say goodbye.

The others in the waiting room turned to see more drama, his escalated breathing confirmation that he was yet another with his own emergency.

He approached the woman at the counter and said, "I'm trying to find my brother Shay Wildridge and also Abby Sinclaire." As she began typing, he turned to face the waiting room. Every chair was taken. Sad faces looked back at him. One man held up a bloody hand, filling out paperwork with the other. A young woman was trying to keep her baby calm. You didn't come here unless it was bad.

Five minutes later, a nurse escorted Brooks through three hall-ways before turning into Abby's room. Brooks saw Shay's back first and then Abby lying on the bed, tubes coming out of her arms, her hair matted.

"Hey," Brooks said.

Abby tried to smile.

Shay turned, revealing a slice across his forehead. "Hey, brother."

"You're both okay? No broken bones?"

Something wasn't okay. He stepped past his brother to the hospital bed. The heartbeat monitor held a constant chirp.

Abby met his eyes; he hadn't seen her this sad in his life.

"What?" he whispered.

Shay placed a hand on Brooks's shoulder. "She's pregnant."

Pregnant. The word echoed in his mind.

"What?" Brooks shot another look at Abby.

"They... We..." Shay couldn't spit out the words.

"We don't know if the baby is okay," Abby said, wiping her eyes, careful not to tear the tube from her arm.

"Oh, God." Brooks set both hands on the bed, balancing himself.

Abby's bottom lip pushed out as she broke into a sob. Shay squeezed her hand, and Brooks didn't know what to do. The shock paralyzed him. And then he began to cry too. Tears dropped down his cheeks without permission.

"What... what?" Brooks looked at his brother, and they locked eyes. He felt overwhelming sadness and pity. "What are they saying?" he asked, finally able to push out coherent words.

Abby mopped her wet eyes. "They're running tests. The baby's alive. They just need to run a bunch of tests. I was thrown from the bike and fell hard on my side."

"How long? How pregnant are you?" He found himself pointlessly counting months since he'd been with her, wondering if he might be the father. He'd ended their relationship last October; the baby wasn't his no matter how she answered.

"I'm seven weeks pregnant," she confessed.

"What?" That meant Abby had known about the child when they'd talked a few days earlier. She'd let Brooks wonder if the two of them still might have a future. He felt sick to his stomach.

Abby whispered, "I'm sorry."

Shay took her hand. "We didn't know how to tell you."

Brooks raised his right hand as if he were about to swear on a book. He closed his eyes. When he opened them, he said, "I... I... I'm going to walk back outside for a minute. Glad you're both okay." He dragged himself through the doors into the hall.

The door snapped shut.

He folded.

52

ONLY ONE THING LEFT TO DO

Nine Days Later

From the back porch, Otis watched Joan walk down to his garden to harvest. The sheep were grazing farther down the hill.

Once Joan was out of earshot, Otis sat in a chair and called Jake Forester. When he answered, Otis said, "We're screwed. I see no way out. There's nothing to appeal. Period. Short of threatening the man, I don't know what to do." Otis took a puff on his unlit briarwood pipe and waited for a reply.

Jake said, "Otis, I hate to say it, but I think you're right. I think we have to accept it. Might be wise to become his friend. No matter what I do, no matter what kind of press we're getting, he's coming. In fact, I get the sense that he loves all this attention, good or bad."

"After everything you and I have done for this place."

"Shit, Otis, I'm just part of your system."

"I don't believe that for a minute. After all we've done, this is what happens."

Otis poured some whiskey into his coffee and sipped. Not strong enough. He poured more. As it burned his throat, he breathed in the heat. This was his second cup of joe and whiskey. He wasn't able to grasp what was happening. Everything he'd fought for, everything he believed was dying. He covered the speaker on his phone and said to himself, "Black cats and broken mirrors. A whole life taking it in the bum." He let his head fall backward and closed his eyes, as if some answer would appear.

"Otis, you there?" he heard Jake asking.

He raised the phone back to his ear. "Yeah, Jake. I'm here. Barely."

"It's time we accept it. It's time we move on."

"I have nothing left. I swear to God, I'm a minute away from going up there and scalping him."

Jake gave a nervous laugh. "I'd say that's funny, but I know you're not joking."

"You're damned right I'm not joking. This mountain is..." He almost said it's all he had left. But that wasn't true. "This mountain is everything I am."

"It's a lot of who I am too, but you can't go bad to make good."

"What the hell does that mean?"

"Violence isn't the answer. Blackmail isn't the answer. We can't go breaking laws and legs and expect good things to come out of it. We can't keep focusing on what we don't want here. People are going to keep coming."

"Let them come. We'll keep stopping them. Whatever it takes."

"Otis, I don't want to get all new age on you, but everything on this mountain came from good vibes. From good people. We have to trust that if we keep putting out those vibes, the universe will protect us."

"You and Joan should spend some time together reading the stars."

After barely acknowledging the comment with a grunt, Jake said, "If we try to filter who gets in and who has to stay on the other side, what does that make us? What does that make our mountain?"

"A dream come true."

"I know you don't mean that." He sighed. "Don't do something you'll regret. You hear me?"

Otis let another sip burn his throat, fuel his anger. He started to say something but paused. "Jake, you do *you*. Don't worry about me."

"All I'm asking is for you to stay calculated. Don't do something that's going to get you thrown in prison next to Henry Davidson. Don't do something that's going to get in the way of you and Joan."

"Yeah, yeah, I got your point. Forget about it."

"I will. Just promise."

"I don't make empty promises."

The conversation pushed on for a while until Otis finally said, "We have less than two weeks. We need to figure out something. I will not let that bastard so much as stick a shovel into the ground over there. As long as I am breathing, there will not be a damned amusement park on this mountain." He raised his voice. "Or anywhere near it!" He took a breath. "Now let me finish my coffee and get on with my day. We have a tractor that won't start, and apparently, I'm the only one who can fix things around here. I appreciate your wisdom. You're a good man."

"Just remember, you are our leader. Keep making decisions that make us proud."

"At some point, someone else on this mountain needs to pick up the flag. Eventually, one way or another, I'm going to reach my end." With that, he ended the call.

In the next hour, he'd finished the bottle of whiskey while leaning against the back patio railing, looking past his vineyards to the sheep. "I'm done, boys. I'm just done." He wasn't speaking loudly enough for them to hear him.

They weren't paying attention to him anyway. Jonathan lay by a stack of lumber with his legs in the air. He didn't care either. Bellflour wasn't going to change anything for them.

Otis wished he could have the same attitude. He wished he could lie down in the grass on his back and let the sun spray his face and not worry about a thing.

With final acceptance, the man dropped his head. Defeat filled his body. He choked up and his eyes watered. Everything he'd done. Even at the cost of losing his family. Wasting so many hours that he could have spent with his two sons. Instead of kicking the ball, fishing, throwing the Frisbee, or even chatting with his sons, he'd spent so much time focused on making world-class wines and preaching the Gospel of Red Mountain. He'd been an okay dad, but his world had been Red Mountain since the day they'd moved here. He'd wrongfully assumed that once he got Red Mountain where it needed to be, he'd be able to sit on that porch with Rebecca and their boys, and they'd be able to look at what he'd done. What he'd helped to build.

So wrong he'd been. He'd wasted his time and all his years. He'd disgraced his family, and he'd brought his bad luck to Red Mountain.

He knew what he had to do. Only one choice. The idea had been percolating for days, but now he was sure.

No more of this. No more fighting a cause he was sure to ruin. Maybe this mountain could go on. Jake, Brooks, Margot, and all the others could perhaps take over, but he was done. Otis had to leave before he made it worse. If he thought long and hard about it, he could surely prove that Bellflour's arrival—shit, even his very existence—were part of that devilish plan the world had lined up for Otis Till. Joan had mentioned more than once that she thought Henry Davidson's destiny had been to pull the trigger on her. Perhaps Henry Bellflour was Otis's Henry Davidson. It was time for Till Vineyards to close its doors. It was time for Otis to get out before it was too late.

With his head and shoulders drooping, leaving the empty whiskey bottle and the empty coffee cup, Otis marched down the porch steps and made his way to the barn. He opened the doors and moved past the two worn-out Cub Cadet riding lawn mowers—as worn out as *he* was—and the line of weed eaters covered in old dead grass, and the shelves of organic sprays, and he set his eyes on the orange Echo chainsaw.

Otis pulled it off the shelf and rested it on the worktable. He grabbed the sharpener from a nail on the wall and sharpened each tooth. As sad as this moment was for him, he felt a liberation that fueled his actions. "It's over," he whispered. "It's over."

Once the teeth were sharpened, Otis tightened the chain and

topped off the gas and oil. Stepping outside the barn, he set the chainsaw on the ground, primed it, and then cranked it to life. The chainsaw roared, and Otis lifted it up and held it high in the air, pulling the trigger, feeding gas to the engine.

He was a maniac with nothing left to lose.

53

THE BOTTLE BREAKS

Brooks was painfully reminded of his solitude in the days after his brother's accident. Shay was a stranger, as was Abby. Adriana had her son and their safety on her mind and had been a wreck since her ex-husband had been released from prison. Brooks wanted to be there for her, but in his current state, he knew he'd be better off staying out of the way. It wasn't that what they had was over. In fact, they had plans tonight. It's just that the news of Abby's pregnancy and Adriana's ex-husband's release had slowed things down to a simmer. Life had gotten in the way.

Brooks found himself visiting Remi, a man he'd grown to admire and appreciate. It was too soon to know if Remi was like the rest of them, but he needed someone to talk to. Even when he was running from everything as a kid, he'd had momentary friends like Rick from Detroit, with whom he'd spent one summer riding motorcycles through western Canada. Those people who walk into your life for a little while, fill your cup, and then they're gone.

By now, Remi had heard the whole story from Brooks. Abby was pregnant. He still couldn't talk about it without laughing. Not a *ha ha* laugh, but an ironic smile and laugh he put out there when things didn't go his way, which seemed to be most of his life.

Today, having exhausted Brooks's pain, they sat in the folding chairs by the Airstream discussing Drink Flamingo. The awning protected them from the brutal afternoon sun.

Remi held Henri in his lap. "I offered him four times what he paid for it. Bellflour said no. He didn't even consider it. Then I offered him eight. I could offer twenty times what he'd paid, and he'd still say no. He's one of those guys who thinks proving a point, standing up and not getting a damaged ego, is more important than money. He doesn't want to go back on his word. He doesn't want to start the project somewhere else and have to do a bunch of interviews explaining the change. I was about to counter again, but he shut the door on me.

"My lawyers are pulling records, trying to get creative. I have another guy looking for dirt. Not much is turning up. I'm telling you, brother, this thing is happening. I told Margot. I used to be that guy. I know his type. When I said no—back in the old days—I meant it. When I set my heart on something, I obtained it, no matter what. And we can't find anything else to hang our hat on. He's clean as a whistle."

Brooks shook his head. "I wonder if he will give us discounted passes to ride the rides."

Remi chuckled. "It's time we start making friends with him, that's for sure. Maybe he'll keep the bleeding to a minimum if no one continues the war." Remi stood and produced a Frisbee from under his chair. "Want to throw?"

"Sure." Brooks jogged down the hill toward the water and caught Remi's first toss. He returned the disc with a perfect spin. Once Remi caught it, Brooks said, "Jake told me he talked to you about the surprise party for Margot."

"Yeah, and thanks for the introduction. He's a good guy." Remi threw the Frisbee and said, "Jasper's coming home for the party."

Brooks dodged a sprinkler and stretched out his right arm to catch it. "Impressive. Margot doesn't know?"

"No. I've been talking to him on the phone. He's not saying a word to his mom about coming. He's anxious to surprise her."

"Good luck with that. You know how secrets are on this mountain?" Brooks flung the Frisbee back and wiped the sweat collecting on his forehead. "Might as well be billboards."

The two men whiled away two more hours, taking in the cloudless blue day and trying to make sense of women, love, and life.

On his way home, Brooks passed Margaritaville Beach and his mind went back to where it had been wallowing for days. Shay and Abby.

They'd been out of the hospital for more than a week now. She hadn't lost the baby. Both of them were okay. But Brooks had promptly kicked Shay out of his house, and he hadn't exchanged a word with either of them since they'd left the hospital.

Brooks didn't handle being lied to well. In fact, there was nothing that got under his skin more than being lied to. Anyone who lied to him was compartmentalized in his brain as the enemy. That's why he could never forgive Abby for her first offense. Now, two of the people he'd let into his world had crossed a line that could never be forgotten or forgiven. They'd first hidden their relationship and then the pregnancy. What could be worse?

He had done what he'd always done. He buried himself in his work. Harvest was coming. Because of the warm summer, he'd be picking whites any day now. He had to focus on that. As long as his head was buried in the vines and he didn't stray from his focus to bottle Red Mountain, he could survive. When he did come up for air, though, when he let his mind wander, he found himself digging a deep hole of anger.

He'd had a week to figure out exactly how this debacle might have happened. Once Abby had realized Brooks wasn't going to cave, at least not at the rate things were going, she'd decided to make it even more personal. She'd figured getting with Shay would get to Brooks. That would be the thing that brought Brooks home.

Did she even like Shay? Now she was pregnant.

Her little plan had backfired. Now, Shay was her new victim—not that he was innocent at all. He sure had played the loving brother card by asking permission to date Abby, but that was after the fact. He'd noticed Shay wasn't always coming home, but hadn't thought much of it. Didn't care that much. He'd made the occasional broth-erly joke if Shay came in at an odd hour. "Ah, the walk of shame. You must have picked up a rodeo chick last night. D'you sleep in her barn? Which tooth was she missing?" Never, not once, had Brooks thought that Shay had something going with Abby. His brother had asked if he minded them dating long after it had already begun, out of guilt, not respect or consideration.

Brooks drove around the last bend before his house on Demoss and saw Shay standing halfway down the driveway. *What's this all about?* Pulling up next to his brother, he kicked out the stand on his Scrambler. With his hands still wrapped around the handlebars, he looked at Shay. His brother was dirty from a morning of work and smelled like compost and farm animals.

"What are you doing here?" Brooks asked.

"You can't ignore me forever."

"I can try."

"It wasn't planned. How would I know I'd fall in love?"

Brooks grinned. "Don't you see? Everything she does is calcu-lated. I know all you see is the good stuff. That beautiful brain. Her great table wit. The way she makes you laugh. What she does for you in bed. That's all fine. But don't you see? You're a part of her plan. To piss me off. And now you both fucked up and have a kid coming. You're going to bring a child into this world and make him decide between his conniving mom and his jackass washed-up dad."

"Watch your mouth, bro. I'm not here to fight."

Brooks tightened the grip on the handlebars. "Then why the hell are you here?"

"To make amends. I want to make this right."

"Then take your life and hit the road. This is my goddamn mountain."

"You brought me here. I'm not leaving, and you're not leaving either. We're going to make this work."

"Oh, good. Yeah, let's move Mom and Dad up here too. Why don't you name your little boy after Charles? Then we can have a beautiful famdamily, and we can all show little Charles the beauty of this world." He punched the air. "This beautiful *fucking* world!"

"You have to know something else," Shay said.

"Oh, I can't wait. What is it this time? You having twins? Did you steal my job? You going to work for Bellflour? That would be perfect."

"Mom and Dad knew about the baby. We told them the day we found out."

Brooks closed his eyes and took a slow breath. Then he looked at his brother for a second before moving his gaze to Rattlesnake Mountain.

Those words cut to the core, and a numbness rushed over Brooks. He didn't feel angry anymore. He felt like he was floating in space, oblivious to the real world. *They knew?* The only hold he had left on normalcy broke away at that moment. Not only had the woman he once loved lied to him and gone after his brother, the brother he saved from deep-frying his life away. Not only all that, but now, his parents were in on the lies. The parents who had left him on a doorstep when he was still nursing. The parents who had gone on to have another child and raise him the normal all-American way, teaching him how to throw a ball and ride a bike. The parents who'd come back to Brooks—so much later—begging to rejoin his life. Those parents had been in on the lie too?

They'd known for at least a couple of weeks before Brooks found out. Who knew how long they might have waited to tell Brooks if Shay and Abby hadn't been in the motorcycle accident? Brooks could see his parents gleefully preparing for the arrival of their first grand-child, not at all concerned about how he would eventually process the news. They had too many things to prepare for: a wedding, the nursery, all the new clothes and toys.

Well, his parents were getting their wish. They would lose their throwaway son over it, but at least they were getting their wish. Finally they could love a child the way they were supposed to. Abby and Shay were going to give them a do-over. They could finally do it right.

Shay shuffled from one foot to the other and put his hands on his sides. "I told them not to tell. Don't be mad at them. Dad said I should tell you. We just hadn't found the right time. We didn't want to derail you."

"When Abby does run off, I bet they'll be willing to take your kid off your hands. You know Mom wants a third chance at being a mom."

"Fuck you," Shay said.

"No, fuck you." Brooks knew he'd crossed a line, that he'd said something nearly unforgiveable, but he was too far gone to stop now.

Shay stepped toward him with his fists rising and his face tensing.

Brooks threw up his left hand. "What? You going to hit me?"

"I don't know."

"Come on. Hit me. You know it's coming."

"I don't want to fight you, bro."

Brooks pushed him. "Don't call me 'bro.' I'm not your bro anymore. You go take your little family and run off. I'm done with you pieces of shit. All of you." Brooks didn't even know what he was saying anymore, but he knew he was looking to provoke his brother, to trigger that flick of the switch that would make Shay throw the first punch. It wasn't about what anyone wanted. Sometimes there's only one next step. Sometimes the fists must fly.

And throw the first punch he did, striking Brooks in the right cheek and causing his head to snap back. Tasting his own blood, Brooks tackled Shay into the driveway. They both grunted as they exchanged punches and rolled back and forth on the pavement, blood dripping down their limbs.

The neighbor across the street ran out and shouted that she was calling the police. It didn't matter. They didn't slow down until they had nothing left.

Brooks pushed himself up and hobbled to the door, fumbling for his keys. "You can have this mountain, Shay. It's all yours. I'm gone."

54

THE CHAINSAW

Wielding his chainsaw, Otis marched up the hill. He would start with the first block he and Rebecca had planted, a now mature syrah vineyard. He had spread Rebecca's ashes there last year. As he reached those vines, he could see her on the day they had planted them years ago, standing there with a post-hole digger; her hair hadn't even turned gray yet. They took turns between digging the holes and plugging in the baby vines.

Holding the chainsaw sobered him up some. The last thing he wanted was to cut his own leg off. When Otis was a kid and his family had first arrived in Montana, Aunt Morgan's husband had taught him how to run a chainsaw. And he'd taught him how such a great tool could easily turn on you. Otis hadn't forgotten those lessons, so as he pulled the trigger and began to saw the trunk of the first vine, he did so with care and precision.

He knew he was doing the right thing, because he was semi-sober by that point and still knew he had to cut his vines down. They'd given him some good harvests, but now, it was over.

Otis yelled, "Timber, ho!"

The chainsaw easily chewed through the trunk a foot above the ground, and the sawdust sprayed sideways onto his boot. The vine crashed to the ground, and he felt the pain in his heart.

Sometimes you have to walk away. Even if it's not the perfect moment. Others could make wine this year, but he couldn't pretend all was well while a man a mile away planned his Red Mountain takeover with his box wine and amusement park.

The people would hear of what Otis had done to his babies. Surely every wine trade journal and wine blog would talk about it. Even the mainstream media would grab this story. Maybe what he was doing would make a difference.

Otis stepped to the next vine. "You've done your duty, and now I'm saving you from the bloody battle that lies ahead. Timber, ho!" Otis screamed and cried as he pulled the trigger on the Echo and cut down another vine. Tears fell down his cheeks. Was this any different than taking a sword to your own child in an effort to protect him?

From the corner of his eye, Otis saw Elijah running down the hill, Chaco and Esteban close behind. Otis ignored their yells and approached the next vine. He felt bad for his men, but he couldn't stop now. The decision was made. He pulled the trigger, and the chainsaw whined as Otis let it chew into the third vine.

Elijah yelled Otis's name and hit him on the back.

Otis released the trigger, only halfway through the trunk.

"What the hell are you doing!" Elijah screamed over the roar of the chainsaw, terror painting his young face, an Irrigation Specialist's hat swallowing his little head. The boy had so much more to learn.

"Don't worry about it," Otis mumbled. A sharp pain in his back revealed itself.

"You're losing your mind! Drop that saw!"

Otis shook his head and fingered the trigger again. "Maybe I am!"

"I can't let you do this!" Elijah yelled. The cords in his neck strained.

Otis stopped the chainsaw. The silence zapped the mountain. "It's over, Elijah." He looked at Esteban and Chaco, felt their disappointment rushing over him. "Time for me to wrap up, boys. I'll help you find other work. Till Vineyards is no more."

"What are you talking about?" Elijah asked.

"There comes a time, my boy. There comes a time. That time for me is now." Otis pushed away any doubt. He had to stand firm with his decision.

"You don't have to do this," Eli pleaded, clasping his hands together.

"You want this mountain to keep going, then it's on you now. But I'm done. Now, let me get back to work."

"I'm not going to let you cut down these vines."

Otis stood tall, fury thick in his veins. "These are *my* vines, boy," he growled. "I planted every damn one. I raised these vines with these hands. They'll die by these hands."

Elijah shook his head.

Otis looked at Chaco and Esteban with their gaping mouths and wide, terrified eyes. They knew better than to intervene. He grasped the starter handle and looked at his young apprentice one last time. He was sorry to scare the boy, sorry to let him down, but like a doctor who'd decided he had to amputate a limb, Otis knew he had to cut away the rotten pieces before they infected the greater whole. "Don't get in my way. I've made my decision." The grapefather squinted his eyes, giving a look that left no room for further discussion.

Elijah dropped his head and nodded. He cursed and kicked the ground, then turned and walked away. He waved off Esteban and Chaco and they did the same.

"There comes a time," Otis whispered again.

He pulled at the handle, and the chainsaw roared back to life, gas fumes filling the air. This would take all day, and his back would hurt like hell, but he wouldn't stop until it was over.

He sawed through half the row before the searing pain in his spine dropped him to the ground. He'd felt the ache, but that last sting wasn't something he could stomach. Was this his body stopping him from doing something terrible? Normally, he could have run that saw for an hour or two before his back stopped him. He shut down the saw and lay flat on his back, moaning. He was covered in sweat.

He wiped his eyes—hoping to clear the blur—and growled at the pain.

The sun was off to his left. Squinting, Otis eyed the blue sky for a while, then closed his eyes again, welcoming some peace and quiet. The pain dwindled.

He felt a lick on his face.

How had Jonathan gotten out? That was the first thought that came to Otis as he opened his eyes again. But it wasn't Jonathan.

It was Cody, the Australian Shepherd.

"Did you break out again?" Otis asked, sitting up, rubbing his neck.

The dog licked him again and buried his snout in Otis's underarm. By that time, Jonathan, who was fenced in down below, began barking. Otis sat up, grimacing at the needles still stabbing his spine. He surveyed the row of dying vines, the aftermath of his assault.

Shaking his head, he returned his attention to Cody. "What are you doing here?" he asked, rubbing the dog down.

Cody barked again, and Otis knew exactly what he was saying.

Down the hill, Jonathan cried like he was caught in a fox trap.

"Settle down over there!" Otis yelled, his hands still on Cody. "This guy's an old friend. At least let him say hello without losing your mind." Jonathan kept going until Otis snapped at him again. Finally, the Great White Beast quieted, but he didn't take his eyes off Otis for the next five minutes.

Lowering his voice, Otis asked Cody, "What are you telling me? That I've lost my mind? Is that what you came all the way over here for?" He grabbed the Australian Shepherd and brought him into a hug. "I know I have. You're the last thing I thought I'd see, but it warms my heart, ol' boy. We went through a lot together, didn't we? I'm sorry I couldn't keep you. You know I wanted to. But you can't keep coming back. Who's going to protect all those animals over there?"

They sat in silence for a while, Otis stroking the dog's face. Jonathan let out the occasional jealous cry. Otis felt revelations bubbling deep within. He couldn't yet put a finger on their meaning, but he suddenly felt weary—a weariness no amount of sleep could transform.

He looked back at his vines and then to the smoking chainsaw. "What have I done, Cody? What have I done?"

55

BLACK EYES AND EX-LOVERS

That evening, Adriana looked across Margot's table, past ripe tomatoes, apricots, and peaches spilling out of a wooden bowl, and rested her eyes on Brooks. She wished she could find more clarity when it came to him. There was no doubt she liked him as a friend and more. Even she could see that. He'd done so much for her. For Zack. He'd brought Zack back to life. He'd been the first man to treat her like a woman in a long time, but they hadn't spent as much time together lately. Everything had been weird between them since Shay's and Abby's accident. Whether or not Brooks would ever admit it, Adriana believed he might still have feelings for Abby.

Brooks had several cuts on his cheek and forehead. His clasped hands revealed more cuts and scabs. He looked at her through eyes swollen from his brother's punches. "I'm leaving this place. Selling my house. Come with me."

"You can't be serious."

"Why is it so impossibly hard for you to see that I like you? Maybe I even love you. I sure like you enough to want to continue what we're doing."

Adriana dropped her head almost to the table and began massaging her temples. This was too much.

"You said yourself, you'll have to leave one day soon. Why not now? Why not with me?"

She looked up, deadpan, and said, "You see that little boy over there?"

Brooks flashed his eyes over her shoulder toward Zack, who was sprawled out on the couch thumbing through his iPad.

She continued, "I've spent every minute of my life since we left California trying to show him a better way, trying to heal him from his awful father. Trying to heal him from dealing with a separation that a boy that age should never have to endure. I'm not going to do that again. You can't board our ship and go for a ride and then hop off at the next port."

"Who says I'm going anywhere?"

Feeling stir crazy, she pushed back her chair and went to the kitchen. Taking a wet cloth from the sink, she began to wipe down the counter. "You mean other than statistics? You think we have something so special that we'll eventually marry and live together forever? You and I take Zack to his freshmen year at college."

"Why is that so hard to imagine?"

"You're delusional. I don't understand why. You've had a terrible life. It's not like you've grown up in a bubble, and you think every-thing always works out. You know it doesn't. So why, in this case, would you think a relationship between you and me would be any different?"

Brooks took his time to formulate a response. "You can't give up. I've learned that. Yeah, you're right, my life has sucked. A lot. For a long time. But we can't give up. Even I, a true glass-is-half-empty pessimist, know we must have faith that things will work out in the end."

"I have faith that if I do everything I can to protect my son, then maybe he'll turn out normal and somehow find a better life than I've had. Than you've had."

"You hover over your son his whole life, he'll find that bubble. And let me tell you, it won't be a good thing."

"Don't!" She lowered her voice. "Don't tell me how to raise my son."

"I'm not. I'm telling you that you're crazy not to give me—"

"What about Abby?" she interupted, feeling some relief in finally spitting it out.

"What about her?"

"You've still got something with her."

"What? She's having my brother's baby."

"That doesn't stop you caring for her. Look at you. You've been a wreck since you found out she was pregnant."

He shook his head. "I've been a wreck because I don't like being lied to. My entire family has been lying to me."

Noticing the trash can was full and needing a break from the conversation, Adriana removed and tied the bag, and with a curt "I'm taking out the trash," she walked out the front door. She rounded the corner of the house, walked past a line of shrubs, and tossed the bag into the larger can. She turned away as the lid slammed down.

"Hey, V," someone called out from the darkness.

She twisted left and stopped cold. The realization settled as if she'd been waiting, knowing he would return. No matter how far she ran. No matter how well she hid.

There before her stood the man who'd been haunting her dreams. Michael. Zack's father. He clasped his hands together in prayer, moving them up and down as he spoke. "V, let's talk. Please, please, please. I just want a few minutes."

"No," she said. "You need to leave." She started toward the front steps, wondering how he'd possibly found her so quickly. She'd planned their escape for months, and it had only taken him a few days to find her.

He followed her, stepping into the light. He'd gotten fit in prison. His body was harder, and his shoulders and arms swelled under his plaid shirt. He'd grown a goatee that was gray around his chin. "I've changed, V. You have to believe me. I miss you two more than anything."

She fired a finger at him, terror rushing over her. "Get away from us. I still have a restraining order against you, and I know you're violating your parole. Do you want to go back to prison?"

"Please don't call the police." He put his hands together in prayer. "I want to see my son."

"We're not a family anymore. I'm giving you this chance now to leave." She placed her hand on the knob, twisting it. "If I see you again, you're going back to prison."

He shook his head. "Don't do that."

"Leave."

"Please, I'm begging you. Have some compassion. You two are all I have."

"Not anymore." She almost asked him how he'd found them, but she was too terrified to speak further.

"Damn it! I want my family back! Did you really think you could run from me? I've known where you were for months!"

Adriana stopped, wondering how he could have possibly known.

"Oh, you want to know how?" he asked, knowing he'd gotten her attention. "Violeta, all I've done is think of you and Zack. I can't live without you."

"How did you find us?" She'd exhausted so much effort in planning and executing their disappearance—saving money, changing their names, leaving everything behind—that she desperately wanted to know the answer.

He grinned. "One thing I learned quickly on the inside, if you want something on the outside, there are plenty of people that can help you. You were very careful not to reach out to your old friends. I was impressed." He wagged his finger. "Your mother wasn't as careful."

Adriana was painfully reminded of her mother breaking their pact and reaching out to her friend, Graciella. She asked, "You had someone tap phones?"

In a sharp, angry burst, Michael yelled, "There's nothing I

wouldn't do to be with you! Tap phones. Hire private investigators. I'd kill to get my family back." He lowered his voice. "That's how much I love you and Zack. Don't you see?"

"Michael, you will never get us back. You hurt me. You hurt our son. You *hit* your son! You have to let us go!"

"I've changed."

"It's too late. Please leave before I call the cops." With that, she hurried inside and locked the bolt. Turning toward the stairs, she yelled, "Zack!"

"What's wrong?" Brooks asked, rushing from the table.

"Call the police. Michael's outside." She was barely able to talk, her body failing her, but the need to protect her son fed her some clarity.

"Don't let him in!" she yelled to Brooks, her foot on the first step. "Call the police!"

She leapt up the stairs. Zack was on the floor in the bedroom, halfway through a pirate ship puzzle. She moved to the closet and reached for the gun she'd hoped she would never have to use. With shaky fingers, she retrieved the bullets from a shoebox under the bed. She loaded the gun and said to Zack, "You stay up here. Okay?"

"What's wrong, Mommy?"

She set the gun down on the dresser and placed her hands on his cheeks. "There's a bad man downstairs. Stay up here. Okay? You hear me?"

He nodded, and she patted his head. "It's going to be okay. The police are on their way. Stay where you are. I'm serious."

Before running back down the stairs, she checked the windows in the room. Just to be sure. As she reached the bottom steps, she heard glass shattering, shards landing on the floor. She yelled Brooks's name as she hurried down the stairs. At the last moment, she remembered the safety and clicked it off. She raised the gun to eye level, her finger on the trigger, and rounded the corner into the living room.

Michael stepped through the shattered sliding glass door in the kitchen with a baseball bat in his hand. Brooks had grabbed a rolling pin and was moving toward the intruder.

"You need to get the hell out of here!" she screamed, raising the gun in the air.

Her voice startled Brooks, and he turned to see the gun. "Whoa, whoa. Set down the g—"

Michael struck the back of Brooks's head with the bat.

Brooks stumbled. Collecting himself, he swung the rolling pin, but Michael hit him in the side of the head, harder this time. Brooks fell down unconscious, the rolling pin smacking the floor and coming to rest next to him.

As long as Adriana had imagined this moment, as many times as she'd fired that gun at the range, as many times as this nightmare had ripped her from her dreams, waking in a shivery sweat, she couldn't have possibly been ready. Despite the motherly instincts that coursed through her, giving her courage, seeing Michael attack Brooks with such fury paralyzed her.

For a long time afterward, she would wonder why she hadn't been strong enough to pull the trigger at that exact moment. But she froze. Her vision blurred, and she froze with the gun pointing toward her ex-husband's knees.

He dropped the bat and ran to her, pushing the gun away and tackling her onto the hardwood floor. As she fell, the gun broke from her grasp, bouncing toward the dining-room table. Michael pulled at her hair and screamed, "You didn't think I'd find you?" He dragged her up to a seat. "You think you can take my son?"

"Stop," she begged.

He squatted next to her, still holding her hair, pulling it with great force and making her bite her teeth in pain. "Where is he?"

He turned and scanned what he could see of the downstairs. "Zack!"

Adriana followed his eyes, hoping Zack would run for safety. Instead, her boy had come around the corner and picked up the gun.

As fear consumed her, her past with Michael flashed before her eyes.

Michael hadn't always been this way. When they first dated, he'd pursued her with almost clumsy innocence, like he'd never done it before. Their first kiss was equally as clumsy. It took him a long time to gain the confidence to try to sleep with her.

There was something about him though. The thirsty eyes that looked into her with a desperate curiosity. He wanted her so badly. And when she played her game, she made it worse for him. With every "no," he longed for her more. He tried different tactics, first the polite courtship of youth, a few texts here and there. She eventually broke him down until he wasn't even playing his side of the game anymore. He flat out told her that he wanted to be with her, that he wanted her with everything he had. Again, she'd said no. She'd watched his eyes puddle as he turned.

He stopped calling. And that's when her switch flipped. She texted him: You're giving up so soon?

That was it. They spent every day together for a year, and he turned out to be the exact gentleman she'd hoped him to be. The one she'd dreamed about in her youth after her father had thrown her against the walls in her room and left her crying and wondering why her daddy hated her. She'd hoped that she could find someone different, and she had.

At least she'd thought so. The only thing that scared her was his drinking. When he drank liquor, he went to a dark place, but she allowed it. She would hold him and bring him back to the sunshine.

He lost a lot of money when the stock market fell. He already had a lot in the market but when it fell, he kept buying in. As their bank account dwindled, his drinking ran the other way. The first time he hit her was the day she told him she was pregnant with Zack.

"We have no money, and this is the time you choose to get pregnant? We tried for years, and you wait until now!"

"This should be the happiest day of our lives."

He stepped toward her, thick with the smell of whiskey. "Happiest day? We have no money. We're screwed."

"We have each other."

"Last time I checked, 'each other' doesn't pay shit. 'Each other' won't get us anywhere. I can't even afford health insurance. I should just send you back to Mexico and be done with you."

She'd slapped him so hard she was surprised he still had his teeth. He'd turned his bloody mouth to her and began spitting curses. He'd punched her as hard as he could.

She'd held her tummy, held the dream she had had since she was a little girl, held the baby as close as she could as he'd struck her in the mouth again.

He'd cursed more and then left. He hadn't returned for two days. She'd sat under a window for most of that time, watching the rays of sunlight slowly fan across the floor, ticking the time of her doom.

When he did return, he'd brought flowers and apologies. He'd promised to get better. He'd promised to stop drinking. She'd taken him in her arms as he'd cried and placed his own hands on her belly, as if he were trying to caress his unborn child. "I'm so sorry, my baby. I'm so sorry. I'll never let it happen again."

He'd stopped drinking; he'd started seeing a psychotherapist. He'd returned to the man she'd married. Then, a month later, something made him slip up. This time, Michael had slapped her hard, and she'd crashed headfirst into their glass-front china cabinet. When he picked her up off the floor—machine-gunning her with "sorry" while picking the glass shards out of her face—she couldn't even see through all the blood.

At the hospital later, she'd lied and told the staff that she'd tripped and fallen into the cabinet. She told her friends and family the same lie. Even her mother. Afterward, Michael had quit drinking again. He'd sought help. He'd returned to the man she married. Adriana had had two surgeries and begun the process of forgiving him.

She should have left him that day, but it took several more years of this abusive cycle before she'd found the courage.

56

MARGOT WALKS INTO THE MADNESS

"You know I'd marry you, right?" Margot said, petting Remi's forehead, loving this man with everything she had. They'd been spending all their time together, and it still didn't feel like enough.

The couple sat in the double rocking chair outside of Remi's Airstream with glasses of wine in their hands, watching the river run and the orange sun fall. He had his arm around her. Philippe and Henri chased each other in the grass. As she said the words, though, she felt trepidation. She held her breath, the seconds counting down at the same rate as her slowing heartbeat.

Had she said too much?

He grinned, his white teeth sparkling as his bushy eyebrow rose above his right eye. He tightened his arm around her. "I'd be the luckiest man in the world."

She touched his nose. "Yes, you would. I'm glad you realize it. On that sweet note, I have to go. Though I love my McDreamy spot down by the river, I do need my soaking clawfoot tub, my mirror, my closets."

"Closets?"

"Of course, closets. A woman can't have just one."

"Fair enough. Then I'll add on to the Airstream. Or better yet, I'll buy another Airstream for your clothes."

"Now you're getting ahead of yourself."

He kissed her. "I want to be with you all night. It's going to get lonely here."

"Why don't you stop by in the morning? Say hi while I'm cooking for the guests. I'll make you a plate." She almost invited him over for the night but was uneasy about it with Zack and Adriana living there.

He stole one last kiss and then let her go.

As he disappeared in the rearview mirror, she rubbed Philippe's ears and yelled in delight, "Oh, my God, I'm in love! I'm in love!" Then she broke into song. The young woman who had taken the stage in New York so many years ago sang, "(I Just) Died in Your Arms Tonight."

She rolled down the windows, and the wind made her blond hair dance behind her as she sang all the way home. Ah, everything was right. As she passed the lit-up *Welcome to Red Mountain* sign, she smiled, remembering the time Jake Forester had busted her singing this same song, not too far away. She didn't care today. She sang loud and proud, and besides, she *knew* she sounded good. Despite a long list of questionable genetics, she'd certainly been born with a beautiful voice.

The moment she began to push open her front door, the Cutting Crew song still lingering in her ear, she sensed something foul. All the happiness, all the positive emotion, was instantly sucked out of her by some unknown force. She pulled the door back, stopping Philippe before he barreled in. As she shooed him back down the stoop, she heard crying and then begging.

Margot peeked through the crack in the door, beyond the dining room table and into the kitchen. Adriana was on the floor with a man standing over her. They were both looking at Zack, who stood in between the bottom of the stairs and the kitchen holding a gun.

All the air in her lungs rushed out of Margot as she gasped and started to scream, but no sound escaped. Something powerful inside gave her the control to stay silent. That same something powerful gave her a sudden burst of courage, and a voice told her to stay calm and help. She sneaked through the door and worked her way left near the television, toward the kitchen, trying not to draw any attention.

With a hand up, the man said, "Son, drop the gun. You don't mean to do that."

Margot now knew for sure who he was.

"Put it down," Adriana pleaded. "Put it down, baby."

Margot was halfway there, moving with determination and clarity. She then saw Brooks lying face down on the floor.

Adriana yelled through her crying, "Don't let your son do this. Please leave, Michael!"

Margot made it to the open kitchen without anyone noticing. On the far side, she silently drew the Shun butcher knife from the block on the counter.

When Zack's eyes finally moved to her, Michael turned too. Margot didn't give him time to react. Without a second thought, she dashed toward Michael and raised the knife high in her right hand.

Michael raised both hands to defend himself, letting go of Adriana. Margot was ready to attack when she lost her footing, tripping and dropping into him. He caught her and slammed her to the floor, but she didn't let go of the knife, gashing the wood with the sharp tip.

Michael swung at Margot, hitting her in the shoulder. Margot felt the blow, but nothing was going to stop her now. She rose to her knees and raised the knife again. Michael threw up his hands to block her, but then Adriana kicked him in the side of the head. His face jarred left, his mouth contorting.

Margot jabbed the knife into his side, and he screamed. She felt the blade collide with bone as blood spurted back onto her blouse. She pulled the knife out and stabbed him again, this time in the stomach. Michael curled up, both hands rushing to the wounds. A pool of crimson collected around him. Margot met Adriana's terror-filled eyes, both of them gasping for air.

Adriana turned to her son. "Put it down, honey. Please."

Zack still held the gun pointed at his dad, his teeth clenched tight. He wouldn't let go.

Adriana crawled to Zack, holding her hand out. "Give me the gun."

Zack ignored her and kept that gun pointed at the middle of his father's back.

Margot said, "Give her the gun, Zack!"

He was going to pull the trigger; Margot moved out of the way. Just in time, Adriana wrapped her hand around the barrel. Zack didn't take his eyes off Michael as she tugged the gun from her son's hand.

Margot breathed a sigh of relief, then looked at Michael again. A pool of blood soaked his clothes. She slid across the floor to Brooks. The side of his head was swelling. She shook him, saying his name, asking if he was okay. She pulled him onto his back. The movement stirred him, and he began coughing.

57

SHOULD I STAY OR SHOULD I GO?

A driana felt as if someone had ripped out her heart and flattened it on the floor. The paramedics rushed Michael out of Margot's house in a stretcher. Brooks let them tend to his head wound but refused further treatment. Adriana tried to convince him otherwise, but his hard head was as tough as his luck lately. She could see the guilt in his eyes and knew that Brooks felt like he'd failed her tonight. That's why he wouldn't go with them.

Not wanting him to feel that way, Adriana took his hand, and the two of them watched through the window as the ambulance sped out of the driveway carrying a man she hoped would die. Blue and red lights of three police cars lit up the drive, and she saw several guests from the inn standing on the front steps rubbernecking. Once the ambulance's headlights disappeared, Adriana turned to Brooks. To add to the cuts, scrapes, and swollen eyes from the altercation with his brother, his ear and the area around his temple were badly swollen from where Michael had hit him.

Adriana glanced over to the couch where Margot was comforting Zack. She held him in her arms, petting his head and talking to him quietly. Adriana turned back to Brooks and touched his cheek. "You should have gone with them."

He shook his head. "I'm fine. I want to be here for you."

"There's nothing you could have done."

He nodded and looked down.

Brooks took Zack up to his room to play with toys while Margot and Adriana dealt with the officers. Adriana told her story to three different policemen scribbling on notepads, her private life laid bare for the first time in more than two years. Now everyone on Red Mountain would know the truth.

Once the policemen left, Adriana lay in bed with Zack until he fell asleep. She spent the next couple of hours sitting around the dining room table with Margot, Remi, and Brooks, hoping that Michael would not make it. She didn't tell them, and she'd never tell Zack, but it was true. She wanted Michael to die. She didn't want to run anymore. If Zack hadn't been there, Adriana would have taken that knife from Margot's hand and finished the job.

The nicest of the policemen called later in the night to tell her Michael would live. Her head dropped. For a long time after that call, she would dream of all the complications she could have avoided had she killed him, fantasizing about a life where she wouldn't have to watch her back.

Around two, Adriana hugged everyone and excused herself. She needed to be close to her son. She didn't sleep a wink, her mind a raging fire of planning and fear and sadness. Her wide-open eyes watched the digital clock on her bedside table count its way through the night, her son, the one who mattered most, sleeping in her arms. She hoped he wouldn't have nightmares of what had unfolded that evening. She hoped he could move past it with relative ease.

One amazing thing Adriana had noticed was the strength Zack had showed. The boy who often cowered in men's presence. Zack had found a strong resolve when he took the gun and pointed it at his father. Why had he done that? Because he loved his mom with everything he had. He couldn't allow anyone to hurt her. That thought had made her squeeze her son tighter, almost waking him as her arms tightened around him, never wanting to let him go.

The morning after, she woke feeling like she'd lost as much blood as Michael. Every bit of her was tired and withdrawn, shattered by the violence. As was customary when someone on the mountain suffered, many came to Margot's house throughout the morning with casseroles or baskets of food and bottles of wine, almost like a wake after a funeral. They brought their gifts and collected on the patio. They talked and laughed and attempted to make sense of it all.

Adriana couldn't make sense of any of it. She couldn't handle all the hugs, all the caring. Though she wanted to love the extended family of Red Mountain, though she wanted to embrace this sense of belonging coming over her, she couldn't. So instead of letting these people in, instead of letting them care for her, instead of allowing her and Zack to become a part of their community, she turned herself off from the connection. Yes, she smiled and let them hug her and even carried on conversations as if they were all friends, but her heart had already turned cold. There was no other option. They had to leave. Sure, Michael would go to jail, but he'd be back, and he'd know exactly where to look for them. It was better to avoid planting their roots there at all.

The Foresters arrived with Abby. Carmen had just returned from rehab. Adriana let a rare smile surface when Margot rose from her seat to welcome Carmen back to Red Mountain.

As Margot pointed from the top of Carmen's head to her feet and back up again, she said, "I want this—all of this. Whatever you did, wherever you went, just wow. Wow. Wow. Wow. Check me in tomorrow."

Luca followed Zack through the shattered glass door to play with the Jenga blocks in the backyard. In no mood to socialize, Adriana had kept herself busy cooking all morning. She was working on a salsa when Brooks joined her in the kitchen. The tile floor had barely dried from mopping up her ex-husband's blood. After a morning of mostly silence, he said, "I'm sorry I couldn't stop him."

She touched his arm. "Stop, Brooks. Just stop."

～

FOR BROOKS, the violence of the night was nearly overshadowed by the shame that weighed down heavily upon him.

While two paramedics worked on Michael, who was still on the kitchen floor bleeding, Brooks argued with Adriana and another paramedic about going to the hospital. There was nothing anyone could say, no concussion severe enough, to convince him to leave Adriana and Zack. After failing to protect them, Brooks wouldn't dare abandon them.

They eventually carried Michael out on a stretcher. As Brooks and Adriana watched the ambulance speed away, he couldn't shake the feeling of having let Adriana down, of not being able to protect her. Everything he wanted to say to her kept dying on his lips.

He almost jumped when she took his hand. Amid flashing lights and policemen walking in and out, she smiled at him and lightly squeezed his hand, and Brooks knew this was her way of saying he shouldn't feel any guilt at all. It was a powerful gesture, and Brooks felt in that instant how much she cared for him. For a while, as he sat around the dining room table with Adriana, Margot, and Remi, he felt like everything was going to be okay.

Adriana changed overnight.

Brooks woke on Margot's couch to find Adriana and Zack coming down the stairs.

"Good morning," Brooks said, sitting up and wiping his eyes.

"Good morning," Adriana replied, but there was no warmth in her words. She barely made eye contact.

Brooks knew she was in pain and terribly confused, so he tried not to bother her. He spent the morning helping Margot and Remi clean and then hanging out with Zack.

Guests began to arrive around nine, and as they collected on Margot's patio, Brooks finally got a chance to talk to Adriana. He walked into the kitchen and started to make another carafe of coffee. "What can I do for you?" he asked.

Adriana stood several feet to his left slicing tomatoes on the counter. She shook her head. "Nothing. I'm fine."

"I'm sorry I couldn't stop him," he said.

"Stop, Brooks. Just stop."

"I want to know what you feel inside. You're totally cutting me out right now."

"What do you want me to do, Brooks? How is this about you? Think about what just happened. Give me a break."

"I'm not trying to make this about me. I'm trying to figure out how I can help. We need to stick together. You can't just turn to ice and ignore me."

Adriana shook her head and set the knife down. She looked at Brooks and said, "You're worried about *us*, our relationship. I don't have that luxury. As I've told you a thousand times, that boy out there is all that matters to me. Stop trying to make this about *us*."

"I'm not trying to—"

The front door opened, disrupting their conversation. Brooks was so tired and lonely inside that he actually felt grateful when Shay came walking in. Sometimes, a shocking event like what had happened the night before can wake you up and remind you what really matters in life. At least he had someone. Shay might not be perfect, but he was family.

"Hey," Shay said, passing the long table on the way to the kitchen, pulling the bandana off his head. "You guys okay?"

"Everybody's outside," Brooks said and looked back to Adriana.

"How's your head?" Shay asked. "You look like shit."

"I'm fine."

"Glad to hear it." Shay started toward the shattered back door.

"Hey, bro," Brooks said, feeling a need to say something more.

Shay stopped and pivoted.

Brooks put aside everything between them and said, "Thanks for coming."

"We're family. Family is forever."

"Yeah." Brooks did his best to offer a smile, but it was little more than the right corner of his mouth turning up, a muscle getting less and less work lately.

Shay understood; they both did. Family doesn't go away.

Family is forever.

58

THE THINGS THAT MATTER

O tis spent the morning sitting among the vines he'd sawed down, so many emotions rushing over him. He hated himself for what he'd done, but he was thankful he hadn't cut more down. The vines would grow back and one day offer their fruit again. Like Otis, grapevines could handle quite the beating and keep on keeping on.

He saw Joan coming up the hill, a basket in hand. Hungry for an early lunch, he walked down to help. "What do you have there?"

"When's the last time we had a picnic?"

"Too long," he said, taking the basket.

He led her to his truck, which was parked in the gravel next to his syrah block. They sat on the tailgate of the truck, their legs dangling, the basket between them. Joan pulled out the bottle of wine they'd opened the night before. Then she set out two plastic wine glasses, a couple of tomato and avocado sandwiches, a bag of raw vegetables, and a container of potato salad. As she fixed his plate, he noticed her hands were much steadier. His baby was coming back. What was more important than that wonderful news? The thought—though positive—made him feel even more disappointed in himself for his mental breakdown.

Yesterday Joan had returned from her house to find Otis sitting in the dirt with Cody. She had held Otis for a long time as he buried his head in her lap. Today he'd woken up with no intention of cutting down more of his vineyard. Whether he was to farm again next year, whether he was to take on another vintage, remained to be seen. He knew that by cutting down his vines, he was letting down the mountain. He was letting Bellflour win. He wouldn't do that.

No. Today, the prevailing thought on his mind was that he'd give his vines to Elijah. Maybe he and Joan would go back to traveling. They could buy an RV and hit the road. He figured Aunt Morgan had given him the trip around the world so that he might learn some life lessons, but all he'd done was wish himself back to the mountain. Maybe he needed more traveling to learn how to let go.

He felt like Obi-Wan Kenobi when Darth Vader finally struck him down, the light saber slashing through an empty robe. It wasn't defeat; it was a moving on, letting the new guard continue the fight. Bellflour would swing his light saber, but Otis would be gone, having done what he needed to do.

He caught an avocado slice falling out of the side of his sandwich, pushed back in, and asked, "What in the world was I thinking?"

Joan grinned and set her hand on him. "They'll tell that tale for a million years."

"At least I gave them something to talk about."

"That you did."

"And now I think it's time to make my exit."

"You've given this place and everyone here your life. Now it's time to do what you want. If that's traveling in an RV with an old hag like me, then lovely. If it's driving your John Deere, tilling your soil, working another harvest, then grand. But at our age, we need to go for the smiles." She crossed her arms and looked at him.

"Go for the smiles," he whispered, pondering her words. "Then I'm going for you, my love. You're the smiles. I didn't get out of bed to taste my wines today. I didn't get out of bed to walk my vines. I got out of bed to be with you. You're the smiles."

As she echoed his sentiments, Joan refilled his wine with a steady hand. He hadn't seen her shake in weeks. He set his hand on her thigh and told her he loved her. And he found that smile. Amid the absurdity of this life, the highs and lows, Joan made it all worth it.

"I realized something yesterday," Otis said. "While I was on the ground and Cody was staring at me like I was crazy, it occurred to me that I need to stop fighting. I wonder if all the bad luck in my life comes from my own resistance."

Joan smiled as if she'd been waiting for months for him to say those words. "I think you're onto something, my dear. You don't always need your fists to get what you want. A little peace in your world wouldn't be such a bad thing."

"Why didn't you mention this earlier?"

She grinned and held up her hands. "You can lead a horse to water but... Well, you know."

59

CUTTING FLESH

As Margot sat with Remi under an umbrella watching Zack and Luca play Jenga, she felt sick inside. She was doing her best to be a good host, welcoming the forty or fifty guests who'd come to offer support, but she couldn't shake off the night before. She'd been killing a man with kitchen utensils in her daydreams for a long time, but she never could have imagined the man would be anyone other than her own ex-husband.

Stabbing a man in real life was nothing like in those merlot-hazed dreams while soaking in her clawfoot tub. Actually stabbing a man, feeling the blade cut into flesh, was evil and chilling. Especially for a vegetarian unfamiliar with cutting flesh of any kind.

More than her role in nearly killing a man, Margot felt Adriana's and Zack's pain like it was her own. She'd spent the past weeks feeling sorry for herself, and that now seemed so insignificant in comparison to what her two housemates were going through. Zack appeared to be okay, considering, but Adriana hadn't been herself all morning. She'd been trying to fake like everything was okay, but Margot knew her too well. Adriana was torn apart inside.

Remi excused himself to take a phone call. As he walked off toward the garden with his phone to his ear, Margot turned to find

Adriana sitting by herself in the grass, apparently unaffected by the blazing noon sun. Adriana watched with hollow eyes as her son pulled a block from the bottom of the Jenga tower. Zack and Luca gasped as the tower nearly fell. Margot and Adriana looked at each other for a moment, and Margot did her best to offer a loving smile. Adriana smiled back and then turned away.

Remi came back from the garden, touched Margot's shoulder and said, "That was Harry Bellflour. He wants to see me."

"What's it all about?"

"I have no idea. Do you mind? I'll be back as soon as I can."

"What does he want with you?"

"You'll be the first to know. I don't want to leave you, but this could be important. Do you want me to stay?"

She patted his hand. "No. No, please just come back as soon as you can."

"Call me if you need me, and I'll come running."

While he was gone, she couldn't believe how much she missed him, how much she needed him, her partner.

Ten minutes after Remi left, Otis and Joan arrived with two growlers of kombucha and a tray of fruit. Otis set the tray on a nearby table and said to Margot, "I would have brought something a little more fun but Joan wants us all to live forever."

"Thank you, guys," Margot said, hugging Otis and then Joan.

"I'm so sorry we're just getting here," Joan said, not letting go of Margot. "You should have sent someone to get us. We were outside and didn't have our phones."

"It's totally okay. As you can see, we've got plenty of support."

"Still," Joan said. "I'm sorry I wasn't here for you. Are you okay?"

"Yeah," Margot said. "I'm fine. Just a scary night."

"I can only imagine." Joan pulled her into another hug.

60

HERE'S REMI!

An hour after arriving at Margot's house, Otis looked up from his chair on the patio to see a man coming from the house with a beaming smile that didn't fit out there, in a place where the rest of them were trying to find a modicum of joy in the aftermath of a nearly deadly evening.

"Please, follow me," the man said to the folks inside. Then, to everyone now assembled on the patio, he said, "I have some great news."

All eyes went to him. He kissed Margot on the mouth, and Otis realized the man in the wingtips was Margot's new boyfriend. Remi Valentine pulled Margot to a standing position and spun her around. "You're not going to believe it," he said loudly so everyone could hear. "I know last night was awful, and I don't mean to take away from that, but I have some grand news."

He wrapped his arm around Margot's waist and faced the fifteen people on the patio. He announced, "I've just bought the Drink Flamingo property from Harry Bellflour."

There were oohs and aahs and gasps.

Otis's mouth dropped to the patio floor, and he felt lightheaded for a moment, like he might faint. An immediate buzz of happiness hit his body, ran through his veins, and tingled his flesh. He launched out of his chair to yell, "What!"

Remi addressed Otis and the rest of the crowd. "I made him a more-than-fair offer last week. Well above what he paid for the property. He turned that and the counters down, and he made it clear that no amount of money would change his mind. Well, things have changed." Remi smiled. "He can't get water. They're already at five hundred feet and ripping through diamond bits. His soil geologist got it wrong. They thought they'd be tapping into the Scooteney Flats Aquifer, the one more south of Red Mountain. But they're not, they're in ours, the Red Mountain Aquifer. The water table's too low. They can't do what they wanted to do. They could barely plant grapes, let alone build anything commercial. They really screwed up."

Otis approached Remi and introduced himself. They shook, and Otis pulled the much taller man into a hug and kissed his neck. "You have no idea what good news this is." Otis had never felt so solid and brilliantly happy. His voice cracked, and his eyes watered. He said to Remi, "You've done a good thing, young man. A very fine thing."

Remi offered a humble nod. "It's not over yet. We have to close, but they're dead in the water. Or dead without water. The D.O.E. won't give them a permit to dig any deeper. They say it might collapse our aquifer."

Otis tried to think clearly, to contain his emotions. Referring to the water Benton County was drawing from the Yakima River, he asked, "What about the L.I.D.?"

"The county won't run lines under the highway. Bellflour already tried that approach. He's done."

Otis said, "I hope you didn't pay too much."

Remi grinned. "A fraction of what he paid. I almost walked away. No one else is going to buy the property, so he'd be stuck with it, but you never know what could happen down the road. Laws could change; he might get his water. I thought it better to take the property off his hands." He raised his finger. "For a song, I might add."

A loud pop stole the silence. Several people ducked, still jittery from the night before. Otis's heart jumped into his throat, and he spun in the direction of the sound.

With a beautifully comforting grin, Joan was standing without her cane by the door. She held a bottle of Champagne with bubbles spewing from the top. "I'd say this news is worthy of an early nip!"

Along with the rest of them, Otis let out a bellowing laugh, and every damned thing in his world suddenly made sense, like he'd been piecing together a puzzle all his life only to have just fit in the last piece. A nearly orgasmic sensation ran through him, and he kept laughing long after everyone else had quieted. He finally found his chair as someone handed him a glass. He raised his glass to the others, raised it as high as he could, and thought about Red Mountain. What was it that Mark Twain had said? Something about spending a lifetime worrying about things that never happened. That's how Otis felt right then. He should have trusted the mountain. She could indeed protect herself.

Otis felt a hand on his shoulder and turned. Brooks—the man he most connected with in life—was staring down at him. He patted Brook's hand. "We made out okay, my boy."

"That we did." Brooks squeezed Otis's shoulder. "Everything's going to be all right."

They both smiled and no more words needed to be spoken.

As Brooks walked away, Otis noticed Carmen Forester had turned down a glass of bubbles, and he was happy to see she was still sober. The first time you quit is rarely the last.

◦◦◦

THREE DAYS LATER, Joan and Otis were at the Conoco getting gas. Otis was talking to her through the open window of his truck while he waited for the tank to fill. He'd just made a comment about the nice weather when Harry Bellflour's Lexus rolled to a stop at a nearby pump.

Otis said, "Look who's here."

From the front passenger seat, Joan whispered, "Please be nice."

"I'm always nice," he replied, but he felt the inner curmudgeon rising up inside him.

Bellflour stepped out, and Otis said loudly, "Well, well, well. I hoped you'd be gone by now."

Bellflour approached Otis, stopped five feet away and crossed his arms. The gold on his fingers and wrist sparkled in the midday sun. "That's no way to greet your neighbor."

"You need any help packing?" Otis basked in the knowledge that Bellflour's plans to bring the circus to town had been thwarted, and by the mountain, no less. Despite the fact that he'd decided to stop fighting everything in his life, he couldn't help but gloat.

"I'm not sure I'm going anywhere." Bellflour looked toward his own house high on the Horse Heaven Hills and then back to Otis with a sly grin, almost as if he somehow thought he'd won. "I kind of like it up there. I can keep an eye on you."

"I'm happy to recommend a good real estate agent." Otis almost laughed at the thought of these two grumpy old men throwing jabs at each other at a gas station.

Bellflour frowned. "I was going to put something great out here, Otis. Something that would have finally made you people some money. Something that would have put Red Mountain on the map."

Processing the comment, Otis returned the gas nozzle to the dispenser and tightened the lid on his tank. "I'd rather burn this place to the ground than get rich off something less than authentic."

"Well, I have a couple of other ideas I'm tossing around. There's too much money to be made around here to walk away." Bellflour noticed Joan and asked, "Aren't you going to introduce us?"

"Don't you hear what this mountain is trying to tell you?" Otis asked, ignoring the Joan request.

"Enlighten me."

"She's saying," Otis cupped his hands on each side of his mouth and continued in a raspy voice, "Go back to where you came from!" Dropping his hands, he said, "By the way, you look all dried up. Shriveled. Can I get you some water? I hear you're having a hard time finding it around here."

"That's funny." He looked at Joan. "He's funny, isn't he?"

"We make classy wines here on Red Mountain," Otis said, feeling a growing rage expanding inside his chest. "But don't think for a minute I'm not too classy to kick your ass all the way back to Lodi. It's time you hit the road."

Bellflour eyed Otis as the light-hearted nature of their conversation evaporated. "You don't want me as your enemy." He thrust out his finger. "Don't start a war you can't win. There will always be property to buy up here."

Otis's jaw tightened upon hearing the threat, but he caught himself before continuing down this aggressive line of conversation. He was suddenly back on the ground, lying next to the vines he'd cut down. The clarity of detail made this flash of a daydream vividly real. He found Cody lying beside him and petted the dog's neck and massaged his ears. In another flash, Otis's imagination carried him to a different time almost a year ago. Otis remembered the day Cody's previous owner, Henry Davidson, had stumbled over to Otis's house, armed and high on drugs. Otis saw the man raise his gun and fire at Joan. He saw Joan fall.

Back at the gas station, standing there in front of Bellflour, a chill hit Otis's bones. For a moment, he thought he'd lost her. He looked into the truck and there she was, looking at him with the most loving eyes he'd ever seen. Her presence washed over him, and the joy of knowing she was okay once again soothed the tremendous pain that burned inside.

Otis let the tension in his jaw dissipate. He was tired of the fight. The day he'd cut down his vines had affected his soul; it had awakened him, in a sense. He'd learned he had to let go some. As Joan had said, he needed to find some peace.

He blew out a heavy breath of air and met Bellflour's eyes. "No more wars. It's peace and love around here." Otis glanced at Joan. "Right, dear?"

Joan smiled with satisfaction written all over her face.

Otis touched his heart and said to her, "No more wars."

"That's a shame," Bellflour interrupted. "I thought we were just getting started." He started back to his Lexus. "I'll see you around."

Otis could think of so many replies but found the true answer in the calm of his heart. "Good luck with your winery, Bellflour." The man didn't turn back and only waved, flashing all that gold.

Otis climbed into his truck and looked at Joan. "I was nice, wasn't I?"

"You never stop amazing me, dear."

Otis leaned in for a kiss. "Maybe one day I'll even grow up."

Joan met his lips and then whispered, "Don't ever do that."

61

HARVEST

Two Weeks Later

Like the winery itself, the land that extended out the backdoors of Lacoda was designed to blend into the landscape. Stone pathways wound through the desert terrain leading to quaint seating areas and rock gardens that looked out over the vineyards now bearing ripe fruit. In one corner, before the vines began to climb up the hill, there was a performance stage shielded from the sun by a series of stretched canvas tarps. A grand piano, a rack of guitars, an electric bass, and a drum kit awaited tonight's performers.

Two men, nearly covered in flour, baked pizzas in the wood oven. Tables offered gorgeous spreads prepared by the winery chef. As was the tradition, the guests brought wines from their own properties and left them along the stone wall for all to enjoy.

While he waited for Margot to arrive and the concert to begin, Jake organized a tug of war match. He split the teams into two groups of ten. As Adriana lined up behind Zack, the symbolism to her own life overwhelmed her—to the point that she couldn't help but laugh at it all. She felt a tugging inside of herself, almost as if the mountain were pulling her toward it. Or *her*, as the others might say. And there she was tugging back, demanding that it was time to leave.

It's true. A part of her didn't want to say goodbye, but she didn't have a choice. Yes, Michael was in jail, waiting on his trial. How long would they put him away? He had money. He had connections. She'd spoken with lawyers who guessed he'd do five years for violating the restraining order, breaking and entering, and attacking Brooks. But he might walk after three. What was she to do then? That's why it made some sense to leave now, before their ties to Red Mountain grew stronger. At some point, as Zack fell further in love with the mountain and her people, she wouldn't be able to drag him away.

As they commenced to tugging the rope, she felt a sense of belonging. No matter how much she tried to ignore the warmth, she felt her cold stone heart come alive. With this feeling emerged a spirit-lifting laugh, but no one noticed because everyone on both sides was pulling with everything they had. And when Adriana's team lost balance and began to fall on top of each other, tumbling into defeat, she cackled even louder, and soon everyone was on top of one another laughing.

After the game, Adriana and Brooks collapsed into two Adirondack chairs to watch the kids play bocce ball. She beamed as one of them handed Zack the small white ball, told him it was called the pallino, and let him have the first throw. He'd left his goggles back home, and he held his head high as he tossed the pallino into the air.

As a rush of emotions struck her and her eyes watered, Brooks reached over and said, "Is this the second time you've ever cried? You're not turning into a softie, are you? I like your tough exterior."

She closed her eyes and shook her head. "Leave me alone."

Watching the boys play, Brooks said, "Zack's happy, isn't he?" As she nodded, he pleaded, "Don't go."

She pulled her hand away and covered her eyes.

"Let's stay here. Together."

"I'm not doing this again, Brooks."

"Yes. Yes, you are. You need to give us a chance. You need to give this mountain a chance."

Even if Brooks didn't have feelings for Abby any longer, even if he truly liked Adriana, there was still Zack. "I have to leave."

"Then why haven't you left yet? Michael's going away. You and Zack are safer today than you've been in years."

She started to say something and realized she didn't know how to answer. Brooks was right.

He continued, "That's what I thought. Be here with me. Let's stay and make this work."

"What about your family? I thought you were going to turn in your resignation notice to Jake."

"He talked me out of it."

"Again?"

"Yeah, again." He pointed to the other guests, the people of Red Mountain. "You see this? You see the love these people have? You can't find that anywhere else. We might have our issues, but we're a part of this mountain. You're a part of it too." He pointed at Zack and Luca and the other children. "They are the future of Red Mountain. Look at your son. He's happy here. Don't take him away. Let us all help protect him. Protect you."

She cried, and he leaned toward her, patting her hand. He said, "I'm here for you. I know it's about your son. I know you don't want to let your heart lead you. But let go. We can try it out here. Let me build a relationship with your son. Let me do the protecting from now on. Let me protect you like you protect Zack. Even if you and I don't work out, I'll be there for you both. Why not give it a try?"

"I'm scared, Brooks. I'm really scared."

"You have every reason to be. This is an ugly world sometimes. That's why, when you find something beautiful, you can't let it go."

"Oh, are you that beautiful thing?" she asked, searching for some light.

"We are. This mountain. These people. Let us help you figure out how to deal with your ex. We want you here. And I'm not letting you walk away. You mean too much to me. Adriana, I'm begging now. You know how Joan told me to say yes more? Why don't you give it a try? Say yes. Say you'll stay. Life's too short to keep running away."

Adriana crossed her arms. She didn't know what to do. She didn't even know who she was anymore. Was she Violeta? Or Adriana? Now that Michael had found her, what was the point of being Adriana anymore? Then again, what would be the point of going back to Violeta? That life was long gone.

Someone yelled, "Margot's coming!" and everyone ran to the front of the building to welcome the birthday girl.

62

WHAT SHE DOESN'T KNOW

F or Margot, things began returning to normal. She and Remi saw each other almost every day, and they were soon going to make wine together at his place. Margot loved the man more and more with each visit. The only thing missing from her life was Jasper, but he'd promised he'd visit home soon. Margot wanted to visit Boston, but Adriana was about to leave, and Margot had no one to run the inn. Not that she hadn't tried with Adriana. She'd begged her to stay.

Tonight was a big night. It was her birthday. Remi was taking her on a real date, to a new place in Richland. They had much to celebrate. Earlier, Remi had closed on the Bellflour property in a rush closing since he was paying cash.

Drink Flamingo was no longer coming to Red Mountain.

If the number of outfits Margot had tried on was any indication of how she felt about Remi, then she loved the hell out of him. You couldn't see one inch of hardwood floor or oriental rug owing to the piles of dresses scattered about.

After spending much longer than usual getting ready, Margot raced down the stairs just in time to straighten up. When the doorbell rang, her heart danced. She raced to the door and pulled it open. "Hi there, mister."

Remi wore a red sport coat and dark jeans. He kissed her mouth. "Happy Birthday. You look absolutely stunning."

"Not too bad yourself. Are those for me?"

He handed her the bouquet. "You're not tired of flowers, are you?"

"That day will never come. Trust me."

Margot invited him in while she found a vase for the flowers. He followed her toward the kitchen. As she clipped the ends of the stems, she said, "Congratulations. You saved Red Mountain."

He rested his hands on the counter. "Red Mountain saved Red Mountain. I had little to do with it."

"Still, you were there at the right time. You were fated to be here."

"I do believe that. Though I love Red Mountain as much as anyone here, I love you more. I'm fated to be here because the love of my life is here."

She liked that. "I want you to meet Jasper. Oh, how I wish he could have come home. You can't really know me without knowing him."

"I know. I feel the same way about my daughter, though I'm not sure there's much I can do about that right now."

"She'll come home to you one day. You're such a nice man. Everyone messes up."

"Yeah, I know. I'll be waiting. Maybe one day we'll be lucky enough to sit at a table with Jasper and Carly. That will be a great day."

Once she finished with the flowers, Remi escorted her out to his truck. He opened the passenger door and waited for her to be comfortable. He kissed her again and gently pushed the door closed. Halfway there, as they passed West Richland, he slowed down and pulled into a parking lot. Turning the truck around, he said, "Uh-oh. I forgot something."

"What?" Margot asked.

"We need to run back by my place."

As he drove back to Red Mountain, Margot tried to extrapolate more information. "What could you possibly have forgotten?"

"Did you see the weather for the rest of the week? I'm so excited for fall." He turned up the yacht rock easing through the speakers.

She turned it back down. "Remi, what did you forget? You're acting weird."

"Before we know it, it's going to be cold. That little trailer isn't going to do it. Maybe I need to build something."

"Don't change the subject."

"I have no idea what you're talking about." He turned the music back up.

It went on like that for a while, but they didn't go toward his house. He turned right onto Sunset Road.

She hit his leg. "What are we doing? This isn't the way to your house."

He was smiling and stumbling over his words. "I, I just need to grab... Just shush."

"I don't like secrets."

"I can tell."

They rode the length of Sunset, past the turn to Épiphanie, past the other wineries. As they rose up the hill, she noticed commotion at Lacoda. A line of cars stretched along both sides of the drive leading down the hill to the winery, and the parking lot was full.

Remi passed the cars and pulled up to the front of the winery. He was saying something to her, but she wasn't listening. Margot eyed the group standing at the entrance.

They were her friends! The cooking class. Joan. The Foresters. Wait, was that Emilia? Down the line she went. All the old and new guard of Red Mountain. And then, lastly, Jasper. Her son! Standing there with a smile plastered on his face and his hand in the air waving. They were all waving at her.

She jumped out of the car and ran to her son, shaking. "What are you doing here, Jasper? What are you doing?"

"Happy Birthday, Mom."

Margot broke into tears, then turned to Remi and asked, "Did you do all this?"

"Happy birthday, honey."

"I don't know what to say."

Jasper squeezed her tight.

Margot said to her son, "You two don't even know each other."

Jasper shook Remi's hand. "We've been chatting over the past few weeks."

"Everybody is here...for me?" Margot asked.

"Of course, we are," Jasper said, and then Emilia appeared and gave Margot hugs too.

Margot wiped her watery eyes. "Oh, my God, I love all of you."

They all hugged and circled around her. She'd never felt so much love in her whole life.

"Are we having a party?" Margot asked through the rivers of tears.

"Mom, you're in store for an amazing night. Remi must really like you."

She pulled away from everyone and found Remi, wrapping her arms around him. She kissed his face. "Yes, he does," she said. "Yes, he does." She hugged him with everything she had and whispered into his ear, "No one has ever thrown me a surprise party before."

"And no one will ever beat this one," he whispered back. "Happy birthday, my love."

63

LITTLE SIPS OF NORMALCY

As everyone returned to the back of Lacoda to hear the first song of the concert, Brooks grabbed Adriana and led her down to a quiet spot by the vines. He said, "Sometimes, we look at this life and think we need to make these big permanent decisions. Like everything until our dying day needs to be decided. How about we put all that aside? How about we both commit to staying here one year? You have a good job, a great place to live. You know Margot wants you, and you might even finally admit that we have something special between us."

"Do we?"

"You're impossible. Just admit it."

"You want me to spell it out?" she asked.

He nodded slowly.

She said, "We have something. I like you too."

He touched her cheek. "Was that really so hard to say?"

"Almost impossible."

With his lips almost touching hers, he said, "She sprouts her wings and flies. Freedom from her chains. It feels good to tell someone you like them, doesn't it?" He kissed her.

She pulled away prematurely. "What about your family? Can you stand living on Red Mountain while your brother and Abby have a baby?"

"Not only that, I'm going to be a *good* uncle."

She laughed at that.

"You don't believe me?"

"Oh, I know you can be a good uncle. I'm just not sure you're ready for family, the real version of family. I understand the child inside you always wanted a family. But now that you're getting a taste, I'm not sure you're ready for reality. The reality of what a family is."

He lit up. "You're going to stay, aren't you?"

She rolled her eyes.

He said with a grin, "You are." He took her hand. "Follow me."

"What?" she asked. "Where are you taking me?"

"I want to show you that I'm ready for the reality of family."

He led her toward the hundred or so people gathered around the stage. The late summer sun poked through the trees. Brooks scanned the crowd with determination. And then he found them. He saw his parents first and then Shay and Abby. One big happy family. He pulled Adriana toward them.

"What are you doing?" she asked.

"Just come on."

He swung by the stone wall lined with wine bottles and filled their glasses. He raised his glass as they approached his family. "I have some things to say, you guys." They looked at him and let him speak. "Mom, Dad. I'm glad you're here. We're going to find you a house that you love, and you're going to find a home here on Red Mountain. Shay and Abby, I'm happy for you. I'm happy I'm going to be an uncle. I know I'm a pain in the ass, but I've learned a lot since we've all met. I just want to say I'm not going to run. Sometimes life isn't what you hoped. Or what you expected. But that's not a bad thing."

He turned to Adriana. "Adriana and I are going to stay on the mountain. We don't know what the future might hold, but we've both agreed not to run from our pasts. Not right now. We may run in a more calculated fashion a year from now, but we'll see what the coming days bring. I'm going to do another harvest. Adriana is going to stay and work with Margot. The reason I'm saying this is because I don't want there to be anything awkward among us."

He blew out an exhausted breath and sipped his wine. "I know I'm at fault for a lot of it. I don't blame you for not telling me about the baby. It's a sensitive situation. But that's over. All is forgiven. What matters is that we are here for each other, and we have a new life coming."

He pointed to Abby's belly, which was now showing the little life inside of her. "I'm going to be an uncle. This little guy is adding to our family. What matters more than that?"

Brooks opened his arms. The family collected into a hug, and Charles said to Adriana, "You'd better get in here too." They'd barely even met her, but it didn't matter.

Adriana smiled as Charles pulled her in.

Brooks took the time to feel the energy of his family. For the first time in his life, he was losing touch with being alone.

As they let go, they heard a commotion near the stage. Brooks turned and saw Jake picking up his guitar. The bassist and drummer they'd used for Jake and Jasper's recent album found their places. And Jasper approached his grand piano, stretched his fingers, and sat down.

Jake walked over to Jasper and whispered something that drew a smile. He returned to his place and approached the mike. He'd been doing this so long, he didn't need to bring the crowd in. They were already pushing up toward the stage, waiting for his words.

"It feels good up here," Jake said. He waited for the sound man to fix a bit of feedback and then, "We're so happy you've joined us." He turned to Jasper. "We're lucky to have this guy back, before he launches into outer space." Jake tuned one of his strings and said, "I like that this special woman, Margot Pierce, the Princess of Red Mountain, is what brings us together yet again. Where is she?" After finding her in the crowd, he said, "May we attract so many more great people like you. Thank you for what you do for this mountain. Happy birthday."

Everyone cheered, and he said, "We talked a lot about what we should play, how we should open up this special night. There was only one song that made perfect sense. If you look back at what we've been through the past year, there's one common theme. One thing that keeps us whole. One thing that protects us. Somehow, this mountain has survived yet again, and it's brought us together even stronger than before. So this one is for you, Red Mountain."

Jasper stood from his piano and faced his bandmates. He snapped his fingers, counting out the beat. Once the rhythm section was with him, he sat and began hammering out the beginnings of a song Brooks knew well: "The Mountains Win Again" by Blues Traveler.

Jasper sang with all the cool in the world and by the time they reached the chorus, the small crowd had their hands in the air and was singing along.

Adriana put her face to Brooks's face and said, "You're the only one who could ever melt me." She planted a kiss on him that he'd feel for the rest of his life.

64

NO, HE DIDN'T

Margot danced and sang. She hadn't felt this way in her entire life. Finally, she was home. In every way, she had found home.

The band played beautifully, and she had her arms around Remi and couldn't get enough of him, the smell, the smile, the way he touched her. He'd done all this for her. He didn't even know these people, yet he'd made it happen.

"I still don't know what to say," Margot said in his ear. "I can't believe you pulled this off."

"You really had no idea?"

"Not a clue."

"Well, I'm not done yet. Follow me." Remi led her to the stage. He raised his hand to Jake, who was still singing.

Jake nodded back.

Margot had no idea what was going on as Remi wrapped his arms back around her.

When the band ended the song, Jake said into the mike, "I'd like to ask Remi Valentine to come up here. He's the organizer of this evening's events. And for those of you who don't know, he's the guy who saved us from Drink Flamingo."

Remi hopped up onto the stage, grabbed the microphone, and said, "Correction. The mountain saved us from Drink Flamingo. Don't assume I had anything to do with it. But much more importantly, I wanted to say something about the birthday girl." He looked at her. "Would you join me on stage?"

He helped her onto the stage and held her hand as he said into the mike, "A lot of you don't know me. I'm the hermit living on Demoss Road in the Airstream. I came to this mountain running from an unhealthy life in Seattle that was consuming me. Here I found Margot. She's the woman I've dreamed about my whole life. She's the kind of woman—or partner—so many of us doubt we'll ever find. I have never met a more beautiful, more intelligent, more kind, more outgoing, more loving woman in the world. She's the only one who can make me laugh for hours on end. And tonight, I've had the great fortune of meeting her son in person and hearing him rip that piano to shreds. I can't believe how lucky we are."

He removed the mike from the stand, reached into his pocket, and knelt down.

Margot raised her hand to her mouth.

"I figured you should all be in on this one, because we're all family here—if you will have me. I want to marry this woman, and I want the whole world to know it." He pulled out a box and revealed a diamond bigger than any Margot had ever seen.

She lost her breath.

"Will you marry me, Margot Pierce? You are the love of my life."

Her cheeks puffed with air as she tried to grasp a breath, grasp reality. "Yes, yes, yes!" She flung her hand out and let him slip on the ring. She held the diamond up to the crowd, and it shimmered under the stage lights. The crowd exploded. The couple stood and kissed as if they were the only two there. A long kiss that sealed the deal for a marriage that would last the rest of their lives.

When they finally broke away from each other, Remi said, "I have a couple of last surprises in store for you...and for my fiancé. Margot has a favorite song that I've asked the band to play."

Margot smiled, knowing exactly which tune.

He took her hand. "Let's go dance."

Leaving the stage, they moved through the crowd toward the front. She looked at the band. Sitting at the piano, Jasper said into the mike, "Mom, congratulations. I've been talking to Remi for a while now, and I think it's safe to say he loves you. In fact, he loves you so much, he thought it would be cool to bring out a special guest for tonight."

Margot glanced at Remi for a second.

He winked.

Jasper said, "You can't sing a Cutting Crew tune without Nick Van Eade, right?" and then looked to the back of the stage.

"No," Margot said uncertainly, pulling at Remi's sleeve, craning her neck to see.

Sure enough, Nick Van Eade, the lead singer of the Cutting Crew, strutted up to the stage dressed in all black. Jake handed him an acoustic guitar, and Nick slung the strap over his head. He took to the mike like the veteran he was. The musician looked at Margot and said, "Happy birthday, Margot."

The drummer banged on the toms, and the band kicked into Margot's favorite song of all time, "(I Just) Died In Your Arms."

When Nick began singing, Margot's legs buckled and she had to fight not to fall. She kissed Remi at least a hundred times and then wrapped her arms around him. She squeezed him tightly, and her smile stretched wider until her mouth hurt, and she fell in love with this man all over again.

As the song finished, she looked up at the stage, looked at Jasper, the professional he'd become. This was her life. He was her son. She turned to Remi. This was her man.

Her man forever.

65

THE LAST GLASS

As the fingernail moon rose and the band played its last song, and as the coyotes began to sing songs of their own, Otis felt chill bumps fire across his body.

Joan turned to him. "How could you leave this? You'd be crazy."

He shook his head. "Why did I even think she'd let me go?"

"She, being the mountain, of course?" Joan asked, lifting her eyebrows.

"Yes, the other woman."

She lifted her cane and then tossed it to the ground. She offered her hand to Otis and said, "That's fine, as long as you save the last dance for me."

Otis was reminded of his promise to his wife Rebecca that he'd return to her after this life. Well, he decided, Joan wasn't talking a dance after death. As always, she was talking about right now. This life. He smiled and pulled her toward him. "The last dance will always be for you." When the song ended and as the crowd cheered, Otis kissed his lover and whispered, "I'm going to go see my desert dogs. I'll find you in a few."

"You do that, my dear." Only she could understand the calling he often felt.

He worked his way through a neighboring vineyard, moving northeast. He'd had enough wine and Scotch by now that he was swaying with a wide-mouthed grin, eager for his typical late-night wandering. For the first time in forever, he didn't feel like cussing the moon or those wild dogs. He was, once again, one of them.

He passed a syrah sign hanging on a post and plucked a few grapes. Popping them into his mouth, he crushed them in his teeth, the juice tingling his senses. *Only weeks to go.* Though he'd be short a few vines because of the chainsaw incident, he'd have a lot more juice than the one barrel from last year!

Chuckling at the sadistic thought, he noticed a figure farther north in the darkness. A man sharing the same drunken sway. The man crossed Sunset Road and stumbled up a gravel drive running between two vineyard blocks. Was this another man pulled toward the calls of the coyote?

His curiosity piqued and with nothing better to do, Otis followed. He crossed the main road as well and worked his way up the gravel drive. The nameless man passed the last vineyard, crawled through an old wire fence, and ascended the steep slope that was host to blocks of granite and slate disks. The coyotes called, and the man went toward them like the walking dead returning to the source.

Breaking past the last vineyard himself and then navigating the fence, Otis reached the final slope that rose to the top of the mountain. There were no more vines here, only the patches of cheatgrass that reddened in the spring and the rocks that made it hard to walk and the Red Mountain dust that rose like smoke around one's legs with each step.

The sliver of a moon didn't offer much for lighting, but Otis had gained some ground on the man and when he turned, Otis whispered, "Bellflour."

His nemesis was now halfway up the last slope. The coyotes had stopped howling. He eyed the black landscape, pushing the limits of his vision, wondering why the sudden quiet.

That's when he saw them. Three coyotes had triangulated Bellflour—each a hundred feet away—all of them moving in. He'd never seen the coyotes go after a human on Red Mountain before, but he knew the dogs were after the man. They wanted blood.

"Bellflour!" Otis yelled into the silence.

The man whipped around in surprise.

"You see these coyotes? You need to turn your dumb ass around."

Bellflour moved as best he could back down the mountain. The three coyotes ran toward him, growling as they went.

Otis saw the dogs start and felt the call of his own inside himself. He ran toward Bellflour too, running as hard and fast as those wild dogs he'd come to know so well. One of the dogs reached Bellflour first, though, and bit down on the man's right arm. Bellflour yelled in pain, doing his best to scamper away. He tripped and slammed into the steep slope of the mountain.

Otis let out an echoing growl, and the coyotes stopped and turned their heads toward him. Even the one who'd bitten Bellflour stopped to look.

"Get out of here!" Otis yelled, still on the move. "Get!"

The dog didn't move. He licked his snout. Tasted Bellflour's blood.

Otis locked eyes with the dog; they'd met before. It was the same coyote he'd met eyes with down at his own vineyard long ago. He recognized the white spot on the right side of his nose.

This time Otis didn't yell. There's a time when a dog must establish his rank in the pack. Every pack, every mountain, must have an alpha. Establishing his dominance once and for all, Otis pointed his finger up toward the top of the mountain, and with unshakeable command, he yelled, "Go!"

The dog blinked his eyes, assessing his rank, then lowered his snout. He looked back at Bellflour, who was trying to stand. The dog turned and ran. The other coyotes followed, and they disappeared up the mountain.

Bellflour cursed into the night as Otis pulled the big man up. "Why would you help me?" he asked.

"That's a great question. I guess I'm getting soft. A better question is what the hell are you doing up here?"

"It's not your mountain, Till."

"Once you've been here a while, Bellflour, you realize no one can own this mountain. If anything, she owns you." Otis pointed at Bellflour's bloody arm and shook his finger at him. "You'll have those bite marks to remind you of that every time you get close."

As they took careful steps back down the steep rocky slope, Otis gazed out over Red Mountain. The moon and stars cast a faint light over the vineyard blocks that ran all the way to the Horse Heaven Hills. He saw the party was still in full swing at Lacoda and heard the band promise to play one more. As their first chord rose into the desert air, Otis heard the wild dogs up high on the mountain behind him begin a song of their own.

If you enjoyed this story, please take a moment to leave a review on Amazon. It makes a world of difference.

∼

For more novels, free stories, updates, and my newsletter sign-up, visit boowalker.com.

boowalker

ACKNOWLEDGMENTS

I'd like to start by thanking Mikella and Riggs, who not only put up with my obsession with storytelling but proudly encourage it. Every sentence I write is for you, and not one of them is worthy.

Thank you to the Hedges and Goedhart families, who taught me everything I know about wine. Your pursuit of authenticity and devotion to Red Mountain give me hope for the future. Thanks to all the other guardians of Red Mountain spreading word of the grand terroir of our place.

Thanks to the editing team at The Pro Book Editor and also my cover designer, J.D. Smith. You two are awesome.

A giant hug of gratitude to my selfless beta readers, who made this story so much better with their hard work. Thank you, Debbie Ice, Nina Krammer, Beth Crittenden, Patty Bonner, Emily Campbell, Bill Lee, Val Noonan, Julie Landry, Paul Dahlke, Michele Dambach, Ruth Koons, David Wallace, Candace Mowers, Jeannie and Jim Ruthem, and Ellen Richardson.

To all of you who support my words, I hope I make you proud.

ABOUT BOO

Boo initially tapped his creative muse as a songwriter and banjoist in Nashville before working his way west to Washington State, where he bought a gentleman's farm on the Yakima River. It was there amongst the grapevines that he fell in love with telling stories.

A wanderer at heart, Boo currently lives in St. Petersburg, Florida with his wife and son. He also writes thrillers under the pen name Benjamin Blackmore. You can find him at boowalker.com and benjaminblackmore.com.

Made in the USA
Coppell, TX
30 May 2020